# THROUGH THE GREY

# THROUGH THE GREY

KAT RICHARDSON

Charlotte, NC

FALSTAFF
BOOKS

WWW.FALSTAFFBOOKS.COM

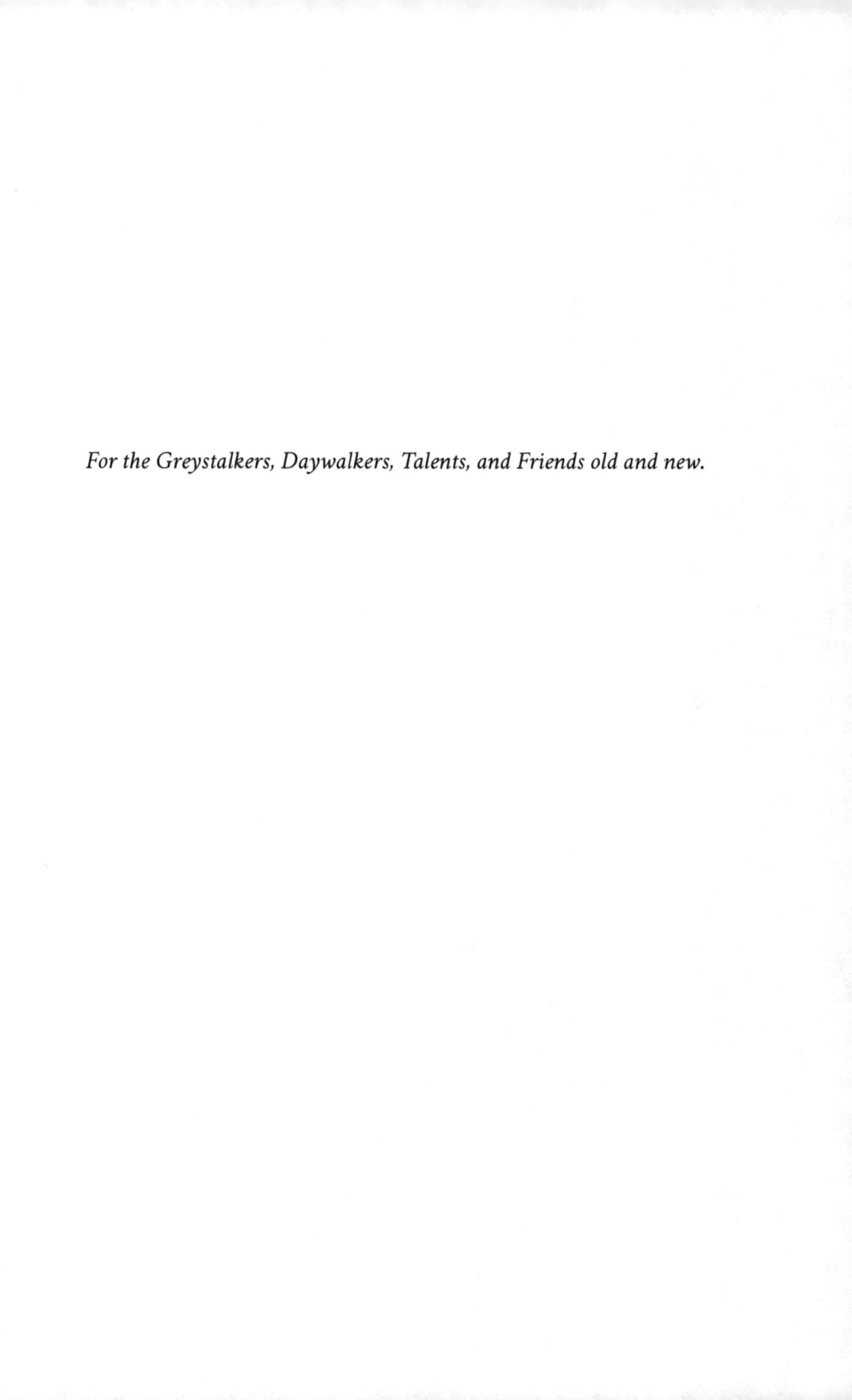

*For the Greystalkers, Daywalkers, Talents, and Friends old and new.*

# CONTENTS

# INTRODUCTION

## BY CHARLAINE HARRIS

I've known Kat Richardson for a long time. My admiration for her work has never flagged. Kat's novels were a great contribution to the field of urban fantasy. Her frequent protagonist Harper Blaine is one of the admirable heroes of the field: brave, determined, confident. You'll meet Harper again in these pages, and other characters who are equally as interesting. Reading over these collected stories, I was reminded that Kat is simply a good writer. Not only are her people complicated and imperfect and therefore real, her stories are told with intelligence and the persistent twists and turns of irony that are unique to Richardson. I enjoyed reading her collected work so much that I am sure you will, too.

*Charlaine Harris is the worldwide best-selling author of the Sookie Stackhouse urban fantasy series, the Midnight, Texas novels, the Aurora Teagarden mysteries, and the Gunnie Rose series. Her work has been adapted into multiple television shows and movies, including the HBO hit series True Blood.*

---

# REINDEER GAMES

I t was in a dark and dingy bar, far from the North Pole and obscured from the city's self-knowledge by a veil of shame and hopelessness. I just came in to use the phone–honest.

I sidled in, keeping a hand on my bag, and leaned on the bar, trying to attract the bartender's attention. The place was so dark that, at first, I didn't realize the patron next to me was a deer. A reindeer, in fact. He had a large, red nose, which resembled a Christmas light-bulb. It wasn't lit, but he sure was. He was knocking back what appeared to be his fifth or sixth glass of Old St. Nick–rot-gut whiskey I wouldn't pour for a junkyard dog.

He looked at me and began to talk, which would have surprised me, if I could have been further surprised after seeing a large ruminant sitting on a bar stool in a low-life bar. Now, I'm not in the habit of listening to sob stories in drinking establishments, but as I tried to attract the bartender, the deer began to tell his tale. I sat myself down and listened as he rambled on. Here's what he told me:

I see you're lookin' at my nose. Yeah, it's big and red, and yeah, I'm a drunk, but that ain't why it's red. It's the other way around, see? I'm a drunk 'cause of my nose. See, long ago I was a sleek, young buck with a nice, little, furry-flapped nose like every other reindeer.

Surprises you, don't it? Yep, I'm a reindeer. Used to run for the Big Guy—y'know: Santa Claus.

But let me tell you, it ain't all fun and reindeer games up at the North Pole. No, siree-bob! Let me begin at the beginning. See, when I was just a young buck, Santa's Elves came around to all the herds, recruiting. Had a bunch of nice flyers and it sounded real good. Easy hours, only one performance a year, educational benefits, room and board, health care and retirement benefits. Now, let me tell ya, when you're wandering the frozen tundra, that sounds like easy street. So, I signed up.

For a while, I was just a second-stringer. Hangin' around, hoping for my big break. I used to talk to all of the other reindeer, trying to get pointers, but some of them were kind of stand-offish. Then, I got my chance: Charlie retired. Never heard of Charlie? Well, you'd have called him Rudolph. See, the team has positions for each name and when you take the job, well, you become the name. You didn't really think they were the same deer, did you? Reindeer don't live *that* long. It's kind of like Ronald Mac Donald. So, y'know, everybody's been replaced a time or two. And some of 'em—well, you wouldn't believe what they're really like.

Let me tell ya, it's rough up there; nothing but wall-to-wall guys, except for Vixen. You could have called her a lot worse than that. But, really, can you blame her? The only girl deer in a herd of eight guys? Not that she had anything to do with Prancer and Dancer, 'cause those two were getting along just fine together, if you know what I mean.

And the elves, man, let me tell you! What a bunch. They used to wear these little pointy-toed shoes until that movie came out. Y'know: *Lord of the Rings*? Then they all got uppity and started wearing long hair and soft-soled boots so you couldn't hear 'em sneaking up on ya. Used to frighten the hay out of us, and then laugh like crazy. Nasty.

But, so, anyway, back to Charlie. See, when Charlie retired, Santa needed a new Rudolph and I wanted to make the first string so bad, I didn't care about the surgery. It was all gonna be OK, right? I mean, the healthcare was gonna take care of it and I was gonna be Santa's Number-One Deer. I was gonna be in gravy and I might even get into Vixen's stall, if you catch my drift. Gravy: boy, there's irony for ya.

So I get the surgery and everything's going pretty good. Heck, I even went for the high-tech, laser-pointer nose option. Every year we get a nice card from Charlie from some exotic place like Madagascar, or whatever. "Having a wonderful time. Wish you were here." Yeah…

Then, one year, things have been going OK, when I get sick. So I go to call in, but I can't remember the back office number. So I call the main number. And what do I get? I get Santa's phone tree! And what do I hear?

"To speak to Santa, press one; to speak to an elf, press two; to order venison products, please stay on the line…"

Venison products!

And suddenly it all falls into place for me. I mean, why didn't I see it before? I mean, this is the frickin' North Pole, fer cryin' out loud! How does a guy running a business on his own manage to weigh three-hundred pounds in that kind of weather without a supermarket nearby? Let me tell you, it sure ain't his wife's cooking. That woman could burn water. He puts away a lot of milk and cookies every Christmas, but it sure ain't enough to keep up that bulk all year. Hell, no!

But every year, somebody "retires." Somebody like Charlie. I was walkin' around in a dead guy's nose! "Wish you were here…" Yeah, more like "wish you were a hero sandwich!"

I needed to get out, but I was too sick to crawl. It was two days to Christmas and I was in deep kimchee. I knew Santa's dirty secret. And I knew I'd be the next Rudolph to "retire". I lay low and tried to build up my strength.

But on Christmas Eve, the worst happened: there was a knock at the door and when I opened it, I could barely see Santa for the fog that had socked us in like poisoned cotton candy.

And y'know what he says to me? Yeah, I can see it in your face: you know. He says, "Rudolph with your nose so bright, won't you guide my sleigh tonight?"

I know what I should have done. I know what the smart thing would have been, but I panicked. All I could see was that smiling, jolly old elf, fat and happy on roast leg of Charlie!

"Fuck you, Fat-Man!" I screamed and I ran for the back door!

I was out and across the field, into the woods and gone in five seconds flat. But I knew they'd be coming after me: the Elves! The elves with their silent boots and long streaming hair and bows!

Bows, I tell ya! I should have realized it earlier. They all had bows, just like that elf in *Lord of the Rings*–what's his name? Leg-o-lamb? That's how they got Charlie! Silently, in the night...

But, my nose was shining like a beacon, that treacherous, traitorous nose! The nose I thought was gonna make my fortune was leading my death right to me! So I ran for the nearest bar and in it I found Blitzen. And he was really Blitzed. I called him a sissy and he took a swing at me and he smacked me right in the kisser. He broke my nose and I thanked him, but the Elves were already on to the place and coming through the door, so I made with the flying trick and sailed on out of there.

With my broken nose, I couldn't see in the fog, but neither could they and I managed to get away.

Eventually, I found a surgeon who was willing to fix my nose so it would never light up again, but it was never going to be a nice, furry reindeer nose again. I'd have to move south, where the air was warm enough to breathe. I started moving, selling my services to petting zoos, then moving on, whenever the Elves started breathing down my neck.

And I've been moving on ever since.

I don't know how much farther I can run, though. It's been a long time. I've been from the North Pole to the South, been to Africa and South America and every little island you can think of, but they keep on coming: the Assassin-Elves. Someday, someday soon, my luck's gonna run out. Then I'll be just another string of venison sausage in Old St. Nick's larder. But at least I'll have told the world the truth about Santa's little sweat shop. I'll die a free deer.

And he tossed back the last of his drink and staggered unsteadily for the back door. He looked back just once and said, "Remember me. Remember Charlie." Then he was gone with an eerie clatter of hooves as he ascended into a cloudy sky, running like... well, like a deer.

When I left the bar, a man came up to me. He was tall and thin and his long, silver-blond hair hung down his back like a shimmering curtain from under a dark fedora. He wore dark glasses and a long, black coat. He stopped me and flashed a picture.

"Ma'am, have you seen this deer?"

"No, sir," I replied. "No deer around here. It's still hunting season."

He glared at me suspiciously, then turned away. I could see the bulge of his bow under his jacket.

I don't know what became of that deer, or if he wasn't just half-crazy with drink, but every time I think of that night in that bar I say a little prayer for him.

"Run, run, Rudolph."

2

---

# SHATTER

A slab of thick, cool glass lay on a patch of weedy gravel, slightly canted up by a rock under one corner. The piece was almost two inches thick, a rectangle the size of a large tea tray. Greg trod on it as they strolled across the field, the sole of his boot slipping a bit on the smooth surface.

He swore and stumbled a little, putting one hand out to catch his balance. A bit of rusted wire, wrapped loosely around a post, sliced into his palm.

"Crap," he spat, sucking on the cut.

Liss stepped over the glass and peered at him. "Tetanus."

Greg swallowed blood and frowned at her. "Yeah, right. Nothing a wide-spectrum antibiotic won't drop in its tracks."

Liss rolled her eyes. "Tough guy..."

"Tough as they come." Greg looked down at his hand, gave it a flick and then ignored the oozing wound.

"When you're in your right mind."

"Yeah, I know. I'm a freakin' head case." He looked around the empty field. The remains of a low, crude fence marched across the scrubby ground at an angle, cutting the open area into two uneven triangles.

He remembered the field from old wartime video. The fence, thigh-high, of posts and razor-wire had been concealed in the tall grass that grew here, then. A man-trap, the barrier stopped the lines of fleeing refugees, tearing living flesh from the first to meet it, until it became a visible barrier of blood and horror. Those immediately behind recoiled, slowed and became targets for the advancing troops. The tough and the desperate used the living and dying bodies of their comrades as stepping stones and fled. Those too horrified to go forward fell beside the fence and rose no more.

Except as ghosts in the imagination, as memories in computer-minds, displayed with agonizing clarity on viewscreens in school rooms, in small displays of personal items like tiny shrines in the cubicles most called home, in the voices of the extremely aged. Unreal to someone Greg's age, or even to Liss, ten years his senior. It was their grandparents' war. Their own was not to be fought in a realm of bullet-torn meat and wet red earth, but of mindspace and memory and whispering electrons.

Greg stared out at it, measuring the regular placement of the posts with his gaze, sweeping the field for anything interesting, anything that he could focus his mind on. Liss started to walk away from him, into the field, parallel to the fence. Greg stood his ground and watched her, crossing his arms over his chest, his fist clenched over the cut. One drop of blood slipped from his hand and painted a blade of grass at his feet.

Liss's long, dark dress billowed in the breeze. It seemed like such an impractical garment, but she'd insisted on wearing it. It covered her legs and clung to them as she walked. He'd seen her body in much more detail, but he couldn't help staring at the way the wind molded the fabric to her, making these legs, defined by the rush of fresh air and smoke-colored fiber, different from the legs she normally wore.

She walked out into the field of a thousand metallic sparkles, head down so her hair swept over her face, stripes of premature gray and white looking like tears in the dark fabric of it. She crouched down and touched something just above the ground.

"This is where my grandfather died," she called back. "Or at least, where they found him. The tag has the right number on it."

Greg took a few stiff steps toward her. Another drop of blood fell unnoticed in his path. "He's on the wrong side of the fence, isn't he?" He did not care about her answer, he only wanted her to keep talking. The breeze moaning over the barbed wire was beginning to sound like distant sobbing.

"He went over the fence like the refugees did and then one of his own shot him in the back."

"Why?"

"Why?" she repeated, rising to her feet. "I don't know. My grand-mother never said."

"Wouldn't the Army database say?"

"I've never bothered to look." She turned toward him.

"You don't want to know?"

"It doesn't matter. He died here, like a thousand others. That's enough for me." She shook her hair out of her face and started toward him again. "You don't like this place, do you?"

"Who would?"

She stopped in front of him and smiled up at his scowl. "I do, kind of. It's a living memory. Alone of many buried, it remains. And it's quiet here."

"Quiet... Not for me. It's an empty field where two hundred soldiers with guns slaughtered eleven hundred people who only wanted to run away."

"It's that, too. See, one thing can have several faces. Depends on where you're standing and what you're looking for as to what you'll see."

"I see a sterile field watered with blood." The singing of the wire fence crept along his spine.

"And for the same reason that, when you look in a mirror, you see a monster, while I see a man."

"I *am* a monster, Liss. I'm useful, and you can dress me up and make me behave, but it's just a nice act, not the truth."

"The truth is sometimes not what you think." She walked past him.

He turned, hoping they were leaving, and followed her, but she stopped beside the heavy glass.

"Look at it," she said, pointing down. "It seems solid, unmoving, hard, but did you know glass is actually a liquid? It never stops flowing, glacially slow. Come down here and look at it." She knelt down, her dress a dark pool around her.

Reluctant, he stooped and looked at the massive, heavy, glass slab. It was so thick it was dark green from the impurities. It glinted slightly as the sun struck it between the shadows of their bodies. The color made it seem that it must be icy to the touch. He started to extend his injured hand, then stopped. Vibrating discomfort down his back gave him pause and he squeezed his eyes shut.

"They say you can reshape glass over time by forcing it to flow where you want it," Liss said. "It flows so slowly, yet, it does move. You could drive a nail through it without shattering it if you were just patient enough You're like this glass, Greg." She reached out and took his hand, pressing his palm against the smooth surface of the slab. Her hand rested, warm, over his. "Strong, hard, pacific, but ultimately brittle when struck hard enough."

The glass went cold beneath his hand and he pulled away, shuddering a little, leaving a smear of blood on the surface. He stood up, suddenly, and Liss had to catch herself to keep from falling over.

"I'm not like that. It's an illusion, a facade. I'm like them, out there: the ghosts who only look like humans," he snapped, sweeping one hand back toward the remains of the fence. "But, inside, they aren't humans. They're hollow at best; at worst, monsters, like me."

Frustrated, lashed by the weeping of the wind, he glared at her and strode away. She tried to scramble after him, but the force of his inner turmoil drove him too quickly for her to catch up.

It raged, boiling in him. He wanted to scream, like a broken pipe venting steam. Distilled fury pumped through him alongside his blood and he felt plucked by its discordant fingers. His sleep had been ungentle, its images still walked with him, gibbering and dancing worship-rings around him like demon children. He was the god of nightmares.

He tried keeping his distance from others; there was no distance to be had, here. He stared at the schematic on the viewscreen before him, but his gaze darted from the crisp lines as if repelled, searching for relief from phantom horrors hanging like a gore-spattered curtain between his eyes and the world around him.

"Forrester..."

Bridling fury by willful effort, he turned his head slowly to look at the man who addressed him. He did not trust his voice and so said nothing, only stared.

Torreni curled his lip in disgust. "Don't you bother with your pops? I need your redesign notes. Akima's waiting for me to check them and you're locking them up. I've been pop-messaging you for an hour."

"I'm not done." Greg's voice ground out between the working mill-stones of his horrors and his will, rough gravel.

The other man hacked an impatient breath. "Well, hurry it up. You're not the only engineer on this project, you know." He turned his back, rolling his eyes and starting away, muttering under his breath. "Freakin' boy-genius..."

"What did you say?"

Torreni kept walking. "I said you're a freak, Forrester."

It struggled to rip from him, pushing him up, and he whirled, stepped out and snatched the man back around. His hands closed into fists on Torreni's shirt. He spun back again and rammed the older engineer backward, into the cubicle wall.

"Freak?! We're all God-damned freaks! Crawling through this nightmare dung-heap we're forced to call home, like diseased earthworms! You're an insignificant piece of shit like the rest of us!" Greg shouted.

Torreni shoved at Greg. "Get away from me! Don't touch me, you spooky son of a bitch!"

"Touch you...?" Greg started, drawing back. Rage coiled back inside him like a spring and he clamped it down.

Torreni saw the recoiling and gathering of Greg's turmoil and launched his own fear before the anticipated wave-front of fury could break on him. He swung at the younger man's jaw.

The inexpert fist thudded against him, jarring Greg's mental restraint as much as his grip, and he let go with a roar. His own fist bolted into Torreni's face, sending the man hard against the wall.

The flimsy cubicle buckled and Torreni collapsed to the floor. Greg stepped toward him down the black-edged tunnel of fury, drawing back to smash the older man.

Akima launched himself at Greg's shoulders from behind. "No! No, Greg! Don't! He's just a windbag. Nothing. He's nothing!"

Greg staggered back a step, then shook Akima off. He heard the dim buzzing of Akima's pleas but could only see the dazed man at the end of the reddening tunnel of his anger. He rocked onto his toes, then back to his heels. Stepped back a pace. Stopped. The rage battered and shook him, burning his bones. He tried to push it back into his head with his palms, pressing them against his temples. It just throbbed against his skull. He clenched it in his hands and jerked away from the men and women gathering around him, back from Akima and Torreni.

With a half-swallowed growl of pain, he whirled and ran.

The rest of the section stared after him, then down at Torreni, who was trying to pick himself up off the floor. Someone moved to help the downed man, then backed away.

Akima stepped forward and pulled the bloody-faced Torreni up.

"That was... that was really stupid. You OK? I mean, except for the nose?"

Torreni nodded, covering his nose and mouth with his hand. Blood leaked between his fingers.

"Take yourself to Medical," Akima directed, "then go get some rest. You... have been working too many hours, maybe. Need some sleep, right?"

Another dazed nod.

"All right." Akima watched him teeter off, accompanied by a helpful co-worker. The senior engineer looked around him.

"Go back to work, OK?"

The engineers, designers, and programmers shook themselves free of violence's spell and returned to their jobs.

———

The cubicle lighting was turned low and yellow, indicating it was now the night-cycle. Liss stared into her viewscreen and scrolled through still more annoying reports. She stopped at one and glanced through it:

*...what we think of as our own feelings are, most certainly, influenced by our relationships with others and with our immediate contacts. In those equipped for a heightened sensitivity, it could be argued that the feelings of the group are, in fact, their own...*

She snorted and flipped to another report.

The doorway chimed and she heard a foot scrape over the sill. She hated having a standard cubicle, but only married couples and special cases got privacy. At least she didn't have a roommate.

"Dr. Laker, I said I'd—" she started, raising her head and turning in her chair to face the door. "Oh."

Greg loomed inside the doorway. His hands were clenched together in front of him. He frowned. "Sorry..."

"No, don't worry about it. Thought you were the boss. Come all the way in, Greg, and tell me what's on your mind."

He remained frozen a moment, then lunged a step toward her and thrust out his open hand. "This. This isn't healing right."

"A little cut is bugging you?" she said and looked down at his hand, taking it in hers.

The slash across his palm looked raw and strange, the fibers of muscle beneath the skin exposing themselves in red relief. It wasn't bleeding and didn't seem to have a scab over it, though it was now several days old. She scowled and recoiled a bit, started to raise her other hand to touch the wound, then stopped.

"Does it hurt?"

"No. Feels weird, but I wouldn't call it pain."

Liss brushed the weal lightly with a finger. The flesh felt solid, though pebbled and hard. She could feel the outline of the scab, but couldn't see it, nor could she feel the raw track of flesh her eyes saw.

"This is really strange. It feels OK, but it looks… well, weird."

"Feels like a constant case of pins and needles. Tingles."

"Did you see the doctor when you first got it?"

"Yeah. Gave me a shot in the arm for the infection and slapped a bandage on it. About what you'd expect."

"Have you been back?"

"Hell no. What's he going to do? Put another bandage on it?"

"There's no more that I can do, either. I'm not a doctor."

"Yeah, I know."

"It bugs you though, doesn't it?"

He nodded and pulled his hand back as she let go of it. He backed up a step and sank down into her other chair

Even seated, Greg towered over her. Most of the younger ones did, though. Liss was among the children born and raised, at least through adolescence, on the surface. For some reason, the generations born in the warrens were tall and thin, like plants seeking light. That's how Liss thought of them: plants without enough light.

It could as well have been that she was stunted in some way, perhaps by exposure to the pervasive, residual radiation that made the surface of the Earth unsafe for full-time habitation. The shielded communities of her youth had been inadequate proof against the insidious radiation and chemicals. Now, thirty years later, she walked on the surface for a few hours with no ill effects. She remembered the scrubby, low-growing plants in the field and knew they were young mutants, finally establishing supremacy over the fading shadow of Death that had once dominated the surface.

"I keep looking at it," said Greg, staring down at his hand. "It's just so damned weird-looking. It distracts me. It's sickly fascinating."

"You need to have something more absorbing to do. What have you been working on, lately?"

13

"The usual: more stupid machines that do the same stupid thing in only slightly better ways."

"Why aren't you creating anything new, anymore? This is not like you. You used to make incredible things."

"I got sick of starving. This pays better."

"Greg, damn it, mere survival isn't everything. If the entire human race had decided that was enough, we'd still be living in radiation-proof domes on the surface and dying of strange diseases."

"'Survival is an evolutionary imperative.' Did I get that right?"

Liss shuddered and made a gagging sound. "You sound exactly like Dr. Laker when you do that, plummy accent and all."

"Yeah, I know." Greg bared his teeth in a cruel grin. "Been practicing. Can't stand that bastard."

"I know. The whole station knows."

"So long as *he* knows, I'm satisfied."

"Be satisfied, then. Laker knows you hate him."

"Good. Maybe he'll stay away from me.

"Doesn't he?" she asked, frowning.

"Haven't seen him in a while, except in viewscreen lectures and that's plenty close enough for me."

"Wish I were so lucky... So, what are you going to do about the hand?"

"Bandage it up, I guess."

"Don't. Just learn to ignore it. Leave it open and let the air and light get at it. That'll be better. And find yourself some interesting work to do. The more frustrated you get, the more likely you are to go off the deep end and that's no way to avoid contact with Dr. Laker."

"Right. What do you suggest? Go back to making those toys?"

"Why not something more ambitious? You've talked about a lot of things you want to create. Surely you've earned some comp time, by now?"

"Yeah..." He narrowed his eyes in thought. "Lots, actually."

"Then you have been doing extra hours, haven't you?"

Greg looked a little sheepish. "About eighty a week."

She closed her eyes in exasperation. "Working every day, right?

14

What are you trying to do to yourself? Do you want to go over the edge?"

"There's nothing else to do! This freakin' place bores the fuck out of me! I feel like I'm in prison!"

"Greg, you need to cultivate a few friends—"

Greg jerked forward in his chair and stabbed her with a look. "I have a friend. I have you. Who else do I need? Not Laker and his ilk, which is almost everybody down here. Who else is there?"

"Buddies? A girl more—?" Liss suggested.

"Fuck that. Well…, you know what I mean. It's just a complication I can't afford."

Liss heaved a disgusted sigh and made a face. "You have to do something. Can't stand the station and can't take the surface. What are you going to do? Hide out in the drafting system and the assembling-rooms for the rest of your probably short life?"

"Something like that."

"Is it good work, at least? I mean, it's no exaggeration to say you're brilliant…"

"What damned difference does it make? If I'm busy enough, I at least don't… hear them all the time. I can't stop them from getting into my head, but I don't have to give them room to make me more insane than I am."

She shook her head. "So you're going to work yourself to death and it won't even be work you want to do. If you're going to burn yourself out, you might at least have some fun doing it."

"Fun…? What is that? No, no: don't start. That's a rhetorical question."

Liss stared at him with a calm face. "How's the hand?"

"Fine. Don't even notice it when I'm arguing with you."

"Which proves my point. It doesn't bother you when you're doing something you enjoy."

"You think I like to fight with you?"

"Argue. You do like to argue with me. You love getting into these little verbal battles with me. You love trying to make me mad."

"Do you ever really get mad? Or do you just pretend to get mad so I can win?" he asked with a grin.

"I never pretend."

"Then you're not angry with me, right now?"

"No. Exasperated, maybe, not angry."

"Can I unexasperate you? Can I take you to dinner? Then we can argue some more and I won't sit in my room and brood over the viewscreen."

"I can't. I have reports to compile for Dr. Laker before the end of cycle."

"Oh, screw Laker."

"No, thank you very much, I'd rather not," she replied.

He barked a harsh laugh. "Don't you get tired of bowing to the demands of the great Dr. Laker?"

"He is my boss, Greg. I have to satisfy at least some of his demands, some of the time, or I'll be wandering around the station hoping someone has some work for me to do so I can support my lavish life-style," she joked, waving her hand, indicating the cubicle.

It was spare even by station standards. Aside from the desk and its administration-quality information interface, there was one narrow bed and ranks of data chip storage where the second bed would have been in most cubicles. Where the second desk would have been, there was a scavenged bookshelf stuffed with real pulp-and-ink books, most of them in rag-tag condition and, though rare, most people thought them worthless.

Most residents could not stand to leave the walls unadorned or the tables and desks uncluttered, but Liss had, for the most part. A flat-view on the wall displayed a plan schematic Greg had given her once, and a dried, pressed leaf from a surface tree was cellophaned to a piece of colored plastic which hung over the desk. But there were no collected bits and pieces displayed on every surface, no manic spots of color and shape. The bed had the brightest thing in the room: a quilt Liss had sewn by hand from scraps of clothing her mother and grand-mother had left in a box.

It had a scent to it that Greg couldn't identify. It was part of the quilt, just like the strange, fragile textiles and the fluffy stuffing. Sitting nearby, he could smell the dry odor, faintly; a smell from somewhere and somewhen else that helped him forget about the dense-packed station beyond the doorway. He preferred her cubicle to his own. Maybe, simply because it smelled like something other than recycled air and chemicals.

"You must eat. Even Laker can't deny that."

"Greg…"

He jumped to his feet. "Up! You must dine. Up, right now! There shall be no saying 'no'. Or I'll pick you up and carry you to dinner."

"Greg!" she snapped. "I can't."

"Yes, you can. You will."

She lowered her chin and glowered at him from under her eyebrows.

"Yes!" he demanded and grabbed her arms, snatching her out of the chair. "Yes. Right now!"

He picked her up and draped her over his shoulder like a bundle of cable. She began kicking and squirming, then she punched him in the back, a few inches above his kidneys.

"Ow!"

"Put me down," she panted.

He put her back on her feet with care.

She glared at him and settled her fists on her hips. "Arrogant. Did you think you could just drag me off? What's come over you?"

"I told you—I'm bored. I'll do almost anything to be un-bored."

She made a face at him and frowned. "Oh, all right. Let me close up the files and I'll come and meet you at food service."

"No deciding not to come, right?"

"Of course not."

"Because, if you don't come in ten minutes, I'll march right back here and then I *will* carry you off."

"I said 'all right'. I'll be there. You win."

"Good. I like winning."

Liss snorted and turned her back on him, shaking her head. "Just get going. I'll be right there."

She heard the door chime as he left. She glanced over her shoulder and saw him striding down the hall. She turned back to her interface and called up a file.

"Greg Forrester... Privacy three." She typed a moment, then saved her files, secured the system and pulled the data chips. Nothing stayed on the system if she could avoid it. It wasn't secure enough for her taste. Not against the curiosity and boredom of someone like Greg.

---

In every public place, the screens glowed with Dr Laker's dignified face, magnified in its disconcerting benevolence. Every week he offered them the comfort of belief in something larger.

"It is necessary to remember that a society is not merely a collection of individuals, but an organism in its own right, which functions for the overall good of the individuals in its collective. Man does not cease to be human within a close-knit society, but he must evolve to a higher state than that of mere animal.

"The animal nature drives him into social contracts such as exist here, at Epsilon Station. We have joined into this sometimes difficult contract in order to survive in a poisoned world. Survival is an evolutionary imperative, and we evolve into a better version of humankind in undertaking this experiment in survival.

"It is incumbent upon us to strive to excel, to rise beyond mere survival, to expand ourselves in our success to the sublime..."

His velvet tones soothed across the proximity-scoured nerves of the ten-thousand, bustling through their subterranean lives like so many moles. Waking or sleeping, the voice trickled into their heads.

---

Greg knew he twitched in his sleep. He'd always been a poor sleeper. He couldn't keep a roommate; his nightmares frightened them even more than they did himself. Being nuts had its compensations: he had a door. But, along with keeping his noises in, it kept the silences in, too. His whimper of fear resonated against the walls and fed back into his dream.

A steel-colored light fell across them all. The field was thigh-high with knife-bladed grass. Ragged people fled past him as he walked against the tide of refugees, their clothing and bodies ripped by the wire of the fence. He wanted to turn around and go with them, run away, but he couldn't. As they passed, their voices called out in his head, building together into a chorus of terror; names and ages and the constant repetition of death.

"Don't go, don't go," one voice began singing. "Come back to us. Don't go. You needn't go, you shouldn't go. Come back to us." The voice threaded, high and clear, through the painful litany of the fleeing.

Come back? He couldn't come back. He didn't dare. That was memory; that was fifty years dead and moldering. Instead, he walked forward, walked toward the oncoming, churning confusion of the refugees as they met the fence.

Some made it over, some didn't. Beyond them, the lines of soldiers and war machines advanced inexorably.

He reached the fence and lifted a little girl over it. She had dark hair and wore a dress the color of smoke. As he set her on the ground, she looked up at him and said, "You don't have to go."

"Yes, I do. I have to fight them. If I don't, they'll win."

"They did win."

He stared at the little girl. She turned away and walked across the field with her head down, searching the ground as she walked through scattered bodies of those who could not continue. Refugees ran past her as if they did not see her: a shadow among shadows

Someone called his name as he stood at the fence, awash in refugees. He looked over the fence and into the blind, black eye of a gun. The soldier at the other end spoke without raising his head.

"Come back, Allberg."

The guns around them opened up with a ripping sound and the fleeing began to fall. Screams and cries twined with the sound as they were cut down: a wave breaking against a leaden shore. Their shrieking mingled with the shadow-cries in his head and wrung his spinal cord. He wrenched himself around, searching for the little girl.

He spotted the small, dark figure, moving slowly. The wave of death surged closer.

"No!" He looked back at the soldier. "I'm not coming, yet."

He started running, back toward the little girl, to the little girl with eyes like Liss's.

He felt the bullet smash into his spine and heard the crack of the shot. His legs folded and he fell into the harvest of death as the little girl turned...

He shouted, slamming onto his knees as he flung himself out of the bed. He caught himself on one forearm and clutched the edge of the mattress with his other hand. He ached. He swallowed bile and choked on the urge to scream.

"Allberg, Allberg," he panted, swallowing again and again. "Who in hell is Allberg?" He pressed his face against the mattress and gasped until his chest stopped heaving. His spine still vibrated with the music of his nightmare, rattling his brain in his skull. He scrambled into clothes and ran.

---

The alarm yapped sharply as he dove through the doorway.

"Liss, Liss, Liss..."

A pale shape like a ghost in the gloom rose up in the bed, the quilt slithering into a multi-colored puddle on the floor.

He dropped down beside the bed, clutching her shoulders, his own violent quivering making her shake.

She blinked groggily. "Wha— Greg? What...?"

Dark shapes crowded the doorway.

"Miss Mori, are you all right?" one of the shapes called.

"I— I'm fine. I'm sure it's fine," she called. "Just go back to bed."

"Are you sure?"

Greg turned toward the door with a vicious snarl. The security patrol recoiled, then started to step forward with clubs out.

Liss shoved Greg aside and bolted out of bed, meeting them at the doorway. She slapped off the alarm.

"It's OK, guys. It's OK. It's just Greg. Just a bad night. It'll be OK. You can go back to... whatever it is you do all night. Really—it's OK."

Shrugging and looking belligerent, they stepped away and started down the corridor, glancing over their shoulders at the glimmering shape of the naked woman in the doorway.

Rubbing sleep from her face, Liss turned back into the room, raising the illumination from "drowse" to the usual night-cycle bronze glow. Greg still crouched on the floor beside the bed and stared at her with wild eyes. She picked up the quilt and wrapped it around herself, then sat on the bed near him.

"What is it?" she yawned. "What happened, Greg? Nightmare?"

"What was—" He stopped and swallowed against an impossibly dry throat. "What was your grandfather's name?"

"Conrad. Why?"

"Conrad... Oh, God... Then I don't know." He stared at the floor in confusion. "What was his first name, then?"

"That was his first name," Liss replied, huddling a bit and pulling her feet up under the quilt.

Greg smacked his head against the side of the bed in frustration. "What was his last name? Mori?"

"No, Allberg. Mori was my father's name."

Greg moaned and scrubbed at his face with one hand. "I need you to look him up in the military database."

Liss blinked and stared toward Greg's downturned face. "Need? Why?"

"Please, Liss." His voice hissed between his clenched teeth.

She scowled and sat still. She sighed. "Oh, all right." She rose and padded across the small room to her desk, trailing a train of quilt, and flicked on the interface. The viewscreen brightened and flashed its "good morning" greeting, playing its little tune.

"Oh, shut up," she grumbled at it. She turned off the voice interface and typed.

Greg crept close. The database responded and scrolled information. He leaned over her shoulder and stared. Text reeled off for a moment or two, then stopped.

"Time, place, location of death," Greg whispered.

Liss typed. The information displayed on the viewscreen. A small icon flashed near the bottom.

"There's video. Play it."

She looked at the screen and not at him and said, "It's going to be gruesome. We all know what happened."

"I need to see it."

She shrugged and touched the icon.

The video image was poor and pixelated, blown up by vast percentages from an old standard. Even enhanced, it was difficult to make out. The crowds of refugees on the field looked like a storm cloud's shadow moving on the trampled grass. A yellow circle marked Conrad Allberg as he moved forward, well ahead of the line of soldiers. He shouldered through the refugees, paused occasionally to shoot, though it was hard to tell what he was shooting or what the results.

He reached the fence and stopped, facing the open field beyond, standing knee-deep in the dead and dying. He slung his rifle, turned twice, then climbed over the fence and stood there, not moving. A dark clot of refugees washed up against the fence near him. At first, he did nothing, then he reached back over the fence and helped them.

Five people crossed the fence alive because of him. Then they stopped coming. There were no more alive to help on that side. And Conrad Allberg just stood there. It was impossible to tell if he was facing the open field that led to safety or the trampled sea of blood and bodies from which he had come. Another soldier came to the fence, approaching him with caution at the length of his rifle. Allberg didn't move for a while, then he suddenly stepped away from the fence and ran into the open field. His compatriot put up his weapon, then rested the butt on the ground and stared after him.

A puff of smoke from another direction and Allberg fell where the tag on the field had been.

The video stopped on the last frame, paused, then reverted to the file icon. Even the archivists hadn't wanted to linger over that.

"Explanation of death," Greg demanded.

Liss typed.

"Accidental: friendly fire."

Greg sat down hard on the floor and shook.

Liss knelt down beside him, draped the quilt around his shoulders, and urged him to his feet. "Come on, Greg. Go sit on the bed. It's cold down here."

Numb, silent, he shrugged the quilt up around his face like a child and walked with her to the bed. Sitting on the mattress, he hunched his long frame into a folded cone under the flowing quilt; he sat silent and staring as Liss slipped into a dress.

She sat down next to him. "Now. Tell me."

"I- I- I had a nightmare. The dead... they play games in my head. They... they... I don't know why they do this to me. Why they picked me. They tell me their names and their stories and they cry in my head."

"I know, Greg. You've told me."

He nodded. "I was walking through the field, not the killing field, the open side. I came up to the fence and stopped. I helped a little girl over the fence and she told me I didn't have to go back because the bad guys had already won. Except that they didn't win, not in the end... And I stood there and thought about it until a soldier came up to me, just like that one did to your grandfather.

"He called me Allberg and I turned and looked at him with the distance of his weapon between us. He told me to come back and I said I wouldn't yet, then I turned away and ran after the little girl, to save her from being shot. And they killed me.

"And she looked like you, Liss, and she spoke with your voice."

"Are you sure that you've never seen this footage before?"

"Of course, I've seen the footage before! Hundreds of times. You can't grow up around here without seeing it, having it rammed down your throat from the first image you ever see. But not this: not these details. How would I know these things? Why would I look for them?"

"I don't know. It doesn't matter. It's funny, though, that you started out on the free side of the fence, not on the side with the soldiers."

"I was just me when I started walking. I often walk through that field in my nightmares. I even walk through it when I'm awake, sometimes. This time, I had to go to the fence. I didn't want to, but I did it. I wanted to run away, but I wasn't allowed to.

"I wanted to stop them. I felt that I could stop them, somehow, that I had to. But then, the girl... In the end I wanted to save one person more than I wanted to save myself or anyone else. Why?" He stared at her over the edge of the quilt. "I'm not a hero. I'm a broken thing, a monster. Monsters don't help people, they don't sacrifice themselves for others. Why, even in a dream...?"

"I don't know, Greg. Maybe you don't want to be a monster anymore."

His eyes grew harder, narrower, and the muscles in the corner of his jaw bunched. "I can't just change my mind and change what I am. It isn't that easy. I almost killed someone a few days ago. I got so angry I was ready to throw him in the tank, after beating the hell out him. I'm not a good guy; I'm a villain."

"Why do you always believe the worst of yourself? You didn't hit him and you didn't throw him in the hypo tank. Did you?"

"I hit him. I hit him pretty hard. A couple, three times, I think. But I didn't throw him in the tank, no."

"Why didn't you, if you wanted to so much?"

"I just... didn't. I dropped him and just walked away." He let go of the quilt and it slipped down into a lumpy arc around his hips and feet. He put his feet on the floor and leaned his forearms against his thighs. "I don't know why I did that any more than I know why he set me off in the first place," he added, sighing.

Liss stared, caught her breath and reached out, touching his near arm with her fingertips, then drew back.

"Oh, my God, Greg... What's happened to you?" she was staring at his near hand.

He looked down at his hand in surprise. The skin was nearly transparent and had a greenish tinge to it. His fingernails looked like disks of slightly dirty plastic. He sat up and studied his hand, turning it over, back and forth, fascinated and slightly sickened.

"I... I don't know. It's been a little stiff the past few days, but... this..." Beneath the surface, the structures of his muscles, exposed veins and ligaments, the yellow masses of fat, were visible as an anatomy lesson. The back surface was slightly cloudy, as if scratched. He brushed at it and some of the hairs on the back of his hand rubbed away, leaving a clear patch. His skin was cold to the touch and rigid.

He flexed his hand and heard a minute crackling noise. His hand flushed pink. Slow, pale blood rose to the surface of his knuckles, lingered in the cracks of his transformed skin and then oozed outward.

"This is... rather disgusting, actually. What is it, Liss?"

"I don't know. May I... may I see it?"

Frowning, he extended his hand to her. She took it in both of hers, examining it carefully.

She could find no sign of the wound on his palm, but, then, she could not properly see his skin. She couldn't feel any scab or cut. As she held onto it, she felt his hand warm up, but the flesh itself remained hard and stiff. Not like a callous, more like some kind of icy plastic, perhaps. She could see that the effect had begun to spread into his wrist and forearm. Though the skin there was still mostly normal, the upper layer was already transparent and cooler to the first touch than the normal flesh just beyond it. She was repelled and fascinated at once.

"Can you feel my touch?" she asked, pressing her fingers against his hand and wrist.

"Yeah. It's fine in the wrist, but in the hand, it's kind of... blunted, like the surface's been anesthetized, or something. Liss, this is giving me the creeps."

"It's giving me the creeps, too. We have to see a doctor. I don't know what this is, but I can guess it's not good. How could this happen? Why didn't you notice?" she demanded, standing up and finishing dressing.

"You told me to ignore it. I've been ignoring it." Greg also rose and hunched his shoulders, stuffing his hands into his pockets. He winced slightly as the strange hand brushed the tight fabric at the pocket's throat.

"That was more than a week ago," Liss chided. "How could you ignore *this*? Your hand is semi-transparent."

"I've been in the tank a lot. Wearing suits and gloves. When I go home, I'm too tired to notice anything except how tired I am. I fall into bed like a cut cable. Then I start dreaming, and I dream about them and I wake up shuddering or screaming, and still too tired to notice anything."

Liss walked out of the cubicle and Greg followed her, talking quietly. "I'm a machine these days, Liss. I work and then I work some more. I want to be too tired and too numb to feel anything else, too tired to dream, too tired to remember. It doesn't work, but I keep trying. I still wake up in the morning and I remember their names and how they died and what they said to me. I write it all down, so it doesn't stay in my head all day. Then I can work without them coming into my head, most of the time. But sometimes, they still come in, with their anger and their pain and I... I lose it. Any little thing will set me off. Like that guy the other day. I wanted to kill him. It's not just that I felt I could, not just that I was angry, but I actually wanted him to be dead, wanted to watch and feel his life ebb away at my hand. I wanted to take it away from him. I wanted to destroy him. I feel sick thinking about it."

Liss stopped walking and turned back to face him. Her eyes ached and she blinked so he wouldn't see the tears building up in them. "Greg, it doesn't matter what you thought as much as what you did. Or didn't do. You didn't kill him. You didn't give in to this monster you always believe you are. We all want to do horrible things, sometimes. We just don't do them. You didn't do anything wrong by thinking. This is much better than you used to be. Remember?"

He closed his eyes, his face twisting for a moment into a mask of torment, then easing back to a near-expressionless smoothness. "Yes," he hissed. "But it's so little..."

She reached out and touched his arm. "Little is a matter of perspective. Compared to you, I'm rather little."

Slowly, he closed his hands on her shoulders and looked at her. "You're not small, even if you're not as tall as I am." He thought he might have done something like this before, holding on to Liss when he felt like the world was too slippery to stand on. It seemed funny that he couldn't remember it better. He never seemed to forget anything else. He felt cold slide down his back, pierce into his chest, and thought he would gag on it. He swallowed hard and shivered. He stepped back from her, reluctantly.

"You OK?" she asked.

"Just... tired, maybe."

"Ah..." She nodded. "I wish you didn't feel you have to drive yourself to exhaustion just to put your mind to sleep for a while."

"It works... sort of." He crossed his arms over his chest and looked down at her. Something struggled to break the surface of his mind and he didn't want to know what it was. He stuffed it back down, scowling.

She frowned up at him and backed away. "All right." She didn't say any more, just turned and started walking again.

He walked slowly next to her.

---

The doctor kept making a disconcerted face. He poked about in his medical database a while longer, but, in the end, he just sat back, shaking his head.

"This is crazy."

"What is it?" Liss asked, leaning forward.

"Well, I've never seen anything like this. I can't find anything really like it in the database, either, so, I don't have any explanation, but, somehow, Greg's skin... Sorry," he added, turning to address Greg directly, "your skin seems to be converting into some kind of hybrid silicate, with all the characteristics of old-style silicon-dioxide."

"What the hell is that?" Greg demanded, glowering.

"It's glass," the doctor replied with a helpless shrug.

"That's just not possible, Doctor," Liss objected. "I know enough medicine to know that."

"Yeah, I know. But, it is happening. As I said: it's a hybrid of some kind, so it's still functioning like skin in most ways, but the material is a lot more like glass, or glass fiber, than it is like human skin or even synthetic replacement. This is totally different and I have no idea how or why this is happening. I have blood samples and I'm going to keep on testing them until I either find something or exhaust the possibilities, but it could be a while."

Greg pushed himself away from the wall he'd been leaning against and stalked toward the doctor. "And what do I do for now? Just watch myself become transparent?"

The doctor blinked at the younger man and sat up straighter, slightly affronted with just a hint of fear under that. "Well, that and try not to break yourself. I could surgically excise the hybrid skin and try to replace it with graft or synthetic, but that's all I can think of. If, however, there is some underlying cause I'm not aware of, then all I've done is push the problem back a little, temporarily, and the hand would be useless to you for about five days while the graft integrated with the rest of the arm. Is that what you want to do?"

"No," Greg spat. "I can't afford to forfeit my time in the tank on a maybe."

"Whoa, whoa, whoa… You're working in the hypo tank? I thought you were out in engineering."

"I was in engineering. I *am* in engineering, but I'm doing prototype assembly in the tank."

The doctor frowned again. "This can't be from the tank, though. I assume none of your suit and glove seals have been leaking…"

"I'd be dead if they had been."

The doctor leaned forward and peered at him. "How many hours a week are you spending in the tank?"

"Forty to sixty."

"Oh… my." The doctor sighed, shaking his head. "Can't stop you, I suppose, but you really shouldn't."

Greg glowered at him in silence.

"All right. Nothing I can do to stop you, but keep an eye on that hand. I don't know what effect the pressure in the tank may have on it. If anything unusual starts to happen, come back here as fast as you can."

"For what?" Greg spun on his heel and stalked from the office.

Liss ground her teeth and started to follow. The doctor caught her arm.

"Please, be careful, Liss."

She laughed stiffly. "Do you think Greg is going to hurt me?"

"I think he could hurt someone."

Liss pressed her lips tight, taking a long breath through her nose before she spoke again. "I didn't bring him here so you could evaluate his emotions, just his hand. He's more agitated than normal, true, but he is also more perceptive than the others and an additional strain like this would, naturally, affect him. But the person most in danger from Greg is Greg. So, let me worry about that, OK?"

He shook his head, resigned, and let her go with a shrug. "Just... you know."

"Yes, I do know. Thanks." She strode out.

The doctor shook his head again, frowning, and looked down at his interface as if it had betrayed him.

---

Liss could not see Greg in the hall. She searched up and down the corridor a while, trying to spot him, but had no luck, even in the sparse early-morning traffic. She hurried to her cubicle, but he wasn't there.

"Oh... drat it," she muttered.

She tried Engineering and Greg's own place, but, again, she didn't find him. She went past the hypo tank prep room, but the assistants there hadn't seen him and seemed just as glad of that. More than an hour passed before she returned to her own cubicle and ran a security query.

He'd exited one of the surface doors.

Liss ran.

---

The air blew a dry, skeleton-rattle across the stems of dead and broken weeds.

Liss stood up from the door in the ground and looked around. The radiation seal warning squealed. She stepped out onto the crumbly earth, letting the door cycle closed, and stared around. She couldn't see Greg. He wasn't near the door.

Funny he should come up just here. It was less than a mile from the domed housing she had lived in as a child. The domes were long gone, of course, the materials salvaged and recycled, where they could be, into parts for the station below. The unusable parts and massive piles of earth and stone had been cast aside, leaving sprawling middens; homes for other types of life too undesirable to be invited into the warren.

It was a long way from this door to the field in Greg's nightmare— a world's nightmares—but he could have done it. Liss began to walk through the awesome heaps of garbage.

A narrow path wound between the rubble hillocks, crossed here and there by detritus that had slid and slithered down the sides. She had to step over several large humps and lumps of unrecognizable waste. The dry wind prickled her skin through her dress. It felt the same as in childhood and she wondered if the wind had always played here, even before the trees had withered and died.

She walked on until the alley of rubble petered out into a flat clearing. Even after twenty-five years, the ground still wore the scars of the heavy equipment that had clawed it raw and trampled it into new shapes. Casts of tractor tread had baked into treacherous pavement of interlaced terracotta Ws in sinuous snake swirls a mile wide.

Liss stood on the edge of it and turned back, looking into the maze of dirt and garbage. Nothing moved but the weeds, swaying and whispering to buried bones. She shouted for Greg again, but if he was there, he was quieter than the wind.

She turned and picked her way along the edge of the clearing into the next gallery of garbage. Though she looked and called, she never found sign of him. At last, she gave up and returned to the station, trailing a scent of red earth and yellow dust.

———————

She stared at the viewscreen, but the neat rows of characters looked like ants dancing. Concentration had eluded her for the past few days. She rubbed her face with her palms and blinked, trying to bring her work back into focus.

"Liss?"

"Hm?" she mumbled, looking up toward the doorway.

The doctor stood just outside the frame and peered in. "May I interrupt you?"

"I'm... I'm not really getting much done, sorry to say. Come on in and sit down," she added motioning him in.

He stepped in and the door chimed politely. He didn't sit, but rocked from heels to toes, his fingers twiddling nervously at his sides.

"Thanks. Umm... I wanted to talk to you before I talk to Greg."

"Oh. Why?"

"Well, aside from the obvious, to be honest, I'm not quite sure how Greg is going to react to what I've found. He's been a little strange."

"Greg's always a little strange. That's the way it is when you carry burdens that don't belong to you."

"I mean stranger than usual."

"Well, wouldn't you be?"

"Yeah, I guess I would. See, he dropped in later the same day you brought him by and asked if radiation could account for whatever was happening to him. I reassured him that it wasn't that kind of thing but he asked me to run a scan anyhow. I already had, of course, but I did another. He was a little high-background, but not unsafe. He almost

31

seemed upset by that and then he left again. But he wouldn't tell me what had happened to raise his background radiation level."

"You've confused me. He was upset that his background level had risen?"

"Sorry, I'm not making myself too clear, I guess. No, what upset him was that his level wasn't significantly over safety limits. Or I think that's what upset him. Do you have any idea why?"

Liss shook her head and tucked her hair behind her ears. "No. Can't imagine."

"Do you have any guesses why his levels went up in just a few hours? What happened after you two left?"

"Well, I don't really know. Greg took off. He went outside."

"He what...? How long was he out there? Where did he go?"

"I don't know where he went, exactly, but he was only out a little over two hours and he wasn't in a high-rad area, to the best of my knowledge. He seems to have an unusually good tolerance for radiation for a warren-born kid. He is kind of unusual, you know. We've been outside several times and he's never shown any illness, not even a little nausea."

The doctor cleared his throat. "He is certainly unusual. Aside from the other... oddities, his baseline radiation levels are higher than normal. Always have been. He's kind of weird that way, so you could be right."

"And that was what you wanted to tell me? His levels went up?"

"No. I've been looking at his blood samples, as I said I would and... This is just so weird, I don't even like to think of what it is, much less how he could have gotten it."

"Some kind of nasty, terminal disease?" Liss demanded. "What?"

"No. Not a real disease. I thought it was a virus until I got a much closer look at it. It was really hard to spot until I found one of the originals. It was pretending to be an organic, but it isn't. The rest are, but the originals that remain, of course, aren't."

Liss shook her head, blinking in confusion. "Could you speak in straight lines, doctor? I have no idea what you're talking about. What is this thing that Greg has?"

The doctor bit his lip and looked on the verge of breaking into hiccups like a frightened child. He fought to let the words out. "It's a nanite."

Liss looked blankly at him. The station muttered and rustled outside the cubicle, while their silence screamed within.

"Nanites are illegal," Liss stated in a flat, bland voice.

"For almost sixty years. Yes, I know. Where did it come from?"

"I don't know. Greg wouldn't have made it and infected himself with it, or at least have guessed that it could be responsible if the infection was an accident."

"Would Greg have broken a law like that?"

"Greg breaks rules all the time. Most of them are never seen by anyone but me. A law's just another type of rule," Liss said. "If Greg thought it was an irrelevant law, he'd just ignore it and take the consequences when they hit him. If they hit him. I think he may have tinkered with nanites before, but just as mechanical toys. He wouldn't set out to build something that could kill him or anyone else. Greg's not that kind of crazy."

"But, what if it was an accident?" the doctor whispered. "What if... what if...?"

Liss stood up and took the doctor by the arm. "Don't 'what if'. What *is* is confusing enough. Sit down. Catch your breath and tell me about this thing that isn't a virus."

He sat down slowly, frowning at Liss. He took some deep breaths and made himself lean back into the chair.

"All right."

———

She walked down to Engineering and found Greg at one of the design suites. He was watching some kind of mechanical simulation on the viewscreen. He paused it and made an adjustment to a series of numbers arrayed on one side of the model, then started the animation again. The machine on the screen stopped and an error message displayed.

"Crap. Piece of crap." He started to reach out again and Liss cleared her throat and stepped closer.

"Mind if I interrupt you?"

He turned and looked up. He had to adjust his gaze down a bit to look her in the eye. Wet hair stuck to his forehead. She noticed that his clothing was damp, as if he had put it on in a hurry after showering, not bothering to towel off first. He kept the strange hand close to his body.

"Hey, Liss. What's up?"

"Do you have a little time to talk privately?"

"Sure. Pull the security door. There's no one else on this side."

Liss turned and hauled the security door closed, shutting off the rest of the station from the design suite. She turned back and saw that Greg had been watching her with a gentle frown.

"All right, what's the big secret?" he asked.

"Your doctor has isolated the vector causing this change to your skin. I figured I'd better come and tell you about it."

"He didn't want to come down here himself?" Greg asked with a cynical lift to the corner of his mouth.

"No. To be honest, I think you scare him."

He gave a bitter grunt. "I scare a lot of people. So, you got to come down here, instead. What have I got, then? Some kind of deadly plague?"

"Well, sort of. It's a nanite."

Greg looked at her blankly a moment, blinked, then grinned. "A nanite. Cool. How'd I get it?"

"He has no idea. What about you?"

He shook his head. "None. Haven't been any illegal builds around here, lately. At least I haven't been doing any and I doubt the rest of these plodders would even think of it. What's the nanite do?"

"Still doing the same thing: converting your skin to glass. I got an exterior schematic from the doctor of the nanites he was able to examine."

Greg's grin broadened. "Show it to me," he demanded, getting out

34

of his seat. He nearly pushed Liss into the chair and pointed her at the interface.

Liss typed in a file address and a pair of drawings loaded to the viewscreen, side by side in a comparison view.

"There're two of them?" Greg asked.

"Yes. The doctor thinks they're the Mark I version and the Mark II version, which was created by the Mark I version to replace itself," Liss explained, tapping the screen to indicate which was which.

Greg bent over her shoulder and stared at the screen. He reached over her and pressed a few buttons, flipping through all possible views, studying and comparing them. He consciously ignored the touch of her hair on the insides of his arms; it sent a shiver over him and a moment of blackness where something else should have been.

"Huh... Mark I looks pretty crude. You know, I ought to be insulted that either of you thought I could design something this shitty. You did think that, didn't you?"

"Not seriously. You'd have guessed it was the nanite if you'd done it yourself."

"Oh, yeah. God, this is great."

"What's great about something that's killing you?"

"Is it? At the moment, it just seems inconvenient and kind of creepy."

Liss peered at him. "Greg, are you all right?"

"Fine. I'm just fine."

His eyes looked out from dark shadow, glassy-bright glimmers of intensity. Under the sheen of moisture, his face was sculpted from milk glass. He seemed patchy and incomplete, wired and held back. The fingertips of his mutating hand were completely transparent, now, and he held the wrist stiffly.

"Show me your hand," Liss demanded.

"No."

She looked coolly at him. "Let me see how bad it is. The glass is well into the forearm, now, isn't it?"

He returned a silent stare.

"You can go show the doctor, if you'd prefer," she said.

35

Greg rolled his eyes and sighed. "All right." He shoved the cuff of his shirt up to his elbow.

The ghostly skin reached for the bulge of muscle below the elbow joint, leaving the mechanical complexity of the wrist and a third of the forearm exposed to view.

"It was advancing faster a couple of days ago, but it's slowed down again," he offered.

"Maybe the radiation exposure energized the nanites so they reproduced faster."

"Maybe. If I had a better idea of what the nanite was designed to do, I could probably figure it out."

"If you knew, would you be able to do anything about it?"

Greg nodded. "Oh, yeah. Once I know what the program and design do—and most importantly how they do it—I could reverse-engineer and then create a new nanite to reverse the process and eradicate the old nanites... What are you grinning at?"

It wasn't a grin and it was a little sad, but Liss was smiling. "It's just nice to hear the old Greg again."

"*Old* Greg?"

"You know: The guy who loved solving problems, built the supply capsule accelerator when he was twelve...? Brilliant, but kind of, uh..."

"An asshole?"

"Yeah, that guy. I miss him."

Greg stared at her for a dazed moment. "I do too." He wrenched his gaze back to the viewscreen. "I could just start tinkering with this, but it would take a lot longer to figure out what the machine and its program do by that method. And I suspect time is a bit tight on this project. Right?"

Liss blinked twice before she replied. "Yes. The rate of change will increase as more of the Mark II nanites are created and then start to create more themselves, et cetera."

"I assume that these original nanites are breaking down and flushing from the system. That's certainly how I'd do it."

"That's what the doctor believes."

Greg went back to studying the drawings. "A two-stage program. They do their primary job until a certain level of wear is reached, at which point they switch to replicating themselves." Liss was not certain that he was talking to her, as much as thinking out loud. "Probably at a set ratio, they shut down and are then dismantled by other nanites for parts. The unusable bits get flushed out of the blood stream and the cycle goes on." He looked at her. "Very neat. The physical build is pretty rough, but the program... that's fucking clever."

Liss only nodded.

"Do you think you could find out more about this machine for me? Schematics, design information? It would make my work go faster, since I can't just drop my other projects to chase after this."

"I think so, but I'm concerned..."

"About what? Getting in trouble for trawling the databases? There has to be some kind of record of this thing."

"Not that. The acceleration of the process means you'll get worse faster and, eventually, the nanites... That is, at some point..."

"They'll reach a new stage of propagation. Is that what you're thinking?"

"That's the doctor's fear. That they'll reach a stage where they begin to look for new hosts."

"Oh yeah. The 'gray goo' scenario." He stepped back and was silent a moment, then turned her chair to face his new position. A frown flitted across his face. "I won't say it's not possible, but only a moron would design something so potentially devastating with no cutoff switch or overrides. I'm not betting this was just some jackass's dumb luck." He crossed his arms over his chest.

Liss shook her head and shrugged. "We don't know where this thing came from, so we don't know how sophisticated its designer was. There's no way to guess at this stage."

"Yeah, yeah, yeah. All the better reason to find out all you can about it for me."

She looked up at him and he looked back. But for his breathing, he could have been uncarved marble. Her mouth quirked.

"All right," she said. "What will you do in the meantime?"

"Go back to the tank. I have to fix this other project before I can do anything else."

"The tank? Be careful, Greg. Don't push too hard. We have no idea what's going to happen to you next."

He ground his teeth. "Liss. You are the one who pushed me to work on this project." His words were clipped and brittle. "I don't have a lot of time and you make it sound like I'm going to keel over any minute. I'm not crazy—not suicidally crazy, at least. I'm not ready to die, yet, but what is worth saving if the life I live is a worse horror than dying? Don't push me in too many directions at once. There's a knife-edge and no more between my temper and the rest of the station. Even with you. Don't assume that you're safe from me."

She held his gaze. "Maybe my safety doesn't concern me that much."

"You've always trusted me more than you should. Don't let me hurt you. I'd... I couldn't live with myself if I hurt you."

Liss smiled a little. "Then you won't."

He snorted but didn't say anything more.

She got up and started to go, then turned back.

"Greg, where did you go?"

He had no doubt what she meant. "I went outside."

"I know that. Where outside?"

"Nowhere. I just ran in a straight line until it was quiet, until I started walking, then I walked back. I can't outrun them for long, but, once in a while, they let me get ahead."

She nodded. "I'll come back when I have something to help you."

He nodded and let one side of his mouth rise slightly into a near-smile. He watched her go. He seemed to see her through a heavy pall of broken memories. He ground his teeth against the disjointed rubble of them, tumbled as pebbles in a stream, and felt recognition just slipping away. Something had risen to separate him from her and he couldn't seem to grab hold of it, much less stop or reverse it. Loss fluttered on the edge of his mind like a moth around a candle. He batted it away.

She combed through archives and databases, and applied to be allowed access to the limited historical archives, when they became available. She hoped there would be something worth the wait, as the connection to the ancient mainframe that served them was difficult to maintain and even more difficult to make in the first place. The old computer was only online to this station once per fortnight.

She had never understood the system's oddities. Why some databases and archives were occasionally unavailable, others available only on a schedule. There didn't seem to be any rhythm to it except sheer perversity.

So far, she had found nothing like these nanites and comparisons of this type were extremely time consuming. She was gambling that the design went back to the war or earlier.

The information she was perusing vanished.

"Source terminated," her terminal muttered.

"What? Wonderful…" She sent a query and got a null reply. She tried to reroute to the database at Sigma station but got put in a holding queue. A query popped up on her screen.

"What are you doing?"

"Trying to recover some information from Sigma's historical database. Who is this?"

"Laker. I'll be right down. Wait for me."

Ice shot down her sternum. Her boss—the great and powerful Dr. Laker—had caught her snooping into things she was sure he wouldn't approve of. She put her hands in her lap and breathed slowly, consciously. Her heart danced uncomfortable tangos as she wondered what Laker would do. She studied her hands and thought they looked like small, dead birds.

The doorway chimed and she looked up.

"Hello, Dr. Laker. What's going on at Sigma station?"

Laker scraped her with his pale blue eyes. His mouth tightened, disrupting his usual public calm. His cultivated silver-white hair was unruffled, his confident face smooth and pink, but the mouth and the lines around the eyes did not belong. They were sour and dissatisfied with what they knew.

"We may have lost Sigma station," he replied, the rich, round tones of his voice jarring against the horror of the possibilities.

"Lost?"

"Yes. The population density, the strain, must have been exceeded. I was talking to their station head when it happened. Most unpleasant."

Liss stared at him. She didn't know anyone at Sigma, personally, but it still jolted. "What happened?"

"To him? I'd rather not describe it. Apparently, it's been building for some time and he was hoping I could help him get them back under control, but his people have gone mad. I warned him, long ago, but he wasn't ready to listen. They're rioting, killing each other. Utter savagery. Once the initial destruction is over, cooler heads may prevail, but we won't know until it happens. This is quite unpleasant. And, of course, it has taken Sigma's data offline. I can only hope..."

Liss frowned down into her lap. "This is terrible, Dr. Laker. Those poor people..."

"Yes. But it is a factor in the Rat Syndrome of which he should have been aware. He simply chose not to face it. Now, it's much too late. All we can do is sit back and wait until the rats stop gnawing on each other. If they don't destroy the facility as happened at Delta station, they may be back. What was it you were after, there? I see you've been spending a lot of time in the historical and technical databases."

"I've been trying to track down some information for Greg Forrester. He doesn't have clearance for these and I don't want to encourage his hacking them."

"That's wise of you. Greg and his unusually strong channels and receptors is certainly a bigger challenge and possibly a greater fascination than I had anticipated. You have been spending a great deal of time with him and working on his files. I'm worried, Liss."

"Worried? It's my job to spend time with Greg. He... he's not doing well at the moment."

"Yes…" Laker sat down in one of her chairs. "Liss, let me be frank. I believe you are losing your objectivity where Greg is concerned. The dreamers are a sort of relief valve, somehow listening in on our fears. Greg is especially… sensitive, I suppose is the best word, and he does require special handling. But please bear in mind that you are not Greg's friend. You are his keeper, to be blunt about it. The intimacy of your relationship may have been appropriate in the past, but it is not anymore."

Liss jerked back in her seat as if he had struck her. "Dr. Laker, Greg and I—"

He waved her down. "I know that you haven't done anything inappropriate in *that* fashion, but you seem to have forgotten how to separate your job from your personal feelings where Greg is concerned. Your reports and your actions demonstrate that you have allowed your necessary contacts to become far too personal. This is completely unacceptable. You may be his friend, or you may be his handler, but you may not be both."

"That's impossible, Doctor," she objected. "I can't do my job without Greg's trust, and he will only give his trust to the rare person who can meet his criteria for friendship. Greg is more intense than the rest, as you say. All his baselines seem to be set even higher. As a result, he's very perceptive and extremely wary. If your theories are correct, then he has to be approached in exactly the right way, managed with exactly the right touch, or we'll lose him, too. It's absolutely required that I be his friend—"

"It is required that you appear to be his friend. Not that you believe it, yourself."

"You can't lie to Greg. I can't, certainly. And I *am* his friend. It's the only way I can do this job. It's the right way and the right thing. I can't shut that off like a switch!"

"Then you have two choices: end your friendship with Greg, or cease to work in this capacity. Obviously, there is no middle ground."

"Dr. Laker!" She jerked forward in her chair, barely stopping from jumping up.

"Liss, when you came here, I had high hopes and you've done very well, but, especially in light of what is happening at Sigma, I simply cannot allow this sort of risk to evolve here."

"But it is exactly the sort of thing—"

"It is not! Management of a single case will not make or break Epsilon! Greg Forrester is not the linchpin that holds this place together. Do you understand why Epsilon is so successful while other stations are falling into chaos? It is because of proper management of the potential stresses of the population due to hyper-density. The dreamers are part of it, but only a part. My theories. My management techniques. This is what has enabled Epsilon to survive and thrive in spite of the pressures placed upon her by the very population we attempt to protect.

"When a population grows too dense with no outlets, it becomes aggressive and self-destructive. It begins to attack itself, like rats in a cage. There must be outlets, there must be routines, there must be strong structures. If it is not properly managed, the population goes insane, becomes murderous and cannibalistic. That has not happened here. It will not happen here."

"Because of proper management of cases like Greg's!" she shot back.

"Cases *like* Greg's, yes, but not specifically Greg Forrester!" He caught himself and leaned back into his seat, breathing carefully. "Liss, please. This is most upsetting. It is inappropriate for you to argue my own theories back to me for a selfish purpose. I am sorry that this may hurt you, but your overfamiliarity with Greg is ultimately of more risk to him and to the proper management of this station than any potential harm which may be done by changing the fashion in which he, specifically, is managed, no matter how exceptional he may be. Now, trust that I know what must be done. Cut off your friendship with Greg or leave this position."

She stared at him.

"I am sorry, Liss. This has been a trying day and I fear I have been harsher than I wished to be. However, I can't change my position on this. Please let me know your decision before the end of cycle. Otherwise, I shall have to make that decision for you."

"The end of cycle? Can't you give me a day? I... this is... What about the others?"

"That will be my problem. Your problem is to determine what is most important to you. I... am sorry. Take your day, but let me know by the end of tomorrow's cycle. I cannot give you more than that."

He pushed out of his chair and walked out of the cubicle.

Liss sat at her desk, gaping, unable to breathe, growing light-headed until she gulped a single deep breath and shivered back into the world. There seemed to be no floor beneath her. She felt that if she moved, she would plunge into some dark abyss.

She rose and stepped away from her terminal.

---

"I don't know what to do," she said. "Obviously, Dr. Laker is monitoring my terminal access, though I don't understand why. He's always left me alone to manage these cases my way. I can't just stop being Greg's friend. That's not how friendship works. But if Laker sees I'm still working on what I admitted was research to help Greg, he'll know I'm not going to quit. I mean I am going to quit, but I have to do what I can while I still have time. I am not going to stop being Greg's friend. I have to find a way..."

"You need a terminal Laker can't monitor, I suppose," the doctor said. "We have to find that nanite. I have a lead, but it's thin and I don't have the kind of access necessary to pry into the databases this sort of thing would be in."

"What have you got?"

"It's military. Old stuff. The markings on the nanite proved to be a manufacturing code. It was referenced in the drug database, of all things, though it is, itself, not a therapeutic."

"I have access to the military archives, but I didn't get a match," Liss objected.

"Not our side. The other side. It would be in the sealed databases or in the original database, if it's still accessible."

Liss looked down at her hands. "I have codes for those. But I can't use them now with Laker watching, and if I give them to you, it'll be even worse."

"You need a terminal that is off the station's network. There must be a secure stand-alone somewhere…" He looked thoughtful.

Liss laughed harshly. "Probably in Laker's office."

He shook his head. "Damn it! Doesn't Laker understand the threat this nanite poses?"

Liss bit her lip. "I didn't tell him."

"Why not?"

"I didn't report it because I wanted to give Greg a chance. If Laker knew that Greg was infected with a wild nanite, I think he would put him outside, regardless of any benefit he offers the community."

The doctor shook his head, brow knit. "Liss, you've exposed us all to a horrible risk."

She pinned his gaze with hers. "The risk was already here, as soon as he got it. Inside, there's a chance we can stop it. Outside, there is only misery and slow death. The nanite action seems to increase with radioactive exposure. Greg will die out there even faster than he'll die in here. What good is that? What if it doesn't stop at Greg? Even if he voluntarily went out, there's no guarantee that this thing won't appear again."

"You're rationalizing."

"Isn't it too late for that to matter?"

The doctor sighed. "I suppose… Look, I can try and get a little closer to this thing through the drug database. I might find a better schematic, or a better reference number, if there's any post-war record of treatment for something caused by this nanite. Assuming that the reference I have is correct and it really is something from the war. I may have some other resources… Let me look. I'll meet you for dinner and tell you if I've found anything. My God, this is all so cloak and dagger."

"If Laker finds out, we'll both be in serious trouble."

"All right. I'll see you at dinner."

She nodded and left his office.

Liss walked along the corridor, past supply corridors and classrooms. Voices droned out of the open rooms, floating lightly on the air, like summer-lazy bees, remembered only vaguely in ancient video.

"...beyond the end of the war. The man who does not remember history is destined to repeat it..."

She smiled bitterly. Merely the memory of history would not be sufficient, though it would go a long way toward helping her, if she could only reach into those machine-memories, somehow. She paused a moment, listening to the lulling cadence of the reader's voice.

"...Starfall device, which unleashed pulses of deadly radiation. In the end, victory by total destruction was preferred over a more difficult political solution. The veritable obliteration of the machines of war put the advantage back into the hands of those who had gone to ground. Previously disadvantaged by a lack of supplies, but blessed with a surfeit of numbers, our forefathers—our grandparents and great grandparents—left us this legacy of poisoned ground in exchange for quick victory, snatched from their enemies after the horrors of the massacre at Crossfield.

"Which has led us to the development of the warren-stations, envisioned and brought to life by men like Eric Laker..."

Liss glared at the floor and moved away from the voice. Her emotions coiled in her stomach and squeezed her chest like snakes.

---

A cloud of disturbance swirled in front of his face. He moved to wave it away, unthinking, and felt the crushing resistance of the medium against his arm. He thought curses which would not rise into his throat. He pushed the movement reset on the back of the suit gauntlet. The dense, liquid medium in the tank lent him a slow, strong grace in every movement.

He repositioned the model and guided the following arm into contact, sending the code for the part to the device. Deliberately, he maneuvered the part into place in the model with a slight lift and a twist that made all the difference, then repeated the action again and a third time. The unbalanced pressure of the medium against the hyperoxygenated fluorocarbon in his lungs made his chest ache; his suit felt as if it was collapsing over his arms and chest.

Vision darkened from the tank's normal ruddy-orange view to streaming red. The usual mild tinnitus was overcome by a keening and howling in his ears. He let go of the part and drifted back from the model. His arms stretched to the side groping for balance he was not losing.

A dark face glared at him through the face plate. He jerked his head against the uncompressible liquid in the helmet, the muscles of his neck twinging against the immovable.

They crushed in on him, a dozen or more, crying and screaming, clawing at him. They clawed through the suit, ripping at his arms and shoulders, crushing him with the weight of their terror. They thrust fingers into his mouth and eyes, prying at him, screaming for help, for succor, for quietus, choking him with their demands.

He tried to scream, tried to push them away. They flooded into him, holding him still, wrenching him against invisible, immovable barriers that ripped into his flesh like the fence of Crossfield.

His mind lashed at them and flailed against their panicked strength. He cried out to them with the voice of his will. "Go away! I can't help you!"

They pushed on, filling him, softening and flowing into him, slowing to a trickle of pain and fright. Then they were past.

Emptiness roared where they had gone.

Greg went limp into the embrace of the tank medium.

The buzzing of pressure on his ears cleared the haze from his mind and his vision. Green phrases floated on the heads-up. He forced his focus to them.

O2: 10 min.

Movement replication recorded.

Next.

Next.

Next.

OK?

Greg? You OK?

He dragged one burning hand to the control pad on the other arm. His skin felt scratched, flayed with flaming knives. Clumsily, he pressed the Acknowledge key, then the Exit Programming sequence and the request for extraction.

They dragged him out of the tank and yanked him out of the suit. Akima caught up to him in the hypo tank prep room.

"You cut it a bit too fine, Greg. I thought we were going to have to call Medical."

Dripping from the shower, Greg glowered at him. "Who cares? The fix works, doesn't it?"

The senior engineer stared at him. His eyes lingered over the disturbing display of muscle and bone under the glassy skin of Greg's arm and shoulder. A pink sheen of diluted blood glowed on Greg's upper arm, lending it a sham of normalcy. The younger man pressed the appendage against his side and folded his stiff, pale hand over his abdomen. His normal skin was ridged by the sharp-pared muscles underneath. Narrow stripes of shadow from the room lights played restlessly over his body as he breathed and moved with nervous flickers.

"Yes, but ten minutes is not a safe margin for extraction. I don't care if the thing works if it fucking well kills you to fix it. You have to stop..."

"No," Greg snapped. "It has to work! Don't lecture me when you get what you want. Don't feed me that bullshit. My job is to fix the son of a bitch. It's freakin' fixed! My God-damned job!" He broke off and spat pink fluorocarbon with a racking cough. His eyes didn't quite focus on Akima. "My fucking life..." he muttered. "They all want something. Just leave me alone to fix what I can fix. I break enough things. Just let me finish fixing these few, before you close the doors on me."

Akima narrowed his eyes and cocked his head. Then he shook himself and turned away. "I'll see you tomorrow. Try to sleep sometime, OK?" Akima plodded out of the room, heavy with some unseen burden.

Greg looked at the floor and nodded, shivering with a hundred sudden finger-touches of the dead on his back. "Leave me alone," he growled at the memory of them.

He tried to shrug them off his shoulders as he turned to dress, but the torn feeling of them stayed on his skin, even through his clothes. He wore the visitation of their fears, bleeding into his own. They'd never touched him in the tank before. And he couldn't remember if Akima had ever sworn at him, before, but he thought not—nobody swore here but himself. The senior engineer was one of the few who tolerated his moods and fits with equanimity. Greg trembled and tried to walk out from under the weight of these thoughts.

He felt himself crumbling and had to stop and be sick. He vomited up pink bile and the last of the fluorocarbon. He stayed a while, leaning against the nearest wall.

As he stood still, panting, an alien memory trickled into his head. It itched over the base of his skull and wormed into his forebrain, illuminating his mental notes on the nanite. For a hot-white instant, the nanite schematic burst into shining detail, exploding outward in an expanding and brilliant sketch of forms and functions, rotating, spinning like the design suite gone mad, clear and solid and complete.

He reached for it and it sparkled a moment on the tip on his finger, a mote of fairy dust. Then it collapsed into darkness with a clang that rang his skull like a bell. He gasped and stumbled back a step, shaking his head to cast out the ache.

He'd had it. For an instant, he had touched it. It existed, if only in a memory somewhere. He could find it again. If he just had enough time... Very distantly, a thousand names began to recite in the back of his mind, a dim chattering he pushed aside.

---

The dining area vibrated with angry sound and harsh light. Liss glanced around, discomfited and wary. She didn't like the feeling. It was foreign to her, who had never felt any cause to fear her close-packed neighbors. Until now. Now she wondered who was spying on her, from what unsuspected place electronic eyes and ears kept track.

The volume and freneticism of the diners sent a frisson up her back. They seemed contentious, loud, frightening and alien. She chided herself for imagination gone to paranoia. Laker's ultimatum, the loss of Sigma, her own imposed pressure to help Greg were working against her normal calm, leaving her feeling hunted.

"Is today some kind of holiday I've forgotten about?" the doctor asked, sitting beside her.

"I don't think so."

"Must be spring fever or something," he commented, shrugging it off. "I almost couldn't get out of Medical for all the sudden drop-ins. I'll have to get back quickly. Here," he added, shoving a data chip at her. "This is what I was able to get. There is a higher-echelon reference number, but the report connected to it is sealed. I didn't even try to get into it. If Laker is monitoring you, he may be keeping an eye on my terminal calls too."

Liss leaned toward him. "Are we being ridiculous?" she whispered. "I can't help myself, but I know I'm acting paranoid. Everything and everyone seems suspicious to me, like there's something dire going on that I can't put a finger on and can't stop."

"Aside from what's happening to Greg?"

"Yes. Or maybe it's just that I'm frightened for him and all the rest of this is making me see monsters in shadows."

"Paranoia seems like a safe mode of operation at the moment. Better too vigilant than not vigilant enough. But, yeah, things seem kind of crazy to me, too. Laker is acting very strange, if you ask me. It could just be that Sigma's blow-up is effecting him badly, though, and the rest of the station is reacting to his upset."

Liss frowned. "I don't know..."

"Can't worry about it, now. If you're still interested in finding that nanite information, you'll have to focus on that. If I'm right, Greg could be approaching a breakover point where the nanites are limited only by the availability of whatever resources they need to do whatever it is they do. Numbers may soon become academic."

She squeezed her eyes shut. "I hope you're wrong."

"Me, too. But it will be irrelevant if you can't get to the information. However, we might have had a stroke of luck. There's a terminal from the old diagnostic system which was installed when the station first came online. If you can jumper it into the main trunk, somehow, you should be able to get into the data system without a location ID. Sounds kind of nutty, but it might work." He shrugged. "Best I could do."

Liss smiled. "Well, it's kind of a crazy problem, so I guess a crazy solution is apropos."

"I wish..." He shook his head. "I... wish you luck, Liss. I suppose you don't want me to come along?"

"No. If anything happens, I'll be the only one in trouble. If I can't manage it, you'll still be around to do whatever can be done. You could always say you didn't know, but if you came along, you'd be just as bad off as me, if something goes wrong."

"Yeah... Be careful. Please." He reached out as if he would take her hand, then pulled back and rose to his feet. "I'd better go. Good luck."

She smiled again. "Thank you." She watched him walk away.

---

Sweat tickled at her temples and down her neck. She could smell the wire insulation in the manual jumpers overheating. The ancient screen flickered as the file download counted down.

She skimmed over the information in the file as it copied to the data chip. Download nearly complete...

*Psychological impact of mimicry/replication is expected to range from disruptive to debilitating. Factoring in additional conversion effects, as well, it is anticipated that average subjects will be psychologically broken by the psycho-emotional complications, which—*

Liss shuddered and jumped ahead in the text, noting in a corner of her mind that the schematic was fully downloaded and the file nearly so.

Lists of names, factors, dates, storage cells scrolled past. She stared at them in horror. "Bastards," she muttered.

The download rate flashed: complete.

She began to pull out.

"Identify user."

"Oh... no." She yanked the data chip from the writer and typed furious keystrokes.

Epsilon's security attempted to lock onto the terminal location. Failing, it grabbed at the user information. Liss jumped up, slipping the data chip into her pocket, and yanked out the jumper wires in the power board.

The wires smoked and burned black strips of char into the palms of her hand. Electricity crackled and popped with the smell of roasting meat and insulation. She whimpered and jerked her hands back filled with smoking jumpers. She stuffed them into her pockets too, and darted out of the room. In the corridor, she slowed to a stroll, squeezing back tears as the hot loops burned against her hands. At the first recycler, she shoved the wires into the slot and hurried on, her mind chewing into the information she had seen.

---

Greg coughed and retched heavy pink fluid onto the floor between his knees. Expelling the fluorocarbon was getting harder. He wondered if it lingered in his lungs, now, eating quietly away at his ability to breathe air. He'd long ago gotten used to the idea of "breathing" the liquid, but his body was beginning to fight the process his brain accepted. He shook his head and puked bright-pink goo. His arms shook with the effort of holding him up after exerting themselves against the pressure of the tank. His elbows gave.

Liss caught him, flinching at the slice of pain through her palms. He gasped for air, hanging in her arms a moment, spitting out the residue of the breathing mixture. Then he shook his head back and rested on his heels, breathing deeply, purging the last of the gel with sudden, choking hacks.

He pushed her aside and climbed to his feet, sharp cracklings of pain ripping along his flesh beneath the suit's skin.

She had come into the tank observation room and demanded that he emerge immediately. His annoyance at the loss of time was wiped out by perverse relief.

"What in hell were you doing in there?" she demanded, backing off only a step, tucking her injured hands out of sight. "The pressure in the tank is killing you."

He glowered as best he could while covered in pink slime. The contact lenses that let him see through the super-dense medium made her an indistinct, dark blur out here.

"It's just the fluoro."

"Oxygenated fluorocarbon is light pink," she said, pointing, "not bright pink and red like blood."

He hung his head back and pawed at the suit seals. His fingers fumbled as his head seemed to spin. He dropped onto a bench.

"Help me out of the suit. Please."

Short though she was, hands stiff from the burns, she was able to wrench the heavy, slime-soaked suit off his shoulders and shove it down to his waist. Air flooded into his lungs, pushing them to full expansion for the first time in hours as the restriction of the suit was removed. He felt faint and the chanting in his ears swarmed up in volume, then dropped slowly back to a dull buzzing.

The air felt cool and tasted like plastic. He became momentarily drunk on it and slumped against the wall.

"What did you want, Liss?" His tongue stumbled over the words.

"I have the build details and schematics for the nanite."

He turned his head to stare at her. Frustrated, he poked the lenses from his eyes, growling. He blinked and looked at her.

"How— Where did you find them? I looked for them myself. I couldn't—"

"Sealed military databases," she cut in. "This was a terrible thing. It was a last-ditch, a sort of 'joke's on you,' just in case. I haven't had a chance to look it all over, but there are things... some of it is really nasty."

He leaned his head against the wall, again. "I thought I had it. I did have it. For just a moment. I thought I could recreate it in the tank, but it wouldn't come back."

"You won't have to do that, again. I hope."

"I can't do it again." He shoved the suit completely off, kicking it away. Tendrils of bright, purple-red blood traced down his arm and side, clung to the shape of his nearly-transparent hand. "I'm falling apart."

She stared. The once-supple body had become tight, fat stripped away until muscle and bone stood out in brittle relief. Patches of cloud seemed to cling to his skin around the shoulder and chest, reaching narrow fingers up toward his neck and down into the curve of pectoral muscle over his heart.

"There may not be enough time," he murmured. He was tired and wound-up simultaneously. His blood seemed to be singing and muttering secrets into his ears which he couldn't quite catch. The recitation of names continued, looping on, endlessly, a constant low tone in his inner ear.

She swallowed. "I will get you some help."

"Without the nanite, there's nothing…"

"I know of someone who can help with the nanite."

"Who would want to help me? I'm despised. Even Akima can't stand me anymore."

"This man won't have a choice. He owes you. I'll see to it."

She put a small packet on the bench. "This is the data chip. Don't lose it. It can't be replaced, yet." Her expression softened and she looked only at his face. "Can you— Will you manage?"

He nodded. "Yeah. Yeah, I'm not dead, yet." He attempted a smile that broke and died. "I'll come around, when I'm… decent. I won't be able to carry you off for dinner, though. Something might shatter."

"I'll look out for you."

She shoved her hands into her pockets and left him as he pushed himself to his feet and shuffled into the shower.

---

"I found your name on a report."

"Which you got from the military database. There was an unknown user report. I should have guessed it was you."

She felt cold in her fury. "It's academic how I got the information. I have it. What I simply cannot understand is how you managed to switch sides and go undetected for so long."

He lowered his eyes and glanced at the viewscreen on his desk. "It's really quite easy when one has money and secrets."

"You bribed someone?"

"I bought my safety. As anyone would have done. I was an intern on the project. I was not a big fish, but I knew a lot. I leveraged that."

Liss looked disgusted. "And we have all believed in you for so long. Well, now I have the secrets to barter with and you will do what is necessary."

"Or you will destroy me with this information?"

"I will let everyone in Epsilon and every station I can reach know what you really did during the war. You are an old man, but they have never ceased to hate what you stand for."

"You are threatening me, Liss?"

"Motivating. I want to help Greg. He needs your knowledge and assistance and you don't want to be exposed for what you are."

"I have only ever tried to do my best, to help—"

"Your help hasn't always been such a raging success, in spite of appearances. You tried to 'help' your side by deploying this wretched nanite and it somehow got to Greg fifty years later. It was the Crossfield deployment, wasn't it?"

"It would have to be, yes."

Liss's gaze turned inward. She murmured to herself. "He cut his hand on a wire..." She felt sudden despair; she had taken him there. She glared at the man before her.

"I—"

An urgent beeping from the message console interrupted them. Dr. Laker looked down and pressed a button. His eyes scanned the message and grew wide. Liss read over his shoulder and swallowed down an urge to retch.

Liss sat in front of her terminal, her fingers manic on the keyboard, scrabbling to recreate a link. Her hair swept forward, touching her cheek and jaw with stripes of dark and light.

Greg raised the corner of a smile at the sight of her. The doorway chimed as he stepped across the threshold.

"Hey," he started. Then he stopped and twitched one shoulder as if bitten by some transient insect. His eyes narrowed as he turned.

The old man on the bed looked back at him with an intense eye, a corner of Liss's quilt clenched in front of his face.

A low growl started in Greg's throat.

"Don't get angry, yet, Greg," Liss requested, turning in her seat. "Laker is going to help you with the nanite. He helped design it."

Greg seemed to vibrate. He stared at Laker, his mouth drawn tight.

"You. At the bottom of anything, there's always you." He stepped across the small space and reached for the old man. His hand touched the quilt first, a shield raised between them, and stopped. One fingertip brushed along a scrap of soft buttercup and wrung a ghost of scent into the air between them. Greg quieted, settled, let his shoulders down, though he kept his fingertip against the worn fabric for a moment longer.

"I remember that smell," Laker whispered, looking steadily at Greg. "That's silk. Yellow silk. There is no more. We destroyed the caterpillars that made it and the moths that laid the eggs. I knew a woman who used to wear silk and she smelled like that, of earth and sun. But no one smells like that anymore."

"Liss does."

"Does she? Then, you and I have even more reason to work together."

"You sound like you're asking me," Greg scoffed.

"I am offering and, in my way, I am begging."

Greg cracked open a bitter laugh. "You. The king of Epsilon, the great savior of civilization, want to help me, the head-case. Why?"

Laker dropped his gaze and watched his hands place the quilt on the bed, smooth it, smoothing, smoothing…

"I owe it to you. I owe it to Epsilon. This nanite… I can help you with it. And we have little time."

"No. *I* have little time. You have all the time in the world. Why the hell should you care what becomes of me? If this toy of yours kills me, what does it matter to you? I'm the freak of the station, I hear voices, I know the dead. Maybe I don't want to keep on living like that."

Laker stopped his hands. "It is not just you, anymore. Akima has found three of the nanites in the hypo tank. They were crushed by the pressure, but he identified them. They are beginning to migrate out of your body."

"Oh, I see. The gray goo isn't just a myth. And here is your side's revenge coming back to haunt you. What was it supposed to do, eh? I haven't had time to read your report."

"It was—" Liss started to answer for him, but Laker waved her down and took a deep breath before speaking.

"It was a mimicry nanite, meant to propagate horror and disease through the remaining population. The program waited for a non-standard sample, then replicated that in its host. If the host—"

"The victim, you mean."

"Please… this is very difficult, Greg."

"I'm not going to make it any easier for you to excuse yourself, Laker. You deployed a terror weapon into a population of innocents. Didn't you? You seeded Crossfield with it, then waited for the survivors to come back to bury the dead. But they skunked you. They set off Starfall and that shut your nanite down."

"No. It is much worse than that. Guidon was deployed after Starfall. The nanites had been prepared and stored. Many were destroyed by the Starfall bursts even through their bunkers, but we had enough to seed Crossfield."

"So, your side deliberately deployed this horror that you had engineered. Because you couldn't stand to lose. You wanted to wreak a little vengeance because the other side had the gall to rip victory from your bloody fists, even though it literally cost us all the Earth. What went wrong?" he mocked. "What spoiled your plan?"

"Conscience. We… just wanted to be able to negotiate. We had nothing left but this. It was illegal. It was horrible, but it was a war and we, like the rest, were desperate and afraid. But, in the end, we simply couldn't do it. We realized what it could do to any chance the human race still had and we threw the switch, turned them off and let the residual radiation do the rest. And said nothing."

"Then how did I get one?"

"I have been racking my brain for that answer ever since I first saw the medical report. I knew what it had to be. Liss thought, perhaps, the wire that cut you harbored one or two. A few of them must have remained viable, but dormant, perhaps they weren't deactivated, or the radiation in the area flipped the switch back on, or they were shielded somehow. So many 'what ifs'… What if they went dormant on a neutral medium? What if they came in contact with some animal or organic tissue and were carried about that way? If they had contact with the oxy-ferrous compounds of blood or bone marrow, they might have maintained a viable population. What if they waited in a dormant state in the very bones of the dead? I simply can't guess."

Greg snarled. "And it didn't matter to you until you thought that your precious station was threatened," he scoffed. "You forgot all about them."

"I never forgot, Greg. I have labored with such nightmares… Please, give me a moment's doubt of my evil. There is something— This nanite was never meant to do… whatever it is that it is doing to you. Something in the program has gone wrong."

"Apparently. So you need me to fix it, build a new nanite, so you can save your precious station. Then what? Go on with my life, listening to every fear and horror screaming in my head night and day?"

"You are feeling sorry for yourself. You weren't meant to feel sorry for yourself, or anyone else. Please stop it."

"What would you know or care about what I feel?" Greg demanded, suddenly sharp. "I am not inside your head the way you and everyone else are inside mine! Why should I do any damned thing to help you and your fucking station? The mere existence of this place is torture to me! Why should I help you save it from your own hubris, you revisionist piece of shit?"

Greg could feel Laker's surprise press against him like wet paper, sudden and shredding to wisps as it touched. Liss was a pool of water in the corner of his mind.

"Yeah," he added. "I figured it out. It's not the dead I hear, it's the living, and they are so much worse. So why should I help you to keep on tormenting all of us? Why not just give up and die? Why not have my own damned revenge on you? You with your Histories and your Theories. The architect of all our pain. Why?!" he shouted.

"You are the only one, Greg. My genius, and you can save these people from my... mistakes. You with that brilliant mind, that defiance, you can make it possible for me to... make up for the past," Laker replied, his voice rising in strength and anger as he spoke. "Epsilon— No. *All* the warren stations were meant to make up for all I had done. They still can, but only if they survive. Delta station burned out. Sigma has gone dark and may be gone now, too. You are a part of all of this. These people, this station, they may go on, but not if you do not help them. Not if you do not help yourself!"

Greg snorted, but he could feel the press of Laker's fear and desperation against his nerves. Now, he could differentiate the metallic tang of it against his senses, though that did not make it any less like being skinned alive. Beneath it was the constant humming and muttering of ten thousand distressed minds, ten thousand ever-dwelling nightmares.

"Don't try to soap me, Laker. You only care what happens to your precious demonstration of your bloody theories."

"For God's sake, Greg! Not the station! Not my bloody, stupid theories! Ten thousand human beings! My ten thousand penances to be repaid. If this thing I helped to make were to get loose it could kill them all. Every one. And it is loose. Three of them in the tank. How many more have escaped?" Laker stood and walked closer to Liss, never looking away from Greg. "And who have they infected? Your colleagues? Your friends? Liss, perhaps?" He grabbed her wrist and turned her hand, showing the oozing lines of burns across her palm to

Greg. He let all his fear and outrage, his panic and guilt, flood out, let it batter against Greg.

Liss gasped in pain and tried to pull her hand from his. Laker's grip was an eagle's.

"Only three in the tank and those are dead, now. But are there more?" Laker demanded. "Are they busying away inside her veins, now, too? Is that horror enough for you? What will they do to her skin, eh? Plastic? Fluorocarbon?" He saw Greg cringe and clap his hands over his ears. He shouted at the young man. "Strip it down to a gas and—"

"Shut up! Oh, you bastard, shut up!" A narrow line of blood trickled against Greg's temple where his nearly transparent hand pressed against his skull.

"No! What will it be, Greg? Make up your mind. Flip your coin. Ten thousand survivors. Ten thousand second chances. Or ten thousand Liss Moris and Greg Forresters. Ten thousand more casualties in a war that's never stopped. Ten thousand more victims—"

"Stop!" Greg screamed. "Stop! You win! You win." Greg dropped down onto the edge of the bed and covered his face with his hands.

Laker dropped Liss's hand and she yanked it back from him, rubbing the bruised wrist. "That was low," she hissed.

"Yes. But it is true. You saw the message. You talked to Greg in the prep-room. The nanites could have been loose in there, too. It only takes one."

Greg mumbled from under his cupped hands, then raised his head. "I... I can do it. In the tank, but..."

"Can't you use the waldo assemblers?" Liss objected. "The pressure in the tank—"

"I don't have fine motor control, anymore. The waldos won't be delicate enough." He raised his head. "I can do it if I just have enough time. I can see it in my head. We can do it."

He stood up and snatched at Laker's arm with his good hand. "Come on, Laker. Liss, call the doctor, tell him to meet us at tank-prep with a blood kit."

He dragged Laker out of the cubicle. The older man caught up to his agitated stride and rushed beside him down the corridor.

Liss called Medical, then sat down on the edge of the bed and stared at the open doorway. People rushed by, outside. She looked down at her own hands, lying quiet and bleeding in her lap. Her mind spun. There was something…

---

The station buzzed like an enraged hive. The corridor slipped blindly away as Laker ran beside Greg, shoving through herds of aimless, urgent people. His heart malleted against his chest and knocked the breath from his lungs in puffs.

"After I'm in the tank, you go straight to the design suite and start to analyze the nanite program on this chip against the new one," Greg began, shoving the data chip into Laker's hand.

Laker glanced at the chip and shoved it into his pocket. "New one? The program in the current nanite, you mean?"

"Yes," Greg snapped.

"Do you have a copy of it, then?"

"No. We're going to get one. My blood is full of nanites. The doctor takes some blood and puts it in the analyzer. We cross-connect the medical diagnostics to the design suite, isolate a live nanite, and extract the program. You'll have to do it. You know the keys and protocols. I need to be in the tank, working on the physical design. It's the only way we can stretch enough time out of what's left of me."

"You think you're going to die."

"Be realistic, Laker."

"I am. You are being a pessimist. Damn it, you're not supposed to be a pessimist. You're not designed for it."

Greg wheeled and cut him off with an impatient wave. "You've forced me into the role of hero. I don't have to believe it. I just have to go through the motions. If we both work at maximum speed, we might make it. But if you think I'm likely to come out of that tank alive, you're the crazy one, here."

"You will come out alive. You have to. I can't…"

"You can finish it without me. The pressure in the tank will break my skin open and whatever else has become so brittle it can't hold, not anymore. Even if it didn't, do you think I have any interest in continuing to dream other people's nightmares? I'd rather crack the suit seals and be crushed into paste. Do not say any such thing to Liss. Ever. Do you understand me? Not one word."

Laker gave a mute nod.

"Good." Greg turned and continued down the corridor to Engineering. Laker ran after him through the surging crowds.

---

She watched the blood ooze into the creases of her palm and saw only red lines, connecting the channels of the burns. Back and forth the information of the blood flowed across her hands. Vagrant whiffs of scent floated upward, disturbed like ghosts by drops of blood upon the quilt.

Phrases from her own reports clattered off the inside of her skull, crashing into words, caroming into ideas and cracking them together into new thoughts, whirling into complex shapes, like molecular models stacking, spinning, growing into structures, into whole creatures, a devouring monster that leapt upon her with a strangled scream from her own throat.

---

The mechanical part was simple, really, merely time-consuming. He had the schematic in the interface memory and the plan in his head was illuminated with a painful insight that glinted off its concept like refraction from diamonds. He ached in every part but set the mechanical arm to spinning before him anyway, concentrating on its slow spiraling into place even as black storms of terror and despair shuddered him.

The heads-up began to scroll.

61

Greg. Your vitals don't look good.

He ignored it. The piece eased into place with balletic precision. He reached for the next and was pleased he could not cough and that the dense medium held him up. His head hurt, but it was easy to let it go in the tangle of other pains and the rushing muttering beneath his concentration. He looked forward to sleeping without dreams.

He could do it, soon. The mechanicals were almost done, then it was just a matter of running the replicator and programming the nanites. He might get to see a few of them drizzle off the assembler, if things went smoothly for Laker...

Laker bent over the design suite interface and scrolled through the program. He had found the broken code quite easily and it wasn't so difficult to remember how to modify the program. He felt a flush of pride as he looked at it. Indeed, there was a chance. He smiled at it and felt the foreignness of the expression tighten his face.

The security door rattled and clattered in its frame.

"Dr. Laker! Dr. Laker! Damn it, open up!"

Laker blinked his screen-dazzled eyes and turned the chair until he could reach the door.

Liss fell in on him and thrust the door closed behind her against the oceanic human flow outside.

"You did it," she gasped.

"Yes. I have the program. All I have to do is make a backup and we can load it. Greg's mechanicals are brilliant. The assembler is working on them, now. We're going to make it."

He grinned at her with a ridiculously buoyant glee. He couldn't remember such elation.

"No. I mean you made Greg, didn't you?"

"What?" he asked, pushed back into his chair with alarm. "What do you mean?"

"When you said 'my genius' you weren't talking about your own abilities, you were speaking in the possessive. Greg is your genius. You caused him to be what he is. Didn't you?"

"Oh, Lord..."

"You told me that the dreamers occurred naturally in response to the mental pressures of the stations' hyper-populations. A relief valve, you said, channeling the destructive pains and confusion of an over-populated system. The sidelight was mental agility and allowing them to be as crazy as they liked would blow the pressure off while allowing their brilliance free rein. What I knew from Delta station confirmed that. But you did something, didn't you? You wanted more. You wanted a dreamer with stronger receptors, bigger channels in his brain for this kind of information to flow through. But you also got the nice little side dish of genius. Was this another nanite? Did you tinker with Greg's brain the way another one is tinkering with his body? Your theory needed a relief valve, so you created it! Maybe they are all your experiments—"

"No! I improved on what Nature had provided, yes, but only that. They do occur naturally, but not enough of them and not strong enough to handle the collective horrors of a whole society. There had to be a better way. A better relief valve. I decided to give Nature a nudge and see what happened. Only this one time. I did not do it for me. I did it to protect Epsilon from what happened at Delta station. From what is probably happening at Sigma, right now. It's the Rat Syndrome—"

"You can't fix one machine by breaking another, Dr. Laker. What you've done is create a scapegoat. The dreamers have always been our scapegoats. We use them up and then shut them outside to die when they get too crazed from our own misery. You have to undo that. You have to stop it, here. We have the chance to fix them. To fix them all. Greg is not an experiment, anymore. He and the rest are not things we should exploit like this. We can find another relief valve. You have to let him have his own humanity back."

"I don't think I..."

"Yes, you can! If the nanites can reorganize a body, why can't they reorganize a brain? You created those mental channels in Greg's brain that allow him to hear these voices in his head. You can program the nanites to shut them down."

"No, Liss. I mean that I don't think I can fix Greg, because I don't think we have time. And I don't think he would let me."

"You do have time. Take the first nanites off the assembler and program them. We can give them to Greg, now. A second-stage nanite can be introduced once his body stabilizes."

"He won't let me, Liss. He doesn't want to live like he has, and why should he trust me? I suspect…"

"What?"

"I can't tell you. I promised him I wouldn't."

Liss glared at him. "Upload your program and start on the next one. Find a way to fix Greg!"

"Liss," Laker began to object.

"Do it!"

She turned and ran out of the suite and fought her way up to the tank observation room. Her dark dress expanded behind her like a cloud in the rising storm of chaos in the halls.

Akima and the doctor looked up at her. The doctor looked bleak. He answered the expression on her face.

"He can't make it. He doesn't respond to us and his vitals are all over the place."

"What about the nanites?" she demanded.

"They're rolling off the assembler," Akima confirmed. "About a thousand of them, so far."

"You've told him?"

"Yes. He didn't reply."

The control computer squeaked and emitted Laker's voice. "The program has been uploaded to the assembler and is being loaded into the nanites, now."

"So, we'll have about a thousand viable nanites in a few minutes," Akima said.

"Then we need to get them into Greg."

Liss leaned forward and began to type into the interface.

Greg's heads-up began to scroll.

1k nanites ready to go.

Nothing came back.

She typed again.

This is Liss. Reply.

Hello Liss.

Come out. Nanites waiting.

The reply was slow.

No. No more secondhand pain.

We can fix it.

I'm FUBARed.

On purpose but not beyond repair.

?

Additional programs can shut it off. Permanently.

Convince me.

Trust me.

They waited and the doctor worried the frame of his monitor with sweat-damp fingertips. Greg hung in the tank, hands clasped to wrists, but communicating nothing. Five minutes weighed upon the feet of Time like lead.

The extraction command came back, at last.

Lights flashed. The doctor slapped the override, stopping the extraction rig from reaching in for Greg.

"No. The change in pressure is more dangerous than leaving him in there, right now. We'll have to send someone in with a box or he can't be pulled out without killing him. The pressure is what's holding him together, right now."

Akima frowned into the tank. "We need one more engineer, I can't run the rig and be in the tank at the same time."

"I can do it."

***

One suited figure slipped like a dolphin through the heavy medium and circled around the other figure hanging limp. A stream of reinforced tubes followed in the first one's wake, nuzzling against the second figure, pale sea snakes. The first one pushed the tubes against the second one, who swayed slowly in the resisting world. A word came back.

OK.

Telltales on the medical monitor strobed and screamed.

---

It was easy to let go. The pain rushed through him, breaking open his heart and brain and the quiet, dense world cradled him to sleep without dreams. No more nightmares.

---

The darkness was warm and soft. The smell of red earth in white sunlight drew him up to consciousness. He remembered the scent. Yellow silk. Buttercup yellow. His head rang with silence.

He opened his eyes.

"Welcome back."

Her eyes were deep and tired and her hair shadowed her face.

"How far did I go?" he asked.

"Most of the way. But you are nothing if not defiant. You don't even go where you want to go, easily."

"I changed my mind about that place." He shrugged. "I'm perverse."

"As always."

He lifted one corner of his mouth into a smile. "Some things don't change. Where's Dr. Laker? He should be here, gloating."

Liss frowned. "He died while extracting you."

"What? He... what?"

"He went in and got you; then he had a stroke..."

"So, who wrote the program?"

"Laker did it. He'd had it there all the time I was arguing with him. But he was debating himself about using it. He didn't know if you were serious about not coming out of the tank, and he said he was afraid to tell you the truth. He designed you, you know."

"I didn't."

"Did the program work?"

"So far, all I hear in my head is me."

"Good. That's the man I need you to hear the loudest. Epsilon is breaking. Laker's theories prove to be as unstable as his past, but without Laker's presence and without you and the other dreamers taking the brunt, the rats have started chewing on each other."

"Then let them go outside. Even rats need freedom and fresh air. They didn't really kill the world, you know. They just buried it prematurely and it's struggling to come back on its own. Laker left us some tools to fix it with. He wasn't all bad."

"But the nanites—"

"Don't say 'but,'" he chided, pushing himself up. "You remember Laker's favorite aphorism? Those who do not remember history are destined to repeat it? We've been burying it, swaddling it in packing and pretending that remembering its horrors is understanding the truth of it. Remembrance is not enough. You have to understand. You can't understand a thing when you wrap it up in lies. You have to hold it in your hands, smell it, feel it. Then you can understand. Then you can fix it. When they understand, they can fix it. When they are free of it, they can fix themselves…"

He looked down at his hand and flexed the supple flesh into a fist, watched the coordinated movement of muscle pull and ripple over the strength of bone, under the flexible, warm sheet of skin. He glanced down at the other hand, identical now. Restored. Fixed by his effort and by the effort of his one-time enemy.

Shattered pieces of memory flowed back in and fixed themselves in his mind, things of his own which had been pushed aside. They bent around the obstacles of pain and the black densities where other people's fear had dwelt, and flowed solid and clear, strong and pacific as glass. The fall of soft hair sweeping over a face, stripes of premature grey and white looking like tears in the dark fabric of it; the push of muscle against working weight; red dust; and the smell of silk.

# 3

## SINGLE-EDGED

It hasn't snowed yet, but it will. And that will be the last straw, Josh Tucker thinks. What else could shit on him today? He hasn't made a significant sale since Omaha and he's halfway through South Dakota, but he's off the clock because no one's open. It's late, his eyes are drifting closed, and the dirty humps of snow that line the endless road barely reflect the light of passing vehicles.

He almost doesn't see the double-tanker hauling 10,000 gallons of dairy fresh milk heading straight for him as his rental car slips across the lane divider. As the truck driver lays on his horn, Tucker overcorrects and swerves back into his own lane, sliding on the icy road.

"Shit! Shit, shit, shit!" Tucker shouts as he fights the car's slide toward the nearest snowbank. The car looks like a salmon trying to do the hokey pokey as it slithers side to side on the slippery road until Tucker finally gets it back on the straight.

Shaking, he pulls over at the first opportunity: a roadside tavern in the middle of nothing. A buzzing neon sign blinks the words "Dan's Double Barrel" above the image of a pig attempting to jump—or hump—one of the titular whiskey barrels, which disappears and reappears erratically, leaving the pig rearing over nothing like a porcine Frankenstein's monster with a bad cause of the DTs. Gritty snow lies in dirty banks around the edges of the packed-snow parking lot that looks like a slab of moldy bacon grease. It's decorated with half a dozen pickup trucks and some larger commercial vehicles that are scattered askew across the surface like they've slid into place with the drunken finesse of a puck on a shuffleboard table. Tucker's economical rental sedan fits in like the nerdy kid at football practice.

A rattling, rustling ringing alerts him to a message, but damned if he can find his cell phone. It was in the console just before the near-creaming of his car... Tucker searches the easily-searched places, but the phone's vanished somewhere in the passenger side. He gets out, slamming the door on the car's annoyed pinging, and storms around to the passenger side to rummage for the phone among the order forms that have spilled out of his sample case. Finally, he sees it glittering under the seat. He has to kneel in the snow and reach blindly, but he snags it and brings it into the light.

Text message from Stephanie: *Divorce papers are on the kitchen table. TTFN.*

Tucker screams and throws the phone back into the car as if it's possessed by the Devil. He slams the door, pounds his fists on the hood for a minute, kicks the beleaguered sedan a few times, then goes back in for the phone one more time, just in case. This time it's managed to get stuck in the footwell's weird plastic lining and he has to lean on the door handle, mashing the buttons, as he gropes for it.

As he grabs it, something sharp zips a straight little cut on his finger and he yanks his hand back, clenched around the phone and dripping blood. There's a single-edged razor blade stuck in the back of his left index finger, cocked at an angle like a jaunty little hat that his knuckle is wearing. It's one of the Platinum Standard samples that has the company name cleverly embossed on the dull edge so he can see it as the corner remains embedded in his flesh.

"Damn it! You slicey little bastard." He plucks it out of his skin and shakes it, making a face, and drops it into his suit pocket—the last thing he wants is to leave a bloody razor blade on the snow or in the rental car. Because that couldn't possibly end badly, right? He puts the phone on the seat and wraps a paper napkin that's been hanging out in the center console since Cleveland around his bleeding finger. Then he picks up the phone again and stands up to look at it in the red-tinted light from the roadside tavern that flickers as the pig continues its quest to jump the vanishing barrel.

The phone's front glass is cracked, but the power button still works, so he turns it on and there's the message, unchanged: Divorce papers are on the kitchen table. TTFN.

He tries to reply, but the phone ignores him, taunting him with the message from its cracked and non-responsive screen. It won't allow him to place a call or even look at his email. "No. No, no, no!" He gives it a shake. "Oh, you heartless technological wonder," he tells the phone. "Fine. Just..." Then he screams at it, "Fuck!" and yanks the wedding ring off his finger, pitching it with fastball speed into the footwell.

The ring bounces and flies back, pinging off his coat button and clattering into the spill of razor blades and order forms on the floor. Tucker throws the phone after it and slams the door one more time before he spins, slips, catches his balance on the hood, and marches toward the bar.

The place is dingy—that's the only word for it—and Tucker feels like a gunslinger walking into a saloon in a hostile Western town. He half expects to hear the theme music from *The Good, The Bad, the Ugly* playing as he enters. But the jukebox is spitting out something else, something reeking of Texas Blues and beer-drenched fuck-yous. Tucker knows this place is hardcore: there's a straight, clear path from the door to the bar so no one has to socialize on their way to a bender. Tucker takes it and no one looks up as he crosses through the boozy fog of cigarette smoke and ancient hangovers. There could be five customers or a hundred and he wouldn't be able to tell the difference.

The bartender has the air of someone who is aging backward and wishes he'd just go ahead and die before he has to endure high school again. Tucker takes one of the two unoccupied stools right in the middle, shrugging his coat onto the back and leaning into the bar with his elbows, looking for the sweet spot in the geometry between stool, butt, and bar that will allow him to abuse his liver for hours without moving more than one hand.

One of those red LED arrays hangs above the mirrored barback, telling the customers what the jukebox is playing—"Why get up?" by The Fabulous Thunderbirds. One of those "my girl left me, took everything, and boy am I screwed" songs backed up by a honky tonk piano and a guitar so blues-laconic it probably has its own name. Tucker wonders if it's a coincidence, or if the jukebox, like the rest of the world, is just fucking with him.

The bartender strolls over after a minute and drops a cocktail napkin with a picture of the barrel-jumping pig on it. Then he gives Tucker a look, sizing him up, and waits. No "What'll it be, Buddy?" no "What can I do you for?" just The Look. Because this isn't the sort of place where the patrons need prompting. Everyone here is here to get drunk.

Tucker almost says scotch but saves himself at the last second. "Whiskey."

The bartender points to the long, long line of bottles behind him and says "Regular, or jet-fuel?"

"I need to kill brain cells—preferably all of those associated with the past twenty minutes of my life. Let's start with the hard stuff and work down as I get more stupid."

"OK, Chief," the bartender says and reaches for a bottle coated in dust whose contents are the leggy, dark-amber color of amnesia. He holds it up and Tucker nods as he slaps his credit card on the bar. The bartender picks up the card with the last two fingers of the same hand he uses to clunk a hefty glass onto the bar in front of Tucker. Then he pours about six minutes of oblivion. Neat.

Tucker downs it. "Nope," he says, "I still remember it all." He puts the glass down.

The bartender pours another dose of anesthesia, saying, "Don't worry. You won't remember it for long at this rate." Somehow, the credit card has vanished.

"I don't know...these fuckers have claws."

"Don't they always?" asks the guy on his left.

Tucker turns his head and looks at his neighbor—he could be a ranch hand on the downhill side of fifty, or a musician on the perpetual uphill side of fame. "I can't remember the good ones—if there ever were any." Tucker picks up his glass and looks at it for a moment.

As the bartender walks off, the jukebox plays something by a group called The Paperboys, about life being a town only seen in the review mirror.

"Yes it is," Tucker says and takes a sip of his whiskey.

The guy on his left looks confused and asks, "What happened?"

"My wife dumped me in a hundred and forty characters or less."

"Man, that's cold. Why would she do that?"

"She says I'm unavailable. I'm always on the road. Says I love my job more than I love her—which would be impossible, because I have the most dead-end job in the world."

"You look like you're doing OK..."

"Do you know what I do?" Tucker asks, just starting to feel the burn of the whiskey as it makes friends with his insides. "I sell the least useful product in the world. Single-edged razor blades." He toasts his crappy job and drinks.

Tucker's new friend blinks. "They still make those?"

"Yup." Tucker digs in his pocket and finds the specimen which has recently invested his knuckle. He flips it onto the bar. "Look at that little beauty. Bite like a mako shark."

The guy on the left peers at it. "There's blood on it..."

Tucker picks up the Platinum Standard with his fingernails, saying "Oh. Sorry. That's mine," and wipes it off on his cocktail napkin before putting it down again. "My boss says I have a gift. Funny thing is, I can't seem to sell anything else—can't even sell my wife on sticking around. Here is the great tragedy of my life: my company's product is useful for exactly three things. Wanna guess what they are?"

The barfly looks nervous and glances around as if hoping to find a way out of this conversation before its predictable denouement. "Uh... no?"

"Aw, come on. Try," Tucker begs.

"Well, shaving, I guess."

"Two more."

"I can't think of two more."

Tucker sighs. "That's OK. Most people can't. And surprisingly, your first guess is... incorrect. No one shaves with single-edged razors—unless they're straight razors. Which we don't sell. Nope. People use single-edged razor blades for" —he enumerates them one-by-one, raising a finger off his glass each time— "scraping off the losing candidate's bumper sticker, chopping cocaine," he has to juggle the glass a bit to manage the last finger without dropping his drink, "and cutting themselves. I do great business in those Stepford-like communities full of housewives and desperation. Especially if there's a private girls' school nearby. And if it's in California or New York I can hit all three market segments at once!"

"Man," says his neighbor, "that's kind of sick..."

"You think so? I think it's sort of elegant." Tucker puts down his glass, picks up the razor blade, and walks it across the backs of the fingers on his right hand. "It's the cure for existential angst. Candidate lost? Not a problem—scrape him off and go on to the next one. Too much money? Also not a problem—invest in a bit of South American marching powder, put our little friend to work, and you'll be feeling much better, and poorer, in no time. Feeling stressed out and unloved?" Tucker stops the blade and catches it between his index and middle fingers and holds it up. "Not for long."

The barfly slides off his stool and gives Tucker a wild-eyed look. "I gotta go... shoot some pool. That's my quarter up. Good luck man." And he scuttles off with his beer cuddled to his chest like an alcoholic's teddy bear. Tucker hasn't noted that there *is* a pool table, but what does it matter...?

The jukebox chides him with The Mighty Mighty Bosstones' "Chasing the Sun (Away)."

Tucker drops the blade again, takes another sip of his drink, and leans into the bar, watching himself in the mirror behind the bottles. "It's a gift."

Tucker drinks through a dozen more songs about trucks, girls, sex, and whiskey, drives off another barfly or two with the sleeping-sickness of his life story, and manages the trek to the restroom and back without taking a dart in the forehead from any of the regulars. He counts this as a victory.

As Tucker returns, the bartender is just making another pass and glances down at the Platinum Standard still lying on the bar. "What's this?"

"Sample. Keep it," Tucker says as he hikes himself back onto his stool.

The bartender picks it up and looks at the blade flashing in the bar lights like a cheap hooker. "You sell these?"

"Yup. Last of the great American salesmen."

"Yeah, I heard. Why not something more… useful?"

Tucker is tempted to shrug, but the liquor is starting to have its effect and he's not sure he won't slip off the stool if he does. "That's what the company makes. That's what I sell."

"Ever thought of changing jobs?"

"Every damn day. But in this economy…"

The bartender nods. "I hear that. Maybe you need a hobby."

Tucker looks at his glass. "This is my hobby."

The razor blade has vanished off the counter the same way his credit card did and Tucker wonders exactly what becomes of the objects the bartender palms, but what he says is, "How does one end up tending bar in a place like this?"

"Well…" the bartender says, wiping the bar and watching Tucker as he does, "I live about five miles off the highway here and, if I want a social life, it's either work in the bar or drink in the bar. Since I quit drinking, the only option left is working here."

"Huh," Tucker grunts.

The bartender nods. "Beats waking up next to a hibernating bear."

"Count yourself lucky that it was hibernating."

"I count myself lucky that it was female."

Tucker isn't sure if there's a twinkle in the bartender's eye or if it's just dust. He doesn't ask. "That would explain why you quit drinking."

Cold air slinks across the floor and winds around Tucker's ankles like a mangy cat. He shoots a glance over his shoulder.

Snow reflections and the moving headlight beams of semis cast a disco glamour around the figure pausing in the open doorway. When the door closes Tucker blinks, trying to smear the silhouette burned on his retinas into something more likely than a seven-eighths scale model of Marilyn Monroe with a brunette paint job. He's just starting to see in color again when something that smells like flash-frozen sin brushes past his right shoulder.

"Mind if I sit with you?" she asks, her voice sweet and sultry like Savannah just before the heat really comes on.

Tucker focuses on the woman beside him. Petite, curvy as a mountain road, and giving him the eyes from under a nimbus of black curls.

The jukebox spins up "She's a Beauty," by the Tubes.

"Uh... Mind? Me? No. No mind at all." Tucker clears his throat and tries again. "That is, I'd be honored if you would."

She smiles like a cat and hitches up onto the stool, letting her fake fur coat slither onto the stool back to reveal a dress as black as things even the devil wouldn't confess to. Tucker thinks he may be staring but manages to shut his mouth and swallow in time for the woman to say, "Thank you." She arranges herself on the seat and somehow manages to cock a hip and cast him a glance that threatens to ignite the contents of his glass—and possibly the glass as well. "I figured you'd be safe."

"Safe? Oh, now that's a pleasant condemnation," Tucker says, taking a drink.

"I meant you look like a gentleman. Not an octopus."

Tucker snorts his mouthful of whiskey up his nose.

She laughs, covering her mouth as the corners of her eyes crinkle up. Tucker wipes his face with his cocktail napkin and shakes the glimmering beads of whiskey off his hands.

The woman waves the bartender over, still giggling. "I'll have what he's having and he will too."

The bartender obliges and as fresh glasses hit the bar, the woman offers Tucker her hand like a duchess in a golden age film. "I'm Jen."

He shakes it. "Josh. Tucker. And thank you."

Jen gives a little squinchy-eyed shrug. "Do I call you Josh or Tucker?"

"Depends."

"On...?"

"How long we're going to be drinking together."

Jen taps a red-tipped finger against her lower lip. "So... if I start at Tucker, do I work my way up to Josh or vice versa?"

Tucker is pretty sure she's just said something wicked, but he can't parse it. He blames the whiskey. "Let's just start at Tucker and not work at all."

"I like that suggestion. Work is the curse of the drinking classes, y'know."

Tucker chuckles. "Oscar Wilde. Good one."

"Thank you."

"So... what is it you're cursed with, Jen?"

"Wire coat hangers."

Tucker blinks at her. "Uh... is that a personal choice?"

"Business. I sell them. You?"

"Single-edged razor blades."

"They still make those?"

"In all their near-useless glory."

"If they were useless, no one would buy them."

"True, but they don't have a lot of breadth."

"You should try comparing paper-covered hangers to coated wire at a dry cleaner's convention."

"How does that go?"

Jen sips her whiskey and Tucker is just drunk enough that he isn't distracted by the sight of her lipstick printing on the rim of her glass. No, he is not. "Much better after a few of these," she says.

The jukebox expresses an opinion about the superiority of whiskey's burn over that of tequila, by way of Toby Keith's "Whiskey Girl."

Tucker ignores it. "So, you drink on the job?"

"Never. I might be tempted to go all *Mommy, Dearest* otherwise. You know, that film almost single-handedly ruined the industry?"

"Seriously?" Tucker asks.

"Yes," Jen says with a nod. "To this day, I can't watch a Faye Dunaway movie. You?"

"Never had that problem. I don't care one way or the other about Faye Dunaway."

Jen's mouth presses together and she looks at him from the corner of her eye. "Smarty pants."

"Flatterer. I'll bet you say that to all the guys."

"Only the ones that are wearing them. So, no ninety-proof give-a-damn for you, either?"

"*Au contraire.*" Tucker reaches into the pocket of his coat and flashes the small flask riding in it. "They should issue these along with the sample cases and order forms."

"Is it safe to drink and shave?"

"Wouldn't know. No one actually shaves with single-edged razor blades."

Jen's eyes widen until she looks like a doe thinking vengeful thoughts about men wearing safety orange camouflage. "No?"

"Not this kind." Once again, he ticks off on his fingers: "They can scrape off a bumper sticker, chop cocaine, or slit your wrists, but they don't shave for shit. And that is why mine is a dying industry. Ha ha."

"Bet mine's dying faster."

"Doubtful. Every dry cleaner in the country uses wire hangers."

"But they don't *buy* them. They recycle the old ones. When was the last time you saw a wire coat hanger in the wild?"

Tucker remembers the tangled mess residing in the closet of last night's hotel. "This morning."

"Cheap hotel, right?"

Tucker nods. "Yeah—the kind that rents by the hour or the month. Don't you wonder about that? I mean, it kind of presupposes there's someone in the world who actually *wants* to live upstairs from hookers and drug dealers."

Jen nods and finishes her drink. "Bail bondsmen and skip tracers."

"You speak from experience?"

"We sell them advertising on the paper wrappers—they're called 'capes.'"

"That sounds like a superhero—The Caped Hanger and his trusty sidekick—"

"Razor Boy." She narrows her eyes, rolls her R, and makes it sound wicked. Her small white teeth flash behind the ardent red of her lips.

Tucker blows out a breath that feels too warm and turns his gaze back toward the row of liquor bottles behind the bar before he can make an ass of himself. The jukebox plays the chorus of Jimmy Buffett's "We Are the People" while Jen muddles through her handbag for a pack of cigarettes.

The bar seems to be getting darker...and emptier. The bartender passes with a brace of long-necks, glances at the massive, shapeless sack of red leather and says, "There's hooks under the bar to hang that on, so it doesn't get wet."

Jen quirks an eyebrow. "Oh?" She looks under the bar. "Oh! Well, look at that. It's like a little hardware convention under here!" She hangs the purse under the bar and grins as she brushes Tucker's knee on the way back up. "Oh, the things I can do with a hook and a hanger..."

There's a promise in that statement that widens Tucker's eyes. "Really?"

Jen gives him the full femme fatale—eyes, cleavage... the works. "Uh-huh... Wanna find out?"

Green Day's "Last of the American Girls" is playing.

Tucker fears this may be true. "Would this include a Faye Dunaway impression?"

She gives him a sly look. "Only if you like that sort of thing."

Tucker does not take up that challenge. "Surely a coat hanger is good for something aside from shilling bond services and cinematic child abuse."

"Do-it-yourself-birth control?"

Tucker blinks at her. "You actually went there."

Jen shrugs in a way that makes her breasts peer over her neckline. "Like it's not the first thing most people think of. Tell me you didn't."

"I really didn't. Guess I'm losing my edge..."

Jen giggles. "Maybe you need whetting..."

Is the jukebox a little louder? The crowd a little thinner? Tucker's not sure, but he holds up his glass. "Working on it."

"Different wet."

"Lady, I sell razors. I know the difference between a whet H and a wet... wet thing." Tucker thinks he may have actually blushed. Blushed! At his age! And he's getting drunk...

"I'll just bet you do."

Jen takes a cigarette from her pack and puts it to her lips. Tucker almost wishes he smoked but it's cut short by the arrival of the bartender, who offers Jen a book of matches decorated with the same plucky pig as the napkins on the bar and the sign outside. Tucker has begun to think of it in terms of a coat of arms: a porcine, pink, rampant on a field of drunkards...

Jen does not take the matches, but leans toward the bartender with the cigarette in her hand and her hand to her mouth. The bartender grins at her, strikes a match, and holds it out, saying, "How're you making out?"

"If we were making out, you'd know it," she replies.

"I'll get my camera," the bartender says with a wink.

"Screw the camera," Tucker says. "Bring the bear."

The bartender looks mildly affronted. "She's a very private person." He refills their glasses and walks off into the gathering gloom at the end of the bar. The matchbook remains.

The jukebox puts up "Take It or Leave It" by The Strokes.

Jen puts her fingers down on the matchbook, the cigarette held between them, and moves it around in little circles. The smoke trails behind, leaving hieroglyphs to rise slowly in the air picking up the spastic flashing of the neon so they look like Portents of Doom in a cheesy fantasy flick.

"He seemed kind of familiar... You come here often?" Tucker asks and immediately wants to kick himself.

"Not here..." Jen says.

"But a million places just like here," Tucker finishes, remembering his own million.

"Yeah. Except for the bear."

"Do you think he really...?"

"Hey, there are times a bear would have been better company than some of the guys I've been with, though I'm not so crazy about the hairy thing. Me, I prefer 'em dark and desperate." She winks at him.

*Is* he desperate? Tucker wonders. He looks up and into the mirror at the back of the bar, past the gleam of the pig's flickering neon and the smoke signal seduction. Yep. That is the face of desperation. "How did we come to this?"

"'Scuse me?" Jen asks and Tucker thinks that she might be a little more than tipsy...

He turns and this time he notices the shabby lining of her faux fur, the slightly thin patches near the seams of her dress, and a run in her stocking that's been stopped with a dab of clear nail polish that just peeps from under the hem of her skirt... It's no worse than his too-often spot-cleaned suit, his ties carefully knotted so the indelible stains won't show, or the gray marks around the insides of his collars that never quite wash off anymore...

"I mean..." he starts, "we're good people, aren't we? Pay our taxes—mostly—don't roll the homeless for shits and giggles, or trip old ladies in crosswalks to steal their retirement checks. We're kind to kids and animals... for values of kind that don't include actually *doing* anything inconvenient. So... we put in fifteen years of ass-breaking work on the road, and this is what it all boils down to? Whiskey and innuendo in Nowheresville bars?"

Jen licks her lower lip and has an intimate moment with her smoke before she replies, "Maybe for you. But I'm all about the cigarettes and meaningless sex."

"Oh, come on. No one really likes this job—not unless they're a serial killer. There has to be something else that keeps you going... Aren't there any other people in your life?"

"There are," Jen says, giving Tucker a significant look.

The clanging of a bell breaks the air for a moment. "Last call, brothers and sisters!" the bartender yells.

As the remaining patrons shuffle and mutter, Tucker leans closer to Jen and says, "I meant for more than one night and sayonara in the morning."

"Do you sayonara in the morning? I usually do that the night before. Like meditating," she adds, holding up her drink and then sipping it while her cigarette continues sending love songs to the pig's shuddering reflection in the barback mirror.

Toby Keith again—this time it's "Stays in Mexico" as the jukebox cautions Tucker against trying to chew too big a bite. Or maybe something else, but who knows?

"Uh... I don't actually do that at all. Married." Tucker looks down at his left hand at the same time Jen does, and spots the wide, pale band of wedding-ring compression that's slowly plumping back to its unburdened state as the alcohol in his system makes his hands puffy.

"I guess that rules out the sayonara," Jen sighs, "since you're clearly already in full-bore contemplation."

"Yeah. Well... She left me." He looks at his watch. "About three hours ago. I'd show you the text message but I broke the phone."

"Serves the little bastard right. Bearers of bad news and all that."

"If only it were always that easy—find the bearer of bad news and *shhkkkk!* Cut its throat," he says, dragging his thumbnail across his neck. "We could just kill them all. Beat 'em with coat hangers and hang 'em up in the closets of cheap hotels—can you kill a man with a coat hanger...?"

"Sure."

Tucker gives her a serious look. "Now we're getting awfully close to that serial killer territory. I was speaking rhetorically—I didn't mean you, specifically."

"I didn't mean me, specifically, either. I mean, do I *look* like a serial killer? Serial thriller maybe..." She winks. "But, y'know... why not? You could stick the coat hanger in an electric socket, I guess..."

"That... that won't do." Definitely drunk, Tucker thinks, but, what the hell...?

"Why not? It's wire."

"I'm more thinking of the position. Electric sockets are never located somewhere comfortable and convenient. You'd have to crouch on the floor to get at it...or next to the bed. You know those crazy beds they have in truckstop motels with the box spring screwed to the floor..."

"Oh, yeah," Jen says nodding like a bobble-head dog in the back of a lowrider. "My sister's chihuahua went behind one once. We had to push him out with a broom."

"Was the dog still alive?"

"Certainly—it wasn't a wire-hair."

"But you see what I mean about that—the coat hanger in the electric socket. If you can't reach it, that's pretty disappointing and you're crawling around on that sticky, fucking carpet with a coat hanger like car thief trying to unlock a mouse hole. But what if it works...? Then they're going to find you on that floor, hugging the nailed-down box spring, with one hand shoved behind it like you're trying to reach a lost sock. It's tawdry. It's undignified. No, no. If you're going to whack yourself, plainly a razor is the superior choice. And while a single-edged utility blade doesn't have the... dare I say *élan* of the classic straight razor, it's got the advantage of a convenient size and shape." He can feel the "roll" coming on, the irresistible persuasion that can sell switchblades to pacifists. This is why he does the job—this high—this is his gift, this monumental swell of words that woos the listener into Tucker's spell and locks the sale like a bank vault with teeth. It hasn't felt this good in a long time.

Jen puts her elbows on the bar and her chin in her hands and gazes at Tucker like a little girl seeing her first movie. Her whole face glows as if reflecting the flickering silver light of a black-and-white film shown in the sort of long-gone theater that has ushers dressed in pillbox hats and red uniforms. She scribbles her signature mechanically as the bartender slides her credit slip in front of her.

Tucker has risen to his feet, holding his glass in one hand and the pen with which he signs the credit card's death warrant in the other. "It's the perfect intersection of grace and practicality," he declares.

"The blade so fine and sharp it can cut *light* without damaging a single photon, but with a simple grip surface, smooth and gently rolled to protect your hand from harm. Your fingerprints will still be perfectly intact with no slipping, no untidy cutting of the palm, or loss of fine motor control."

From the corner of one eye he sees the last of the patrons making for the doors. He is alone in the spotlight of the bar's reflected beer signs and the flashing pink nimbus of the prancing pig.

"And the best thing—the *best thing*—is that you can do this in the comfort and privacy of your bath! No mess, no muss, no fuss, no pain. Cradled in the warm embrace of water like a return to Mother Sea and as easy as pulling on your shirt. Score a simple line from forearm to wrist and you're free!"

He flings his hands into the air and the last, forgotten drops of whiskey in his glass patter down like summer rain.

Jen claps her hands in delight and beams at him "Oh, Bravo! Bravo! You could sell swampland to Satan, Josh Tucker. You're my hero!"

Tucker puts his empty glass on the bar and bows to Jen, the jukebox, and the bartender. "Thank you, thank you, and thank *you*. It's been a great run and you're a wonderful audience. Be sure to tip your waitress."

"Waitstaff went home an hour ago," says the bartender, "and we're closed."

Tucker shakes back his hair which has fallen into his face and stands tall, making a grand gesture toward the door. "Well, then. Shall we?"

Jen stands up and Tucker helps her into her coat and shrugs into his own before offering his elbow. She giggles and tucks her arm through his. "Last of the Great American Salesmen."

As they stagger toward the door, the jukebox stutters the chorus of Boingo's "Goodbye, goodbye."

Outside, the temperature has dropped, the highway is silent, and the parking lot is nearly empty except for two cars, a tow truck, and a pickup without a single undented panel on its whole body. Tucker's rental car stands alone, distant from the bar. As they trudge toward it, the lights of the bar go out, casting them into starless gloom as snow-stuffed clouds sink against the hissing sulfur light of the last remaining street lamps.

"So, are we off to end it all?" Jen asks as they stop beside the sedan parked askew to everything.

"Sounds like a plan to me," Tucker replies with absolutely no irony. "I have the appropriate instruments in my car—about six dozen of 'em." He turns to give Jen a smile and then stares over her shoulder.

He would swear that he saw a bear wearing a pink bow around its neck follow the bartender to the pickup and jump into the back. As the pickup starts up and rolls away, he's no longer sure—the shape in the bed could just be a shadow—and he can't hear anything above the tubercular coughing of the engine.

"What?" Jen asks, craning her neck to look over her own shoulder.

Tucker shakes himself. "Nothing." He reaches into his pocket for his car keys.

They aren't there.

He tries each of his pockets in turn and then again, patting, pawing, digging... but no keys.

Staring through the driver's side window he sees them gleaming right where he left them: dangling in the ignition switch. "Fuck!"

Jen peers into the car and begins laughing. "Oh... my... God... You locked your keys in the car!"

Tucker heaves an exasperated sigh. "Yes. I did." Cutting his wrists might not be such a bad idea after all...

Jen waves her hands in the air as if she can wipe out the error. "No problem! I have a wire hanger..." She turns and Tucker turns with her.

Across the lot, the tow truck rolls away from a fire hydrant with a basic-bland sedan in train behind.

"... in my car," Jen finishes, blinking at the retreating lights of the truck and her rental car.

Then "Phone!" she cries and freezes, clutching her arms and looking around. She is naked of that most-essential of female accessories: "My purse..."

Tucker can see it in his mind's eye, still hanging like a side of desiccated beef on the hook under the bar.

Jen looks to him and he points at the locked rental car. "Broken."

They stare at each other and then toward the bar.

Dan's Double Barrel is dark, even the pig is no longer leaping and the beer signs have ceased to glow.

They walk back to the building and all the way around in hope, but it's locked tight—steel grilles and security doors pulled shut. The pay phone on the outside is missing its handset and phone book, but it has acquired deep gouges and the heady reek of urine in their place.

They return to Tucker's car and peer through the windows one more time—just in case the keys have magically escaped from Buick Hell.

No luck.

Tucker shrugs, picks Jen up around the waist, and sets her on the car's front hood. Then he hikes himself up and sits beside her. They stare at the empty highway and huddle against the cold.

Tucker fishes the flask from his pocket and listens to it slosh—nearly empty, but not quite. He unscrews the cap, pours a tot into it, and hands it to Jen. He raises the flask in an ironic toast. "Well… here's to us."

"Yeah," Jen says. "Freezing to death."

And the snow begins to fall.

# 4

## CHEMOTHERAPY

### A GREYWALKER STORY

My would-be client started off by standing in the door, his face and front sticking out of its surface like Han Solo out of carbonite. His puff of white hair looked like laundry lint arrested in its earthward-drift by something sticky on the door's inside panel. He wasn't quite looking at me. In fact, he was dead, which made getting information out of him a bit tricky.

I knew I didn't want the case—whatever it was—but it's often easier to say yes to the dead and inhuman than to say no. They can make persistent pests of themselves, turning up at odd times, knocking on the walls, and being general pains in my backside if I refuse. I'm the only PI in Seattle—possibly the only one anywhere—who can operate in their world as well as the normal one, and they all seem to know it.

"They killed me." His voice quavered with distress and indignation. "They killed me."

I nodded. "All right. Why don't you take a seat, give me some details, and I'll see what I can do for you?" I suggested, but he just continued on the same complaint.

I rolled my eyes in disgust: a repeater. Ghosts come in a lot of varieties, from the ephemeral wisps and harmless unexplained cold spots in the hall, to wraiths and revenants—conscious and alive in all but body. Repeaters have limited consciousness, looping through thoughts or events left over from their lives again and again. They're difficult clients; not very helpful if I can't knock them off their loop, and they never pay.

I tried another tack. "Who are you?" I demanded. "What's your name? Who killed you?" Questing ghosts often respond to offers of help or requests for information, but not this one—he just kept blithering.

I heaved a sigh and got up to lock the door. I'd have to conduct this interview in the Grey if I were to get anything useful out of him, and I'd need assured privacy to do that. I didn't want any casual clients to freak out if they dropped by.

Working in the Grey—the slippery overlap between the normal and the paranormal realms—is exhausting for a naturalized citizen like me, though it's native country for ghosts and such. Most people ignore the odd flicker in the corner of the eye, but I tend to go a bit ghostly when I sink into the Grey, and I appear to be talking to or dancing with wisps of light and darkness. That can be unsettling.

I had to stick my hand into the ghost's left arm to reach the dead-bolt. A shock of cold electricity ripped up my forearm and plucked a profound chord on my ribs. I stifled the urge to gag and flicked the latch over, pulling my hand back as fast as I could. Greywalking got easier with time, but it didn't get more pleasant.

The ghost jerked and stared down at his arm where I'd intersected it. Then the moment of volition ended and his gaze de-focused again.

I rubbed my now-aching elbow, then took a deep breath, and let go of my hold on the normal world.

The cold, unraveling feeling starts in my chest now. When all this began, there was a curtain between me and the Grey and I'd have to go through it. Now I just let go, and the Grey wells up around me, but the feeling of it starts at the knot of Grey-stuff that had been rammed into my chest way back at the beginning.

The Grey power grid snapped into view: bright, hot lines limning the dark world in neon. The ghost in front of me was just a hazy mess afloat in a blazing wire-frame world. I'd sunk a bit too far, too fast. I concentrated on it, and the world became an icy overlap of misty images on top of images—time and place stacked on each other like overlapping film projections. It was noisy with whispering and clanging that had nothing to do with anything I could see. And cold that stank, suddenly, of disinfectant over persistent mold and old death.

In this mist-world, I found myself face-to-face with a black man in his late sixties or so. He was well-dressed in a suit he'd probably bought at Nordstrom and worn often to some office job—his residual concept of himself, complete with a memory of aftershave. He was a little stooped at the shoulder, but was still a tall guy.

"Hi," I said.

He blinked at me and looked me over as if I were the ethereal one. "They killed me..."

"So you said. How 'bout you come all the way in and sit down, and you can tell me why I should give a damn."

He didn't move. "You're certainly rude enough for the job, young woman."

At least he'd gotten off his loop, though the tenor of the comment could have been nicer. I took half a step back before trudging across the misty floor to sit down in the gleaming shape of my desk chair. "I'm the only game in town. So get to it, or go away."

In the Grey overlap of the room's past and present, ghosts of long-gone furniture stood among the shadows of the current stuff, some sticking out of the living fog of the walls, and no more substantial than my potential client. He finally came in and seated himself in one of the missing chairs—a Scandinavian memory from some late-80s incarnation of my office space. But then he stopped. At that speed, it was a miracle he'd gotten to me at all. I had to lean over the desk and poke him—literally—to get his attention again.

"They killed—"

"Yes," I interrupted, nodding. "OK. What's your name?"

"Francis de Fayette Parker."

"And you believe you were murdered?"

"My family killed me like a dog in the pound."

You can't count on ghosts to tell the truth, or even to know what it is. Death doesn't impart wisdom. Or common sense. "Who in particular?" I asked. "Which of your dearly beloved did the dirty deed?"

"They killed me."

I sighed. "And what do you expect me to do about it?"

"Stop it!"

I leaned forward and braced my arms on the unseen surface of my desk. I was tired already. "Bit late, Mr. Parker. You're dead."

He glared through me. "They killed me! They killed me! Stop it!"

Damn, damn, damn. Looping again. I was tempted to hit him, but it's not easy to smack someone who's only sort of there. I get lucky, sometimes, but it's not a sure thing, and touching ghosts isn't pleasant. The dead press into me as much as I into them, and they bring along whatever emotional and physical turmoil they're still carrying around. And the dead part is just nasty.

Attempting to be both alive and dead at the same time is life- and sanity-threatening. This wouldn't be a problem if every even-remotely conscious dead and undead thing west of the Cascades didn't drift in and play hob with my life whenever the fancy took them. Plenty of live ones have a go, too.

I watched Francis Parker chant for a moment. He was a wreck, for a ghost: short trigger radius, short loop, low energy. He seemed to have retained his intelligence, but only by some on-again-off-again act of will. Must have been hell—like being a paralysis victim who retained a fine mind, but could only blink to express it.

That decided me.

"Parker!" I yelled at him. "Frank!"

He went on.

I braced myself and snatched at his wrist.

It felt as if he'd punched me in the gut. He flooded into me on a rip curl of chill, sucking my breath out, and cracking me open. Gasping, airless, burning from the inside, ice-sheeted skin, crumble-boned in toxin-wracked flesh.

His eyes flared into incandescence and glared into me, breaking the loop. My body resonated with his voice. Poison! It burned into us, through the age, and the illness, and the exhaustion.

I tore myself loose like leaving skin behind on a hot stove. I swallowed convulsively and caught my breath as I kept my distance.

Parker stared at me, his eyes as bright and alive as if he still wore flesh. Then the dulling started.

I couldn't just let him go. "When did you die?" I demanded. "I'll find out what happened, but give me a place to start."

"Feb'wa..." The left corner of his mouth turned up as he slipped into a seam in the mist.

I ripped my way out of the Grey and slumped at my desk, shivering and uneasy. There was something more than usually strange about Frank Parker.

---

I headed up the hill to the County Records Office to dig up Parker's death certificate. I finally found him in February about two years earlier. He'd died at seventy-two, of complications related to cancer and his chemotherapy. This didn't look like a murder, but the corpse was convinced. Maybe he'd believed his pain pills or chemo were meant to kill him. I'd have to poke around, if I was going to get him off my back. I took notes for follow-up, then made a phone call.

Detective Solis answered his own phone. His Colombian accent puts the emphasis on the second syllable: "Sol-EES."

"Hey, it's Harper Blaine. Can you answer a question for me?"

"Maybe." The noises in the background sounded like the Criminal Investigations office in the black-glass Justice Center a few blocks away. I imagined he was hunching the old phone into his shoulder as he transcribed from one of his scribbled notepads, a frown creasing his round, pock-marked face.

"First, was there ever any kind of homicide investigation into the death of a man named Francis de Fayette Parker in February about two years ago?"

He paused before replying, "None I see here."

"And what would be required to open one?"

"On a two-year-old non-suspicious death? Strong evidence. Maybe a confession, medical report, some physical evidence. Otherwise, we're too busy here."

"What about an autopsy?"

"You have a suspicious report?"

"Nope. Death was while under doctor's care. No autopsy."

"Then you need an exhumation—if you got a body. If you got ashes, you're probably out of luck. But you need evidence to convince the M.E. to issue the exhumation order."

"That's nicely circular."

"Eh. Nine times outta ten on a cold homicide, the perpetrator confesses as soon as we show the badge. Most people, they can't live with the guilt. You get a confession, you can get an exhumation to confirm it."

So, I'd have to solve the case to prove that there was one. Or not. I did not bless Frank Parker for bringing his death to me.

Seattle has a reputation for cancer treatment, but there are still only a handful of hospitals doing long-term care. The doctor's name was on the death certificate, so it didn't take long to find out where he was working and make an appointment to see him. Parker's oncologist didn't remember him, particularly. He was in a hurry, and aside from confirming the cause of death, he had nothing to say.

The hospice Frank Parker had died in was just down the street from the oncologist's office. I walked there and had to steel myself against the brush of ghosts and streamers of emotional residue that hung the walls and fluttered past me like rotting drapes as I entered. The dull-white building hummed with fear, pain, and despair amid the odor of chilled flowers, bland food, and cleaning fluid.

I asked around until I found a nurse who'd been there when Parker was a patient and was willing to talk—up to a point. She wasn't any less tired or harried than the doctor, so I suspected she was using me as an excuse to sit down for a little while. She paid no attention to the swirling fog of switched-off lives that flowed through the place as if it were an oxbow in the stream of the afterlife.

"I can't tell you anything about the patient's condition or care. Only that two sons and a daughter-in-law came around a few times. They all seemed nice," she said, her aura a thin smog of exhaustion around her. Her face creased with thought, then she smiled, a momentary blush passing through the dull color of her energy corona. "The couple had a toddler with them once or twice. Rambunctious little thing. Sad way to see grandpa, though. Hmm. There's a note in here about the unmarried son carrying in a gun, once. We asked him not to come back, but we didn't enforce it."

"A gun?" I asked. "Why?"

She shrugged. "Who knows? Probably just a punk acting tough."

"Did anyone else visit Parker, volunteers, friends from church?"

The transitory color around her died. "No. We do have a few volunteers, but... They call this Death Row, y'know. Every patient here's gonna leave in a bag. It's kinda depressing for the kids, so they bring us coffee and drop things off, read to some of the more lucid patients, but they always keep it short. The older volunteers are better, but even they don't linger."

That was sad, but it didn't help me figure out what was driving Frank Parker out of his grave. "Were any of the family here when Parker died?" I inquired.

"They all were," she said. That didn't make it any easier for me, since it didn't narrow the field of suspects.

Maybe motive would be more enlightening. "What was Parker like —was he an easy patient?"

"I really don't remember," the nurse replied, shaking her head in an off-hand manner, little green spikes of dishonesty dashing away from her and into the darkness that lurked at the corners of the room. "At that stage, they're usually in pain most of the time, on a morphine drip. I think he had bad reactions to chemo: nausea, pain, rash, vomiting, headaches, hair loss. He had fever a few times, was too weak to move himself, needed a lot of help. The family pitched in a lot."

"Could his symptoms have been poisoning?"

She looked bemused. "That's what most chemotherapy is—calibrated doses of potentially toxic substances to kill off the cancer, but not enough to kill off too many healthy cells. All drugs are potential poisons, and a lot of the drugs we use are heavy metals in the same broad family as arsenic and so on. Toxicity is all about dosage. Chemo is low-dose. Poison is high-dose. And morphine only reduces the pain, so once they're at that stage, we're just waiting it out."

She made a face that hardened into a shell of professional distance, her aura going darker and colder before she went on, "Let's be real. This place is the bargain basement of oncology. We're not going to work any miracles in a county facility with no research funds and patients who are at the end of their insurance money. We do our best, but everyone knows this is the last stop, and if we let every patient into our hearts, we'll go crazy. We can't let ourselves love them or become angels to the family. Some nurses do weird things when they think they'll be loved for this. The family can be just as bad. We can't let that happen, for all our sakes. It's bad enough knowing that some of these guys could go just a little easier, but we don't have the legal option to let patients opt out of life. If you think that makes me cruel…well we're the cruelest bunch of stone-hearted monsters you're ever going to meet."

She colored under a sudden red flush of impotent anger, and stood up. "I have to get back to work."

"Just one more question," I said. "Do your patients ever…get a little help out of here from their families or friends?"

Her eyes narrowed to wary slits, colors flickering in her energy corona like suspicious satellites reflecting distant suns. "I wouldn't know."

"Afraid of cracking that stone heart of yours?"

With a snort, she turned her shoulder to me and began stalking down the hall, the colors around her form shifting to the hue of a dark green sea. "I bleed gravel."

I shook my head and left the hospice. I already knew about Parker's family from the death certificate and obit files: two sons, a daughter-in-law, a grandchild. If he'd been poisoned, it would have to have been one of them. The grandchild was out, being a mere toddler at the time and not likely to have slipped something clever into grandpa's medication cup. I'd have to talk to the sons.

I put in another call to Solis. My mysterious leads had paid off for him in the past, so he reluctantly agreed to meet me at the address I provided. But he didn't like it and he said he'd be late. That was fine with me.

I used my cell phone to call ahead. Daniel Parker, Frank Parker's younger son, was just as reluctant to talk to me as the doctor, but he agreed, since I was nearly on his doorstep. He let me in when I arrived.

Daniel was about thirty and had the trim, quick wariness of a feral cat, and a dark, old scar down the length of his left temple and cheek. He had a curious yellow-orange light around him as he ushered me in with a finger to his lips. "Tanika just fell asleep. Today's been rough, so can we keep this quick and quiet?" I guessed the color of his aura was anxiety over something that wasn't just me.

"Sure," I said, following him into a tiny home office lined with heavy tomes and stacks of discarded bar-review guides, files, and scribbled yellow pads. "Is Tanika your daughter?"

"Niece," he said over his shoulder as he closed the door behind us. He took a seat near me. "She's been sick a while. Been a rough couple years for all of us, y'know, with dad and all. What did you want to ask me about him, anyway?"

"I wanted to ask you about what happened at the hospice."

He closed his eyes and shook his head. "Man, that was two years ago. Who'd make a big deal out of that now?"

I just kept my mouth shut and my eyes level on his face.

He dropped his gaze and rubbed one finger nervously over his scar. "Look, I was a stupid kid, I ran with the wrong guys. It was hard, but I was trying to get out. Studying for my bar exam. But some of those guys...they don't let go easy. They kept showing up. The gun was the only way I thought I could be safe, then. I wasn't gonna shoot anybody. I just wanted to be left alone. If it comes up now, I could be disbarred. But it was nothing. Nothing happened. Why ruin my life over that?"

A thin scraping sound moved down the corridor outside.

"You didn't poison your father, then."

He jerked and stared at me. "What? No! Dad died of cancer!" His professional demeanor and careful speech slipped back to his gang days. "Why you think anybody'd kill him? He was dyin' already!"

"There's a reason they call it 'mercy killing,' Mr. Parker."

He stared around the tiny office as if trying to find an answer in the dim, book-filled corners. "God...they couldn't..." Something thumped into the door. Daniel's eyes widened and the muscles in his jaw bunched, making the scar writhe. He jumped to his feet. "The little mother—"

He yanked the door open and nearly stepped on the tiny child who tumbled into the room. He stooped and scooped her into his arms. She shivered and made a gagging sound against his chest.

She was the smallest five-year-old I'd ever seen, and to my senses she flickered in and out of the Grey with the sighing of wind over dry grass—the flickering of someone slowly dying. She was skinny, mahogany skin patched with rashes like ash smears, and wispy dark hair that grew unevenly on her head. Something about her symptoms seemed horribly familiar.

Daniel Parker cuddled her close, in spite of the reek of vomit that clung to the child. "Baby, baby. How y'doin', girl?" he crooned to her, still kneeling on the rug, rocking, with his whole body wrapped around her.

I had it. "When did she get sick?" I asked.

"Year, year-and-a-half back," he mumbled. A couple of miserable tears squeezed from the corners of his eyes before he could bear to look at me again.

He started to say more, but a woman ran into the hall and saw us. I guessed this was Janeece Parker, Daniel's sister-in-law. She was too thin, but beautiful in it, burning with an unpleasant inner glow that shone through from the Grey like ancient wrecker's lights through coastal fog, sending hungry green tendrils seeking in all directions. She stopped a moment, then darted forward, holding out her arms.

"Give her to me, Daniel." Command resonated in her voice, and she gleamed brighter with unnatural avarice and twisted love. Her horrific aura thrummed and sent toxic creepers over Tanika, stroking and tightening with possessive pride. The sight made me ill.

Daniel's jaw bunched again, and he started a retort, cut off by the doorbell.

I looked Frank Parker's daughter-in-law in the eye, almost feeling his presence against my back, like a bad spy. "That's probably the police. Answer the door. We'll take care of Tanika." I can be pretty commanding myself, and there was no way I'd let her near the girl; the ugly green threads of psychic avarice and sickness that tied her to the child told me she was responsible for Tanika's condition. I just needed some proof, which might be found in Frank Parker's remains.

Janeece flared her nostrils and glared at me, but she turned and went to the door to let Solis in. Daniel and I followed her into the living room.

Janeece jabbed an accusatory finger my direction. "That woman broke into our house! She's trying to steal my baby!"

Solis looked at Daniel and Tanika. Then he turned his impassive face back at me.

"I believe she's been poisoning this child for more than a year," I explained. "My guess would be arsenic or another heavy metal." The rash and hair loss, the perverse pleasure her mother took in the girl's wasting illness, had all clicked into place with the nurse's description of Parker's final illness, and I knew what must have happened. I glanced at Daniel and lifted my eyebrow. Should I go on...? He gave a grim nod over Tanika's bowed head. "My guess is she poisoned her father-in-law, Francis de Fayette Parker, also. Exhumation should prove the link."

"What are you saying?"

We all looked around at the new player standing in the open front doorway, clutching an attaché case. In thirty years, he'd be a dead ringer for his father.

"You're Frank Parker Junior?" I asked.

"Yes. What's going on here?"

Solis fell back and to the side where he could see us all. He offered his ID to the newcomer. "Detective Solis, Seattle P.D. Homicide. I'm sorry. I'm here to arrest your wife for poisoning your daughter and your father."

Frank Jr. stared at Solis in horror, then looked at his wife. "Dad wanted to go. But...not our little girl...Janeece? Why—"

Daniel lost it. "You killed Dad?" he shouted. Still holding Tanika, he started toward his older brother, his scar dancing as hard feelings flickered across his face.

I could hear Solis muttering into his cell phone for back-up.

I grabbed Daniel by the shoulder. "Don't. You're all she's got."

He stopped moving, but quivered where he stood, clutching Tanika to his chest and staring at his brother and sister-in-law.

---

Four of Seattle's finest arrived a few minutes later and broke up the party, arresting both Frank and Janeece Parker. Family Services would come later for Tanika, but for now, she was still in her uncle's arms and, I thought, safe.

Solis shook his head as I slipped out in the press of cops.

I found my client lurking by the door. He wafted behind me for a block, then stopped. I opened my cell phone and pretended to make a call.

"They killed you because you asked them to, didn't they? 'Like a dog in the pound' you said. An old, sick dog that any decent human being would put out of his misery. But the law says you can't do the same for a man."

"Frank is a good boy. Always does as he's told," he replied.

"And Janeece?"

"Janeece used to bring me custard every day—my favorite."

The oblique replies annoyed me, but there wasn't much I could do.

As a repeater, Parker's communication was limited, but he made do, just has he had in my office.

"You gave them up to save your granddaughter. But you know it's your fault, don't you? Janeece was a martyr to your illness—even while she killed you—and I'll bet she liked being admired for her apparent selflessness. The nurse on your ward warned me about that. Once you were gone, Janeece just replaced you with Tanika."

Parker looked past me. "She's the shining star of my life, that child."

"Yeah. Well. There's still a long road ahead for her and Daniel. You could have moved a little sooner, you rotten old corpse."

He finally looked right at me. I wished he hadn't. He grabbed my elbow, his phantom fingers sinking into my bones with a jolt of energy. I felt time reel and stumble. I wrenched myself away and looked at my phone. Six minutes had vanished in an instant. "All right. Point taken. I stopped Janeece from killing Tanika the way she did you. When you said 'stop them' that's what you meant, isn't it? That's what you asked for. Are you satisfied?"

The left corner of his mouth lifted into a smile, then he flashed into brilliance and faded away.

I would have to content myself with the thought that a young life was probably saved. The gods knew there was little else to prize in that situation. I rubbed my eyes and closed the phone.

## 5

# CUTLASS

The car sported a young man's corpse on its long hood, head down toward the bumper and one foot caught in the busted windshield. The paint had probably been mint green originally; now the oxidized finish was soaking up blood and turning the spinach-colored bodywork the sort of brown you scraped off your shoe. Solis and Brickman studied the car and its macabre passenger from across the street.

Cop cars and barricades cut off traffic for two blocks around the Marine Bank of Seattle leaving the street a messy tableau of broken glass and near-hysterical bank customers who'd been corralled near the shattered bank doors. Another, smaller knot of people huddled on the other end of the block, farther from the bank. Some woman near the cars was crying. A Medic One truck, three civilian cars, and two cop cars littered the road. One of the civvie cars was turned sideways to the lanes, creased like an envelope down most of the driver's side front quarter. The car with the corpse had a matching crumple on the driver's side rear and a severe front-end buckle where its passenger side bumper had plowed a parked car before it rocked down and kissed the curb.

"Ten to one the deader's our bank robber," Brickman said as they nudged past the barricades, flashing ID at the nearest patrolman who was holding back the gawkers.

They looked an odd pair: Solis a short, slim, Latino kicking middle age; and Brickman a big, blonde mutt who still had his college football player tone and 'tude. They presented themselves to the first officer on the scene, a foot-patrol uniform named Gerard, who frowned at Brickman's FBI credentials and addressed Solis instead.

"Bank robbery started about thirty minutes ago, Detective. Ended about fifteen minutes ago. The two robbers attempted to leave the scene in that car," he added, pointing at the body-draped vehicle, "after taking a few thousand in cash from the tellers at gun point. That's about when I got here. The driver seemed to lose control or maybe she panicked and slammed on the brakes. Anyhow, one guy fell or got pushed out the door and the other went out the windshield. That's the hood ornament."

Brickman smirked at Solis. "Told ya."

Solis shrugged, dismissing him, and looked back at Gerard. "Where's the driver?"

Gerard pointed at the smaller group near the cars, where the Medic One team was lifting a laden gurney onto its legs. "That's her on the cart. Lois Wilkins. Seventy-two years old." The crying had stopped. "You want to talk to her, you better hurry."

"A granny getaway driver?" Brickman scoffed. "What, crime's the family business?"

Solis shot the fed a scowl. "I don't like it. You take the bank manager, I'll talk to the driver." He ran for the medic team without waiting for Brickman's reply.

The elderly woman on the gurney had her eyes closed and her hands clasped over her sunken chest. If they hadn't strapped an oxygen mask on her face, Solis might have thought she was dead. The medics didn't stop for him and he had to trot beside them toward the bright red Medic One truck.

"I need to talk to her."

"You can follow us to the hospital."

"I can't ask one question?"

"Do it quick."

Solis touched the woman's shoulder to get her attention as the medic lifted the mask off her face. She wasn't nearly as frail as he'd expected, or as small, and he changed his question. "Mrs. Wilkins," he asked, "how did you end up here?"

Her breathing was ragged and after only a single look at him, Lois Wilkins squeezed her reddened eyes shut, tears oozing from the corners and into the thin white hair at her temples. "That awful, awful boy. He wanted my car…"

---

Lois had disliked the young man on first sight. It hadn't been the piercings or the ratty hooded sweatshirt, not even the stubby black gun he'd waved in her face. It was the sneering disrespect that really got her goat.

"Nice wheels, gran'ma," he'd said, yanking open the passenger door and jumping in as if she'd stopped at the light only to chauffeur him around town. That was some nerve. "How's 'bout you put the pedal to the metal and take me where I want t'go?"

"Why should I?" she'd demanded. "I have an appointment. I can't be running errands for the likes you."

The boy's face got mean. "Why?" He echoed. Then he'd reached under the back tail of his shirt and pulled out a compact automatic that he jabbed into her ribs. "Because I got this gun, that's why, you old bitch. Otherwise, I pop a cap in your gray-haired ass, take this fine piece of American steel away from you, and leave you fuckin' bleedin' in the fuckin' gutter. You got it?"

Cars behind her honked impatiently. She started to put her foot into it, knowing the Oldsmobile still had it in her, but the boy'd dug the gun harder into her side. "Nice n'easy, gran'ma. Don't want no cops pullin' you over, now do we? I gots me a 'pointment too."

She'd gritted her teeth and let the car roll out from the line as stately as a Presidential limo.

The horrid boy settled in on his side of the car, but kept the gun low and pointed at her. He ran his free hand over the white bucket seat and the center console with its Hurst shifter and fake burl wood trim. "Nineteen-seventy Cutlass Suuuu-preem. Nice. How's an old lady like you rate a ride like this? Huh? You can't barely see over the steerin' wheel."

That was patently untrue as well as unfair. Lois was old, but she wasn't any shrimp. "It was my husband's car."

"You musta took him good in the divorce, am I right?"

"He died."

"Shit. Ain't that the way. All the fine, fine things be in the hands of them what can't appreciate 'em."

"You really are insufferable," Lois snapped at him.

He'd glared and waved the gun at her again. "You keep your eyes on the road, old lady, you know what's good for you. And you gonna have to *suffer* me a little longer. Less you wanna stop sufferin' altogether. Dig?"

Lois bit her tongue. She knew what happened in carjackings.

The thug nodded. "That's better. Now, you got to take me to get my crew."

---

Brickman caught up to Solis beside the owners of the other two cars. The medic unit had rolled and been replaced by the Coroner's team, and the surviving bank robber was already booked and cooking off in holding. Solis was just picking up pieces and looking for a fit. A fine prickling of rain had started up again, making him hunch his shoulders as he glanced at his notebook and walked toward the middle of the street where their conversation wouldn't be overheard.

"Carjacking," said Brickman, shaking his head and making rapid notes so sloppy Solis pitied the FBI transcriptionist who'd be stuck deciphering them. "Jesus, what a pair of dopes. The surviving asshole's a local gangbanger named Jamal Rosewood—'Shotgun Rosie.' Already lawyered up, but he's leaking so fast trying to shift blame to the dead guy, I'm guessing they'll plead out."

"You guys going for felony murder as well?" Solis asked.

"Yup. Always take 'em to the mat and make 'em beg for mercy. And since this is strike two for Rosie, we'll probably end up going for twenty-five in Sheridan. Bet ya he'll be out in less than ten, and swinging for strike three within a year. Your guys'll take the carjacking rap to court, I suppose, but it'll just be icing on the cake."

"So, just the two robbers? No inside guy?"

"Bank manager says no. Just two idiots with guns and the driver."

Solis grunted.

"What did you get on her?"

"Lois Wilkins? Nada. I'll have to try again at the hospital."

"You think these guys targeted this old lady at random?"

"I don't think it *was* totally random."

"So…you're saying she was in on it."

"No. I think they picked her for a reason: She told me they wanted her car."

Brickman shot a look over his shoulder at the battered Oldsmobile. "That piece of junk? What the hell would they want that for?"

"Because it looks like a piece of junk. You know witnesses are unreliable about cars. One out of ten can't tell you what color a crime car really was, what model or year, how many people were in it, or what the license plate was. You ask all ten, you get ten different answers. If you close your eyes right now, can you tell me what color that car is or how many doors it's got?"

Brickman snorted, turned his back on the car and shut his eyes. "Sure. It's, uh…faded silver gray, two doors."

"What color roof?"

"Black."

"It got a door pillar?"

"Yeah."

"Anything else you remember about it? Make, model, approximate year, license number…?"

"No. It's just some kind of old sedan, like…maybe mid-seventies?"

"Take a look."

Brickman turned around and opened his eyes. Not turning, Solis began to recite: "It's a 1970 Oldsmobile Cutlass Supreme SX without the badges, faded metallic green with same-color roof, two-door coupe, no door pillar, original Washington plates front and rear, which means Mrs. Wilkins is probably the original owner."

Brickman frowned. "How do you know the badges were removed?"

"Because there aren't any now, but there aren't any holes or signs of recent removal. And that car has the dual exhaust and the Hurst shifter. The car's not a street rod project, so they weren't retrofitted, they're original. The owner must have removed the SX badges when the car was new."

"*If* she did, that's pretty weird."

"Not if you wanted the ultimate sleeper. It's got no hood scoops or striping or anything to tell you it's a muscle car. It looks almost exactly like the base model. Which looked almost exactly like five or six other cars. I'd like to know who Lois Wilkins really is."

"She's a little old lady who got carjacked. What does it matter who she is?"

"Why does an elderly woman drive an old sleeper? So she's an attractive mark for a couple of gang members who want a powerful but anonymous car for a bank job? No. She's owned that car for forty years. Why did she buy it?"

"Maybe she was a hot number back in 'seventy. Maybe she just liked it. I don't know."

"Well, I would like to."

"Go for it, Solis. You want to run yourself down on a carjacking rap that'll be buried under the other charges, you do that. But I gotta say, I think you're making a lot out of this old lady. What is it? She remind you of your mother or something?"

Solis frowned. "She does, a little..."

The boy with the piercings gave Lois directions to an apartment complex on the south end. The city's attempts to make the area respectable had failed again and again and though it was officially White Center, a lot of people still called the area "Rat City." That was how Lois thought of it, too, but it wasn't because of the rodent problem.

They pulled into a graveled parking area across the street, between a school and a park that looked like they'd been dropped there by accident.

Another young man in a similar hoody ambled toward them from the apartment and motioned them to follow him into the muddy park.

The carjacker twitched his gun at Lois. "Get out th'car, gran'ma."

Her stomach heaved and she knew she would have thrown up if she'd had anything to eat that morning. But she managed to say, "No."

"Say what?"

"I said no. I'm not getting out. You're just going to shoot me and steal the car and I'm not going to make it any easier for you." She was shaking and felt hot and cold with fear, but she sat defiantly behind the wheel and gripped it with white fingers.

He swore, reaching for the keys.

Lois snatched them before he could and tried to nip out the door, but her two seat belts—one across her lap and the other, separate, across her chest—got in the way. He booted the other door open and came around the car to yank her out of the driver's seat as she stuffed the keys down her blouse.

Rolling his eyes, the boy hauled her onto her feet and shoved her toward his friend waiting beyond the fence. "You see what playin' by the rules get you? Fucking seat belt just slow you down. Now we gonna talk to my man, see what we gonna do with you, crazy-ass bitch. And don't think I won't go for them keys, old lady. Your flabby old tits don't scare me none."

He stuck the gun into her back and prodded Lois forward. Her knees were wobbly, but she marched ahead, telling herself if he was going to shoot her, he'd have done it already, and he wasn't half as scary as some of her husband's friends had been... He was just here and he had a gun and that was bad enough.

"Hey, Ringo, what you bringin' me a geezer for?" the other thug called out as they got near. "What we gonna do with that?"

Oh, goody: another stupid boy who thinks he's a gangster, Lois thought.

"Gonna take the car, man. Right after we ice this bitch," Ringo replied. "What you think? Where the rest of the posse?"

As she'd expected, they were going to kill her. She should have been scared, but mostly it just made her angry to think of these two punks shooting her and stealing Duane's car. They were just kids but they thought they were tough guys and they were going to shoot *her*. This sort of thing wouldn't have happened back in the day... Her eyes prickled with furious tears.

The other boy shrugged. "They ain't comin'. You want t'prove you got the balls, man, you got to do it your own self."

"Fuck!" Ringo shrieked. "Fuck those motherfuckers!" Enraged, he shoved Lois and she stumbled to her knees. "You think I gonna rob a bank on my own, Rosie? Fuckin' errand boy?" He jerked the gun up and pointed it on its side at his friend. "Think I'm gonna make my way dealin' for small change and greasin' motherfuckers for Fat Dog? This my *score*! This my *mark*, man! You gonna come wit me. You gonna crack that bank wit me, or I gonna blow you all over this fuckin' park!"

Rosie shook his head and sighed. "Put the heat away. Ringo, I ain't got no dispute wit you. I come along, you want me to..." He shrugged. "But who gonna drive that piece of shit you got?"

"Don't you call my husband's car a piece of shit, you potty-mouthed SOB," Lois muttered. Her chest hurt almost as much as her knees did, sunk into the cold mud. This was doing her health no good at all. She was cold and she was hungry and she wanted to piss. But, maybe...if she played them right, she might still see her doctor tomorrow. Practical, that's what Duane always said: "Got to be practical about these things." He'd said it just before he ratted out his bosses. And about an hour before someone blew his brains out for it. Still, an hour was an hour...

Rosie and Ringo both stared at her. "What you say, gran'ma?" Rosie asked, turning his head on its side to look at her. He was better-looking than the boy with the jewelry in his face, but still no Rock Hudson, and all he had in common with Rosie Greer was his color.

"I said," she gasped, "my husband's car isn't a piece of shit." Lois raised her head and glared at them. "Duane would die if he heard you say that—if he wasn't already dead, rest his soul. He loved that car! I still take it to the shop twice a year."

Ringo stuffed the gun into the back of his belt and nodded at his buddy. "She right. Look like crap, but it run nice. An' it a *classic*. We get another couple gee for that. Once we done."

Rosie shrugged again. "Whatever you say, dog, but...who gonna drive it? Can't go park it like a citizen, or bust the bank while five-oh tow your ride."

Lois pushed herself to her feet, panting and wincing from the stiff protests of her joints. "I can drive it. "

"You? You crazy, gran'ma?" Rosie inquired. "We ain't takin' no blue-hair on no bank job."

Ringo looked doubtful. "I dunno..."

"Ringo, you lost your fuckin' mind? She gonna drop us off, then tear-ass over to the po-po turn us in. She a citizen," Rosie added, looking over at Lois. "Ain't you, gran'ma?"

"You boys have no idea..." She tried a grandmotherly smile, but she was pretty sure it looked more like the rictus of a corpse.

---

Brickman went with Solis to Harborview. He claimed he wanted to interview the witness himself, but Solis suspected he just wanted to see if the SPD—in his person—fell on its face. On the way, Solis made a lot of phone calls for information on Lois Wilkins. There was something he felt he should know, but he couldn't put his finger on it...

Mrs. Wilkins' doctor met them outside her room in CCU. "She's not doing well," he warned them. "She missed a cardiology appointment this morning and we were already worried about her. Trauma to the chest from the impact with the steering wheel is making a bad situation worse. So don't upset or excite her. You can have ten minutes, but then you'll have to go. You understand?"

Solis nodded. Brickman was too busy checking messages on his iPhone to do more than grunt. They started toward the room, but Solis's phone rang and he paused to answer it. He listened to the caller, thanked them, and shut the phone off. He looked puzzled.

"It was her husband's car," he muttered. "She inherited it."

"Huh. Who was the hubby?"

"Duane Wilkins. Should I know that name?"

Brickman pulled an incredulous face. "You don't know who Duane Wilkins was?"

"No. Should I?"

"If you ever handled a corruption case in Seattle, Wilkins's name would have come up. He was killed in '73. 'Made man' as the lingo has it. Informed on his bosses during the indictments of '71 and '72. Found in a garage, shot in the head, which was taken as a warning since the usual method of offing rats in Seattle is drowning in shallow water. You should remember that the next time you find a vic face down in three feet or less."

"I was eight years old in 1973. You weren't even an itch. So how do you know this ancient history?"

"Drugs are still the number one field of study at Quantico. We know every notable mob murder in the last fifty years."

Solis grunted. "Drowning. They used to do that in Cali, too."

"Colombia? The cartel wars?"

"*Si*. My father was a cop in Cali."

"Runs in the family, then?"

"Not so much." Solis turned away from Brickman and went into Mrs. Wilkins's room.

———

She'd shown them. First she showed them the gun in the glove compartment. That had been Duane's too, but she didn't feel any attachment to it and she didn't mind so much when Rosie took it away from her. She'd given them the car's registration and her driver's license, too.

"That's insurance," Ringo said, as if it were his idea. "So's you don't run off on us."

Lois pressed her lips together and didn't say a thing.

Then she showed them what Duane had taught her about driving the Olds. It was harder than she remembered, even with power steering, but she did all right. She'd always done all right. Her chest ached, but she ignored it. Another hour and she could go to the doctor. She just had to get through with these stupid boys.

Ringo, the punk with the piercings, whooped it up as Lois maneuvered the car around the streets of south Seattle. "Check it, dog: granny kickin' it old skool!" And he'd laughed at his joke. "You pretty fly...for an old lady."

"I'm old, not dead."

"Yet," Ringo reminded her. "You want t'keep it that way, you just drive that good on the backside of this job. We might even let you keep this fine car. What you think, Rosie?"

Rosie scowled and she knew he wasn't any more taken in than she was. "Whatever you say, bro. Whatever."

Lois kept her mouth shut. Her initial dislike of Ringo had already been surpassed, but she knew better than to talk. Not in Rat City. Driving wasn't the only thing she'd learned from her late husband.

She drove them up to the industrial district, to the Marine Bank, at Ringo's direction. It was an old building and mostly alone in the midst of parking lots and warehouses beside the train tracks. There was plenty of open space to turn the car, even with business traffic, and lots of directions to go once the job was done. She had to hand Ringo that: he'd picked a good spot.

She slid into a loading zone in front, hung up her handicapped placard, and watched the boys run into the bank. She kept the engine running, unlatched her shoulder belt, and started beating the inside of the windshield on the passenger side with the heavy steel buckle.

---

Lois Wilkins looked tiny in the hospital bed, though she wasn't really a small woman; she was, Solis thought, taller than he was. But her toughness was failing. The strength he'd felt in her arm on the medic gurney wasn't going to be enough for this fight: he could hear it in her breathing, like he'd heard it before. Her voice trembled as she struggled to answer his questions and her pain made him feel ill.

He tried to ask the questions gently, but he didn't think he'd have time to ask twice. "So they carjacked you and made you drive them to the bank. Why did you wait for them? Why didn't you drive off?"

"They knew where I lived..." Mrs. Wilkins whispered. "I was afraid...they'd tell someone to come after me."

"Like someone came for your husband?"

Mrs. Wilkins began to cry. "They said they just wanted the car. But, but...I thought...they were going to kill me. I couldn't let them... take Duane's car..."

---

The bank alarm started clanging as the two young punks rushed back out, bags bulging with small bills, and Lois was waiting. They didn't notice the crack.

Ringo jumped in first, screaming at her and waving his gun without a care for where he was pointing it. Rosie was a second behind him, but it was a second too far.

As Rosie reached for the car door, Lois stomped on the accelerator.

The Olds burst forward, spinning Rosie onto the sidewalk. Lois gunned the car toward the lane of oncoming traffic as she clawed the unbuckled shoulder belt from under her arm.

"What you doing, crazy bitch?" Ringo shouted, trying to bring his gun to bear on her as the Olds lurched and scraped into the car in the other lane, fishtailing away from the impact. Lois turned her head and body toward the young punk as he was tossed around, unbuckled, in the white bucket seat.

Lois ground down on the gas pedal with one foot and yanked on the wheel, overcorrecting as she turned and whipped the heavy metal end of her shoulder belt into Ringo's face. "Granny's kickin' it old skool, you little bastard!" she screamed.

She lashed the belt across his hand, knocking the gun away as the car careened into another parked by the curb. Then she hit the windshield with the belt as she wound up to smash him in the face one more time.

Blood flew around the inside of the Olds as it rocketed forward, ruining the white upholstery and the fake burl wood dash as the car lurched and slid.

Lois twisted back into her seat and stood on the brakes with both feet, bracing her arms on the top of the steering wheel to protect her head. The disc brakes grabbed all four wheels and locked up, the Olds screeching and rocking up onto its front fender.

Lois slammed forward as the car stopped, banging into the steering wheel hard enough to knock her breathless.

Ringo was flung up against the cracked windshield with a grotesque, wet thud and a snap of his neck. The glass ruptured and he crashed outward in a rain of a million tiny glass puzzle pieces. His foot in its oversized sneaker caught in the twisted frame and his body thumped onto the hood, broken and still.

Blood spread across the faded green paint job.

---

The patient monitors were screaming. Doctors and nurses rushed into the room, pushing the policemen aside. Solis could barely hear Lois Wilkins saying "I couldn't let them take my husband's car. He loved that car..."

Brickman backed out of the room shaking his head, dazed. "Jesus. She fucking killed him."

Solis shrugged. "Self-defense. He was going to kill her and take the car."

"That's a bit more than self-defense, man. She laid a trap. She still remind you of your mother?"

Solis nodded. "Yes. My mother killed three men in Cali when I was twelve. They tried to rape her because she was married to a cop they didn't like. All she had was one shotgun shell and a kitchen knife. Imagine what she could have done with a Cutlass?"

## 6

## DRAFTY

A twig prodded Kes in her upper left thigh—right where the tasset should have been and wasn't. "Plague take it!" she spat and all the woods around went silent. "Whosoever designed this so-called-mail should be forced to wear it himself. With pattens and one of those ridiculous hats!" She slashed at the offending shrubbery with her sword.

The falling-stones sound of Angeli's laughter came from behind her. "Oh, but I think your outfit is quite cheeky," the little dragon said, with a giggle that set a small bush on fire.

Kes patted her free hand against her buttock and found a considerably greater degree of flesh exposed at the bottom of the brief... umm...brief than she had realized. She whipped around, glaring, and pointed her sword at her draconic companion. "I'll thank you to stop sizing up my backside, wyrm, or *you* can walk in front and clear the way."

It was an outrageous outfit: mail it may have been, but the hauberk was little more than a bandeau that shaped to her breasts with the familiarity of a drunken lord's groping hands—and not much larger than the same—while the lower business was neither leggings, nor even chausses, but something far more akin to the tiniest of small-clothes that covered her derrière like peach fuzz. Steel peach fuzz that tended to pinch, chafe, and yank out any strand of pubic hair that happened to curl round the leather-bound edges. In addition, she had nothing like a proper gambeson and the rings pinched her skin—especially any bits which happened to be somewhat upstanding by dint of the irritation of cold steel nipping like a thousand insects. And it had a draft like a blacksmith's forge in full roar. It rubbed Kes quite the wrong way, but it was all the covering she currently had, aside from inadequate boots and a hair ribbon. She'd donned the ridiculous ensemble that morning and used the ribbon to secure her hair in a plait, which she now twitched over her shoulder.

Angeli ducked its head and attempted an abashed expression—which resolved poorly on a face so scaled and inhuman. "It's a nice backside...for a squishy-two-legs."

Kes clonked the dragon on its snout with the flat of her blade. "It is not an ornament for the delectation of spark-wits. And extinguish that shrub before the whole copse is afire, if you please."

Angeli grumbled a bit before it said, "Oh, all right, Grumpy." It turned aside to pat out the flames with one partially-unfurled wing.

"I am not grumpy," Kes said, kicking some dirt over the nearest smoldering plant life. Though, certainly she had a right to be.

"Are too."

"Am not! Ow!" she added as an ember burned through her thin leather soles. "Blasted things!" They weren't even proper sabatons—just soft boots. Fine for hunting, but not up to a real battle—or dragon fire. "I shall definitely kill the blackguard—"

"When we catch up to him," Angeli said.

"Oh, we'll catch him up. I've a good idea just where the toad's got off to. Is all flora and fauna extinguished now, Angeli?"

The dragonet looked around, spotted a small smoldering weed, and sat on it. "All clear, My Lady Kes. Not even particularly singed, I'd say."

"What *you* would say, my dear Angeli, is quite likely to get us both thrown out of even the lowest bawdyhouse. You have the tact of a leprous pickpocket."

"Yes, but I'm charming about it! And I always leave a tip."

Kes snorted. She hadn't wanted the whelp, but it had arrived a few days before her twelfth birthday and nothing could make it go away. Six years on, whither went Kes, so went Angeli, and she was, by now, used to it, its bad jokes, worse timing, and fierce companionship. Truth to tell, she'd hardly know who she was without it—but she would never admit such a thing.

---

They left the scene of the minor conflagration with Kes in the lead and walked west. The sun was just behind them, but coming up quickly. The woody landscape was all very much the same and Angeli scuffed along in Kes's wake. The dragonet snaked its head back and forth on its long neck, looking for something interesting in the underbrush, and frightening small animals and birds with little puffs of steam. It was quickly bored with their skittering, chittering, and running, and went back to merely dragging along behind the woman in the measly mail.

After a while, Angeli asked, "Are we going to High Tower?"

"Where else?" Kes replied. "Now hush."

"But we don't like High Tower. Do we?"

"It is of no consequence whether we like the place. It's Assembly Day and therefore it is undoubtedly where our quarry has flown—"

Angeli chuckled. "Hah! Imagine that one flying! He hasn't any wings! Silly squishy-two-legs."

Kes turned around and gave the young dragon a disapproving glare. "While you, ruler of the slop heap, have two perfectly good ones that you never use."

Angeli huddled to the ground in the dragonet version of a sulk that nearly hid it from view among the brush and tree trunks. "Are you implying that I'm too fat to fly?"

Kes looked the miserable creature over with a critical eye and started to reply.

There was a crashing from the brush behind her and a voice called out, "Hold, and hand over your purse, sweetheart."

Kes clamped her mouth closed and narrowed her eyes. Then one eyebrow rose, pulling her face into a singularly sinister expression. Angeli tucked its head under one wing, muttering, "Uh-oh," as she turned slowly around.

Three rough-looking men had arranged themselves across the path ahead, armed variously with a cudgel, a crossbow, and a plain but serviceable sword.

"Where do you imagine I might conceal a purse in such harness as this?" Kes demanded, spreading her arms. All three men goggled at her largely-undressed form. None seemed to notice she held a sword of her own in one hand, or that a small dragon cowered behind her barely-booted legs.

"Maybe you've tucked it under your bubbies," the one with the sword suggested. "We'll search you, eh?"

The one with the cudgel said, "And if your purse is truly empty, maybe we could lend you a yard or two to put in it." The others laughed as he started forward.

Kes flicked her sword upward with a chilly smile on her face. "Come closer, and I'll take your yard and serve you my own."

The advancing bandit stopped and swallowed, watching the gleam of sunlight off the edge of her blade. "What's a pretty thing like you need a nasty great sword for?"

"For skewering meat."

"Well, if you didn't want our attentions, why d'you go walking the woods in little more than your skin?" he asked.

"Perhaps I'd a mind to feel the sun on my hide. Or perhaps it's no business of yours what I chose to wear, anymore than it's mine if *you* choose to go unclothed in the wildwood, yourselves."

The one with the sword cast a nervous glance down, possibly wondering if he was displaying anything that was better off hidden. "We're not undressed."

"You might as well be," said Kes. "Not a whit of armor among you all." She let the sunlight flash on her sword again.

"But...there's three of us..."

"And that should give you pause," she said.

The bandits looked at one another, confused. "Why ain't she afraid of us?" the one with the crossbow asked.

"Exactly," said Kes.

"Them mail smallclothes...maybe they're magic..." the bandit with the cudgel whispered. "Why else would she be walking around, brazen as that?"

"Maybe we should just—"

While the bandits were distracted, Kes dove sideways toward the one with the crossbow and shouted "Angeli! Storm up!"

Angeli may have been young, and small, and something of a coward, but it knew when to follow orders. The dragon leapt up, unfurling its wings with a mighty crack and a gust of air that sent two of the three bandits staggering and dropping their weapons. True, its wings weren't much for flying, yet, but they made an impressive display.

Kes knocked the crossbow upward as she rammed a shoulder into the bowman's gut. His bolt shot off into the trees and he fell backward with a grunt. She wrenched the crossbow from his hands and whirled to deal with the other two, but they'd already taken to their heels. Their companion scrambled to do the same. She smacked the flat of her blade across his backside to hurry him on his way.

Angeli bounded after them a way, snarling and blowing puffs of flame. "Yah! Run, cowards! Scared of a woman in mail smallclothes! Nyah!"

"Enough, Angeli," Kes said.

"Aren't you afraid they'll come back?"

"They may, but all the better reason to take our leave."

"Awww...but then you could run them through—or I could eat them!"

"Curb your bloodlust, dragon. We've more important things to do than spit fools on their own swords. Withdrawal being the wiser course upon occasion—a strategy clearly unknown to the fathers of that lot."

Angeli did its best to rein in its enthusiasm, but was still bounding and puffing most of the way to High Tower.

---

The gate guards at High Tower were apparently cut from the same cloth as the bandits in the forest. They leered at Kes and one said, "What's this? Come for a bit of sport on Assembly Day?"

"Make mock at your own peril," Kes said and pointed at Angeli. "I've a restive dragon and a sword as keen as my temper."

"But dressed as you are—"

Angeli looked over her shoulder. "I wouldn't say that if I were you. She beat three bandits in the forest for such talk."

The guards gave way. Kes and Angeli continued into the courtyard and through a gathering crowd. At the bottom of the tower's wide stairs, another guard hailed them with a similar observation.

"What ho! A dainty that comes unwrapped and ready to be served!"

Kes rolled her eyes. "Turn a hand to such service, and your fist will never know another weapon."

"Oh, a spicy one! Surely such a clever tongue—"

Angeli poked its head around Kes's side and gave the guard a toothy smile. "Oh goody! She slew three bandits in the forest for better turns of phrase than yours. It was fun, but now I'm bored, and a little bloodshed is so entertaining!"

The guard retired swiftly.

Near the top of the tower yet another guard stopped them, as sure of his clever observation as all who'd come before him.

"Oh, a wench with her own chain!"

Kes leaned on her sword and sighed. "If you imagine yourself a wit, you're only right by half."

"That's bold for a woman in a—"

"Oo," Angeli said, looking over Kes's shoulder. "We skewered and ate three bandits in the forest for less. But maybe you should chatter on, morsel—I think I could manage a bite of dessert by now."

This one also discovered silence and a pressing need to step aside.

Kes and Angeli passed through the doors and onto the tower's roof. The westering sun gilded the stones. A man stood at the north parapet, looking down on the assembly of people below. Golden light reflected off his armor and fair hair. The armor could have been better burnished, but it still glinted in the sun and, from any distance, he was an impressive sight.

"Take it off," Kes said.

The man turned. "Why...Kes!" he said with a smile. "How delightful to see you! You look...perky." He was a handsome beast, but it cut no ice with Kes.

Kes raised her sword and narrowed her eyes. "Take off my armor."

"But you're wearing so little," the man objected and smirked.

Kes growled and took a step closer. "Speak neither of *your* wit, nor of this travesty you left behind when you absconded, Ormand. Remove *my* armor," she said, tapping the point of her sword against the breastplate. "The armor you *stole* from me."

It chimed at the touch, startling Ormand. He cleared his throat and said, "But it fits me so well, it couldn't possibly be *your* armor."

"Adaptability and perseverance are the nature of a woman's plate," Kes said. "And it's the nature of men like *you* to think someone else's pride always looks better on them."

"But you're a *girl*! You don't *need* armor! Men are the ones who go out and fight!" Ormand objected.

Kes scoffed. "Say rather, it's vainglorious men who go out and *pick* fights and women who are left to defend themselves with what weapon comes to hand." She shifted the point of her sword from his chest to the gap between the tassets that hung down from the breast-plate to his thighs. "Now, off with it, or I'll *unmake* a man of you and let Angeli loose to finish off the rest—and you well know what a mess that will be."

Angeli spread its wings and stretched upward so the sun shone through their membranes, scarlet as blood. "Ah, a skirmish! I knew I'd come in handy, though you always say I'm so inconvenient. Inconvenient *this!*" it added, with a well-aimed puff of flame.

Ormand yelped as the blast warmed his hind parts. Then he scrambled to remove the stolen armor before the dragon—or the lady —could take further offense.

The crowd below muttered and gabbled. Ormand blushed, but kept his mouth shut until he stood in nothing but his smallclothes. The pile of Kes's armor lay between them on the stones.

"Well, there," Ormand spat. "You've made a mockery of me and left me bare besides."

"If *that* were mockery, it's you who've made it of yourself," said Kes. "While I've come all this way covered in naught but a wisp of mail and the aegis of my wits."

Ormand started to say something and Angeli snorted a stream of warning smoke in his direction. The man stepped back and glowered at Kes. "Fine for you. But what am *I* to wear, now?"

Kes took off the paltry mail, donned her armor, and tossed the tiny woven-chain garments to Ormand. "You may have these back. I'm certain they'll offer all the protection you need, as they have withstood so many barbs already."

Ormand slumped and sat down against the nearest crenellation, digging his naked toes into the cracks in the floor. His mouth turned down in chagrin and he cast his glance anywhere but at Kes and Angeli. "Small comfort," he muttered.

"It is what you make of it," said Kes. She sheathed her sword and started back toward the stairs with the dragon in her wake. The plate, now on its proper owner, shone bright and golden in the sun.

"Pretty," Angeli said. "It fits so well. But I think you were just as fearsome in the other stuff."

"Of a certainty," said Kes. "But this is warmer. Though I think the draft I felt before was as much from holes in wit and common courtesy as the gaps between the rings."

They went down the stairs and across the courtyard. A few of the crowd murmured or whispered, but not a single lascivious comment was foisted their way. They stepped out the gate and onto the road again in peace.

Angeli looked around and grinned. "Can we go teach those bandits a lesson in manners, now?"

Kes tried a disapproving frown, but it broke into a laugh. "Perhaps next month."

# 7

## HEART'S DESIRE

I have no choice but to kill you, heart of my heart. It is all that is admirable in you—love, compassion, resolve—that seals your fate. Now I trudge up the tower stairs blinded by tears that burn with bitterest salt. I hear the golden eagle's wings beat the air as it lands on the parapet, the stone still chilly in the pine shadows thrown by the rising sun.

I cuff the water from my eyes, though the bird will not care that I weep. "Where is he?" I ask.

*Many leagues, by morning's light,*
*No closer still by dark of night,*
*Across the river that mountain stream*
*Delights by glacial freshet.*

"Bother you and your metrical poesy, bird." The eagle is too much like me—a killer who fancies himself a poetical soul. Perhaps you will find me as amusing to begin with, as vain and flowery as the bird. "Does he know of me? Does he come hither?"

The bird spreads his wings and bobs his head. *He prepares, Mover of Stones. His distance is yet great and I have had to seek many of my cousins to learn his flight.*

"On the far side of the river, beyond the mountains..."

The eagle bobs his head again.

"I had not expected him to rise so far away," I say. "Is it not strange that this should be?" Oh, liar that I am, this comes as no surprise, but I enjoy the bird's discomfort at being asked a question any deeper than a dish of salt.

The eagle shuffles side to side and tilts his head. *Perhaps one of my cousins carried him in her gullet when first you cast your stone.*

I throw my hands up in frustration. "And perhaps the wind gave wings to pebbles and the gravel speaks to the river that passes over it —each just as likely since nature gave beauty to such a one as you."

The eagle ruffles his feathers in annoyance. *Why belabor me, Mover of Stones? It is no fault of mine if my answer does not please. I shall take my lovely self away if I offend you so.* Piqued, the bird extends his wings again and makes as if to vault into the sky.

"Oh, bird, bird, don't be so quick," I say. "I am intemperate this morning." No more so than ever, but the eagle is easily hoodwinked since of Power, Beauty, Brains he has only two. I take one of the scraps of rabbit flesh from my pocket and hold it aloft. "And I have brought you a tidbit."

He lets out a cry of delight and leaps into the air as I toss the meat upward. The morning light gleams from his golden feathers as he wheels and snatches the bait. You will find him as easy to dupe, I have no doubt.

The eagle lands again and tears the meat, devouring it. And I speak to my spell, which twines through him as he dines upon it. He feels it stir and change him, growing like the thicket that springs up around my tower, but he is too greedy to stop eating the enchanted flesh until it is too late. *Oh, wretched creature!* The bird screams and springs upward, talons extended. *You have poisoned me!*

I lunge and throw my arms around his neck as he expands. My weight pulls him back to the tower's roof and though he rakes me, rends me into pieces, I do not bleed.

The eagle shrieks and flutters, content that he should escape my grip if he cannot kill me, though that is, of course, as impossible as the other.

Now he is as large as a hunting hound.

And now as large as a horse.

I let go and lie on the roof as the torn shreds of my body draw together again.

The eagle flaps his wings, but he is too heavy, now, to fly. *I shall take your eyes, betrayer!*

I roll myself small beneath him and say, "But how shall I behold your loveliness if you blind me, Eagle? And you are lovely—more beautiful than the sunlight on water."

The eagle hops back and perches on the parapet as I rise again. He cocks his head to stare at me with eyes now as large as golden cauldrons. *You think me lovely now? But I am huge and cannot fly! What beauty is that?* He tilts his head in curiosity. *Water comes from your eyes. Is it pain that brings it—I hope so!*

"It is your beauty that brings tears to my eyes," I lie to him, for it is only regret. But he is much too foolish to question my flattery. "And I can restore your flight."

I throw the other piece of meat onto the farthest apron of the tower roof.

The eagle regards it with hunger, but he does not lunge for it yet, though I can see his constant appetite in his gaze. *What will you inflict upon me this time, Mover of Stones?*

Already he forgets his ire. "Only what I have promised," I say. "I will restore your flight and you will remain as mighty and beautiful as you are now. But there is a task..."

The eagle lets out a small sharp cry. *As always!*

"You are bound to me by our mutual nature, no matter what you will," I remind him. "And do you not delight in proving your strength and cunning as I do...?"

He eyes me and clacks his beak as if he imagines how delicious my innards shall one day be. I doubt he has the brain to realize that prey that cannot die is prey that can be tormented for eternity. Alas for us both when he does.

He shuffles foot to foot and spreads his wings, casting a shade over the tower. *What would you have me do?*

"Go to him. Lay a trap. Let him think you in his debt or power. In discharge of this debt, carry him safe across the river and the mountain, so that he will come here all the sooner. But tell him nothing of me."

*But to fly so far...and carry one of your kind!*

"It will be as nothing to you—see how vast and powerful you are! Once you dine upon the meat, you can fly across the valley in a single beat of your wings."

The eagle considers it, turning his head side to side. Then he snatches up the bit of rabbit and gulps it down. My spell enfolds him, illuminates his form in light more golden than the rising spears of the sun.

He launches into the sky and beats high into the brightening blue. Oh, how glorious is this thing I have made for your doom! And the horror of it pains me until fresh tears well from my eyes and I clutch the stone edge of the tower so that I shall not fall to my knees. I am a wretch, and you bring me to this.

The bird returns, raising a wind as he cups the air to land on the parapet again, so pleased with himself that he stops to preen. *Soar! Oh, flight and feathers! I rule the sky!*

"And shall you undertake my task, Eagle?"

*Yes! But. But, how shall I entrap him?*

"He is a human and believes all animals are stupid," I say. "Leave one of your golden feathers in his path—even the smallest of them will be as long as his hand—just where the river is widest or where I have cast the mountain sheer and daunting in his way. When he picks it up, you have but to descend and attempt—unsuccessfully—to take the feather back. But fail carefully or all is lost. Once he believes he has the upper hand of you, tell him you will carry him toward his heart's desire in exchange for the feather. He will, of course, accept, and as this tower holds his heart's desire, you will carry him to the edge of the wood. No farther. For a goal too easily won is a prize without value."

*Your kind is strange. I prefer the prey that comes easily.*

I shrug. "Indeed, as what truly intelligent creature does not?"

He preens a bit more and there is barely room enough on the roof for us both.

"Fly, my friend. Find him."

The eagle leaps into the air and beats away. When his form is a distant shape against the mountains, I sink to my knees and weep.

***

I have shared such dreams...dreams that draw you to me by the weakness of your nobility, visions of perfection and irresistible desire. Lies and truth bound up as we two are bound together in life and love and death. I have sent them each night since I knew what I must do. While you tarried, the tale spread, bringing others who batter themselves against my obstacles to drown, to fall, to die pierced by thorns and crushed by vines. Not one survives while my forest and my brambles drink their blood. Had you only heeded my sendings earlier, they would not have died.

I climb to the tower every night before I dream. The bat arrives first and then the owl as night thickens. The hedge below the tower grows denser by the day, winding between the trunks of the lofty evergreens as thick as marsh fog and more dangerous, but no news comes...I begin wondering if the eagle has failed me, for he has not yet returned. Perhaps I should send the owl...

But as the darkness draws in tonight, the bat flutters to the tower top and hangs himself on the bare limb I've left there for him, wedged into the crenellations of the parapet.

*There is a breeze from the mountain that smells of carrion.*

"Indeed, Master of the Evening Sky?" I ask.

*Would I tell you something that was not true?*

"You never have."

*And never will. I have no need to lie, Swarmcaller.*

"Everyone lies."

The bat chirps his laughter. *I shall bear that in mind when I converse with you.*

My grief for you has made me incautious, and I would regret my candor, but regret is something I shall have to learn to live without. And the bat, at least, has the virtue of humor—a trait I share with neither the eagle nor the owl, who possess it not at all.

"What does this wind tell you?" I ask.

*A man draws near—flies leap from the trail of his leavings and they taste of his journey. The eagle accompanies him, so he has neither eaten the man, nor been killed by him—though that might be a battle worth seeing.*

"What would you know of battles, Leatherwing? Your kind does not duel or fight."

*My kind are wiser than to kill each other over a bit of land. But battles draw such delicious insects, spiced with tales! And your kind are amusing in their battle array—surging together and churning like a confluence of rivers. It's a good thing your kind have not learned to fly, for then we should have to learn to fight! Would we not look proper fools flapping through the night bearing tiny swords?*

I chuckle at the thought. "Like a battalion of idiots."

The bat bares his tiny fangs in mock anger. *Do you call me an idiot? Perhaps you mistake me for an eagle...I fear I've been insulted. Should I challenge you to a duel, Swarmcaller?*

I look at him askance, but smile as I say, "That would not be wise— as the challenged, I choose the weapon."

*But pity me! Would you be so dishonorable as to choose one I cannot wield?*

If I were an honorable creature, I would not, now, be plotting your death. A sudden pang squeezes my chest and I must shut my eyes against it, shedding a tear as large and hard as a pearl. "I will choose that which suits me," I reply.

I cast a spell into the air and send a buzzing cloud of gnats toward the trees below, rife with my own sorrows and stories.

The bat looks first to me, before he makes to fly away after the fast-moving flight of his supper. *Coward.*

Then he falls from his perch and swoops to follow the swarm away into the twilight.

I send away my only friend and draw you to your fate here, where you will be powerless against me. For yes, I am a coward, as much as I am a monster, but I am not a fool.

---

For two nights I see neither bat nor eagle and return to my chamber alone to cast my dreams. The forest of thorns has grown thick and full all around my tower and there is no path to me but by my art or through the air. I have made it difficult for you, knowing you as I do; like me, you crave challenge and have no time for that which is acquired without effort. So much comes easily to you now, that it was inevitable that you would seek me, though you do not know the price that you will pay in finding me. I am the prize that holds a hidden sting, death at the heart of love. I despise myself, but this will pass...

Late in darkness the owl comes, swooping to the parapet on silent wings like a windblown flurry of snow.

She lays a shimmering crystal on the parapet and turns her head to regard me with a somber gaze.

I pick up the pretty rock and bow. "Well met, Queen of Night. What passes?" I ask and put the stone away in my pocket.

*I have taken a mouse that crept into the forest from the shadow of the eagle this afternoon.*

"What did it say before you devoured it?"

She hacks and spits its rendered carcass—only bones and fur and long tail—onto the parapet between us. *Ask it yourself. I do not cross-examine my dinner.*

I take up the pathetic bundle and sort it with my fingers, muttering memories to it, willing it to recall its shape and life. The remains rise and take their form, bones assembling into skeleton, fur wrapping about, until the dead mouse stands in my hand, squeaking. I listen closely to its tale, holding it near my ear, feeling the twitch of ghostly whiskers at my cheek.

*Sharp beak by evening, where the bramble roots make a den beneath the hazel. As I cross a field of grass, the eagle—monstrous large—roosts above an oak waiting for daylight.*

I consider what it's told me. "At the base of the hills where an oak stands beside a field that spreads to my woods. The owl caught you near the bramble and a hazel tree, only the distance a mouse could run from evening into night...I think I know the place," I say.

The owl blinks at me. *Another day will see him to the edge of the thicket.*

"Yes. And then another to the tower, if he can pass the thorns." My breath stumbles in my chest and I look back to the mouse. "I will ask a favor of you, little one."

The remains squeak and tremble—even dead it is afraid of me. I part its tattered fur with my fingertips and take two of its tiny ribs. The creature's cries wring me with pity. "There, Mouse, it will soon be over and you will live again. Find the man and lead him to your ribs, which will rise up into a gate. When he is through, touch your bones and they will return to their proper place as you will return to life. Then scamper fast back to your home and be at peace."

*But he is far...*

"Never mind it. I will bring him closer." I work my magic over the sad bundle of remaining bones and fur and the mouse stands again as if alive, though it is only an illusion for now.

I breathe into its mouth and ears and it looks up, speaking like a man, "My thanks, Mage."

"Do not be foolish with my gift, Mouse."

It trembles again. "Never!"

I place it on the parapet and watch it scamper away down the vine-grown walls of my tower.

The owl regards it hungrily, then turns her gaze back to me. *You place much faith in the rodent.*

"It will do as I ask."

*Why trust such a one? They are foolish and easily frightened. Why not ask the bear to drive the man to your hidden path?*

I shake my head. "The bear could not resist his impulse to do the man harm. I would rather that he comes without violence."

*Why?*

"Now that he walks in my domain, every drop of his blood shed is as a drop of my own. The longer he takes to come to me, the greater the danger."

My plan proceeds and the ache within me builds with every step you take in my direction. I walk to the edge of the parapet and look over, but the view down is obscured by night and the constant stream of my tears.

*You should find some other way...*

"It is none of your concern, Owl," I snap. "There *is* no other way. I have studied and I have searched and if I would gain the greatest potential of my power, it must be thus."

*But this pains you.*

"Little worth doing comes without pain." There would be much more if not for my plan. I shall not abandon it, though it means your death and my own agony.

I pick up the tiny bones and hold them out to the owl. "Take these to the place where the hidden path lies at the edge of the wood and lay them on the ground there. Then summon the bat to me. And leave the mouse to his own devices."

The owl stares long at me, keeping her own counsel. Then she blinks and takes the bones in her beak, flying away with neither word nor sound.

---

You must not delay, nor wander far afield, for I cannot bear this much longer. The path is strewn with horrors—with the bodies of those who would have the prize that was not meant for them and met their end, instead. By your gentlest feelings I will compel you quicker to my side.

I draw my knife and weave my sending around your name, my illusion of perfection cast to dreaming night—for you would never come to me were my image otherwise. Then, I stab the blade into my chest and fall to the tower roof, blood drawn from those who've died before you spreading all around as I cry out into your dreams. I know you hear me, see me fall, and feel my pain as your own. I hear you in the darkness, startled from sleep and shouting your distress, compassion, love... You will rescue me; you must. And soon, for my creatures and my plan ensure it.

But for me this pang, this bleeding, is nothing. You must come and you must die and that is the greater torment. I sob for you until I sleep, wrapped in blood and watched by cold stars until the bat comes.

His fluttering awakens me and he leaps to roost as I climb to my feet, streaked in blood.

*Are you clumsy, Swarmcaller? I have never seen you fall before.*

"I do not fall—I sleep."

*I don't care for your pajamas...*

"At least I do not ask you to wear them. I have another task for you."

*I guessed as much. What now?*

"Only this," I say. "Take your kin and drive the man across the field and toward the hidden path. He will encounter a mouse in the morning who will show him the rest of the way. Be sure to leave the creature in peace and only harry the man faster toward the tower once night is falling. I'd have him here by tomorrow's sunset."

The bat snickers. *You grow impatient.*

"That should be warning enough for you, Leatherwing. Your charm may not be proof against my temper."

*But will your temper be proof against my charm?*

"We shall see..."

---

By morning the eagle has stooped to my tower and I have restored him to his natural size—I need him no longer, and his appetite is as gargantuan as he is. I fear for my woods were he to continue in such a state.

He stands at the edge of the parapet and glances at the forest below. *He comes.*

"Well I know it, bird," I say. I feel you close.

*And yet, you cry. Why does this not bring you joy? Or is it that you mourn my beauty now that I am diminished again?*

"Bird, you are as beautiful as ever, so there is nothing to mourn."

*But you are not as beautiful as I...*

"Think you that I should be jealous? Who could be as lovely as you?" I ask. But my vanity is pricked and I call forth the semblance I wear in your dreams—tall and fair as dawn, kind-eyed and cherry-lipped.

Startled, the eagle cries out and bolts into the sky.

I feel your attention turn toward my tower and in the moment a thorn tears your sleeve, pricks your arm...I gasp and feel the poison burn your flesh.

You must not die. You must not. Not yet. Not but by my hand. I cast a spell out to the thorn and take your wound to myself. Agony like wildfire rages through my body and brings me to my knees, but I must not cry out, since you will hear me and turn again, drawn to my aid. I could fly to you and end this, but that would not accomplish my goal, for the spell has a mind of its own and you must come to me of your own will, no matter the hardship, else my heart will be too weak and we both shall die.

I go below to my rooms in the tower to heal myself and prepare. I needn't stay above now that you are so close; I feel your presence as my own true north and know every step you take. I drink the draughts and cast the spells, cure my wounds, and lay the treasures of my love aside.

I know of your amazement in meeting the small ghost of a mouse. I feel the rush of wings as the bats drive you to the gate and through it to my path. Your fear and resolve wash through me as the gate vanishes and you must wind alone along the path to my tower. Your wonder ignites in my breast as you see the white stone walls rise before you at last.

I climb again to the tower's top, clad in my fair illusion, and walk awhile where you can see me before I descend again without acknowledging your presence. Elation leaps within you as it does in me and you rush to the wall that separates us.

I feel you press against the door, heart beating fast, flushed with yearning that warms me like a fire.

You break the lock with your sword and begin up the stairs.

Round and round, rising up the interminable steps, your breath fast with excitement. I leave my chamber and return again to the roof, panting with you, rushing toward the light that you might see the sun one last time before you die.

You follow, drawn by the fleeting glimpse of my hem, my sleeve, my hair...always out of reach, tantalizing. Oh, how your heart beats, how it thrills, and I am entwined in love that binds like cutting wire.

Upon the roof of my tower I cast my circle wide and you ascend within it.

My back is turned, my illusion still intact. I feel your breath stop in your chest, feel your heart leap. You raise your hands to touch me, even from a distance drawn to me. My own breath comes short and wild.

You take a step, then two to bring us close.

I slam the door and turn to you—my heart, my love, my life—as the sky begins to flare toward sunset. And in its changing light I am myself alone.

You stop short. Your confusion is like cold water.

"You are not she," you say.

I smile my bittersweet expression, for you are as beautiful and beloved as ever in my dreams and scrying. And you are here, drawn to your fate. "But I *am* she," I say, and let the face that you have loved take form across my own. I let it fall away to leave my own true face, dark where you are bright, a mirror of yourself. "And I am he. I am you, as you are me, heart of my heart."

You scowl and step back, filling us with your fear and horror. You draw your sword. "You are a sorcerer and mean me ill," you say.

My remorse and resolution twine in our fear and my tears flow again. I tremble with effort. "Not yet a sorcerer, but I do mean to kill you, my heart—for that is what you are and a sorcerer needs no heart."

You strike at me as I draw close—close enough to touch you. But your stroke is no more mortal than the raking of the eagle's claws—you cannot kill me, for I do not bleed.

But you do, and I stab my knife into your throat.

We fall together as your blood flows over me, covering my skin, filling my mouth, blinding me. I lay your body on the tower roof and kneel beside you.

My guilt compels me to speak—if I could only leap through time until this were over I should hold my tongue, but, though I try, I cannot. You are my weakness, even as I feel you dying. "Once we were one, my heart, but I put you from me—all my better feeling, my mortality, and frailty. I cast you as a stone, far away. But perhaps I should have held something back, for such was your goodness and humanity that you sprang up again as a being more perfect and more pure than I, yet tied to me. My own beating, living heart, eternally mine. You plague me with your emotions, your desires, your love. I do not want them. They are my weakness. So today, heart of my heart, I shall murder you and be plagued no more with mortality or feeling."

You say nothing—what can you say, indeed, with your throat slit from side to side?

I plunge the knife into your chest and cut to draw forth the tiny sliver of stone as black as jet that is all that remains of the once-large heart I threw away. The greater perfection around it has grown to be you and this hard cinder is the one cold, hard thing within you—the one thing that ties me to you, still.

My breath steadies and I grow colder as you die, all feeling flowing from me like the blood from your body.

I draw the shimmering crystal from my pocket—the stone the owl brought to me—to bathe it in our blood. This will serve as my heart now. The stone has turned black but for a single brilliant star.

I hear a rustle of wings and look up, the two stones in my hands.

The eagle, the owl, and the bat assemble on the parapet as the last red light of sunset touches it. They watch me with cold eyes as the bond between us dissolves.

Your life snuffs out like a candle, and the kernel of my heart crumbles between my fingers. I—too late—know I have been a fool, reached for immortality and the chill of power unleavened by emotion and all that remains in me now is horror, swiftly fading.

The creatures watch me without feeling—the feeling that I endowed them with by my fancy and the empathy by which I bound them, now as dead as you are. What I saw as weakness was the sinew and fiber that binds resilience to power into true strength, and what remains without it is as brittle as ice. I have deceived myself to my own doom and slaughtered you for nothing.

The crystal in my other hand goes black...

Now they come for me, heart of my heart.

# 8

## THE HOLLOW HOUNDS

He was still a young man, though his tall, slim body was much battered and his face no longer handsome beneath his luxuriant blond mustaches, but when the news came, his commanders were as glad to send him home: a patched and broken soldier, old at twenty-six, and no good to anyone at the front—not anymore. No good to anyone at home either, for there was no one there, nor family remaining east, west, north or in the war-torn south. How bitter the irony that while he stood in the hellfire of war and emerged changed but still living, his wife and child, safe at home, had died of fever and remained forever as they had been in his memory, but only there.

He had returned to bury them, and then found no reason to stay. Carrying nothing but what lay in his pockets, he returned to the station and boarded the first train heading away from all he knew—west past Kansas until the train could go no further. He disembarked at the rural station in an unknown territory and begin walking. Just walking. Looking for...what? Something to set his heart by, perhaps. Some purpose. Or some reason to stop.

He'd walked west, seeing no one and caring little who or what saw him, for a day and a half when he came to a crossroads in the woodland through which he trod. He paused beside the stout signpost there, the sunlight through the trees dappling his pale hair as he looked down. He checked his watch—like its owner, a battered thing but running still in spite of all it had passed through—then took a key from his pocket as if he meant to wind the mechanism up and stood staring at the key a moment. He'd looked up at the fingerboards pointing from the post and down to the key again—as if the key would help him decide which road to follow—when he heard a sound all too familiar: an explosion like those made by the infernal torpedoes to which he had lost a good horse on the battlefield and taken no small injury himself.

The not-so-old soldier shoved the key back into his pocket as he ducked and scrambled under the nearest cover, expecting a hail of dirt and stones thrown up by the blast that had sounded so near at hand, but there was no such rain of debris. Instead he felt a rude and insistent shoving at his back, which he had pressed against a sheltering rock outcrop.

"Devil take it," someone groused at his rear. "Give way!"

He jumped forward, whirling to see what and who prodded him in the backside so persistently and why they spoke in such impatient tones.

From the depths of the rock emerged a disordered man who shoved wide the camouflaged door that had been hidden in the deep shadow of the overhang. The soldier saw that the door was in fact wood, cleverly painted. The rock around it had been carved away in some fashion to create a niche just deep enough to ensure the door would remain shaded all the year and preserve the illusion of stone, but not so deeply set in the rock that any animal would choose to make their den on the threshold.

The man, portly and balding, wore sleeve gaiters and a long leather apron covered in bulging pockets over his clothes. He closed the door in haste against a billow of smoke as acrid as that from any battlefield and stepped out into the sunshine near the signpost and there stopped to stare at the soldier from behind the thick, round lenses of goggles that gave his eyes a bizarre, insectile appearance.

"What, by Jupiter, are you doing here?" the man asked, pulling the goggles off his face as if they might be causing him to hallucinate. "No one walks through these woods nowadays."

"If they are regularly troubled with explosions beneath their feet, that would hardly be a wonder. Shall I assume that was your work," the soldier asked pointing to a few wisps of sulfurous smoke, "since you came from a door in the rock that clearly leads to wherever that explosion originated?"

The disheveled man peered at him, his uncovered eyes sharp with speculation. "An observant man, I see. Do I take it rightly, by your dress, sir, that you are but late returned from the battlefields of the southeast?"

"I am not returned at all, sir," the soldier said, taken for a moment by a perverse humor. "But I am, indeed, late from the war."

"I don't recognize you," the man said, "and I've lived in these parts nigh on five years."

"I am not from these parts. I find myself at loose ends and thought I'd take a walk until I tied them back up again."

"What, no family nor friends nearby?"

"None. Not nearby nor anywhere. All dead."

"A tragic tale, friend, and perhaps too common in this time of conflict." The man shook his head in sorrow and then offered his hand, "My name is Conscience Morton and you have my sympathies."

The soldier took his hand and shook it stiffly, but offered nothing more, for there seemed no further reply to make.

Morton continued after a moment's clumsy silence, "Well, friend, if you have no destination, perhaps I might persuade you to do me a small favor...? Though you are wan—perhaps still suffering from your wounds?—you seem a strong man and clever. Educated, I would guess. And what I would ask of you requires no great strength, but is quite out of the question for one...encumbered by such flesh as I am."

The soldier nodded at him to go on, or in agreement that the gentleman before him was, inarguably, rotund and unused to physical labor.

"Below," Morton began, "lies a great maze of caverns and tunnels in which are secreted such marvels as would amaze even the most jaded collector, and gold enough to send a miser into transports of joy. Now, among this treasure lies a small music box—quite an ordinary sort of thing carved from a pretty bit of wood, bound in brass, and no larger than a lady's prayer book—that I made...for my late wife." The man watched the soldier from the corner of his eye as he spoke and must surely have noticed the other's unhappy expression as he added, "She died of a brain fever and nothing to be done for her, poor thing."

The soldier bowed his head and shook it in sympathy, his eyes sparked with tears.

"So you see," Morton continued, "how dear such a keepsake is to me."

"I see," the soldier replied, dashing the moisture from his face with the back of one scarred hand.

"I would give all the gold of Midas to retrieve that box. It was stolen from me by a rival: a mad inventor, a very devil of a man who has turned his hand to building vile mechanisms—but I let my emotions run away with me. Forgive me. It is only recently I've discovered that he keeps the music box in his secret laboratory, which lies below."

"In caves beneath our very feet?" the soldier asked, with a hint of doubt.

The weighty Mr. Morton gave an adamant nod. "Exactly as you say. And I have tried to gain access to the place to reclaim what is mine, but this man—beast that he is—set traps at the door which I, unsuspecting, set off and the explosion has sealed this entry. There are other ways in but only to this one did I hold a key. And now I cannot pass through it."

The soldier drew himself up, frowning in thought and looking at the man before him as if he could weigh the truth of his tale in his gaze. "How do you propose to get below and reclaim your treasure?"

Morton's face lit up and he exclaimed, "Ah, such penetration! I knew you were a clever fellow the moment I clapped eyes upon you. And you, you see, *you* are the very answer. There is, nearby, an air shaft disguised as a lightning-blasted tree and a slender fellow such as yourself should find no difficulty in shimmying down it. I might assay it myself, but I fear I am not a vigorous man and should fail of the attempt. If *you* would go down and retrieve the box, I should be most grateful."

The soldier frowned. "If you'll pardon my saying so, sir, I don't quite perceive what reward there is in this venture for me," he said. "Saving the satisfaction of returning your beloved wife's trinket to you—which is a kind-hearted gesture, I do admit it—there seems no further inducement to *me* to take such a risk, for such an impulse no longer shivers in *my* breast. I have lately laid all my worldly happiness and all I possess on the altar of my country and placed my life and limbs in the hands of men who cast me aside once my usefulness was done, and my heart is no longer kind. So tell me what I am to be paid for this service."

"My dear friend," Morton replied, "you mistake me entirely. There is treasure in plenty below—gold, silver, and gems. Merely take what you will—be discrete in your choices for the builder may recognize his toys if you should take one of those—but of materials, he shall miss nothing if you temper your avarice with common sense. It's a veritable trove down there!" he added, throwing his arms upward with enthusiasm. He knocked the backs of his knuckles against the fingerboards on the signpost and winced, missing the soldier's swift, ironic smile.

The soldier schooled his expression into one of careful thought and then nodded. "Very well. Lead on to your air shaft and I shall go below and see this dragon's hoard for myself."

Morton led him perhaps a half a mile into the woods, his path wobbling between the boles of larger trees and the spindly growth of smaller ones, to a large, blackened stump. It stood a couple of feet taller than the soldier—who was taller than Morton—and was more than twice as big around. The remaining top of the tree was ragged and had only one branch that stuck out at a crooked angle.

The soldier raised his arms and jumped, aiming to catch the branch and pull himself up, but the branch hung just out of reach. He thought to ask Morton for a leg up, but observing the pudgy man's physique, only raised an enquiring eyebrow.

"I have with me a rope," Morton said. "If you could scramble up and tie the rope off to that branch, I should be able to climb up behind you so as to pull you back up once you've found the music box."

The soldier nodded. "The height is just a bit more than I can leap and the trunk too large to shin up easily. Perhaps I could step on your back..."

"What?!" Morton objected.

"Dear fellow," the soldier replied. "It *is* in a good cause, isn't it?"

And so it was that Morton knelt on the ground at the base of the false tree and the soldier wrapped the rope around his body and stepped up, light and quick, caught the branch with ease, and swung himself up to look down into the blasted tree.

"Hollow as a hound before supper," the soldier observed of the tree as he tied off the rope to the branch and prepared to swing his legs over into the void.

"Just a moment, friend." Morton called, dusting himself off before struggling to ascend the tree with the help of both rope and soldier. And an arduous journey it was.

When Morton sat, panting and sweating, on the branch, he said, "Before you descend, you must know this: the owner of this cavern has three guardians below and they stand vigil over his most precious inventions—and no doubt the music box as well. These guardians are clockwork beasts of a horrible aspect, but they may be easily overcome with a small invention of mine own." He took a small box from one of his pockets and a sort of round brass plate that he popped open into the shape of a cone, telescoping much in the manner of an opera hat that extends from its flattened state with a flick of the gentleman's wrist. He screwed the cone thus made into a hole in the box and offered it to the soldier. Then he passed him his goggles as well. "But touch the button on this box and it will emit a field from the cone that will temporarily disable the mechanical beast. Wear my goggles and you shall be able to see the field and any others like it that my rival may have placed below. They aren't terribly dangerous to men—make one a bit queasy is all—but they play hob with mechanical things for a time. If he has used these fields for alarms, walking through one will allow the bell, or whatever diabolical engine at which it has been aimed, to begin functioning again, so these fields are to be avoided if you wish to emerge again alive and free. Just remember: point the cone at the beast and press the button. You may then leave the emitter on the ground in front of the creature until you have finished your inspection. I've calibrated the effect to last several minutes after the generator is removed, so you may carry on out of the creature's sight where it will not perceive and pursue you. They will not detect you otherwise but with their eyes."

The soldier accepted the goggles and the device, carefully dismantling it and putting the parts of it into his jacket and pockets so he could have his hands free to climb down. "Just be ready with the rope when I come back," was all he said before he vanished down the hollow tree.

It took several minutes to slither down the pipe using his back and legs braced against the opposite sides, for the space was much wider than he'd at first thought and he was not so tightly tucked in as he would have liked. Morton might, in fact, have eased in, but the inventor was clearly not fit enough to climb.

When he neared the bottom, the soldier paused to don the goggles and survey his proposed landing site. A dim or distant lamp cast poor illumination on the area and the goggles darkened it still further, but he saw no sign of mysterious fields or roving mechanical beasts of a diabolical nature, so he let himself down with care and crouched below the air shaft a moment while he assembled the emitter. He could barely hear the constant dripping of water somewhere below a low whine that filled the air much like the sound of the monstrous engine he had seen prowling the Confederate skirmish lines at Shiloh. It had been no rail locomotive—though just as large—and it had raised lightning around its metal body that struck at the Union men and ground around them. It had seemed the hand of Zeus himself flung the bolts on General Johnston's orders until that man was, himself, brought down and the engine silenced. In this shadowy cavern, the memory of death whispered close and the soldier shivered.

He crept across the floor to the nearest wall and inched along its length toward the sound until he came upon the thing, crouching beside a buried stream of water on a bed of steel and rubber. In the low light made dimmer by his goggles, he inspected it, for it seemed unlikely to attack him, fettered as it was to the ground. It took only a minute to recognize it for what it was—an electricity generator, driven by the spinning of a handful of propellers sunk from the machine into the buried stream of water below it like some cockeyed metal water mill. Thick cables clad in rubber and guided by hoops of rubber-lined brass carried the electricity away into the cavern to power the dim lights hanging in cages pegged to the walls. Here there were no gas flames or sputtering torches, only the lowered, chilly light of the heavens' rage tamed by Man. Nearby, a regiment of switches marched along a metal panel, carefully labeled, but in no wise helpful, for the soldier couldn't imagine what they truly did and had no desire to call unwanted attention to himself in this place.

He prowled onward, taking care to avoid anything that looked like the field Morton had warned of. It was in avoiding one of these that he came suddenly around a corner and face-to-face with a dog. It was about the size of a big hunting hound but it gleamed metallic gold and red in the low light and its eyes, as large as doorknobs, glowed the pale blue of electricity. The soldier jerked to a standstill and stared at the beast, his own eyes nearly as wide as the dog's.

The mechanical beast scratched one iron forefoot upon the floor, sending sparks flying from the stone as it growled like a freight car rolling slowly over gravel. The soldier leapt backward, and the metal dog crouched as if to spring, but the soldier held Morton's emitter between them and, praying more from habit than hope, pressed the button. The box made a click and a squeal, then what looked like a hash of black and white lines shot from the cone and enveloped the dog, who stopped stock-still, half-crouched, the cold fire in its gleaming eyes extinguished in an instant.

The soldier put the box on the ground in front of the mechanical beast and walked toward it, curious. But as he stepped into the beam, a wrenching pain tore through his chest and he reeled, stumbling aside and falling against the wall, his sight dim and his ears filled with an unnatural silence. He lay still against the wall for a minute or two, as still as death, until at last he heaved a mighty breath into his lungs and dragged himself back to his feet.

"'Makes one a bit queasy,'" he mocked. "Hah!" He turned to regard the dog, but it was as motionless as before, unmoved and unmoving, its eyes still dark. "But it does work a treat on you, old boy," he added, and forbore to pat the brass-bound hound on the head. He stepped with care past the dog and into the chamber it guarded.

Shelf upon shelf groaned under the weight of brass, copper, and steel parts and boxes filled with the tiny sapphires and rubies watchmakers used in their art, of which he poured a few into his hand and put them carelessly into his breast pocket. Spools of wire, coils, cylinders, and sheets of metal rolled thin enough to bend and shape were stacked beside bins full of screws, pins, gears, springs, valves, grommets, pistons, chain...and things so foreign he had no word for them. Ranks of tools waited in racks on the walls. Upon the tables set across the room, quiet under a thin blanket of dust and cobweb, sat dozens of mechanical creations. Seeing only the glitter of jewels and no spark of electricity in their eyes, the soldier walked up to the first table and found himself in the midst of a wonderful menagerie of automata: birds, beetles, snakes, rabbits, puppies, squirrels, chickens...all such small, familiar animals rendered in shining metal and each with a key protruding from its back. The second table was filled with more sophisticated and bejeweled miniature human figures poised to demonstrate various clever tasks: a tumbler dressed in jester's motley of set gemstones, a lady with face and arms of carved ivory and hair of silk thread seated at a tiny piano; even a soldier dressed in British red enamel with a small ebony and brass musket in his hands, and so many others it was hard to count them, each more gloriously adorned than the last and all left to gather dust. The final table was much cleaner and held more frightening models: a tiny guillotine that raised and lowered its own blade and diligently disposed of the severed bits of its wax victims into a box below, all at the flick of a lever; a sort of reverse torture rack that screwed itself down to crush the dolly victim within; a metal box that seemed capable of opening by itself to spew out its unpleasant secrets; balls covered in the sturdy spines of detonation triggers; and cylinders with valves and timers that whispered in his memory of deadly gasses creeping across the Georgia ground like killing fog.

He shuddered and stepped back, wanting nothing from this chamber.

He turned warily toward the dog, but it was as inactive as ever. He edged past the cone of strange light, careful to stay entirely out of it, and pressed the emitter's button. The field vanished and he picked up the box. Still the dog made no motion, its eyes remaining dark.

He walked on, passing yards of cable burdened with electricity and fixed to the cavern wall with loops of rubber-lined brass as he went.

Around another corner he encountered a second dog. This one was the size of a great mastiff, its horrible sparking eyes as large as artillery shells and nearly on a level with his own. This one let out a bark that shook the soldier in his boots, but he thrust forward the emitter and pushed the button...

and the dog froze as if encased in glacial ice, the light in its eyes winking out.

The soldier let out his held breath, put the emitter on the floor in front of the massive hound, and stepped around it with wary care.

The chamber beyond was much larger than that he had just come from and it was filled with great mechanisms and engines built to run on steam, all gleaming bright with polish and glistening with oil. Though not as pretty as some in the previous chamber, these far surpassed the others' mechanical sophistication with their apparent—and not-so-apparent—abilities. Here a machine that cleaned, dried, and pressed clothing; beyond it another that appeared to be a self-contained and automated forge, and still another that seemed to be some kind of massive, pressurized pump covered in couplings, valves, knobs and coiled lengths of hose.

Farther on stood a conveyance like a pony trap that rolled around under its own steam power and another larger version had, not wheels, but an endless chain of spiked plates that dug into the ground and clawed the engine forward—no doubt meant for conveying freight over rough or muddy ground a horse and wagon could not pass. Another machine seemed to be a kind of self-propelled augur on six articulated legs—perhaps a drilling machine? Beyond that lay a large armored ball with another set of the clawed tracks running around it and a door to a passenger—or driver's—cabinet within. The soldier had no idea what it was meant to do for he couldn't imagine how it moved, though it clearly was meant to.

As he wandered through the room, the mechanisms, as before, grew bleaker in their purpose. He saw great guns with valves and tanks stinking of kerosene and hoses leading to nozzles where the muzzle should have been and others that propelled themselves on legs or wheels, directed by huge empty eyes like those of the inert hound outside the door. An experimental poke at the muzzle of one gun produced a spark and a moment's blue flame that suffocated as the dregs of its fuel burned away. Beyond that lay an iron cask that stank of gunpowder, its surface all scored to break apart once it had crept on moving belts to its destination. Still more dread mechanisms lined up beside it.

Against the wall stood a rack of cylindrical machines nearly as long as he was tall with something like a stiff metal rotating fan at the tail and the fins of a fish along the sides. The lean metal bodies led to empty heads that plainly awaited the mounting of some large, round thing. Beyond them he saw the bulbous, unpleasant shapes of land torpedoes such as the one that had claimed his horse and guessed these were the objects the swimming machines were meant to carry to ships. The farthest wall held racks of rolled paper plans and he had barely the heart to open a few and see their descriptions of even worse machines of destruction before he rolled them up and shoved them back into their pigeon holes.

He turned aside, disgusted, and spied a small version of the very lightning machine he had seen at Shiloh.

"What manner of man owns this place?" he whispered.

Forsaking the plans, which he knew would be worth a small fortune to men who practiced war, he ran from the room, barely remembering in time to dodge the field that immobilized the massive mechanical dog before he bent to retrieve the emitter.

As with its smaller kin, the mechanical dog remained unmoving and unlit as the soldier walked away.

He passed through more tunnels, taking care this time to check around each corner in search of other fell guardians, but he saw only room after room of empty tables, marked with the dents and scrapes of heavy objects removed in haste. Judging by what he had seen already, he had no desire to confirm his suspicions of what those things had been.

He heard a sound and turned back, to see the second dog drag itself slowly past and into the room where the electricity generator hummed. Following it, the soldier saw the dog stop beside the generator and lie still. In a moment, the dog seemed to glow and arcs of blue lightning grew from the end of the generator to stroke the dog, which sat up, its eyes igniting again with their eerie blue light.

The soldier withdrew quickly, lest he be spotted by the dog, and hurried back to his search, wondering what had become of the first dog and if the second had awakened sooner than the first. Was it possible the emitter was weakening, its charge lingering for less time with each use?

Ahead, the light gleamed brighter and more yellow, like a hot welcoming fire, and he quickened his steps toward it without thinking.

Perhaps he made too much noise, or cast a shadow, but whatever the cause, he had only a moment's notice of the beast's proximity before it pounced and bowled him to the ground with a roar that shook dust from the ceiling.

Blindly, the soldier waved the emitter in front of himself, holding down the button with his thumb. When he was not killed, he put the emitter down to rub his eyes clear of dust and then looked around.

A mechanical dog whose shoulders were as tall as a door and its body almost as wide loomed over him, its head lowered and jaws poised to snap the soldier in two. The man's breath caught in his throat, but it was obvious the dog was as immobile as its brothers had been before, its gaze as banked and dark.

Beyond the dog, the chamber gleamed, but this time not in shades of copper and brass, but the bright hardness of electric light glittering on gold, silver, and gems. He stepped past the mechanical beast, awed by the beauty of the light that reflected from such a pile of wealth, his breath trapped in his throat.

With such engines of destruction at his call, the soldier supposed it was no difficulty for the inventor who kept these caves to amass such a treasure and yet it was thrust and piled and spilled into the chamber as carelessly as if it were so much trash. This, indeed, was a dragon's hoard and nothing in this chamber—much smaller than the ones before it, but guarded by such a monster—was ordinary, nor of base materials. Except the one box of brass-bound wood lying as if discarded near the feet of the huge dog.

The soldier was loath to reach into the beam to retrieve the box and he wasn't sure that the dog could be held in its sleeping state for long if, as he guessed, the emitter was truly burning out. He looked about the room until he came across a life-sized figure of a man. The gilded figure was something like a giant doll with arms and legs articulated at each natural joint.

"You'll not mind, I hope," the soldier said, addressing himself to the automaton. Then he twisted and pulled until one of the arms came away at the shoulder socket with a pop. He carried the heavy arm as close to the strange light of the emitter as he could and lay it on the floor, pushing and rolling it until the cupped hand curled around the music box. Then he pulled the arm back and picked up the box.

Stuffing the music box into his jacket, the soldier carried the arm back to its owner. Then he turned to the glittering trove and picked out a fortune for himself in silver and gold coins and gold nuggets with which he filled his pockets.

At last he picked up Morton's device and returned to the room where the shaft had first deposited him. He saw no sign of the dogs on his way, but he could hear the generator in the far room humming and a clanking sound that reminded him that at least one fell guardian was awake and feeling its mechanical oats.

"Morton," he called up. "Throw down the rope."

"Do you have the music box?" Morton demanded, peering over the edge from his perch on the branch.

"Of course I do," he replied. "Lower the rope and I'll give it to you."

"Toss up the music box, first."

The soldier had no intention of doing anything so foolish, but before he could say so, he heard the clanking and sparking of a great machine coming toward him. Looking back, he saw the two smaller dogs racing toward him. In the distance, he thought he could hear the grinding of the larger one making its way through the tunnels as well.

"We've no time for these games," the soldier shouted back. "The hounds are coming and I doubt I'll hold them off for long!"

"Throw me the music box and I'll let you up."

There was no time to reply, for the first of the mechanical beasts was upon him. The soldier kicked at it, sending the smallest of the beasts skittering across the stone floor, but it righted itself and turned to come back. The soldier slammed his finger onto the button of the emitter, but this time it only gave a squeal and a click and the dog faltered, but the fire in its eyes remained alight.

The second dog now dashed at him, its dreadful jaws agape. He threw the emitter at it. The hound snapped it up like a biscuit and ground it between its metal teeth, staggering a moment as the box crushed in its mouth, spewing out a final, dying pulse of light. The soldier tore off the goggles and leapt up, using the stunned dog as a stepping stone, and scrambled upward to grab at a rubber loop that hung from the bottom of the air shaft. The dog shook itself awake again and snapped at the dangling soldier who swung his legs up into the shaft, but couldn't find enough purchase at such an angle to wedge himself into the pipe. Thus his legs swung back down.

Now the first dog returned to the fight, making mighty jumps the larger dog could not assay and snapping at the soldier's dangling bootheels. It bit into one and ripped the boot from his foot as it fell back to earth, growling and savaging the leather as it would, no doubt, savage his body if the soldier fell.

The soldier pulled the music box from his pocket and waved it in the light of the air shaft for Morton to see. "Pull me up, damn it, man, or I'll throw this to them next!"

Wide-eyed, Morton finally tossed down the knotted end of the stout rope. The soldier, breathing hard, shoved the music box back into his pocket and swarmed up as the chamber below him shuddered and rang with the sound of the third dog breaking past the narrow doorway.

As he pulled himself out of the false tree stump, a gout of dust and a frustrated roar from the throat of the third dog rushed upward behind him. He tumbled over the edge and barely caught the branch to stop himself falling to the ground.

Morton, still perched on the branch, stared at him and put out his hand for the music box. "Now, the box, my friend, or I'll shove you back in."

The soldier hauled himself up onto the branch and locked his legs around its girth. "To the devil with you, you miserable, lying swine! You never meant to let me up, but to leave me to die below." And he grabbed the inventor and heaved him, headfirst, into the air shaft.

Morton screamed and plummeted down the pipe, lodging for a moment head-down before his screeching was cut short. The soldier looked away, not caring to see what work the hellish hounds would make of him, but the sound alone was gruesome enough to raise the soldier's stomach into his throat.

He let himself down to the ground while the scrambling sounds faded below. Limping along with but one boot, he returned to the crossroads and took the road to the nearest town.

---

The place was called Stone Crossing and even at a distance, he could hear the sound of rail workers at their toil, laying the iron road across the vast grassland to the west. The town was busy with railroad men, farmers, cattlemen, and merchants offering every sort of goods and services to the caravans of settlers passing through as they escaped the strife of the war to make their way into the empty territories beyond, hunting a fortune, or simply a new start. The soldier took a room in a boarding house run by a careful, plain-faced woman named Sarah—the widow of a railroad man who'd been blown to smithereens by a misplaced dynamite charge—and set to spending his fortune in merry pursuits that lightened his mood only temporarily.

He was accounted by most to be a generous and pleasant-enough companion, if one wasn't bothered by his silence, his scars, and his ever-present expression of sorrow. Such was his discretion in all things from his person to his rare speech that his acquaintances took to confiding their own troubles to him. Even the widow Sarah spoke more easily to her taciturn boarder than to anyone else in the house. Thus it came to his ears in the rising heat of a blistering summer that the town of Stone Crossing was in dire straits.

Over dinner one Sunday evening at the boarding house, another guest—one of the railroad men passing through—complained, "I thought the land problem was going to be the worst of it here, but if this heat doesn't break soon, we'll have to halt work. The workers are dropping like flies and we've near run out of water as it is."

"And you won't find any for miles," Sarah replied. "The creeks have all shriveled up or gone underground. My own well's nearly dried out and I'll have to ask you gentlemen to take your baths at the barber shop from now on, or there'll be no water to cook with or clean the pans. I've already stopped mopping the floors as it is. I swear our situation wasn't much better when Morton was still around, but at least you could usually get him to arguing with Halprin and stand a chance of getting something for your trouble when one or the other won out. I've almost developed a soft spot for Conscience Morton now that he's gone—a less well-named man there never was."

The soldier pricked up his ears. "Who're those fellas—Morton and Halprin?" he asked.

"Well, they used to own pretty much the whole town between the two of them and most of the property beyond until Morton up and disappeared a few months ago," Sarah replied. "Utterly mad for inventing things, the pair of them, and small-minded with it. Such a rivalry you never saw—as if making a better spinning wheel were the be-all and end-all. If I had to guess, I'd say Halprin finally found some way to drive Morton off—or kill him and hide the body. The Lord knows they tried to get rid of one another often enough, though I'd as lief it were Halprin who vanished—he's a vile man who kills sheep for his own amusement with his terrible inventions. And greedy beyond imagining, though he's very rich from selling his murderous inventions to anyone as will pay—Union or Confederate. He and Morton fought for a whole year about where the rail right of way was going to pass and the town was a mess because of it. Halprin only half-won that argument."

"And now the railroad may have to make a jog around Morton's property," the railroad man added, "since he ran off without leaving a clear deed to the land to anyone. We've tried to apply eminent domain on the abandoned property, but Halprin is fighting us in court—ironically to 'protect Morton from being taken advantage of while he's missing.' I suspect he's just doing it to gain time until he can find a way to get the property for himself."

"I wouldn't put such a thing past him. He's a cruel creature is Mr. Halprin," Sarah added.

The soldier looked back to Sarah. "What business is it that you're wanting Halprin to do?"

"I'm wanting him to let us drill for a deeper well. We all know there's an aquifer below the town—just look at how the cottonwood trees are still green even in the heat and dry: they must be getting water from below the topsoil. But Mr. Halprin won't allow it. I've asked the council and I've asked him and the answer is the same—which isn't surprising considering the council is no more than Halprin's puppets these days. And I wouldn't countenance what Mr. Halprin suggested."

The soldier raised his eyebrows, but it was the railroad man who asked, "Surely he didn't impose himself...that way?"

"I'll content myself with saying Mr. Halprin is no more a

gentleman in that respect than one could suppose from his other deal-ings," Sarah replied. "And he did not get what he wanted, though I very nearly had to run from the room to make it so."

The soldier frowned and asked, "Why can't you dig your own well?"

"I don't own the land and Mr. Halprin has made it very clear none of us are to go around digging holes on his property without his permission—which he won't give. So I tried to convince him we should drill for a public well, since that benefits everyone and we could use a bit of Morton's property on the south side of the main road—since Mr. Morton can't be found to say no to it. But Halprin refuses to consider it—same argument as he's giving to the railroad, but really, it's because he'd like some of Morton's tenants to up and leave. Without water, it's certain that some of them will. And soon."

"Won't he lose some of his own tenants?"

Sarah gave a wry smile. "Of course, but that makes no never-mind. Once the railroad is through, there'll be plenty of people lining up to buy every scrap of land, built on or not."

The soldier looked thoughtful and made a sound in his throat, nodded, but didn't say any more.

After dinner, he retired to his bedroom, pacing and wondering if he could do anything to help, for he'd taken a liking to the widow Sarah and hated to see her and her neighbors so abused by both nature and a single, greedy man. He also regretted having killed Morton—though not much. His thoughts ran in circles and eventually he sat down on his bed, wishing he had some distraction such as music or cards, but as it was Sunday, the saloon was closed and he didn't dare disrupt the house by going down to the parlor to play Sarah's piano—badly. His eye fell on the music box he had brought out of the caverns, sitting where he had put it down months ago on his chest of drawers. He picked it up, but it had no key. He tried the key he always carried in his pocket. The fit wasn't perfect, but he was able to wind the mechanism one turn before the cylinder began to revolve with a sudden chord that gave way to a strange tune.

Before the song had ended, he heard a scrabbling sound outside his window and when he opened the sash, he was confronted with the face of the smallest of the mechanical hounds from the cavern. He fell back, making room to do battle with the beast, but it only stepped delicately into the room and looked up at him with its flickering electric eyes.

After a moment of stilted silence the dog spoke: "What would you have me do, Master?"

Thunderstruck, the soldier sat down on the hard chair beside the door. "Who would have thought…?" he muttered.

"What would you have me do, Master?" the mechanical beast repeated.

"Can you dig a well?"

"I cannot, Master. But I can fetch the digging machine to you."

"Can you, indeed, little dog?"

The gleaming metal dog nodded its heavy head.

"Then fetch the machine and take it to the field beside the last building on the southeast side of the main road of this town. Bring it in darkness or someone may try to stop you, and we'll drill a new well so deep the town will never run dry again."

The mechanical dog nodded again. Then it bounded out of the open window and was gone from sight in a moment more.

Once darkness fell and the last lights of the town were extinguished, the soldier went out for a walk and strolled to the eastern edge of the town where he sat on the edge of a dry horse trough, lit a cigar, and waited to see if the dog would turn up. Moonlight silvered the ground and the earth sighed the day's gathered heat into the air, swirling up eddies of fine grit that looked like fairy dust enchanting the cloudless prairie night.

In a while, the soldier could see something coming down the moonlit road from the woods. It marched along on six slim legs and in front of it ran the metal dog. The soldier stood up to meet the dog and its strange companion, which proved to be the walking augur machine he has seen in the cavern so many weeks ago. He pointed to what looked to be a good spot for the well, but the dog sniffed at the ground a while and led the machine to a different location.

"Well, all right, then," the soldier said. "Let the drilling begin."

The machine began to drill into the ground, the dirt and rock spewing out and piling up around the edges of the hole as the bit dug in with a deep grumbling noise.

The soldier stood by and watched the machine. The augur dug steadily for hours with only a few adjustments by the soldier while the town slept on. After a while the sun started peeping over the eastern woodland and the soldier could hear people stirring and beginning their morning chores.

He turned to regard the stalwart mechanical beast standing beside the tireless augur. "Best hie yourself home now, dog. I'll look after the drill, but I think it better if no one gets a glimpse of you."

The dog made a smart turn around and loped away, vanishing into the trees as the sun broke over their tops. The bright orb had barely sent its fingers down to touch the gleaming drill when a geyser of water erupted from the hole it was digging, knocking the walking augur into the air and tumbling it end over end to the very edge of town.

The sound of the machine falling attracted attention and in a minute a few men and women had gathered to stare at the spring that had appeared overnight in Morton's field at the edge of town. It wasn't long before a crowd had encircled the muddy ground and begun talking about the miracle and praising God for it. The soldier edged to the back of the crowd, but not fast enough to elude the eyes of two people who came running along the street to see the source of the ruckus: Sarah and a beanpole of a man wearing a very fine suit and an expression of fury.

The widow hailed him and the man came along. "What happened?" Sarah asked.

"A spring seems to have erupted from the ground while we slept," the soldier replied.

The tall man scoffed. "It just…appeared here overnight?"

The soldier shrugged. "By the grace of God."

But the man had already turned his sharp gaze to scour the land-scape and he spotted the broken augur lying like a crippled spider at the edge of the woods. Ignoring the wondering crowd, he ran to the machine and looked it over. When he returned, his expression was thunderous, but he said nothing, merely brushing past the soldier with a glare and ignoring the calls of "Mr. Halprin, Mr. Halprin!" that followed after him. A small number of men detached themselves from the gawking crowd and scurried after him.

Sarah let out an amused snort at the sight. "There they go, kissing Halprin's backside, but I think they won't let *this* be taken away. Even the city council needs water." Then she turned to regard the soldier with a clear eye. "I suspect you have some idea how this 'miracle' came to be."

"It's hardly my place to guess at the motives of the Almighty."

"I was thinking of someone closer to home," she said, reaching out to take his nearest hand and turn it over to see the light smears of dirt and machine oil that smirched his palm and fingers.

The soldier cast his gaze down and pulled his hand back.

But Sarah was disinclined to let him get away so easily. "Why don't you come home with me and fetch some buckets? Be a pity to let that water go to waste when there's so much to clean and cook, and bathe..."

The soldier nodded and followed her, meek as a lamb, but with a smile on his face.

It took two days to build and cap a proper wellhead and most of another to mount the large, gleaming pump donated by Mr. Halprin, but the folks of Stone Crossing went to the job with a will. It took two more days before the city council had declared that there was enough water and pressure to consider Mr. Halprin's suggestion of a proper civic plumbing project that would pipe water to every building on the main road by the end of the year. Sarah and the soldier both applauded the announcement, but Halprin himself, though hailed publicly as a great man—and privately as a miserly bastard—wore a sour countenance throughout the proceedings, turning a suspicious eye on the soldier and his landlady. But nothing came of his bitter looks and the town reveled in its wonderful new water supply. The miraculous walking augur was repaired and a second well was drilled west of town to irrigate the fields so that they flushed again with greenery even in the heat, the railroad workers continued their din of industry, and everyone smelled a stretch more pleasant.

***

Things went on as they had before the drought, except that the soldier smiled once in a while and was seen on occasion strolling with the widow Sarah along the edges of the woods on Sunday evenings. The summer burned out the last of its fury and the town was left adrift on the golden autumn sea of scythed fields.

As the trees dropped their leaves, red as garnets, on the ground now touched by the silver fingers of frost, the railroad moved west and the folks of Stone Crossing laid up stores for the winter. The soldier began thinking he should do something more than smoke, gamble, drink, and read books in Sarah's parlor, but what he might do eluded him, for he had known no other trade but war. Should he stay or move on? He grew more fond of the widow with every day that passed and he liked the town well enough, but he did not know what place there was for such a man as he. He pondered on it in the night and was, therefore, the first to see the dreadful ruddy glow that illuminated the western sky when all should have been blanketed in darkness.

The soldier threw open his window and leaned out to see what caused the light. A thread of smoke came on the wind and the whisper of a distant fire, crawling on its ravenous way across the stubbled fields toward the town. For a moment he was seized with a terror of this mindless, devouring thing and he thought to flee, but he knew he could not outrun such a conflagration even if it were not a coward's act. Then he thought of the metal dog and plucked the music box from his dresser.

He turned the ill-fitting key in the mechanism, but the tune did not ring out after the first wind. He turned it a further revolution and now the cylinder rotated, starting up with a harsh chime of chords, one and then a second chord, before the queer little song began to play.

He slipped down the stairs and ran outside in his night clothes to meet the dog. He gazed toward the woods and saw it coming, bounding across the ground in great leaps, but as it drew near, he realized it was not the knee-high beast that had come to his first call, but the larger dog that had guarded the second room and its machines of destruction. He stiffened his spine and waited, for he could no more run from this beast than from the fire advancing on the other horizon.

The massive hound stopped before him, its sides of copper and brass reflecting red in the distant firelight. "What would you have me do, Master?" the dog asked, its voice rumbling like a rockfall.

"Do you see the fire that comes toward this town?" the soldier asked.

The mechanical beast nodded its brass-bound head, red light flickering across the rivets as large as the soldier's thumb that picked out the lines of the creature's face.

"Take the pumping engine from the cave and place it on the crawling wagon, then bring it to me by the western well. Quickly!"

The massive machine-hound turned around and bounded off again without a word.

The soldier began running toward the fire. Soon he was joined by a handful of his neighbors who grabbed up buckets and rushed along with him, though by their frightened words, he knew they held little hope of stopping a prairie fire with nothing but pails and strong backs. As they ran on, the fire gobbled up the western fields and lit the iron rails of the train tracks with orange light that made them glow like blades fresh from Hephaestus's forge.

As the soldier and his neighbors neared the edge of town, a wind from the east passed violently by them, blowing back the flames for a moment. The townsfolk turned their heads aside to keep the dust from their eyes, but the soldier did not and saw that the wind came in the path of the metal mastiff that towed the crawling wagon in its wake. The dog dashed on to the well at the edge of the blazing fields and the soldier followed it.

At the well, the soldier clamped the engine's hose to the pump and began to fill the tank as rapidly as he could. The townsfolk were slower, but coming toward the well also.

"Quick, dog," the soldier said, "bring fuel for the crawling wagon!"

Once again the dog ran away and returned in minutes bearing cans of fuel in its massive mouth.

"Good dog!" the soldier cried and took the fuel. "Now run around the far edge of the fire and dig for all you're worth—bury the flames if you can. We'll water them away here and meet in the middle."

The tireless hound bounded off, disappearing in the smoke that billowed from the burning fields.

The soldier's neighbors stared and rubbed their eyes, but there was no time to wonder if they had truly seen a giant metal hound and they turned their frantic hands to filling the pumping tank and firing up the motor of the crawling wagon. In minutes, the engine began to creep forward. One of the men from the town climbed up into the wagon to steer it while the rest ran beside it, supporting the hoses and turning them on the flames as the soldier ordered them, low to the ground where the fire ate its fill of the harvest stubble.

Water hissed and steam rose and more and more townsfolk appeared to relieve the men who held the hoses and guided the crawling wagon back and forth along the fire line. As the night wore on, they pushing the flames back and back, down and down. Through the smoke and fierce light some swore they glimpsed a giant beast scurrying back and forth and throwing up clods of dirt as large as pigs that smothered the fire where they could not break through.

By dawn the fire had been extinguished and the empty fields lay blackened and wet, the warped metal of the railroad curling through the wasteland like petrified snakes and the tracks of the crawling wagon laid over the ashen mud for a mile. But Stone Crossing stood untouched. Shrouded in the steam and lingering smoke at the middle of the burned field stood the wagon, nose to nose with a tarnished metal beast.

The soldier, steam-scalded, burned, and dirty, sat on the front of the wagon and patted the monster on the snout, its glowing eyes dim, but burning still. "You've done well, old dog. Can you return home now on your own?"

The brass beast nodded its massive head and trotted away, its stride covering the miles with ease.

The soldier slid down from the wagon and staggered toward the town, exhaustion weighing his every step as he wove his way across the field. He emerged from the steam and lingering smoke like an apparition and fell to his knees. Near to fainting, he took the little key from his pocket, but before he could do more, Sarah rushed to his side and helped him back to his feet.

"You marvelous fool," she said, hugging him much closer to her side than necessary. "Don't say this was the hand of the Almighty at work."

The soldier slipped the key back into his pocket unseen. "Your preacher says the Lord moves in mysterious ways."

"I doubt the Lord plunked down a pumping engine in the middle of our fields," Sarah said, "but I won't refuse the gifts He *has* given us. I know a good man when I find one."

She walked with him until they were enveloped in a crowd of their neighbors. The relieved and ragged folks of Stone Crossing carried the soldier home, right past the scowling face of Mr. Halprin as he stood at the outer edge of the town, alone and white with fury.

At the boarding house, the widow put the soldier to bed, and it wasn't particularly remarked upon by anyone that she took it upon herself to bathe his burns and care for him. It was also no further business of theirs that when she kissed his cheek he kissed her back or how those kisses lingered and slid into something more. Some would not even have been entirely surprised if, like the morning sun, they had peeped in the window a day or so later and saw the widow Sarah snuggled against the soldier in his narrow bed and clothed in nothing more than the sheets.

The soldier, however, was taken quite by surprise at these developments, for he had thought the joy and peace he found in her arms had vanished from his heart forever. When she murmured sweet words and stroked her hand across his chest, her fingers lingering and then stopping on the strange scar that lay in the arch of his rib cage like a keystone, his elation crashed to the ground and he stiffened, holding his breath.

"What is this?" Sarah asked. "Does it pain you?"

"It pains me no more, except that it may send you from me."

She would have inquired further, but a rumpus had begun downstairs and she took herself out of the bed, cursing and putting on her dress in haste. Barely had she closed the buttons when the bedroom door burst in to admit Mr. Halprin and her other tenants in his wake.

The men of the boarding house stopped on the threshold, their eyes wide with surprise, but Halprin bulled forward until Sarah blocked his path.

"Step aside, woman," Halprin demanded.

"I don't think I shall," she replied. "You have no right to assault my guests in my house, Mr. Halprin, and I will ask you to leave at once."

"I'll have my say before you throw me out of this house where you consort like a whore."

Sarah slapped him with such force that it turned his head full stop to the side. Then she spoke in clipped tones, "These gentlemen will escort you to the door, now."

Halprin glared over her shoulder at the soldier and jabbed a warning finger his direction. "You stole my dogs and you've ruined everything! I don't know how you managed it all, but if you are still here come morning, you'll live only long enough to wish you hadn't come here."

The soldier gave him a glance as cold as winter midnight and said, "I mean to stay, sir. Make no mistake: I like this little town and I'll like it just as much without you in it."

"Are you threatening me, you miserable scrap of a man?"

"No more than you are me. But you'd do well to recall what befell Morton."

Halprin straightened like a tree bough snapping back from being bent down and his nose went up in the air as if the soldier's words put a stench up his nostrils. "You will regret your trespassing and your meddling before I'm through," Halprin declared. Then he turned and glared at Sarah and her boarders. "As will you all!"

And he stalked away, brushing past Sarah as if her touch were acid. The rest of the boarders fell in around Halprin and conveyed him out the door and down the stairs with chill courtesy. For the first time in the history of Stone Crossing, they barred the door behind him.

Sarah turned back and looked down at the soldier, who had propped himself up in bed and was reaching for the key he always carried in his pocket.

"Do you truly mean to stay?"

"I do, if you'll have me."

Sarah looked down at him, puzzled. "Have you? Haven't we just—?"

"I meant that I should like to marry you, if you will have me once you know the truth of…this," the soldier added, touching the keystone scar on his chest.

Sarah offered him a bemused smile. "Of course I'll marry you, fool! How can you imagine that I would run away now? I know these scars are from the war. I know what you have been through, that you have fought—"

"And died," the soldier said.

Sarah was taken aback, but she sat on the edge of the bed as he patted it for her. Then the soldier told her his tale: how his horse had stepped upon a torpedo and been killed beneath him by the explosion and the sharp metal scrap that cut through the poor creature; how the flying barbs tore into his own face and body, one piercing his heart; how he lay dying, watching his fellows charge ahead on the disarmed ground vouchsafed to them by his noble horse; and how he had awakened again in a makeshift hospital with a clockwork heart ticking away in his chest—the "gift" of a half-mad surgeon driven to save whomever he could by whatever means, no matter how unnatural.

At first the soldier had been confounded, then amazed, happy, frightened, sorrowful, guilty…so many emotions crowding into him that he could not think. Until his commanding officer ordered his return to the battlefront and he discovered that now he could not feel, and feeling nothing, he did not care. When the letter came about the death by typhus of his wife and child, the army was glad to send him away at last—a broken toy soldier, a mistake they wished they'd never made.

Sarah stroked his cheek. "You are no mistake, my love."

"Am I your love, truly? A man who must wind up his heart like a watch?"

"I don't care *how* your heart beats, only that it does. I loved you when it was a mystery, and I love you still, now that it's not."

"Then hand me that key, beloved, for I have much to do before Mr. Halprin springs his traps."

"Do you believe he means the things he said?" Sarah asked, passing him the small brass key from the dresser.

"Oh, yes. He means to kill me," the soldier replied, fitting the key to the odd scar on his chest, "and he'll no doubt take half the town with him, for he's clearly quite insane."

"You mustn't let him hurt you," Sarah said, her face going pale, though who could tell whether it was from fear for him or the sight of the little brass key sinking into his flesh...?

The soldier did not look up as he wound his clockwork heart. "I don't intend to. Nor let him harm this town any further. I've stopped him before and I'll stop him again. I'll regret it mightily, but if I must put him in his grave to do it, I will."

He drew the key away at last and raised his head to look at Sarah. Her mouth was set firm, but there was a softness in her eyes that was neither pity nor tears. "I am sorry to present you such a terrible betrothal present," said the soldier. "You can still refuse..."

"No, in fact, I cannot." She smiled gently and kissed his cheek.

The soldier and Sarah sat together for quite a while, talking of their own future and of Halprin's threat. Sarah informed the soldier of Halprin's past in greater detail—which was sufficient to turn even that battle-hardened man pale.

"Halprin is a very monster," Sarah concluded. "I don't doubt for a moment that he set that fire himself, though why he should burn his own properties I can't guess."

"As you said once, there will be no lack of buyers once the railroad is through."

"But the fire ruined the new-laid tracks," Sarah objected.

"Only those that run beyond the town. The station and warehouses at the edge of Stone Crossing remain untouched."

"And those warehouses belong to Mr. Halprin," Sarah added. "No doubt filled with his horrible devices ready to be shipped back to the war in the east."

The soldier looked startled and Sarah asked him what was wrong.

"I am suddenly reminded of something that was missing…"

"What? Has someone robbed your room?"

"No, my love, but there may be a worse problem. Pass me the music box from the dresser, please."

"Why?" she asked, even as she handed him the key.

"I fear Mr. Halprin's threats may be all too real and we may need a great deal of help to counter his plans, but I must ask a question of a dog, first."

He put the key to the music box and turned it once, twice, thrice. The chimes rang out in three dreadful chords and the tune began to play. Its strange, discordant notes still shivered on the air when they heard the sound of metal feet clattering against the roof outside the window. Sarah helped the soldier to the window and threw up the sash.

The smallest of the mechanical dogs stepped inside, its copper and brass no longer so bright as when the soldier had first seen it, but its eyes glowed as if lit by hellfire. Beyond it the head of the largest hound peeped over the roof ledge, gilded a dull silver by the cloud-shrouded moon.

"What would you have us do, Master?" the dog asked as before.

"Are both your brothers outside?" the soldier asked.

The dog nodded.

"Then I will go down to meet them."

The sun was long gone by this time, the late-autumn night clouded and the wind speaking of snow soon to come. The soldier dressed warmly and went down to the porch to speak with the mechanical dogs. If any of his neighbors peered out of their windows, he made no remark upon it.

The first dog scrambled down from the roof and joined the other two, making a row by ascending size: the first normal sized, the second huge, and the third a giant whose head overtopped the doorway to such a degree that the soldier commanded it to lie down and thus ease his neck from craning upward to see the beast.

"Now tell me, has your former master returned to the caverns lately?" the soldier asked.

The first dog shook its head and the soldier marked it as by far the cleverest and most nimble of the three.

"And has anything more been taken away since I first called upon you?"

All three dogs shook their heads and the porch shuddered as the largest dog knocked one of the pillars with its snout. This one, the soldier thought, was the juggernaut of the company—ponderous, but as near unstoppable as a comet hurtling through space.

The soldier pointed at the first dog and named it, "Scout—for that is what you are—can you record information?"

The smallest dog seemed to give it thought, and then nodded. The soldier nodded also. "Very well then. Take yourself stealthily to observe your former master and what preparations he may be making. Then return and let me know what you've discovered. We have only until daybreak to lay our plans."

While they awaited the dog's reconnaissance, Sarah sat down beside him and asked where the dogs had come from and what their purpose was. The soldier replied that he had found them in a cave filled with mechanical wonders and metal nightmares, and as to their original purpose he was not sure, but as of now, their charge would be to protect the people of Stone Crossing from Mr. Halprin's machinations.

The moon had just tipped past its zenith when Scout returned. The dog's metal body was soiled with dirt and soot and marked with scratches. It paced off a large circle and began to draw in the dirt with its forepaw. Sarah brought more lanterns so that she and the soldier could examine the drawing: two buildings, two long parallel lines, and many rows of small circles backed by more rows of oblongs. The couple stared at the drawing for a while, not knowing what it represented, while the dog-shaped machine trotted across the circle to draw some more: a collection of boxes and lines.

"That's the town," Sarah said, pointing to Scout's newest drawing.

The soldier peered at it. "If that's true, then these lines to the northwest must be the train rails, and that would be the station house beside them and Halprin's warehouse beside that."

"What are all these things spread outside it?" Sarah asked, pointing to the circles and oblongs.

"I don't know, but I suspect..." the soldier started. Then he looked at the dog. "Did these things come from the cavern, once?"

Scout nodded and the other two dogs mirrored its movement.

The soldier remembered the empty room beyond the middle cavern where the plans for machines of war and destruction had lain and he thought of the lightning generator at Shiloh. "I'm not certain, but I suspect they are engines of devastation, meant for the war, but now arrayed against all of us. Can he really mean to attack the whole town for the anger he feels toward me?"

Once again the dogs nodded and the chill wind sent shivers down the humans' spines. A terrible guilt struck the soldier. He stood up. "If I am gone by morning, perhaps this madness won't come to pass." He looked at Sarah and she looked back, shaking her head.

"And perhaps pigs will sprout wings and fly across the Alleghenies every spring," she replied. "Have you not understood all I've told you of Mr. Halprin? He is more than half-mad, cruel, and uncaring for his fellow creatures. Did you not see that for yourself? It is not against you alone he swore his threats, but against all of us. I believe he means to carry out his revenge in the worst way. What shall we do?"

"*Si vis pacem, para bellum,*" the soldier muttered. He studied Scout's drawing a while longer then looked up at the dogs. "We shall be ready for him, but we must ensure his first strike does no harm." First he named the dogs from smallest to largest for convenience' sake: Scout, Bucephalus, and Juggernaut. Then he told them all his plan and sent the dogs to their duty, bringing everything that walked or rolled from the caves while he and Sarah went to rouse the house and town.

---

Well before dawn, the grinding sound of gears and the grumble of heavy feet began rising in the northwest. By the time the first rays of light had pierced the clouds, the townsfolk were arrayed in trepid wonder at the western edge of Stone Crossing with great piles of chain and rope at their feet, staring out at the burned fields where a cotillion of delicate automata danced and gamboled slowly west in the pink light. Just beyond, ranks of brass and iron machines spewing steam and smoke walked implacably southeast to meet them, some on four legs, some on six and some on cleated tracks. They bore a variety of weapons from the spiny heads of torpedoes to huge guns and the shining upright tubes of mortars that looked like hellish calliopes.

At the northernmost edge of the town the soldier stood with Sarah, the massive dog he had named Bucephalus—for his head was surely as large as an ox's—and Scout, and watched the mechanical army descend. "So, this is how a general must feel, playing with his toy soldiers," he said.

"Yes, but none of these soldiers are flesh and bone," said Sarah.

"So we shall hope. For if this plan fails, it falls to men and not machines to fight these monstrous things that come upon us."

"It will not fail," Sarah replied, staring out at the blackened ground filled with golden toys.

In the field, a gleaming rabbit of brushed copper and brass gave a mighty hop into the air, windmilling its ears. Three of the walking guns swiveled toward it and a shattering hail of bullets tore the toy to glittering shards. The townsfolk gasped and recoiled at the sight. But the soldier nodded his head and muttered, "He may have the force, but he hasn't any strategy at all."

In a moment the first of the walking torpedoes clashed against the tumbling jester in his jeweled motley and exploded with a roar of gunpowder. Gleaming metal confetti and mechanical entrails scattered outward in all directions, setting off two more of the explosives.

The rain of shrapnel drew the attention of the walking guns and they began firing in ragged volleys, sweeping back and forth so long as the cloud of metal hung in the air. A bullet ripped through the soldier's sleeve, slicing a hot groove in his arm and he winced.

Sarah reached for him, but he pushed her back. "No," the soldier said. "Fall back, now. Take them all to the engines. Remember: our goal is to turn his line south of the town and flank him, not to make dead heroes."

"What of you?" she said, her voice sharp.

"I've been a dead hero once—I've no need to do it again."

Sarah, gave him one last look and ran toward her neighbors. At her command, the townsfolk ducked and scurried away as the field filled with the gold-dusted explosions of dozens of murdered automata. The battle line turned slightly south as the walking guns tracked to each new blast of destruction. Behind them the mortars crouched down on their articulated legs and fired off their first ranging volley.

The ground between the automata and the town erupted, throwing dirt clods and burnt stubble into the air with a roar.

The soldier looked to the smallest of the mechanical dogs. "Now, Scout, go!"

The mechanical beast, brown and rusty as a dirty penny now, dashed away beneath the cover of the earthen explosion, heading southwest to a lonely stand of trees and vanished into their morning shadow. In a minute it emerged again, circling back to snatch a knotted rope between its metal jaws and run northwest.

Juggernaut broke from the stand of trees, clutching the other end of the rope in its own massive mouth, its head held low as if on the scent. The ground shook with each step the giant dog took across the field, pulling the makeshift cable of rope and chain taut, inches above the ash-covered ground.

As the dust began to clear, the mechanical dogs raced on west, dragging the patched-together hawser between them until it pulled against the legs of the front line of walking death machines, toppling them backward and sideways into the machines behind them. The first three ranks exploded with a roar that shook the earth. The torpedoes all destroyed, some of the remaining walking guns staggered and fell, some toppling on their sides while others righted themselves and walked on in random directions. But most only corrected their path to the south—toward the largest mass of falling machines—and marched on, spewing bullets and fire over the gleaming bodies of the machines in front of them.

The soldier turned to the last dog and said, "Now, Boo. We're off to find the villain himself."

The large beast bent down and the soldier climbed on his back. He felt absurd riding astride a metal dog, but the time for vanity was long past. The huge mechanical beast leaped forward, running to meet Scout in the north end of the field.

As they hurtled onward, the soldier turned his head to see Juggernaut racing up and down among the stumbling guns, throwing up clods of dirt and metal debris in all directions, luring them steadily southeast and destroying what it could. The nearest guns rotated to open fire, and shot their own kind instead, the giant dog bolting past under the whine of ricochets and the hissing of escaping steam.

Then, two engines roared onto the field: one from the southwest and the other from the northeast. A long stream of water shot from the pumping engine as some of the townsfolk drove it into the shattered line's flank from the livery at the south edge of town. The other, clanking forward from the north end came forth spitting fire from twin barrels that poked out of an improvised shield of steel plates hiding two men who drove the smaller machine, sweating with heat and fear, but going forward nonetheless.

Streams of fire and water smashed into Halprin's walking guns, battering them with opposing forces of heat and moisture. Heating them, melting them, then cooling and shoving them. When the cold water hit the gleaming sides of hot metal and straining boilers, the machines on the south end of the line exploded with a screech of scalding steam, rivets and metal flying wide and raining down again like metallic snow. The townsfolk crouched beneath the engine and let this Devil's rain fall. On the north flank, flames from the other wagon melted the chains of projectiles that fed the guns and they ceased firing, walking onward with no purpose but to smash bodily into the buildings of the town while their companions staggered and fell in warped piles of metal, hissing and bursting in clouds of steam and exploding ammunition, or going down in conflagration from their own ruptured fuel tanks.

The townsfolk swept the streams of water and fire across the broken line of machines as the mortars crouched again.

This time the mortar shells struck the first buildings of Stone Crossing, throwing wood and fire into the sky as the buildings were blown apart.

The water engine turned to put out the fires while the flame-spewer and Juggernaut converged on the rest. Fire washed over Halprin's devilish calliopes until the shells exploded inside their tubes, rupturing the mortars and sending their pipes spinning into the sky. The townsfolk who could be spared from the water engine attacked the disarmed machines with whatever came to hand: axes, poles, or shotguns. They battered the automated army, knocking it down piece by piece while Juggernaut wreaked havoc on the remaining armed guns, pouncing from behind and flinging them into the air to shatter on the ground. The clanging and roaring of destruction and fire deafened the ear and the fumes of burning metal and wood clouded the fields.

The soldier rode on toward the train station, bolting from cover to cover.

Scout raced across the churned field in wild zigzags, turning sharper than a dancer as a single heavy gun fired at the mechanical dog from the warehouse. Bucephalus and the soldier—ever the cavalry man at heart—swung out wider, heading for the rear of the building from its blind side as the gun continued to try to score a hit on the smaller, swifter metal beast. In the distance, they could feel the pounding of Juggernaut's dashing and digging shaking the ground.

As soon as the soldier and Bucephalus were safe beyond the warehouse's front wall, Scout took a sudden turn and bolted south toward the disintegrating remains of the mechanical army.

The soldier and his strange mount crashed through the back door of the warehouse, the building shuddering as they came inside. In the loft, Halprin spun to stare at them, staggering under the weight of the large gun he cradled in his arms.

"Bastard," he shouted as the soldier slid off the back of the massive hound.

Halprin, a moment too late, squeezed the trigger of his gun, sending a smoking stream of bullets just over Bucephalus's back and across the top of its head. The soldier hit the ground face down and the brass-bound dog turned its head upward and opened its jaws, one burning eye extinguished.

Then the dog launched itself up the stairs toward Halprin, making a terrible roaring sound as it went. The soldier jumped up, calling "No, Boo. Stop!" but, apparently by its own desire, the creature of brass and copper and steel had set its path and leapt forward without heed.

A cheer rose outside as if a crowd were drawing near to urge the mindless copper beast onward. The soldier ground his teeth and started after the massive dog.

Halprin reeled back, the gun chattering as bullets rattled against the hound's chest and head. And then they tore though, the heavy metal beast lurching forward as its gears blew apart and ground to a halt. Mighty Bucephalus fell with a thunderous clatter, collapsing the stairs and dragging the loft flooring down with it as it plunged to the floor.

Halprin tumbled as the earth shook. The soldier ran to the side of the shattered hound, its body bullet-ripped and its huge eyes darkened forever. It was only a thing of gears and metal—it could not think or dream or hurt—but he hadn't felt such sorrow in a long time as he felt for this unlikely beast.

Halprin scrambled backward toward the front door, rolling to scoop up his fallen gun, saying, "Look at what you've done to this place. Look at what you've reaped by your meddling."

"This is what *you* have done, coward!" the soldier shouted back. "You sent your machines against innocent people and it was other machines that stopped them."

Halprin swung the gun's muzzle around. The soldier ducked behind the wreckage of the dog as the gun coughed and then stuttered silent.

The ground continued to shiver and heave as he glanced over the ruined machine beast. Halprin threw down the useless gun and turned for the doorway.

Outside a swift shadow bolted toward the doorway, half-hidden in rising sun. The soldier drew his revolver from his belt, aimed over the back of his fallen hound, and squeezed the trigger.

As the hammer dropped, the streak of brown and gold rammed into Halprin's legs and he tripped, tumbling headfirst out the doorway as the soldier's bullet passed through the air his head had recently occupied.

The soldier cursed, jumped up, and ran for the doorway, stumbling across the bucking floor. Scout darted inside and dragged the soldier out of the building behind Halprin. The soldier tried to shake the mechanical dog away, furious and set on taking his enemy's life.

Outside Halprin scrambled to his feet and tried to run across the shuddering ground as Scout harried the soldier aside.

A shadow fell on Halprin and he glanced up, then froze at what he saw.

Juggernaut, dripping oil and water, his metal skin torn open and blasted by steam and gunpowder, let out a howl as of a million angry souls shouting for vengeance, and pounced on Halprin with his iron jaw agape.

Halprin shrieked in terror as the giant creature fell upon him and crushed him to the ground. A cloud of dirt and metal flew into the air, knocking the soldier and Scout backward as the massive dog came to rest at last.

His breath heaving in his chest, the soldier pulled himself up by holding onto Scout—filthy, dented, indomitable Scout, the last remaining clockwork dog. He stood there still, his revolver loose in his hand, when Sarah and the citizens of Stone Crossing arrived, by foot, on horseback, or riding on the crawling wagons with their battered engines.

Sarah took in the wreckage all around, the broken dogs, the warehouse as tumbledown as a shanty, and the sickening remains of Halprin. Then she looked to her beloved soldier, sorrowful and unmoving with Scout beside him.

She took his hand and drew him closer to her. "Did you shoot him?" she asked in a soft voice. "I'm sorry if you had to."

"I didn't kill him. It was the dogs. Even torn to shreds they did not stop."

"You told them to protect us and they did."

The soldier shook his head in wonder and sorrow. "I never ordered them to kill. I never ordered them to protect *me*. Their duty was to you—to all of you. Hollow hounds they may have been, but they had hearts the size of giants.'"

Sarah took her soldier back to Stone Crossing where they were married at Christmastime. They lived in the town for many years, filling the house with children and dogs, but it was always the one dog, the odd one with the metal hide like dirty pennies, that the soldier kept at his side. Two of a kind: their mechanical hearts wound up by something more than a key.

# 9

# THE THIRD DEATH OF THE
# LITTLE CLAY DOG

Trouble radiated from the black figurine like some kind of dark neon at the Devil's own fairground. Not that I could actually see any such thing even in the Grey, but an electric prickling sensation zipped up my arms and down my spine when I touched it and that was close enough; I know human hair can't literally stand on end like a dog's, but I would have sworn mine was trying to.

Nanette Grover was still standing at the side of her desk, looking at me and the little statue. Her fanatically neat office flickered silver, smudged with red and orange and sad shades of green she would never see—the emotional and energetic leftovers of her clients still hanging in the Grey like smoke. A ghost or two lingered in the corners with sour, accusing faces and the odor of misery, muttering their cycles of frustration. They weren't interested in me, so I ignored them and put my attention back on Nan.

She was impeccable as always: her straightened, deep-brown hair was smoothed into a perfect French twist, her stylish tweed skirt suit was unwrinkled even after she'd been behind her desk since five a.m., and her smooth, dark skin was highlighted by delicate makeup that didn't show a single crease. Even her energy corona was cool and constrained to a narrow bright line, except when she stepped onto the stage of the courtroom floor where it alternated between hypnotic veil and legal scalpel. In spite of her beauty she had all the warmth of a steel pipe in the snow—which was part of her appeal as a litigator, but not as a human being. One of her opponents in court had referred to her as "the Queen of Nubia" and, in spite of the intended insult, it wasn't hard imagining Nan on a war elephant chasing off Alexander the Great—even her allies found her intimidating. "Well?" she asked, the word leaving amber ripples in the air.

"Well what?" I responded, shrugging off the commanding effect of her voice.

"You're supposed to accept or reject the conditions."

"What happens if I say no?"

Her energy closed back down to an icy line. "Then I have instructions regarding the disposition of the item."

"What are those?"

"Not your business. Yes, or no, Harper."

"What was it the client wants done with this, again?"

Nan sat down on the other side of the desk, the mistiness of the settling Grey giving her a deceptively soft appearance, and blinked once, long and slow—like some kind of reset—and explained again, with no heat or change of inflection from the first time. "A colleague of mine in Mexico City forwarded this item to me upon the death of his client. His client, Maria-Luz Arbildo, had left you a bequest in her will, with conditions. Namely, to personally hand-carry the statuette—this little dog figurine—to Oaxaca City in Oaxaca state in Mexico, and place it on the grave of Hector Pure-cete on the night of November First and attend the grave as local tradition dictates until daybreak of November Second. Additional specific instructions for the preparation of the grave will be provided. All this to be done in the first occurrence of November First following his client's death. Ms. Arbildo died earlier this month."

"The twentieth of October," I added. "A week ago."

Nan nodded.

"November First is the day after Halloween. Doesn't that seem strange to you?" I asked.

Nan's ice-smooth expression didn't change. "No."

"And I never met this woman, never heard of her, but she sends this thing all the way to Seattle so I can take it all the way back to Mexico—the far end of Mexico I might add. Still not sounding kind of weird?"

"I don't question the conditions of clients."

"Is this sort of thing even legal?"

"Perfectly. If it flew in the face of public interest, then it would be illegal, but this does not. The condition also does not require you to do anything illegal either here or there, nor to violate your professional ethics, nor take on unreasonable expenses—everything will be paid for by Ms. Arbildo's estate. If you choose to follow the conditions of Ms. Arbildo's bequest, you will receive the thirty thousand dollars, once the condition has been completely and correctly met. Sum to be paid through this office."

I was raised in Los Angeles County California, so I'm not totally ignorant of Mexican culture—just mostly. I knew the First of November was the Mexican equivalent of Halloween, but I didn't know the details. My experience as a Greywalker, however, makes me wary of any date on which the dead are said to go abroad among the living. I know that ghosts—and plenty of other creepy things—are around us all the time, it's just that most people don't see them. I do more than just see them; I live with them and I've discovered that days associated with the dead are usually worse than most people imagine —they're veritable Carnivales of the incorporeal, boiling pools of magical potential. So being asked to take a folk sculpture to a Mexican graveyard on the Day of the Dead sounded like a dangerous idea to me. Especially when the client is deceased.

On the other hand, I can at least see what's going on. As someone who lives half in and half out of the realm of ghosts, monsters, and magic, I stand a chance against whatever strange thing may rear its head in such a situation. And the money was attractive. The work I regularly did for Nan—investigating witnesses and filling in the details of her cases prior to trial—paid the majority of my bills, but it wasn't an extravagant living. Even with all the rest of my work added in, thirty thousand dollars was a major chunk of what I usually made in a year and it would only take about four days.

I looked back down at the statuette. It was a hollow clay figure of a dog, about a foot tall and long, give or take, and about four inches wide. The shape was simplified, not realistic, with stumpy legs and tail, a cone-shaped muzzle, and a couple of pinched clay points for ears. It had been painted with a gritty black paint and decorated with dots and lines of red and white that made rings around the limbs and a lightning bolt on the dog's side. It also had two white dots for eyes, but no sign of a mouth.

Peering at it, I could see the little clay dog had been cracked and repaired at some point, the casting hole in its belly covered up with an extra bit of clay and painted over with more of the black paint. A hint of Grey energy gleamed around the repair seam, but beyond that, I couldn't tell anything about what might be inside the dog. The statue itself had only a thin sheen of Grey clinging to its surface like old dirt, as if whatever magical thing it came from had withered long ago. There wasn't any indicative cloud of color or angry sparks around it as I'd seen with other magical objects, yet I was sure there was something more to it than met the eye.

I looked back up at Nan, who hadn't moved so much as an eyebrow. The silence in her office would have unnerved some people, but I found it pleasant as contrast to the incessant mutter and hum of the living Grey and its ghosts.

"What about the lawyer?" I asked.

"What about him?"

"Is he legit?"

Nan didn't crack either a smile or a frown. "Yes. His name is Guillermo Banda. He does a lot of maritime and international work."

I admit I had some reservations but I was also a little intrigued by the mystery of it—I'm a sucker for mysteries—and the money was pretty good, so I shrugged and said, "All right, I'll take the thing to Mexico."

Nan waved to the small shipping carton from which she'd originally removed the dog at the start of our conversation. "You can put it back in its box while I get the papers ready. I'll need your signature on a receipt to prove that you picked it up and I have a copy of the instructions for you as well."

I nodded and wiggled the little clay dog back into the snowstorm of paper shred that had sprung from the box when Nan had opened it. We finished up quickly and I left with the papers in my pocket and the box full of probable trouble under my arm.

The aluminum and glass tower that houses Nan's office has lousy cell reception, so I had to wait until I was just outside the lobby doors to make a call.

"King County Medical Examiner's office. May I help you?"

"I'd like to speak to Reuben Fishkiller, please," I replied.

I was put on hold for a few moments while someone located the forensic lab technician for me. I'd met him during an investigation into the deaths of homeless people in Pioneer Square and Fish's connections to the local Salish Indians had certainly come in handy. But he'd been a bit upset when one of his ancestral legends tried to kill us, and I hoped he wasn't still too freaked out to talk to me.

"This is Fish, what can I do for you?"

"Hi, Fish, it's Harper Blaine."

He paused. "Oh. Hi, Harper. You, uh…need something?"

"I do, if you're willing to do it for me."

"Does it have anything to do with monsters in the sewer this time? Or Salish holy ground? Because I really didn't enjoy the last time."

"No monsters, no Salish, no sewers. I promise. I just need an x-ray."

"We only x-ray the dead."

"This thing is inanimate, is that close enough?"

"What is it?" he asked. I could almost see him narrowing his eyes with suspicion.

"It's a clay statue of a dog."

"You're sure it's inanimate? Things act weird around you…"

"I promise it's just a hollow lump of baked clay, totally incapable of movement or pretty much anything else. I just want to know if there's anything inside it."

Fish sighed. "Okay. I can take a look, but it'll have to be quick. Get here at lunch time and I'll see what I can do."

I agreed to come while most of the staff was occupied with food, and thanked Fish before hanging up.

It would be just my luck to spark off an international incident and get arrested for smuggling if the dog had anything significant in its hollow innards. I hoped Fish and his x-ray machine would tell me if there was anything to fear. The easy-money aspect of the situation bothered me; I don't believe in harmless, eccentric benefactors. There was a sting of some kind in the little dog's tail—or belly—and I wanted to figure it out before I got hit by it.

I killed some time at the library before heading down to Pill Hill, where the major hospitals cluster like trees in a concrete forest. Fish met me at the front desk of the morgue and we walked back through the chilly chambers in the basement of Harborview to the x-ray room. His shaggy dark hair with premature streaks of white, hanging over his square face, still reminded me of a badger, but a more wary and grumpy badger than he'd been before. He'd become a bit nervous since our run-in with living myths, as if he, too, could now see the steam-billow shapes of the dead that wandered through the old hospital, or sense the tingling power that thrummed in the neon-bright lines of magical power that shot through the Grey.

"What have you got?" he asked as we pushed through the door to the x-ray machine and other lab paraphernalia.

I put the white cardboard box down on the machine's table and carefully removed the little dog statue. He started to reach for it, then stopped.

"You—um… it's OK to touch it without gloves, isn't it?"

"I think so. I've been handling it bare-handed all morning." I had supposed I'd know if there was anything toxic on the figure's surface, but there really wasn't any way that I would. I looked at the small black dog as I clutched it by its middle and hoped it wasn't dusted with anthrax or the like.

Fish paused to pull on a pair of purple gloves before he took the figurine from me. Then he scraped a bit of the black paint into a glass tube and repeated the scraping on the bottom of the dog's foot, where the mellow orange clay was bare of glaze or paint. The sheen of Grey on the sculpture's surface rippled and squirmed as he scraped, but it didn't flare or change color—either of which would have been bad signs. He added some chemicals to the tubes and put them aside in a large, white machine.

"I'll run a couple of tests on those while we're at it," he said. He poked some buttons on the machine. Then he turned back to the x-ray table. "Now, let's look at this little guy…"

Altogether, Fish took three views of the dog. Since the morgue had updated to digital x-ray, we didn't have to wait for the pictures to be developed, but just viewed them on the computer screen behind the radiation barrier.

"What's that?" I asked, pointing to a bundle of faint lines that showed on every picture. It was in a different spot each time.

"Something loose in the hollow interior. Let's crank up the resolution."

Fish poked a few keys and the image of the bundle got larger and more clear.

"Looks like hair or threads knotted together. Whatever it is, there's not much of it," Fish observed. "I could pull it out and examine it if you didn't mind reopening that hole in the dog's belly."

The condition of the bequest was that the dog statue be put on the grave intact by me and only me. I didn't think it would qualify as "intact" if part of its secret bundle were missing, not to mention the plug of clay in the figure's belly. And I didn't have much time to sit around in Seattle: it was already October twenty-eighth, the trip was going to be a long one, even by air, and I didn't know where in Oaxaca City Hector Purecete was buried. I wasn't fool enough to think there was only one cemetery in town, so I'd have to do some investigating in Oaxaca before I could complete the conditions of the bequest, as Nan insisted on calling them.

"I don't think it should be removed, unless you suppose it's something illegal," I said frowning at the picture.

"That small? Nah, not likely to be anything drug-related, or human remains. Unless it's hair, like I said, in which case it probably got in there while the dog was being painted. It's too fine to be plant matter and there's not enough of it to be worth much if it's any other fiber. It's not dense enough to be metal strands, either. Without actually seeing it with my own eyes and running tests, my best guess is still human hair." Then he shrugged and added, "Or a few strands of some really long-haired animal's fur or tail. Maybe horse tail..."

Noises in the hallway and a sudden agitation among the ghosts indicated the post-lunch return of Fish's coworkers. We packed up the figurine and Fish led me back out, promising to call when he had the result of the tests on the clay and paint. I headed back to my office to clear off my schedule and check on the flights Nan had promised to book for me on behalf of the estate.

Only Nan's work had any specific deadlines on it, so it wasn't difficult to rearrange my meetings and appointments—I don't make that many anyhow. The biggest hurdle was finding someone to look after my pet ferret while I was gone, and that was taken care of by tracking down Quinton and depositing the tube rat with him. I suspect Chaos prefers him over me, since he will happily carry her around with him all day in one deep pocket or another while I usually have to leave her at home. Anyhow, she didn't look grieved to see me go, even if Quinton did.

We sat in the glass picnic shelter beside Ivar's Acres of Clams on the waterfront and talked while we ate our fish and chips. Chaos helped us with the chips and ignored the gulls screaming outside, even in the late-October chill, for their tithe of greasy fast food. Ivar Haglund may have loved those damned birds but to me they were a nuisance worse than persistent haunts: ghosts don't poop on you.

"Oaxaca?" Quinton questioned. "Why?"

"Some nonsense with a bequest. There's a set of instructions—sorry: conditions—that have to be fulfilled."

"Like in one of those movies where you have to stay in the haunted house overnight or change your name to Gaggleplox?" he asked. "Those usually don't work out well—most of the cast ends up dead or the inheritance turns out to be a stash of counterfeit bills."

I made a face. "That's in the movies. This is just a job. Find the right grave, put the dog on it, and wait for daybreak."

"And in between is when all hell could break loose. Which seems pretty likely considering your talents."

"It's possible," I conceded, "but the money is pretty attractive and I don't get a sense of danger from the statue—just trouble."

He snorted. "Just trouble. And why did this woman pick you? Did you know her?"

I shook my head and pinched off a bit of fried potato for the ferret. "No. I didn't know her and I don't know why she picked me for this job. I assume she somehow knew what I can do, but how she knew, that's the big mystery. And why I agreed to go. Maybe there's some clue to be found about why this happened to me and not to every person who's ever had a near-death-experience. There must be someone who knows more about all of this than I do, or the Danzigers do, or every vampire from here to Vancouver seems to." I felt a flush on my face that didn't come from the space heater overhead and realized I was getting angry. Not at Quinton, but at the shifty fate that had yanked the rug out from under me when I'd died only long enough to have my life wrenched into a shape beyond my control.

"But if it was this Arbildo woman, she's already dead," Quinton said.

"Then I'll hunt her down in the Grey." At least my change of life had come with useful skills. I was still figuring them out more than a year later, but I no longer hated and resented them.

My flight was set for 11:40 that evening with a five-hour layover in Dallas before I could fly on to Mexico City and from there to Oaxaca, but even with the delay, I'd still have a few hours once I got to Oaxaca City to find the records office and start looking for the grave of Hector Purecete.

I finished up my food and gave Chaos a final scratch around the ears. Quinton got a lot more than an ear-scratch, which annoyed the ferret, judging by the way she kept pushing herself in between us and snagging our kisses for herself. Jealous little furball.

The trip was smooth. Right up to Mexico City where they broke the dog.

The customs agent was going through my bag when it happened. There was the box with the little clay dog inside. He held it up.

"Is this a gift?" he demanded in a crabby, tired voice.

I'd have guessed he was near the end of his shift if it wasn't quite noon, but maybe he was aware in his own way of the cranky, dispirited, over-excited motion of the Grey as much as I was. The customs area was aboil with the flashes and clouds of hundreds of passengers' emotional energy giving shape and color to the loose power of the magical grid. It chafed and roared and twisted through the space around us like angry lions in a too-small cage. The sound of the Grey was a strong, steady hum with a sharp edge, like barbed wire under silk.

That sharpness was probably why my response was inappropriately flippant: "No. It's a dog," I said.

One really shouldn't joke with security people of any kind while they are on the job; most have had to leave their sense of humor in their locker with their civilian clothes. He raised his eyebrow and opened the box, rooting inside with his blue-gloved hand—every employee at airport security looks like they're about to play doctor in some very unpleasant way these days. He snorted in surprise and jerked his hand out with the figurine not-quite gripped in his sweat-sticky glove. You'd have thought the little dog had bitten him from the way he moved. His hand yanked back, jerking upward a little as the statuette cleared the edge of the box. The black object moved up, popping out of his loose grip, and arced into the air, ripping a slice of glove with one pointed ear as it went. It was like slow-motion film watching it rise from safety and crash to the hard linoleum beneath our feet.

As it hit the floor, it flashed a panic-bolt of silver white into the Grey. The little clay dog shattered, a tiny bundle of dark fibers bouncing onto the floor amid the terracotta shards. With a silvery gasp, the flash rushed back toward the broken figurine and coalesced into the ghost of a dog.

The ghost dog looked around, then looked at me, and whined piteously. It was a rangy, mongrel beast with the shape of a stunted greyhound and the coat of a shaggy pony. It sidled up to me and leaned against my legs and I felt its cold, Grey shape press against me with its memory of weight.

The customs agent looked at the smashed figurine and bent to pick the tiny knot from the wreckage. "Eh?" he mumbled. "What is this?"

I shrugged. "Hair?" I guessed.

He looked at it, rubbed it between his fingers, sniffed it. Then he motioned to one of his coworkers who walked over and rubbed a small cloth swab over the little bundle. He put the swab into a machine while the first man moved me and my bags to another table deeper inside the security zone. Someone else swept up the bits of clay and put them in a plastic bag. The dog stuck to me like a shy toddler.

"Nada," said the man with the machine. "Esta es pelo."

They put a little of the clay dust from the broken figurine into the machine, but that also yielded "nada." The customs agent looked sad as he finished inspecting my bag and closed it up, handing it and the bag of shards back to me with what almost looked like a contrite bow, and an apology for breaking my dog.

"De nada," I replied. Then I asked for the knot of fluff back, which he thought was odd, but dug into the trash and retrieved for me anyhow. I dropped it into the bag of broken ceramic—it wasn't intact anymore, but better to keep it all together, just in case, I thought.

He handed me a claim form to fill out if the dog had been insured, and I took it, even though I doubted the figurine was valuable. I was sure it was the ghost that was the important thing.

The spirits of Mexico hummed and roared. The ghost dog pasted itself to my heels and shadowed me around the halls of the Mexico City airport as I tried to find a place to put down my bags and make a phone call. Of course, the place I found was a bar.

I threw myself and my bags down and ordered a beer while I called Nan on my cell phone. Seattle being close to the other border, I'd had international calling added to my service long ago. Sometimes I wondered how I'd gotten along without a cell phone so long. Other times I wished I still had my pager.

It took a few minutes to get connected to Nan.

"What is it, Harper?"

"Mexican customs broke the dog."

"Is it reparable?"

"No. But I have a major part of it," I added, looking at the cowering ghost at my ankles.

"Where are you?"

"Mexico City airport."

"Banda is located nearby. He may have instructions for that contingency."

She gave me his number. I wrote it on my cocktail napkin, as is traditional in that sort of situation. "If I call this guy, I may miss my connection to Oaxaca," I warned her. "I'm already running tight because of the mess at customs."

"I'll have Cathy reschedule you to a later flight and call you back with the information. Is there anything else?"

"No. I'll let Cathy know if anything is still out of whack when she calls."

"Good. Stay in touch." And she was off the phone as fast as that.

I finished my Negro Modelo and called the number on the napkin. I felt itchy from annoyance and lack of sleep—I don't get more than a fitful doze on planes, since my long legs end up cramped and head-rests are never in the right place for me. I always longed to upgrade to first class, but the PI business usually comes with an economy-class budget.

Guillermo Banda answered his own phone. He spoke English like a New Yorker as soon as he heard how bad my Spanish was.

"Miss Blaine! You're here! This is excellent! How is the perrito? The little dog?"

"Customs broke it."

"Fuck! Pardon me. My client would be very upset to hear it. If she weren't dead."

"Which is why I'm here at all." Talking to this guy was like talking to Lou Costello and I was afraid I might start laughing. "I do have part of the dog and I could take that up to Oaxaca, if you think that would be in the spirit intended."

"I don't know..." There were noises in the background and he muttered away from the receiver something about Puerto Vallarta which was rejoined by a feminine giggle.

I tried to keep him on track. "Well, if you could tell me what it was your client had in mind with this condition, I'm sure we can figure out a way to satisfy the spirit, if not the letter, of her request."

"That I also don't know. Miss Arbildo wasn't very...forthcoming."

"How long had she been your client, Mr. Banda?"

"Oh, years! Years and years! But we never spoke. She came in to update her will last year and before that we'd only seen each other twice. I inherited her account from my partner who died a few years back in a plane crash. Horrible."

"Did your firm do any work for her aside from the will?"

"Well, the specifics are confidential, but yes. We did a little background investigative work for her and for her father—mostly routine checks. We managed her estate—her father's estate—and of course we'd been doing work for his company for many years. We work primarily with international and maritime law and his company was involved in quite a bit of international shipping. Handling Miss Arbildo's will and so on was more in line of a...courtesy."

"I see. Do you have any idea what her relationship was to Hector Purecete? The guy on whose grave the dog was supposed to be put."

"None at all."

"Damn. I wish I knew what she expected. This is kind of a pain in the butt. You don't have any idea what her intentions were in the will instruction?"

"No. Like I said, the woman was very strange."

I sighed. "Maybe if I could see the will itself we could figure this out. May I come to your office?"

"Oh no," he said. "You'd never get here and back before your flight."

"I've already called Nan to change it."

"No, no, you don't understand—the traffic. Here's what I'll do. I'll bring it to you at the airport, if you have time."

"I'll make the time." I told him where I was and that he should bring as much of the paperwork as he had. He said it would take him an hour to get to the bar and I said that was fine. After all, I was still waiting for Nan's secretary to call me back.

I was thinking about ordering food when the phone went off, showing me Nan's office number on the ID. It was Cathy with my flight change and some additional information.

"Nan's booked you into a guest house in Oaxaca City—it's one she's used before. The owner speaks English and can help you with the records search if you need it."

"Thanks. I only hope I'll get there before the offices close."

"I think you're going to have to re-arrange your schedule. The earliest flight I could get you was five-fifty. I'm sorry. But the provincial offices should be open Friday."

Terrific. My two days for research was now down to one. I'd have to hope I got what I wanted the first time or could work up some local contacts very fast. "I'll make it work," I said, then continued, "Umm...I talked to Banda. Nan said he was reputable, but he seems a little...odd. Is there anything I should know about him?"

"About Guillermo? I don't know much except that he's the biggest New York Yankees fan in Mexico. And I'm not even sure that's unusual."

"Baseball?"

"Yup. Baseball is big in Mexico City. A few years ago he had season tickets and flew up to watch the games—I swear that's why he took his international courses at Columbia; so he could go to Yankees games—he even tried to take Nan to one, but she's not a sports fan. Don't get him started on any conversation about baseball or you'll miss your plane."

I said my goodbyes and started thinking while I waited for Banda. It was after one o'clock already. I'd have to get lunch at the airport and see what I could do by phone. I'd miss the open hours in person today at whatever government office might have the burial records and I'd only have Friday to do records searches before the holiday weekend hit—if they didn't close early or not open at all. I'd have to get to that office first thing on the thirtieth if I was going to stand much chance of finding the right grave. I only hoped that whatever I could turn up about Hector Purecete in that time would help me get information from Maria-Luz Arbildo. If she showed up at his grave. Definitely no time for "Who's on First" discussions with Guillermo Banda that afternoon—I hoped he didn't look as much like Lou Costello as he sounded or I might lose it.

Fish called me before I could get anything done with directory assistance, saying there was not much to report on the scrapings he'd taken from the clay dog, except that the black paint was colored with crushed charcoal and volcanic sand, with just a touch of human blood. Not your average pottery glaze. No sign of dread diseases or drug residue. No unusual clay substrate, just plain terracotta. I mentioned that the dog had broken and dropped the bundle of hair out.

"So it is hair?" he asked.

"It looks like it. My Spanish is lousy, but I heard the inspector call it 'pelo'—which I recognize from my shampoo bottle as the Spanish word for hair," I replied, gazing into the plastic bag of shards. "Five or six strands here, dark brown and black, with a red thread holding them together."

"Two different kinds of hair?"

"Two different colors, but they have the same look and texture."

"Interesting. I wonder if the DNA matches the blood in the paint. I'd love to take a look at it when you get back—if you're game."

"I don't know if I'll be able to bring it back. It might have to stay here," I added, glancing down again at the phantom hound. Once the knot of hair had come free, so had the dog, and I wasn't sure if it was the hair or the sculpture which had held the spirit in the clay shell, but I wanted to know more before I let any of the parts out of my hands.

The dog ghost leaned against me and seemed to doze. I envied it; the beer had made me feel more tired than ever. Resigned, I stuffed the bag of pottery bits into my purse and went back to fruitless phone calls for the next hour. Outside of Mexico City directory assistance, most of the people I talked to had no better English than I had Spanish—and my Spanish was embarrassingly poor. The dog stirred and I could feel its low growl as it pressed against my leg.

A man of medium height with short black hair stopped beside me and looked me over as I tried to make myself clear—without much success—to a clerk in a provincial office somewhere in Oaxaca. The man carried a leather briefcase. He wore a gray suit, had a bland, oval face made interesting only by a boxer's crooked nose and basset-hound eyes. He smelled of laundry starch. The aura around him jittered and jumped in flickers of vibrant orange and blue as his eyes moved over everything, evaluating, cataloging... He seemed to have a hot-sauce stain on his tie, but it could have been part of the pattern.

His eyes flicked down toward my feet and he blinked, but I wasn't sure if he saw the ghost dog or if he just didn't like my boots. He turned his restless gaze back to me, waited until I hung up in frustration, and said, "You gotta be Harper Blaine."

He didn't look at all like Lou Costello, not even a Hispanic version. He didn't look like an international law practitioner with an advanced degree from Columbia, either. He looked like a guy who worked in an office eight-to-five; like an insurance adjuster or a mid-level manager in a very expensive suit.

"You must be Guillermo Banda," I replied.

"Willy. You can call me Willy." He hoisted himself onto the bar stool next to mine, keeping his feet away as if I might kick him without warning.

Considering my ex-boyfriend was named Will, that particular first-name didn't sound like a good idea. "I'd rather not," I said and wondered if he could see the ghost dog—he seemed a little wound-up.

He shrugged. "I'm sorry if I offended you, Miss Blaine." He put the briefcase on the bar and snapped it open. It held a single manila folder and a business-size envelope. Banda picked up the folder. "These are the last three versions of Miss Arbildo's will. I don't have to show them to you, but since a will in probate is a public record here, just as it is in the US, you could get most of this information by searching the district probate records—"

I cut him off. "Mr. Banda, I'm not offended with you and I'm not trying to put your back up. I'm just at a loss to understand this. I don't know why I was named in your client's will—I've never met her or heard of her. I just want to understand what I'm doing. I don't want to be stuck with some creepy mystery for the rest of my life." I did not look at the dog, but I could feel it still rumbling and pressing to me. "The conditions say I'm to put the dog on the grave intact. What am I supposed to do, now that the statue is broken?"

He put the folder down in the case and picked up the envelope, offering it to me. "That's easy. You take the money and run. I'm sure Miss Arbildo won't even know. She inherited a truckload. Thirty thousand U.S. is a drop in the bucket."

I was sure she would mind. Very much. I shook my head and didn't touch the envelope. "I can't do that. Maybe if I knew why she wanted the dog put on Purecete's grave, I could agree, but I don't. What is with the dog?"

Banda laughed—a tired laugh but genuinely amused. "It's a tradition. A really old one. You don't see it around here much anymore—up in the mountains around Michocan and Yunuen, maybe in Oaxaca, but even there it's dying out. It's from the Aztecs. They used to sacrifice a dog and burn the body on the funeral pyres because they believed the dog could lead the spirit of the dead to Mictlan. Now we just use a statue.

"See, the Mexican Land of the Dead is kind of like Dante's geography of Hell—it's got rings, only nicer. In the middle is Mictlan—where the dead live just like we do and from which they can someday be reborn. But it's a long way for a soul to go and there's a river you have to cross as well, so you need a guide: the dog, because tradition says dogs can always find the way home. Every year, the dead come back to visit us during el Dia de Muertos. The really traditional people put a statue of a dog on the ofrenda—the offerings on the family altar—so their dead relatives don't get lost coming and going."

"OK, I get the dog, but why me? Why would your client want a perfect stranger from two thousand miles away to take this specific dog to Purecete's grave?"

Banda shrugged again and dropped the envelope back into the briefcase, glancing down. "I don't know. Before you ask, I don't know who Purecete was or what his connection was to Miss Arbildo, either. You want to see the will for yourself?" he asked, looking back up at me.

I nodded. He pulled a draft copy of the will from the folder and handed the long pages to me. He pointed as he talked.

"See how she left her money to all these charities? That was pretty much unchanged from the first version I ever saw—one Jimenez, my partner, drew up for her. You can tell she was kind of an oddball when you look at the list." He pulled out another version of the document. "In an earlier draft of this will, she'd designated Jimenez as the recipient of the dog as you can see. She did it right after he died and she was very upset with him. Then she changed her mind—out of the blue —and named Purecete. Just a few months ago, she marched into the office and she handed me this."

He fished a creased scrap of paper out of the file. It was the hard white of a cheap notepad, torn along one side to make a ragged square from a longer piece of paper. The handwriting was similar to the signature on the will, but more crabbed and wandering:

Harper Blaine

Seattle Wash USA

The letters were cramped up against the left edge, but became more expansive and arched as they moved to the right, as if she hadn't thought she'd have enough space when she started and tried to stretch the words out to fill the page as she finished each line. It looked odd.

"She just held it out to me and said 'this is the one' and I knew better than to argue with Maria-Luz. So I wrote you in." He offered me the collection of drafts. "Take a look, you can see she had pretty definite—if crazy—ideas about her money. The woman was kind of loopy."

I glanced at the will again, making mental notes of the recipients of her bequests. They were mostly church charities for the unfortunate, the homeless, the poor, the dispossessed. There were a few odd animal charities as well, such as support for retired racing greyhounds, a rabbit shelter, llama farms, and care for retired circus elephants. None of them had conditions. And there were no individuals named other than me and Purecete.

"Didn't she have any family, or friends...employees even?" I asked.

Banda laughed and pretended he was coughing. "Miss Arbildo? No. She was the last of a literally dying breed—the Arbildo family died with her. And as I said, she was pretty strange and she wandered around a lot, didn't settle down much after a certain age, didn't make a lot of friends. She was kind of fond of Jimenez once—like I said she put him in the will at one point—but about the time he died she was furious with him. She stormed into the office screaming about it; 'Why did he do it? Why, why?' I almost thought that she would have dragged him back out of his grave and killed him if she could."

"What was she so mad about?"

"Well...his dying on her. She worked Jimenez pretty hard—he used to say if he died suddenly it would be her fault. His death shook her up. She was irrational. You know how some people get mad instead of grieving..."

I nodded; I was familiar with that phenomenon. Arbildo sounded like a difficult client, and I could understand not wanting to argue—or console—with one like her. But there was something incredibly strange about both the wills and Banda himself. I just couldn't pin down what was bugging me.

As I pondered the problem, under cover of checking the wills, the ghostly dog at my feet began whimpering and moving restively, then it got up and walked a few feet away from the bar, toward a column of thick mist that was forming in the Grey between the bar and the doorway. I adjusted my position on the bar stool so I could watch the dog and still seem to be reading the documents. The dog stopped near the smoky mass, then looked back at me with that pleading look dogs have. It looked at the ill-defined shape, whimpered, then glanced back to me.

The form that interested the dog was vaguely human in size and shape, but it had no features. There was no face and after a few moments, the dog turned and trotted back to me, whimpering and scratching at my legs with its cold, incorporeal paws. The specter drifted out the door. I didn't know what it was or where it was going, but the dog seemed to be urging me to follow it—or at least humor the dog's desire to do so. Banda would still be in Mexico City in a day or an hour, but whatever the ghost dog was after might not last another five minutes.

I wanted to ask him more about Arbildo, but I excused myself from Banda and said I'd be right back. Let him assume I needed the washroom, if he liked. I stood up and the dog darted out of the bar and into the main concourse. I hoped my luggage would be all right with the lawyer for the time it would take to chase the dog.

And it was fine, since the dog only got a few feet farther into the concourse before the shape seemed to fall apart and drift into the clutter of thousands of passengers' energy coronas moving through the silvery space of the air terminal. A few shapes had no living person within them, but most of those were simple repeating ghosts or fogs of happenstance and emotion left over from some altogether human interaction. The shadowy dog trotted back to me and pushed against my legs again.

Banda was looking impatiently at his watch when I returned to the bar.

"I can't stay longer. Have some clients to meet in twenty minutes and the traffic is getting bad. I have to go." He took a card from his inner jacket pocket and offered it to me. "If you have any more questions, call me. My cell phone number is on here. Good luck, Ms. Blaine," he added, picking up his briefcase and heading for the door.

"Hey," I called. "Aren't there any other documents? And what am I supposed to do about the dog?"

"Any other documents in Miss Arbildo's file are none of your business, Miss Blaine. As to the dog, the check is right here—you could just turn right around with it in your hand and call this thing done, as far as I'm concerned. But if you feel you have to, take the broken bits up to Oaxaca and leave 'em. Stick 'em back together with Superglue if you want."

"What about the grave? Where is it?"

"Damned if I know," he called back. "Pick one!"

He waved and ducked out before I could ask him anything more. It appeared that Guillermo Banda just wanted shut of Maria-Luz Arbildo and her nutty will and I was as convenient a way as any. I followed him a few paces out the door, saw him duck past the Customs area, waving to the guards on the other side as he went past —old friends? Something odd was going on with Banda, but I wasn't entirely sure what. I did pause to wonder if the breaking of the dog was entirely an accident… I shook off that thought and went back to my seat, the Grey dog scampering along in my wake.

I ordered some food and ate in a hurry before heading to the Mexicana Airlines desk to pick up my new boarding passes and check my luggage for the flight to Oaxaca. The phantom dog stuck to my side the whole time, casting glances around the room and sniffing for sign—of what I didn't know.

For just a moment as I boarded the little prop-plane I wondered what to do with the dog before I remembered that no one but me would even be aware of it. It huddled under my feet the whole hour we were in the air and again on the ride from the airport, which reminded me of the regional airports I'd grown up near in Los Angeles County with their push-cart stairs and wind-blown tarmac. A white van was standing at the curb outside, offering rides to down-town Oaxaca City and the ghost-dog and I shared the vehicle with a family of six and two couples who all seemed excited beyond my ability.

The van driver dropped each group off, leaving me at a tall, Spanish colonial building on the edge of the downtown core. As far as I could tell, the whole area was late Spanish colonial, though at that elevation, darkness had already fallen and it was hard to see details beyond the streetlamps. The road was layered thickly with silvery ghosts and loops of memory, playing like old movies in a two-dollar theater. I saw a discreet sign on the buttercup colored plaster wall that indicated the carved wooden door before me led to my guest house. I pulled the bell handle as instructed and was greeted with a flood of light and the odors of spicy cooking as the door was opened wide.

"Soy Harper Blaine—" I started.

"Oh! Miss Blaine! Si! Come in! You were bumped to a later flight?" the dark-haired woman in the doorway asked, snatching my bag indoors with one hand as she waved me in with the other. "We have dinner for you if you like it."

She turned her head and called for "Miguelito!" who proved to be a teenager as tall as a professional basketball player and as dramatically emo as a Cure album cover. "You are in manos de leon," she continued to me while pointing at my suitcase without shifting her gaze from my face. "My nephew will take your bag. You can wash and come back down to the sala for some food."

I was almost dizzy with exhaustion by then, but I know better than to argue with whirlwind women. I followed "little Miguel" up the tiled stairs and around an open gallery to a door with a painting of a magenta coxcomb flower on it. Miguelito unlocked the door for me and put the suitcase just inside before handing me my key and slouching off with an insouciant nod.

I glanced down over the railing before I went into the room. In the courtyard below I could see people gathered around a ceramic firepit that gleamed with heat, serving themselves from a nearby table laden with food. The cool mountain air settled gently from above through the open center of the building's roof, drifting down to meet the swirl of spark and heat that rose from the gathering below.

I was so tired I didn't make it back down that night. I woke up in the morning of October thirtieth with one boot on and one off and the ghost dog running in and out through the closed door, whining. Someone was tapping on my door. Groggily, I stumbled to it and opened up.

Miguel-the-not-so-small was slouching there—clad in black jeans, black t-shirt, black boots with his naturally dark hair hanging over his eyes—probably hoping I hadn't heard his timid tapping and could lope off to whatever he'd rather do than wait on me. The energy around him was a dun-colored cloud shot with red lightning bolts of annoyance—or something short-tempered and pissy—while thin gold lines trailed off his fingertips in a way I'd never seen before. In the face of his determined gloom, I smiled at him with perverse malice, in spite of being still half-asleep.

"Buenos tardes, Miguel!" I chirped—fairytale princesses had nothing on me for chipper.

"Yeah, yeah... Good morning to you, too." His accent was still pretty strong, but his English was clear. And abrasive. I could almost see the expletive deleted from that sentence still hanging in the air in all its F-bomb glory. "Tia Mercedes said I'm supposed to show you around the city 'cause you have some kind of business thing..."

"Yup! Busy-ness. Busy, busy! Gotta find a grave."

He frowned at me. "Grave?" he asked, as if I surely didn't know what I'd just said.

"Yup. I have a mission to do something with a grave and I don't know where it is."

"Today?"

"No. On Sunday, November First."

"Oh." Was that disappointment? "Dia de Muertos. Yeah."

"Is today special or something?" I asked as he started to turn away.

"Yeah. There's, like, a whole series of Days of the Dead. Todos Santos—November First—is just the big one the tourists are all crazy for. Today's, like, the day for the spirits that died by violence. Tia Mercedes doesn't celebrate that in the house—we have to go outside so the mad ghosts don't come in and mess stuff up." He shrugged and started to turn away, having lost all interest in me, now that I was no more interesting than the average tourist.

I grabbed his arm. "Hey, where y'going, Miguel?"

He huffed his hair out of his face and glared at me. "Call me Mickey."

"Not Mike?"

"No." Like, duuuuh, I thought facetiously. Was I this snotty as a teenager?

"Mickey Mouse fan, then? Mickey Mantle?"

He snorted, and pulled his arm out of my grasp. "Tia Mercedes has breakfast downstairs in twenty minutes. Then we can go look for your grave. OK?"

I didn't miss the implication of whose grave, but I did ignore it. "OK. Be right down. Thank your Aunt for me."

He skulked away as I retreated into my room. I took a very fast shower and threw on clean clothes.

I'd been given a room with its own bath, which I suspected was an unusual luxury in an antique house. And there was no denying the building—some wealthy man's town home originally I'd have bet—was exactly as old as its style indicated. It didn't mimic Spanish colonial, it *was* Spanish colonial.

Downstairs the food was endless and lush: eggs scrambled with corn tortillas, green salsa, and cheese; fried plantains; grilled tomatoes; bread and sweet pastries only distantly related to the greasy churros found in American malls. Coffee, chocolate, and milk were all available as well as horchata and fruit juice. My hosts, the Villaflores family, felt that their guests during the holiday should be well fed before they faced a day of hiking up and down the mountainous elevations of Oaxaca City and its environs. Mid-day meal would be on our own, but dinner with the family was open to all, Mercedes informed me—she was the proprietress I'd met the previous night. I thought I'd have to find an excuse to dodge it or I stood a good chance of gaining five pounds before November Second, hiking or no.

Miguel-call-me-Mickey was not so enthusiastic, picking at his food and jumping up the moment I was finished, telling his aunt we had to leave and get to the "palacio de gobierno" that morning or we'd never get in before they closed. He sloped off to wait for me outside while I thanked Mercedes for breakfast.

She smiled. "Gracias. I hope you won't mind Miguelito too much —he is bored here. I don't know why he came at all—such an odd boy —but at least he can be some help to you. If he doesn't make you scream and leave him in a ditch by the road."

"Oh...I think we'll be OK," I replied, thinking there would be ample opportunities to knock a hole in Mickey's attitude if I wanted to. Angsty teens aren't much of a challenge after vampires and vengeful ghosts and monsters in the sewer.

Stepping through the door, the sound of the Grey really hit me. Where Mexico City had been a strong, steady song of steel and silk, Oaxaca was a wild roar. It sounded like the Battle of the Bands in which someone had forgotten to tell the musicians not to all play at once. Layers of contrasting melody and meter, song and noise flooded the mist-world and made the lines of energy around me spark and throb. Strata of time and memory seemed to juggle and flow, like Einstein's river. It was tiring just to stand in it.

Mickey lounged against the wall outside, smoking a noxious-smelling cigarillo and shifting his fake-sleepy gaze around the street like a hoodlum in a black-and-white film looking for a chump. I stood on the doorstep for a minute while he ignored me. Then I nudged his foot with mine to get his attention. He jerked like I'd kicked him and muttered a phrase under his breath even I knew was an insult.

"Hey, I thought you were in a hurry," I said.

He grunted and threw down his smoke, grinding it out under his toe with more malice than the horrid thing deserved. "Yeah, right." A sentence that seemed to mean nothing when he said it.

He gathered himself after a final glance around and turned his back to me, heading out into the street. "This way."

I wondered if his shoulders got tired carrying the weight of that chip.

I was there because of the holiday, yet I hadn't thought of some of the implications of its presence beyond the possibility of office closures and an increased presence of the dead. Once out on the street with Mickey, it became obvious that el Dia de Muertos was a much bigger thing than Halloween and there was more to contend with, both living and dead, than bureaucrats on holiday. We walked down the wide, gray-bricked road, hemmed in by a mix of adobe and buildings of pale green stone, none newer than the late 1920s, many painted, like the Villaflores house, in rich shades of red, yellow, orange, or the native pale green. The bricked street boiled with ghostly traffic on foot, in cars, on horse- and donkey-back, even a group of ancient Spanish soldiers marching with pikes pointing at the sky.

I was startled to note that unlike the ghosts of Seattle, most of these looked like skeletons in clothing and not like the remembered-shapes of live people. Skulls grinned and empty eye sockets gleamed with only the memory of eyes. They were completely aware of us too, watching us as we went and seeming amused. It was unsettling to be observed through eyeless, unblinking sockets and so much more closely than I was used to.

We scuffed through the legions of phantoms without talking for a while, to a huge central plaza. Miguel paused and pointed into it, saying in a bored voice, "That's our famous zocalo. Where the Federales shot all those teachers a couple of years ago. That was in front of the old palacio de gobierno, but it's a museum now. We'll have to go through the market to get to the new one—I hope you don't want to stop and go shopping," he added with a sneer. He didn't know me very well.

I rolled my eyes and ignored the jab—for now. "I'm not much of a shopper. I just need to find this guy's grave by November First."

"You know which cemetery?"

"Nope, just have a name and a date of death."

"Yeah, right. We'll go to the Registrar of Deaths." He said it with such relish I had to stifle a giggle. "We have to move it, though, 'cause they'll close early. Dia de Muertos is a major holiday. It's like your Christmas, only with dead guys. The market's crazy-full with old ladies like Tia Mercedes and all their kids doing the shopping for the ofrendas and all that. And tourists. And you want to get inside before the ghosts of the violently dead return." He gave me a sly glance from the corner of his eye to see if I'd bite, but I didn't.

"Then we'd better get going," was all I said.

We continued down the street to the market with the ghost dog tagging at our heels and the gold threads that dragged from Mickey's fingertips spinning out through the crowds of spirits that thronged the streets already crowded with the living. He seemed unaware of the vibrant threads spooling from his hands. I wished I knew what that shiny energy strand was all about, but I'd have to wait and see.

We threaded our way through the periphery of the market crowd and cut across the corner of the zocalo—partially "opened" by the ruthless removal of towering trees, the memories of which still threw phantom shade over the raised, central "kiosk" where the state band played on Tuesdays, according to a notice nearby.

I could see the memory of the original plaza like a projection over the new design, with huge, thick-trunked trees and Victorian iron benches set along the narrower, shadier paths, and the not-so-long-ago stench of tear gas floating on the warm breeze and an echo of screams. Shadows of the dead protesters glimmered over the memory of blood on the stones in front of the old government building. I could hear the shouts and the shots mingled with the scent of flowers and fresh, spiced bread from the market nearby. The combination made me queasy. No one in their right mind would want to linger there that night.

We turned from the market, the shops, and the cafes that lined the sunbaked zocalo and headed down to the government offices a few blocks away. We entered the usual bureaucratic maze of once-grand rooms chopped into offices and cubicles with flimsy, movable walls, repulsively out of place in the building that predated World War I.

The man behind the registrar's desk, however, fit in perfectly. He had a small mustache with waxed points and wore his shirt collar buttoned up tight under his conservative tie.

"Hi," I started, hoping I could manage to make myself understood in English. "I need to locate a grave."

The clerk's nostrils pinched in annoyance and he shook his head. "No habla Ingles, Señora."

I cast a glance at Mickey, who was leaning against a wall again. He shot me back a snotty look. This was going to be fun.

"Mickey, would you translate for me?" I asked.

With a sigh, the teenager heaved himself upright and ambled to the desk.

He made a gesture at the clerk, who gave him a look nearly as disdainful as the one Mickey had given me.

"La gringa está buscando un sepulcro," he said.

"La gringa." Well at least I wasn't "puta" this time.

The clerk heaved a shrug and spat back something that I imagined was "Yeah, aren't they all?"

There was a bit more wiseass chit-chat before I put a restraining hand on Mickey's arm.

"Mickey. Just translate. Commentary isn't required."

He rolled his eyes. "Yeah, right." Then he gave me a blank look.

"What?" I asked, feeling the ghost dog brush past me to lie down on the floor near the door. I didn't look down, just stared at Mickey.

"So...? What am I supposed to translate?"

I closed my eyes for a moment and breathed, then said, "Ask him if there's a form I need to fill out and what it will cost for him to find the information right now."

Mickey made with the rolling eyes again and looked back to the clerk who was glaring at us, even though there was no one else waiting in his cubbyhole. Mickey seemed to be repeating my request, but this time in a slightly singsong, high-pitched voice.

The man frowned a him. "Forma? Para qué?"

"He says 'A form for what?'"

"Yeah...I figured that part out, Mickey. I need to know if there is a form I am required to fill out in order to find out where a certain person is buried here in Oaxaca. If so, I need that form and I wish to know what fee I have to pay to get that information immediately—while I stand here and wait. Now, can you be that specific with him, Mickey?"

He huffed and turned back to the clerk, parroting my request in his mocking voice.

The clerk was annoyed by it too, but he grunted an affirmative and handed over a form and said something about pesos.

"He says it'll cost a hundred dollars to do it right now."

"No, he didn't Mickey. He said 'cinco cientos pesos.' That's about fifty bucks. My Spanish sucks, not my math."

"Yeah, right." And the eye roll. I was getting too familiar with the routine already.

I filled in the form as best I could with Mickey's non-help and fished a thousand pesos from my wallet. I put it down with the form, saying "Apesadumbrado," and jerking my head toward Mickey. Even as bad as it is, I can manage a few important words in Spanish: please, thank you, beer, toilet, keys, and sorry.

A smile almost cracked the man's wooden face as he accepted the form and the overpayment, with an amused snort. "Momentito," he said, taking the form away behind a screen.

I sat down on one of his two cracked green vinyl-covered chairs to wait.

"He only goes back to the computer," Mickey groused. "He just wants to make it look important."

I shot him a quelling glance, but said nothing.

The phantom dog got up to chase a phantom cat around the room. I ignored their antics and so did almost everyone else, except a skeletal clerk who tried to give the dog one of his finger bones to dissuade it from barking. The dog wasn't having anything to do with the clerk's finger and backed away, bristling, leaving the ghost cat free to dash out of the room to the relative safety of the hall.

The flesh-and-blood clerk, who looked nothing like his bony predecessor, returned with a sheet of paper. "Hmph," he coughed, then launched into a rattling discourse aimed somewhere in between me and Mickey as if he couldn't decide which of us he was supposed to talk to—Mickey the brat or the illiterate gringa.

Finally the clerk let out an impressively heavy sigh, shrugged, and shoved the paper forward for one of us to take. "Buenos dias," he added, turning his back and stomping off to his sanctum in the back.

Mickey grabbed the sheet and held it out to me after a second's perusal. "You're fucked. There are three graves for your guy."

"Three? Not for the same date."

"Yeah. Look."

I took the page and looked it over. And there were three gravesites given for Hector Purecete, all with the same death date in 1996. "That's gotta be wrong—it's not a common name, is it?"

"No."

"Great," I muttered. "I guess I'll have to go look at all of them and see what shakes loose."

I stood up and walked out of the government offices with Mickey and the dog trailing me.

We'd started back across the zocalo, passing closer to the site of the teachers' fatal protest than I liked, when Mickey finally decided to talk again.

"What do you want to find this guy's grave for anyway?" Mickey asked. "Some kind of creepy ritual or something?"

My turn to sigh. "No. I told you before, I just need to find it and leave something on it. On November First."

"Yeah, right."

I stopped, burning in the high altitude sun and the hot Grey energy of the massacre. "Mickey, is it just for me, or do you always have a bad attitude?"

He turned his head and muttered under his breath, starting to walk on. I snatched his arm and dragged him back to me, through a red blotch of remembered blood and pain. He flinched a little and tried to wrench himself out of my grip, spitting nasty Spanish words.

"Damn that's a lot of endearing little nicknames you have for me. How 'bout we make this easier on both of us. You can just call me the G.P.—"

"Huh? The what?"

"The gringa puta. And I'll just call you brat-boy. It'll be so much easier, don't you think?"

He glowered at me and pulled against my hold. I let him go and sighed.

"Mickey, look: I appreciate the offer of help, but your attitude is just not flying with me. You can straighten up and stop acting like a punk, or I can do without you. What's it going to be?" My ghostly dog-companion circled around us, growling as if to keep something unpleasant at bay.

Mickey seemed to consider my statement seriously, sidling into the sun and away from the crying red energy of the teachers' deaths. "OK...GP. We'll have to get to the panteons soon. It'll be a lot busier tomorrow. And you really don't want to be out tonight."

"You're serious about that ghosts of the violent dead thing?"

He nodded. "You Norte Americanos think el Dia de Muertos is just a funny tradition—not real—but we don't. Not up here. This is the ghost country. We're not afraid of death—not like you. We live with it."

"You might be surprised."

He ignored me. "But we don't do foolish things like stand where people were murdered on their Day to return from Mictlan. That's just fucking stupid."

I nodded. "All right. Let's get someplace better then. Like the panteon—a panteon is a cemetery, right?"

"Yeah. It's actually pretty safe right now. But we should get the car. Those three aren't close to each other."

I was surprised at his change of attitude. He was still kind of surly, but at least he seemed to be helping me instead of making more work. We walked back to the house and Mickey borrowed his aunt's car—a dusty silver Chevrolet Chevy, which amused me.

I took the passenger seat and held the door open for a moment. The ghost dog stopped at the car's doorsill and sat on the ground, looking pathetic and thumping its stumpy tail, but wouldn't step up into the car.

Mickey looked at me. "Something wrong?"

"No...no I'm fine." I closed the door and the dog vanished from view. We drove away without any sign of the phantom canine until we got out at the first panteon on the list.

The first stop was the municipal cemetery of San Miguel. We drove around a small carnival that was setting up in a courtyard in front and walked across drifts of flowers and greenery that had escaped from the bundles carried by a stream of people entering the panteon ahead of us. The dog trotted up, materializing out of the road dust and Grey mist to rub against my legs and bump its head against me impatiently until we walked through the cemetery gates. The dog ran ahead, into the crowd of animate skeletons and live humans who filled the graveyard.

Everyone was busy, the living and the dead, and I paused to stare. "There are a lot of...people here." I said.

"Yeah. The graves have to be cleaned and decorated, the family ofrendas made, and the cooking has to be done before Todos Santos on November First. It's a Sunday this year, so they gotta be done today and tomorrow or the Church might be offended. Most of these guys won't bring their feasts until after sundown on Sunday."

I glanced at him with a curious frown. "Feasts? In a graveyard?"

He snorted something that was almost a laugh. His tone still left a bit to be desired, however. "Yeah. I keep trying to tell you: it's like a party. El Dia de Muertos is a cycle of life thing. We have all this stuff at home—the ofrendas and stuff—but we come to the panteon in the evening to party with the family ghosts. We know death, but we don't worship it or freak out about it. It's just...part of life. We aren't afraid of the old bony woman. Just look at the skeletons," Mickey added, pointing at a pair of children waving paper skeleton puppets at each other in an elaborate pantomime punctuated with much chattering and laughing.

The puppets had jointed legs and arms controlled with strings the children pulled with their fingers while clutching the sticks to which the paper skeletons were mounted. One was a musician with a guitar and a top hat, while the other was a girl singer with a fur stole and long skirt. The kids pranced ahead with their puppets. The ghosts of several other children tagged behind, giggling, as the impromptu cabaret act headed for the family plot. The group was herded along by an aging man carrying an elaborate iron-work cross under his arm and followed by a cold boil of silver and red energy—the imminence of those who died by violence, perhaps.

"Those guys are gonna clean the graves of their family and put that new cross up," Mickey lectured me. He was almost spitting. "They're not sad—they're happy. They work hard today. They remember the dead. 'Cause they know we're all gonna die. That's the big deal you

Norte Americanos don't get. You can't 'cheat' death. You just have to know it's there and remember. We all got a skeleton inside us."

The skeletons. As I looked around the panteon, I saw few ghosts of the type I was most familiar with—the memory manifestations of the dead. Nearly all the ghosts in this cemetery were skeletal with only the barest hint of faces or flesh, a few were purely bones while a smaller handful had the shape of the living people they had once been. These were the only ghosts I saw that seemed distressed or confused, wandering among the raised graves as if desperate to find something they'd misplaced, blind to the throngs of living and dead around them.

I got it: the manifestations of the Grey depended upon the minds of those who shaped it. Here, where skeletons were the symbol of the dead, embraced, even beloved in all their bony glory as just another part of the cycle of life, most of the spirits of the dead looked like skeletons. In the US where death was the end of life, most ghosts manifested with the memory-shape of their formerly-living bodies. But they could have been anything, like the discorporate entities I'd met once or twice, manifesting as changing shapes, or inconclusive features on a mutable column of fog, or the roiling anger of the slaughtered.

The ghost dog trotted back from its peregrinations through the crowd and sat at my feet, tongue lolling, looking happy for the first time since it had appeared. I almost reached to pat its head before I remembered that most people don't see ghosts. Even as comfortable with death as the Oaxaquinos were, I doubted they would understand my stooping to pet a spectral hound. Mickey would probably think I was crazy and say so. I didn't believe he'd suddenly decided to respect me; he just didn't want me to kick his ass. But he wasn't above a few more needling comments.

I cleared my throat. "Where do you think we'll find the grave? This a big place."

"Caretaker will have a list of the plots and tombs." He was pretty savvy about graveyards, but I supposed that wasn't unusual here.

We pushed through the crowds to a large stone building with colonnades filled with niches on one side and open to a large courtyard on the other. The patio of the mausoleum was full of people walking or crawling on the paving stones to lay out pictures in mounds of colored sand: cavorting skeletons, Virgins of Guadalupe; flowers and crosses and skulls. Mickey called these "sand carpets." We found one of the caretakers assisting a sand painter, laying out a border of small bricks to keep the moist, colored sand from dribbling into the walkways. We picked our way closer, careful not to disturb the developing sand carpets. Mickey called out to the caretaker as we got near.

The woman looked up from her bricks and said something I couldn't follow. The caretaker was darker-skinned and had a more pronounced nose and cheek bones than Mickey—probably related to some local Indian group. Mickey replied in a language I knew wasn't Spanish. The kneeling woman stood and began to talk very fast. Mickey pointed to the paper we'd gotten from the Registrar of Births and Deaths. The woman frowned and pointed off across the cemetery, making motions with her hands to indicate turns. Mickey nodded and seemed to be thanking her, then turned and tugged me back into the mausoleum's colonnade.

"She says it's out in the edge, near the back fence, but she thinks this is wrong. The grave's been around a long time. You *sure* 1996 is right?" he added with a touch of sneering doubt at my brain power.

"Yup."

Mickey shrugged so hard his eyes rolled. "All right. Let's go look at it."

We set out through the graveyard, trailed by the dog. Distracting myself from Mickey's volatility, I tried to imagine the scruffy mongrel as a skeleton. I didn't succeed, to my relief.

We found the grave under a pile of people who were busily scrubbing the headstone and stone fence clean of dirt with stiff-bristled brushes. As we watched the inscription came clear: Hector Purecete, died 1888. Not even close.

Mickey grunted and shot me a smug look. Oh yeah...that showed me, all right.

He started to turn back, but before he could move away I waved to the oldest woman in the grave-cleaning group. She peered up at me and I tried to ask her if she knew of Maria-Luz's Hector Purecete, but her English was non-existent. Groaning in disgust, Mickey stepped in.

After a rapid exchange, he held her off with a gesture and glanced back at me, his face creased with curiosity. "This is Señora Acoa. She says this is the only Hector Purecete she knows about. But she says a man came asking the same question a few years back. Señora Acoa couldn't help him, either. She says Hector, here, was a soldier. Sounds like a real pendajo. She's his, like, great, great, great niece. She doesn't live here anymore and is going back to Coyocan tomorrow, but she figured they should come and clean up Hector's grave every year. She didn't even know where he was buried until that guy showed up."

"Does she remember the man's name?" I asked, looking at the elderly woman who stood by her ancestor's grave.

Mickey translated for me and this time he was dead serious.

The elderly Señora Acoa replied in a streak of words I couldn't begin to follow, her voice wavering. Then she swayed, putting her hand to her chest. The energy around her shut down to a thin, white line that grew more and more translucent, then began to shift and rise away from her as a messy skein of gold and white light.

I started to jump between them, knowing that the old woman was dying right in front of us, overcome by heat and excitement, her mortality rising off her corporeal form. But Mickey kept talking, his tone going gentle and cajoling, as the gold strands at his fingertips waved and stroked at the old woman, calming her down, smoothing the rising knot of her soul back into its body, easing her back into herself. It was an eerie effect coming from such a determined jerk, and he didn't know he was doing it. Finally the old woman plumped herself down on the edge of the grave with a huff of breath, and fanned herself with her hands until one of her staring family handed her a paper fan shaped like a grinning skull. She cooled herself, catching her breath and settling her life back into her oblivious body as my reluctant assistant returned his attention to me. Nothing in his demeanor showed he knew what had just happened, anymore than her family did. He didn't know he'd saved her life, or that he seemed to have some kind of power. He was just Mickey the jerk again.

"She wants to know why you want to know, but I told her you're doing a family a favor. I think she said the other guy's name was Jimenez. A lawyer maybe? She's kinda confused. And a little loco—she thought she had seen this Jimenez guy just today."

I gazed at the tired old woman who was still living in spite of everything. I blinked slowly, getting my thoughts back to the case. "Maybe she did. He died a few years ago in a plane crash," I said. "And yes, he was a lawyer." Hadn't Banda said he knew nothing about Purecete? But his partner had been to this grave...

Mickey's eyes flashed wider. The word that dropped from his mouth was unknown to me, but it was inflected just like "Cool!" He had no idea what was really cool, here.

I wondered if Señora Acoa had actually seen Jimenez, maybe her proximity to death had made it possible—this was the day for the violently dead to return, and I couldn't imagine a death much more violent than his. "What else did she have to say?" I asked, trying not to stare too much at the old woman.

"Not much. She said Hector didn't have any kids, so there's only her and her family to look after his grave. She's worn out, but she's afraid her family will forget him after she dies. So she makes them come here every year so he doesn't die the third death."

"Excuse me. What's the third death?"

The lecturing tone was back as he explained. "The first death is the death of the body. The second is when they put us in the ground. Then we can go to Mictlan—the land of the dead—and, y'know, live among the dead. But we can come back for the Dia de Muertos feast with our families, so long as they remember us. That's the third death —being forgotten. That's the real end, when we don't come back 'cause there's no one here for us. But we can be reborn once everyone forgets, so it's not so bad. That's the three deaths."

"How do you know all this stuff?" I asked.

He shrugged. "It's tradition around here. I'm kind of into the death-magic thing. And my, like, great uncle was supposed to be a black sorcerer or something. It's cool."

Typical baby-goth fascination, though I suspected his went a little deeper and from a more personal angle, whether he understood that or not. To me, the life-magic "thing" he'd just done was a lot cooler.

We both looked at the family who had returned to sprucing up the grave of Hector number one. We watched in silence a while. Then we turned away, letting them get on with their task as we headed back to the car with the ghostly dog in tow.

"You said Mexicans were not afraid of death," I said. I didn't want to ask him about what he'd done yet, that would only get off our track, but I hadn't forgotten it.

"We aren't. But no one wants to be forgotten. That's why we have all these parties in the graveyard. We bring the dead all the stuff they loved in life so they can party with us, and that way we remember them like they really were. Not like a body in a casket. Or some saint. It's kind of funny: you're keeping the third death away, but you didn't even know Hector Purecete."

"I'm not sure Maria-Luz did, either."

"Who's Maria-Luz?"

"She's the woman who wanted a dog laid on Hector Purecete's grave."

We were nearly back to the cemetery gates, deep in the twining, boiling mess of the carnival and the confluence of the living and the dead. Mickey wheeled and stared at me. "Not that dog!" he asked, pointing right at the canine phantom panting at my heels.

Startled, I turned and looked for another, corporeal dog, just in case. But there was no animal near enough to be the one he meant. I pointed at the ghost. "This one?"

Mickey nodded. "Yeah."

"Umm...this dog's already dead."

He peered at it and the ghost-dog let its tongue loll out in a huge yawn. I could see right through its transparent, silver-mist skull to the ground below. Apparently Mickey could too, because he jumped a little and then looked back to me.

"Fuck me! Where did it come from?"

"I'll tell you in the car on the way to the next cemetery."

We climbed back into the Chevy and again the dog refused to come in. We drove away, the dog vanishing into the misty Grey as we pulled out of the lot.

"How is it that you can see the dog?" I asked as he started the car.

"I just—I just can." He looked a little uncomfortable and hunched his shoulders. "Why are you taking it to this guy's grave?"

I told him about the dog statue—after all there was no seal of secrecy or confidentiality on the bequest—how it had come to me and what had befallen it at Customs. I told him about Maria-Luz Arbildo's odd last request that the statue containing the dog's spirit was to be placed on the grave for which we were searching on November First.

"Weird," he said as we wound onto a narrow road. "Why did she wait so long to give him the dog? He's been dead since 1996."

"She didn't seem to know where he was buried."

Mickey shook his head. "Weird," he repeated. "Hey, at least we've narrowed the search to just two graves. That Jimenez guy must have done the same thing...so why didn't he put the dog on Hector's grave?"

I shook my head. "I don't know. Miss Arbildo was still alive then, so I assume she wanted to do it, but didn't get around to it for some reason." But if she had known which grave to put it on, wouldn't she have given that information in the will? I guessed that Jimenez hadn't told her. But why not?

Mickey scowled. "That's messed up." But he didn't say any more and we reached the next panteon in silence. The dog greeted us at the gate to the cemetery of San Antonio and ran ahead, barking like a puppy chasing butterflies. Mickey watched it dash into the bustling crowds in the graveyard and shook his head.

"Maybe the dog knows where the grave is," he suggested, "but it runs so fast..."

"I'm not even going to try to follow it," I said. "If the grave is here, maybe we'll find the dog nearby when we get there."

"Yeah, right."

The courtyard of Panteon San Antonio was filled with people building elaborate table displays.

"Competition ofrendas," Mickey explained. His sneer wasn't quite as pronounced now. "Each group makes an offering in a traditional style and they compete to see whose is the most authentic, or whatever. Home ofrendas are more plain, they usually have more food and personal stuff. This is mostly for the tourists." He pointed at one table where a pair of men were lashing tall, dusty-green plants into a seven foot-tall arch attached to the front legs. "That's sugar cane—it's traditional. Those guys are Purepeche Indians. See the little clay dog? That's really old-school." He stared at me. "Hey...was your statue like that one?"

I glanced at the table and saw a small, black figurine, much like the one I'd started off with. I walked closer and the men stopped work and stared at me. One of them said something I couldn't translate.

"He says 'can I help you?'" Mickey supplied.

"Ask him about the dog," I replied, pointing to the small clay figure, sitting on the table with a pile of other items waiting for its place. "Where did it come from? Are all the little dog statues the same?"

Mickey asked and translated his reply. "It's from Mita—that's a village near here. It's a traditional design."

"May I look at it?"

The man listened to Mickey, then shrugged and picked up the clay dog. He offered it to me with a half-smile.

I smiled back and took the dog, turning it over and studying the rough shape and paint. It was the same shape, but the black glaze was very ordinary—I'd bet there was no blood or volcanic sand in this one's finish. The lines around the legs were the same, but there was no lightning bolt on this one. The hole in its belly was unpatched, open, and had a fine lip where the glaze had tried to drip around the rim. I handed the dog back to the man, who grinned at me, showing gapped teeth stained by tobacco and coffee.

"Could you ask him if he ever met Maria-Luz or Hector Purecete?"

Both men frowned and shook their heads, apparently telling

Mickey they'd never heard of either. We thanked them and headed off to find the caretaker and look for grave number two.

"That statue is almost identical to the one I had that broke," I said as we walked away. "But mine had a white lightning bolt on the side."

"A glyph to keep the spirit inside the dog. Someone worked magic on it."

"I guessed that, but how do you know?"

Mickey shrugged, "Like I said, magic is kind of interesting."

Mickey seemed to have been studying more than he'd admitted. I decided to fish a bit. "I was thinking that the bit of hair that fell out was part of the magic, too."

Mickey shot a startled glance at me. "Hair? There was hair inside the dog?"

"Yeah, a little bundle of five or six strands tied with red thread. It looked like human hair, not animal."

"Tied with red thread? Inside the dog? With the lightning bolt?" He looked both excited and scared. "That's witchcraft."

I frowned at him. The only witch I knew was good-hearted and friendly, but Mickey was plainly not acquainted with the same sort of witch—and like a lot of young morons, he seemed to think it was kind of sexy.

"It's death magic," he explained. "The dark side stuff."

"I thought you guys weren't into that death worship thing."

"Not normal death—y'know: the cycle of life stuff. The hair-thing's death cult stuff. It's black magic from the colonial days—half native magic, half Christian mysticism stuff. It all about Santisima Muerta— Most Holy Death, the reaper of souls, Death triumphant over Man." Frightened reverence resounded in his tone and set his aura sparking red and gold. "Your Maria-Luz used black magic to hold the dog's spirit inside the statue. Trust me: I know this shit."

"It didn't feel like evil magic when it broke," I said.

He shrugged, pretending sudden disinterest he then undermined by saying, "I wonder why she wanted to put that thing on this guy's grave."

I didn't know, but I wanted to. If I knew who Hector Purecete was to Arbildo, maybe I could figure it out. But we'd have to find his grave first.

Once again we were directed to a grave and picked our way through the people who were cleaning and decorating throughout the cemetery. Here, the families and friends of the dead were making sandcastle-coffins over the graves, mounding the wet sand up into caskets and even the archetypal long pentagon. Some were bordered with cement block or brick to retain the wet sand, others were free-standing. Other groups were just beginning the process of clearing off the weeds and grasses that had invaded the cemetery during the year, attacking the plants with hoes and hands and, in one case, a machete, to get down to raw earth.

Panteon San Antonio bore no resemblance to the carefully-mani-cured cemeteries of Seattle, with their endless lawns or Victorian markers. This was a place of gritty brown earth, punctuated with riots of gold and purple flowers and green foliage. The plants and flowers were being arranged into patterns or pictures on the sand coffins, or lashed into little huts and ofrendas that would straddle the graves when finished. The scent of marigolds was thick and spicy on the air along with the smell of turned earth and sweet, green sugar cane.

Once we had cut a path through the crowd, we found a short stone obelisk with a list of names carved on it. Hector Purecete's was there, but listed as one of a dozen men lost at sea in 1982. No grave, wrong date, wrong Hector. The Grey was thick as oatmeal and ghost-dog gamboled around the base of the stone, snapping at the marigold petals floating on the breeze. It glanced up at me and seemed to laugh, giving me a doggy smile.

Mickey glowered and the energy around him pinwheeled orange sparks that looked just like the flower petals. "That guy at the regis-trar's office just took the money and gave us a list of all the Hector Purecete graves he had," he groused. "He didn't even try to get the right one!"

"Yeah, because your attitude was just so endearing," I reminded him, but I was looking at the dog, which was now pawing around the base of the obelisk with incorporeal paws.

I crouched down to get a look at whatever had caught the dog's attention and saw a loop of blue energy protruding from the ground. Warily, I caught it on my fingers and pulled it up. It came like a long-rooted weed from a flower bed and popped out of the ground with a small crackle of electricity.

A skeleton-man wearing a yellow fisherman's coat appeared where the blue bit of energy had left a hole in the ground. I had the impression that he was blinking, even though he had no eyelids or eyes to cover with them.

Mickey stared and jerked back half a step, but the bony ghost didn't notice. He let out a glad exclamation I heard in my head and bent down to ruffle the ghost dog's fur. "Iko! Look how big you got!" He wasn't really speaking English, but the words seemed to come clearly into my head.

The dog frisked around and whined in glee, taking slobbery licks at the skull in between joyous wiggles.

"Is that your dog?" I asked.

The skeleton in the slicker glanced at me. "He was the cook's dog, but we all liked him. He was just a puppy when the old *Dulcia* went down."

"So…was Hector Purecete the cook?"

"Hector? No. Hector was a deckhand. I suppose he must have saved Iko. Neither of them drowned."

"His name's on the memorial," I said.

The skeleton looked at the obelisk and laughed, clacking his teeth. "It's wrong. Martin Ramirez got off in Bermuda and was replaced by an American named Lofland. And see, there I am, but they spelled my name wrong," he added, pointing to the name Ernesto Sanchez. "It should say 'Santara,' but my writing on the contract was so bad, they had to guess. No, they must have just taken the crew list from Señor Arbildo and assumed we all died."

"Arbildo?" I asked, surprised.

"Si, he owned the boat."

So there was a connection, but not a clear one. "What became of Hector, then?"

The bony shoulders under the slicker shrugged. "I don't know. He must have been picked up by someone. He came and looked at the memorial once or twice and used to clean it up for us every year, but then he stopped and people began to forget about us. Most of the crew are gone now, since no one comes to remember us. I have a sister who is building the ofrenda right now at home. I can feel her thinking about me and I can go soon and see all my nieces and nephews..." He trailed off, his empty eye sockets directed just over my shoulder as if he could really see them, just there, in the field of graves behind me.

"Ernesto," I said, hoping to recapture his attention just a little longer. "Hey, did Hector have a family? Was he married? Had kids?"

"Eh? Oh, Hector? No. He was our Don Juan—always charming the ladies—he couldn't make himself get married and settle down, he said. His family here was all gone. He said. I don't know. We were shipmates, and you know how sailors are with stories..." Now he was pulled away, drifting into the air like a dandelion puff and wafting toward the cemetery gates. "Goodbye, Iko," he called, without looking back. "Be a good dog..."

He vanished into the crowd of living and dead, heading for home, I supposed. I stood up, dusting off my knees and butt, thinking that the memorial must have been raised before anyone realized Hector wasn't dead, so it wasn't really wrong, just premature. I wondered how long he'd been "lost at sea" before he'd shown up again in Oaxaca.

Mickey was gaping at me, but I'm used to that. Most people give me strange looks when they catch me talking to ghosts. But Mickey had seen Ernesto, also, as well as the dog, Iko. "How long have you been seeing ghosts?" I asked.

He was too shaken to lie. "Me? I've always seen them, but only during Dia de Muertos. You too?"

"No. I see them all the time. They aren't usually so helpful, though."

"He didn't seem very helpful..."

"He identified the dog and it seems like a safe bet Iko was rescued and raised by Purecete. But that doesn't really answer how Arbildo had the dog's spirit or why she put it in the statue."

"Yeah, maybe..."

I agreed and started for the car.

Mickey caught my arm. "Hey...how come *you* see ghosts? Mi madre says it's because my birthday is Todos Santos. Are you...?"

I shook my head, slipped his grasp, and kept walking for the car. I wasn't sure this was a good conversation. Or that I liked the sudden avid expression in Mickey's eyes.

"C'mon! Tell me!" he yelled. "Please!"

"I'll tell you in the car. This isn't a good place for it," I conceded.

Mickey nearly dragged me back to the parking lot, flinging open the doors for both of us and sliding behind the wheel clumsily in his frenzy.

As soon as the doors were closed he turned to me again, but I shut him down with a look. "Start the car and drive. It's getting dark and I want to get inside before it's full night."

"But—"

"I'll tell you as you drive. If you don't kill us."

He ground the car to life and drove like Mario Andretti to get us out of the parking lot.

"OK," I started. "I died. That's why I see ghosts."

"Died? No way!"

"Yeah, way. Don't ask why, 'cause I don't know. It just is what it is."

He muttered, prayers or curses, I didn't know. "You don't look dead."

"It was only two minutes. But it was enough. Trust me."

"But you didn't just talk to him. What were you doing? Magic?"

"No. I just...pull them out. If they want to talk, they do. Sometimes they don't. Sometimes they try to kill me. Most of them are useless."

"Yeah. I see those, too! They don't really know we're here."

I nodded. "Somehow she must have known..."

"Who? Knew what?"

"Maria-Luz Arbildo. She never met me, but she put me in her will to do this job. She must have known about me, but I don't know why or how or what she expected me to do. I hope I can figure it out before Todos Santos."

"She must have been a bruja," Mickey muttered. "Doing black magic and stuff. I'll bet she scryed you out somehow because of the ghost-thing."

"Maybe," I conceded. "How would I know?"

"Umm... the Santisima Muerta magic goes backward. Y'know: right to left and down to up. Counterclockwise and stuff like that."

"But I never saw the woman do any magic," I reminded him. "I didn't know her."

Big-eyed, Mickey nodded and drove. But I could see his thoughts grinding and the gold strands from his fingertips wrapped the steering wheel like a frantic vine.

We approached the last grave on the list as the sun was beginning to paint its farewell on the slice of sky above Oaxaca's mountains. We'd taken a long drive into the hilly countryside to find the small panteon of San Felipe del Aqua and then trudged through the crowds and the boiling Grey to discover an abandoned burial plot far in the back, under a stunted tree. Grass and weeds had grown over it undisturbed for years and no one was making an effort to clear it. I heaved a sigh of annoyance and got down on my knees to rip up the corn stalk-like growths obscuring the memorial stone. Mickey knelt down and helped brush the dirt aside, scraping the carving clear enough to read in the dimming light.

This time the list was right: Hector Purecete, born 1929, died 1996. Sixty-seven years old.

Mickey sat back on his heels and studied the filth-crusted memorial stone. "He's been forgotten here."

"Maria-Luz remembered him," I said. I didn't know with what emotion she recalled Hector, however, or what she'd been up to with the dog and its black magic spirit bundle. I'd have to take a look and see if the red thread wound counterclockwise around it.

"That's an irony," I said, looking at the stone and thinking aloud. "The only person who seems to remember this guy is already dead and has been for years."

"You mean that other ghost? Ernesto? Yeah. And Iko."

I nodded. "Yeah, that's a problem. Iko seems like a nice dog, but who knows what will happen—if there really is black magic involved, here? I was hoping to find Hector's family or someone who knew him or Maria-Luz. But the registrar will be closed tomorrow and it's not likely I'll find anyone who knew what their relationship was at this point."

"The ghosts know."

I rubbed my face, breathing in the scent of the broken grasses, the turned earth, and the spicy odor of the marigolds that had already been placed onto the grave decorations and ofrendas proliferating throughout the burial ground. I didn't enjoy interviewing ghosts, even when I knew where to find them. Obstinate, limited beings—when they qualified as beings at all—with axes to grind and personal quirks more annoying and unhelpful than a ward full of recovering heroin addicts. "Yeah, but how would I find the right ghosts?" I asked, tired and, I admit, disappointed. "This is going to suck. Purecete's grave wasn't even in Oaxaca proper but way out in this little mountain village."

Mickey jumped up, beaming in the sudden magenta flare of mountain sunset. "You can call them here! You know how and the ghosts will find you if you make the right offerings—it's the Day of the Dead! The living have forgotten this guy, but the dead haven't!"

I stared at him. "I'm not sure I'm following you. The instructions just said to clean the grave and put the dog on it."

"Yeah, yeah. Clean the grave, but you should do the whole thing. Decorate, make an ofrenda. Put out food and drink and stuff—throw a party for old Hector Purecete, and the ghosts of his friends will show up for it! It's not just the living who come visiting the graveyard, you know. Tomorrow is for the angelitos—the little kids. We can make an ofrenda and bring it here for them. If he ever had any kids, or if his family ever had any that haven't died the third death, they'll come. Then on Sunday we can make the party for the rest of 'em—and Hector. I'll have to hang out with Tia Mercedes, but I can help you first and come back later. Tia's big on this stuff, she'll understand—she'll probably even cook extra food for you if we go shopping early enough."

I tried not to groan at the thought. "What about the dog?" I asked.

He frowned. "I'm not sure. Maybe if you don't bring the clay bits and hair, it won't matter, even if his ghost comes along."

The ghost dog had come back from a nose-guided tour of the graveyard to sit down beside me and pant through his doggy grin. He looked increasingly like a real dog and less like the remnant of one. I wondered what he'd be like come Sunday night.

I looked around and saw the deepening colors of the sky. Shadows writhed with the spirits of the violently dead waiting to emerge once darkness fell. I shuddered and hoped we wouldn't have to go past the zocalo and its slaughtered teachers tonight.

"Let's get out of here," I suggested.

Mickey jumped up and we nearly ran back to the car. Once in it, he chattered half in excitement and half in relieved terror, trying to persuade me his plan was solid. I would never have thought of throwing a party for ghosts. Mickey waxing enthusiastic over it was kind of unsettling. He dodged silvery clots of horror as we barreled through the falling twilight.

Back in the guest house, normalcy reigned and most people would have no idea of the gruesome sights and sounds playing out in the night beyond the doors. Over dinner Mickey wheedled his aunt into agreeing to cook extra food for my ghost-party. He finally let me go at the door of my room with a warning to be up early for our shopping trip. I hate shopping... especially in the morning. The surreal quality of the whole day left me dizzy and grateful to crawl into bed.

Bundled up against the chilly morning, we had to shed our coats by the time we were carrying home the third load of the stuff on which Mickey had insisted: colored paper and strings of paper banners; armfuls of flowers; incense cones; food; sweets; candles; tiny toys; papier-mâché skeletons going about their daily business, including one lady called Catrina in an elaborate hat; and a set of combs and brushes for the dead to tidy themselves with, once they arrived for the party. If I didn't know better, I'd have thought he was enjoying himself, but of course Mickey managed to drag me thither and yon with disgusting amounts of energy, while still slouching, glowering, and shooting barbed comments though almost none of them were now directed at me. I bought him a sugar skull with his name on it as a birthday present, getting a twisted, uncertain smile in return.

Iko followed us back and forth, barking and running through the stalls, playing with skeleton children and chasing skeleton rats. The odors of food and flowers and cones of copal incense waiting to be burned mingled with the odor of wet streets and warm bodies. Color rose in dust-devils from the power grid of the Grey and spun off Mickey's shape like the golden rays of a religious icon. I felt light-headed and found it difficult to tell the Grey from the real, if not for the hard shapes of skulls and bones where I would normally expect flesh. More than once I excused myself to a specter after stepping on it and each time they nodded to me as any living person would. Mickey stared at me with a strange yearning expression that disappeared under the glower as soon as he noticed my attention.

I wasn't sure this crazy plan was going to work, but it was the best thing either of us had come up with. And frankly, it was nice to get out of the guesthouse before the smells of food overwhelmed me. Mercedes Villaflores and her daughters had been cooking since before dawn, starting with the pan de muertos—traditional loaves of bread that smelled of orange and spices and had dough bones crossed on top. By the time I'd gotten up, there'd already been half a dozen of them set on the patio counter to cool.

After our shopping, Mickey dropped me off at the cemetery in San Felipe del Aqua to clean the grave site, promising to come back with the ofrenda supplies later. Then he dashed back down the hill to join his family for their own work party. As I crossed the cemetery gate, Iko the ghost dog appeared and followed me to Hector Purecete's plot, making scent-led loops and discursions across the path as we went.

The morning was giving way to afternoon and in the thin air at 5,500 feet, the sun warmed the graveyard and sent the odors of earth and work, flowers and food toward the blue crown of the heavens above. Iko performed an inspection of the site and gave it his doggy approval as I rolled up my sleeves and began clearing weeds, hearing the chatter of others working at family plots, or setting up vendor booths in the square and street nearby. Some musicians started practicing in the distance, serenading our labors in fits and starts. After a while, the ghost dog hied off to hunt ghost rodents, leaving me alone with the weeds.

A while later, I paused to wipe the sweat off my face and found an old man in a wide-brimmed hat squatting at the edge of my efforts, grinning at me. I had to look hard through the thickened and colorful Grey to be sure he was no ghost, for he looked more like a vision than a man. But that might have been the elevation and my own sleep-deprived brain talking.

He held out a clear glass bottle. "Aqua?"

I took the bottle gratefully, muttering my "gracias," and sipped the warm water. It tasted of deep rock wells.

"I never see a gringa working out here before," he said, watching me drink.

"Never been here before," I replied, pushing my clinging hair back and returning the bottle to him.

He put the bottle down, digging its bottom into the dirt I'd softened with my weeding at the edge of the grave. "You come for this man's angelitos?"

"I don't know if he had any. Did you know him?"

The dark-tanned old man shook his head. "No. I live here all my life and I never hear of him until they bury him here. And no one comes to this grave for a long time. Until you. Why?"

"A woman named Maria-Luz Arbildo died last week and she wanted me to come here and take care of the grave."

"Huh. But she never come here. I never see any woman here before."

"No. She didn't know where the grave was. I had to find it. You ever heard of her?"

He narrowed his eyes and searched the ground for his memory, brushing pebbles and bits of weed away from the headstone. "No. Antonio Arbildo lived here, long time ago, but he moved away. Old man, then. He get rich, the whole family go to the D.F.—Distrito

Federale, Mexico City," he explained with a nod. "I'm a little boy, then —so tall," he added, holding his hand up about two feet from the ground, and cackling. He shot an amused glance at me from the corner of his yellowed eyes. The ghost of Iko trotted back from his hunting and threw himself down in the dirt about two feet from the old man with a contented dog sigh. The old man made no comment.

I nodded. Another interesting connection, but not complete. "Are there Arbildos buried in this panteon? Maybe Maria-Luz?"

Again he shook his head, his gnarled-stick fingers digging into the ground to pull a weed. "Not her. Some a long time ago, si. Not now." He pointed to a group of equally abandoned graves nearby. "There."

Hector Purecete had been buried within sight of the Arbildos of San Felipe, yet it seemed Maria-Luz had never found him on her trips to Oaxaca. But with the two false graves Mickey and I had found, maybe that wasn't so strange. Of course the Arbildos of San Felipe and those of Mexico City weren't necessarily the same family, but I doubted it.

I nodded to the old man and got up, unkinking my work-stiff knees and back, to go look at the graves of the Arbildos. The most recent had been buried in 1943. When I got back to Purecete's grave, the old man was gone, but his water bottle still stood in the soft earth between the gravestone and Iko's napping form sprawled in the dirt. I looked around for the man. A dozen hats identical to his bobbed in the field of graves, but I couldn't spot the old man under one. I took another sip of the water and went back to work, thinking Iko had it good.

By two o'clock I'd gotten the weeds cleaned up and the plot squared away. Some helpful live children helped me find stones to replace the missing border around the grave, begging, in return for "mi calavera," which confused me until Mickey showed up.

He made a face at them and started digging into one of the boxes of ofrenda decorations. "They want these," he explained, dragging out a box of small sugar skulls, coffins, and lambs we'd purchased in the market that morning. "Like your trick-or-treat, but with extra skulls."

He handed me the box and snapped at the kids to go away as soon as they had their "calavera" in their sticky fists.

"Need to work, here!" he added to me, unfolding a small card table he'd snatched from the guesthouse. "Usually the ofrenda's at home, but yours will have to be here."

The ghost dog sat up and watched us work. We got a few odd looks from the humans too, as we put up the decorations, but no one came to ask what we were doing. Mickey helped me bend long, slender poles into arches over the table and attach them to the legs. Then we put colored paper over it all and hung up the paper banners, which were decorated with punched silhouettes of skeletons dancing, riding bicycles, eating, and generally carrying on. We made patterns on the grave with the marigolds, magenta cockscomb flowers, and greenery, edging it all with white candles in tiny glass jars.

Mickey looked around. "You should go wash while I put out the food—and bring back water in the big bowl for the spirits to wash in, too."

I shrugged, not minding a pause to clean the dirt and sweat off my face and hands while Mickey took over—he had managed to avoid the really filthy work of weeding, edging, and shoring up the grave, after all. Iko dogged me to a standpipe where a few other people were washing up and filling containers with water for flowers or washing. The old man was standing near the water spigot and grinned at me as I approached.

"It is going well, your ofrenda?"

"I think so. Does it look OK?"

He glanced toward Purecete's grave. "Si. Is very nice for the angelitos—white is good."

"Mickey picked the color."

"Really?" the old guy said, raising his eyebrows. "Surely for him, red is more likely."

I turned to glance back at Mickey. He did have a lot of red in his aura.

"You mean Mickey?" I asked.

"Your amigo joven, si. So very angry..." He shook his head.

I stared at the old man. "What is it about Oaxaca? Is everyone around here tuned in to the freaky frequency?" I asked.

His laugh was like sandpaper. "Only you, pequeño faisán. But, you are staying to see the angelitos?"

"Si," I answered, turning back to the immediate, putting my hands under the cold water that streamed from the pipe, and then throwing several handfuls onto my sticky face. Iko stuck his muzzle into the water and tried to drink it, but I wasn't sure any was making it down his ghostly throat, no matter how fast his spectral tongue was going. "Maybe it's not so bad that Mickey's supposed to be home with his family tonight."

"Maybe." The old man nodded. "I also must go tonight, so I bid you buenos noches. Dress warm—the night takes the heat away. And give your amigo good wishes from Tio Muñoz, eh?"

"I will, gracias," I replied, filling the wash bowl for the spirits of dead children. My hands full, I nodded again to him and turned to head back to the plot, wondering what Mickey was up to.

"Buena suerte," the man said with a chuckle as I started off.

I turned my head to look back at him over my shoulder and saw him scratch Iko's head, smiling. I guess I wasn't even surprised. Then he turned and walked away, vanishing into the crowd with a golden glitter in his wake. I stood a moment staring after him, not sure what he was, nothing about him seemed ghostly, yet in the mess of the active Grey of Oaxaca, I hadn't noticed he had no aura. What was he? I frowned, holding the heavy bowl of water. Iko pawed at my knee and barked, prancing impatiently on the path.

I shook off my surprise and walked to rejoin Mickey.

While I'd been gone, Mickey had laid out a small feast of sweets, soda pop, and pan de muerto as well as some more substantial food— all provided by his aunt. Small plastic toys were scattered among the cockscomb flowers that we'd piled up around a stack of empty boxes at the back of the table and an arc of small tea cups and saucers surrounded a dish for the copal incense. A dozen more white candles now stood on the boxes. It looked like an album cover for something gothy and fantastic.

"Nice, huh?"

"Umm…yeah. These ghosts eat a lot."

Mickey shrugged. "They eat the spirit of the food. My cousins say the food they leave behind has no calories." He barked a derisive laugh. He pointed to the end of the table. "Put the water, comb, and towel where the hot bottle is."

I saw a large vacuum flask where he pointed.

"Tia Mercedes made hot chocolate. You can put it on the ground till you need it," he said. "Pour some for the angelitos after you light the candles and the incense—they should come when they smell it. And there's a box under the ofrenda with some food and a blanket and stuff for you. Think you can make it?"

"It's not as cold as a stake out during a Seattle winter."

He snorted. "Gonna be empty up here. Most people do this at home." Mickey gave me an assessing look that clearly found me a bit wanting.

"I think I can handle it," I said.

Yet another shrug as he started gathering up the excess supplies. "The angelitos come at four and stay until the morning. You'll have to do it all again tomorrow for the adults, too. I'll pick you up when the sun comes up."

"Hey, Mickey, Tio Muñoz says Happy Birthday."

He jumped back from me. "What?"

"An old man near the water pipe said I should tell you he sends his good wishes."

He stared at me. "Tio Muñoz? Mierda! He's a legend in my family. He's a…a…"

"Ghost? Didn't look like a ghost."

Mickey was shaking his head and gathering the excess stuff in a hurry. "No, no. He's the one—you know: I said about my great uncle? What's the word…a bad wizard."

"Warlock?"

He shook his head. "No. Not a brujo. He's…a black sorcerer. Undead." He threw the last of the materials into a box and snatched it up against his chest, eyes wild—which was not what I'd have expected. "I'm going back to Tia Mercedes. You'll be fine, yeah?"

"Yeah…" I said, not sure why he was freaking so thoroughly, since his Tio Muñoz wasn't any kind of undead I knew.

"Yeah, right. OK. I'll be back for you in the morning. Don't go talking to Tio Muñoz! Don't believe what he says!"

Iko and I followed him with the rest of the boxes and loaded them into the Chevy under the weight of Mickey's red-and-orange brooding. Then we watched him drive away, leaving the ghost dog and I in the emptying panteon as the hour of dead children approached.

The last of the homeward-bound walked out of the gate—two small children in slightly rumpled clothes—strewing a path of marigold petals for the dead. In a mood of strange solemnity, I watched them lay the deep orange line down the road until they disappeared around a bend. I walked back to the grave, Iko dancing before me all the way.

The ghost dog seemed more real than ever, if still a bit translucent. As the long shadow of the mountain began to steal the light, that became less apparent, but a new oddity began to show around him: a blue glow like marsh light that flickered over the dog-shape and cast it into strange silhouette against the pockets of twilight forming in the cemetery as night crept forward.

I unfolded a camp stool from the box and set it aside, paused to put on my coat, and dug deeper for a box of kitchen matches. As the church bell began pealing four, I lit the candles and the copal, sending the sweet, musky scent into the cooling air. The breeze stirred the grasses near the fence to rattling. Smoke and Grey mingled, sparking with gold and white lights. I could hear the Grey humming, the shapes of the mountains glowing in the silvery mist as great bulks of power.

Something splashed into the water bowl and I turned with a jerk to see nothing, no small shape lurking near the table end, as I'd half expected. I shivered as my skin prickled with a premonition of movement nearby. The darkness was still only a threat, but a sense of presence seemed to gather with it, though nothing stepped forth. Yet.

I poured hot chocolate into one of the tea cups and sat down to wait while afternoon advanced toward evening. The ghost dog lay down beside me and smiled with secret thoughts. We waited, swirled in the dizzying odors of the night and the sound of distant music from houses just out of sight, alone in the hush of sacred anticipation in the doorway to the land of the dead.

Something brushed past me, giggling. Iko barked and chased the formless whisper of laughter across the burial ground toward the iron gates. Then nothing. The ghost dog returned and threw himself down on the ground with a dog sigh. Candles smoked and the stream of incense swayed upward like a charmed cobra. The muttering emptiness of the cemetery held sway long past sunset, past the eight o'clock peal from the church tower.

I renewed the hot chocolate in the cup and sipped a little myself, finding it more bitter and spicy than American chocolate. It went better with the sandwich Mickey's aunt had packed for me than the coffee did, but I thought I'd better save it in case of tiny haunts. Maybe it was because I was thinking of it, but that was when a little cup of chocolate on the table rattled and I looked again at the ofrenda.

One of the cups was moving in its saucer, tilting forward and back. Tiny silver-mist hands clutched for it and missed again and again. I stood up and picked up the cup, saying, "Here, let me help you."

I held the cup low and filled it to the brim. Then I offered it down around my knees, holding it still until I felt something tug on it. I let myself slip all the way into the Grey looking for whatever was pulling on the cup.

A skeleton child, barely as tall as the table, reached for the cup. Its bony, incorporeal hands met the porcelain, but couldn't grip. I tipped the cup and watched the steaming chocolate dribble onto the ground while the foggy skeleton seemed to nibble at the edge of the cup. It pushed the cup away and clacked its teeth in satisfaction.

The toys on the table moved. Smears of color hovered around the ofrenda, lined up in front of the other, empty, cups. I poured chocolate into all of them and watched shadows of the cups tilt and rise as spectral hands reached for the sweets. There was a burst of chatter—like radio static—and a dozen small skeletons dressed in the memories of their best clothes, appeared around the table. They weren't as well-formed as the adult ghosts I'd seen—as if they hadn't had time to get the knack of being alive before they were dead. None of the chatter was quite understandable to me—unlike the adult ghosts I'd talked to—coming through to my mind only in Spanish.

Iko jumped to his feet again and began trotting around the little ghosts, sniffing them, but he returned disgruntled and disappointed to my side and sat down with a huff of breath. Apparently none of the skeletal kids was familiar.

I felt small hands on my knees and plucking at my sleeves. I looked down and found two small skeletons dressed in cloudy white dresses looking back up at me with empty eye sockets.

I'm not much of a kid person, so I never know what to say or how to act when faced with children. I had no idea if the ghosts of children knew any more than they had when alive, but even children have information. I squatted down, feeling my bad knee pop.

"No hablo Espanol muy bien," I said, probably mangling what little I remembered from years living in Los Angeles. With my luck they didn't speak anything else, but sometimes ideas came through with ghosts, even when the language was foreign, as they had with the ghost of Ernesto Santara. "Ustedes habla Ingles?"

They turned their skulls on their slender spines in unison: no. They didn't bother to talk at all, but, with a shiver, I knew they were twins then, and they wanted to know why I was in their graveyard. No one had come for them in a long time and they were lonely—was I a relative of theirs? How I knew these thoughts I couldn't begin to tell you.

I shook my head and pointed to Purecete's memorial stone. "I'm looking for him. And for Maria-Luz Carmen Arbildo. Maria-Luz y Hector."

Two skulls tilted in curiosity as if to say "why those two?" while a toy truck pushed its way across the dirt nearby guided by a misty skeletal boy.

"Umm..." I started, not sure how to explain. "Como Maria-Luz...

umm… knows?" I stumbled through the language, tapping the side of my head and hoping the sign translated somehow, "Hector?"

The skulls consulted each other with a glance of unseen eyes. They turned back to me and spoke as one. The words pushed the concept into my head, naked and complete, but not in English. "Él es su padre."

Their father. Whose burial place she did not seem to know, whose name she did not have. "Oh," I breathed, the situation both more clear and less. Why the black-magic present, then? What was the nature of that paternity that she sent such a dubious gift?

The twin ghosts beckoned me to follow and they drifted toward the Arbildo plot. Leaving the chocolate and the ofrenda behind, I followed them and Iko followed me.

The graves of the Arbildos were crowded with tiny skeletons and strange, half-formed shapes of silvery energy thick as clay moving in some somber dance. The two skeletal girls floated through the weird party and stopped before a grave with an unusual double cross of gilded iron from which the gold had flaked until only shreds remained. "Nuestra madre y nosotros."

This was the grave of Dulcia Maria-Carmen Ochoa Arbildo, wife of Antonio, and her two daughters, Carmen and Lucia, who had all died April of 1936. The girls had been four years old. Dulcia had been twenty-five.

"Por qué—" I started, but the ghosts of Carmen and Lucia pointed their bony fingers at the crowd of small spirits.

"Vea: nuestros hermanos y hermanas."

I looked. Beside the grave huddled a knot of unformed shapes, the features of lives they never lived flickered and changed, fluid as water, over half-faces the size of my fist. I'd seen this before; they were transient souls, in flux between one life and the next. Grave upon grave across the plot was littered with the reminders of children who had never been born, or died while still infants and toddlers. They were everywhere, generation after generation of the family's bad genetic luck and horrific accident. It seemed as if the Arbildos of San Felipe had been cursed.

Maybe, against all tradition, this was something the family

preferred to forget. Hardly a wonder, then, if Antonio Arbildo had removed his family from this place as soon as he had the money to do so. Not too surprising if he had named a boat for his ill-fated wife, or that the boat had been lost with everyone aboard, except a single man and a dog.

A dark shape started to push the grid into some new form, struggling against the strength of the Grey's energy lines. Iko barked suddenly and the deep humming of the Grey hit a sour note. The ghosts flickered out with a collective gasp. The shape collapsed back into darkness and I was alone again in the graveyard.

I still didn't have all the pieces, but an idea was forming in my head. Dead children and a daughter by the wrong father... I returned to my camp stool and sat again beside Purecete's grave, pouring the last of the chocolate and wondering if the ghosts would return.

They didn't.

Dawn came up slowly in cold shades of blue, while I huddled, expectant and ultimately disappointed, in the empty panteon. It was still lit only by candles and drifted with copal smoke when Mickey arrived.

He avoided my glance and packed up the food and containers, the toys and gewgaws in glowering silence. I let him. My body was too tired and my brain too full of strange threads weaving slowly and incompletely into a tapestry I didn't yet understand to want to add the frustration of cross-examining my volatile escort to the mix. I followed him back to the Chevy, hardly noticing that Iko had disappeared with the dawn and didn't follow us to the car this time.

Back at the guesthouse, I fell into bed and slept eight hard hours. I was still a bit groggy when I turtled out of my bedroom and down to the empty sala about noon. The visitors had all gone out, most of the family was at church or in the kitchen. Mercedes Villaflores glanced out of the kitchen window and waved to me to come inside.

"Buenos dias! Did you enjoy your evening?" she asked, immediately putting a cup of coffee and a plate of food on the counter for me.

"Yes," I replied, not sure if "enjoy" was the right word, but certain I'd learned something, if I could shake it into clarity. "Where's Mickey

—Miguel?" I sipped the coffee and felt it kick my system back up to speed. I looked for Iko, but didn't see him and was just wondering about that when Mercedes replied.

"Oh, he's still asleep." She shrugged and returned to her stove, chatting over her shoulder. "Teenagers. You know."

Thinking about the missing ghost dog and Mickey made me think of the cemetery. "Mercedes... Who's Tio Muñoz?"

"Tio Muñoz? Where did you hear of him?"

"Mickey mentioned him."

"Ah! That boy...he's such a trouble. Muñoz is...the family boogey man. You know: the crazy uncle your mama tells you will take you away in the night if you don't finish your supper. Totalmente loco en la cabeza," she added, knocking a knuckle against her temple, as if sounding a melon for ripeness. "He was accused of working black magic long ago, but he ran up into the hills and disappeared. I think, if he is alive, he is no trouble to anyone, just a crazy old man. If not... maybe he'll come to dinner tonight, eh?"

She laughed, clearly she didn't feel the same horror as her nephew, but then she wasn't fascinated with black magic, as Mickey was.

"Do you know anything about the Arbildo family that used to live in San Felipe de Aqua?" I asked.

She just shook her head.

I poked at my food and thought. I was seeing a picture that was not at all pretty. I wished I was sure what had turned Maria-Luz from sweet on Jimenez to sour. Why hadn't Jimenez told her where Pure-cete was buried? Was that the key? Or had she discovered something else?

I fished the little baggie of statue shards from my jacket pocket and stared at the bundle of hairs, tied with red thread, wound counter-clockwise. The magic goes backward... Like the writing on the paper. I could see the slip of notepaper clearly in my mind: the letters cramped on the left, expansive on the right, as if it had been written backward, running out of space... She'd scryed me out through the Grey, talking to ghosts through a magic connection as Mickey had described. Death magic, blood magic... Had Maria-Luz sacrificed the dog? No, Iko was dead long before she knew about me—possibly before I was a Greywalker—back when Jimenez died in a plane crash. Just how long had Maria-Luz had the statute waiting for the right grave? Why had she wanted to put Iko's spirit, wound in black magic, on Jimenez's grave?

Tio Muñoz seemed more interested in Mickey than in me. But if he was—or had been—some kind of sorcerer, maybe he was interested in the black magic I was carrying in my pocket as well as his great nephew. You can't count on much about black magic or boogey men, though he didn't seem to approve of Mickey's personal darkness.

I needed to talk to Maria-Luz or Hector Purecete. I hoped one or both would show up once darkness fell at San Felipe de Aqua.

Mickey scuffed into the kitchen looking morose and wan.

"We still on for tonight, Mickey?" I asked.

"Huh? Tonight?"

"Yeah. My little ghost party at the panteon, remember? You're going to help me with the set-up, right?"

He looked relieved I hadn't said anything about Tio Muñoz. "Yeah, right. Set-up. Sure."

"What time do we need to head up the mountain? Four?"

"Dusk. Whatever. Tia Mercedes won't mind if I'm late back for the party here."

She said something in Spanish that sounded like she'd be happier the later he was.

"OK," he replied. "We can leave at four with the food and stuff."

"Cool. See you down here, then," I agreed, carrying my empty coffee cup to the sink and allowing Mickey to escape.

I walked down to the zocalo and found a cafe table to occupy while I made a phone call. The layers of spirits and magic were thicker and brighter than ever, surging like an ocean in the plaza and spilling into the streets leading to it. I dialed Quinton's pager and waited for him to call me back. Quinton was still paranoid about the possibility of being re-discovered by his ex-boss, so the easily-tracked technology of cellphones was one he chose to do without.

About half an hour later, as I was working on a sunburn, he returned my call.

"Hey."

"Hey, yourself. Need a favor."

"Shoot."

"I don't have Internet access here, so can you run some searches for me and get back with information before four p.m. here?"

"That's...two here. Yeah, I can do that. What are the search terms?"

"I need everything you can find on the death and bio of a Mexico City lawyer named Jimenez. Sorry I don't know the first name, but he was the partner of a guy named Guillermo Banda. Jimenez died in a plane crash a few years ago. Also anything on the Arbildo family that owned a ship or boat called the *Dulcia* that sank in 1982, based out of Mexico. And look for any connections between Jimenez's firm and Arbildo—especially anything shady or questionable."

"Arbildo. That's the woman who left you the dog."

"Her family and her lawyer, yeah. There's something strange going on between them and, so far, death hasn't proved to be much of a barrier. I'm also wondering if Maria-Luz was adopted, but it's doubtful there'd be any record of that on the Internet."

"You never know. I'll see what I can get and call you back."

I thanked Quinton and hung up before going out to walk around the zocalo and take a closer look at the Grey grid of Oaxaca. There were a lot of things about the way energy flowed here that were different from Seattle's grid and I didn't want to be surprised that night. I needed a little local practice with the power lines before I felt comfortable about my ability to deal with the potential conflicts that might be in store. I tried a variation of the ghost-pull that had brought up Ernesto Santara and got Iko, as I'd hoped. I was pretty sure I'd be able to banish him again, if I had to. I still had no idea what part he had been intended to play at Hector's grave.

Quinton called back and I took notes about the perfidy of lawyers; hard financial times; an unhappy school girl with bad, black habits; and the sinking of insured boats while leaning against an old church wall, cooled by the shade of the stones and the ice-water feeling of the rising tide of ghosts. The ghost dog panted at my feet, tongue lolling onto the bricks of the plaza.

A silvery skeleton dressed in a dark vest and trousers paused to pet the dog and raised his head to me. "Este su perro?"

"Hang on," I told Quinton. "My dog? No," I replied to the skeleton-man. "You know this dog? Uh…Usted…uh…" I stumbled through the language as badly as ever, but the ghost seemed to know what I meant.

He shook his skull and clacked some words I didn't catch, but the meaning seemed clear enough. It wasn't his dog, but it might have been Estancio Rivera's dog. I pointed at Iko. "Esta perro?"

The skeleton nodded his skull vigorously. "Si! Es Iko!"

Iko rolled over in the spectral dust and offered his belly for rubbing.

I returned to my phone call while the skeleton man gave Iko some attention. "Is there any mention in those files of an Estancio Rivera?" I asked Quinton.

"Not that I've seen, but Rivera is about the most common name in Mexico after Garcia. This is in Oaxaca, right…?"

I could hear his fingers speeding on a keyboard. "Yeah."

"Huh. This is kind of weird. A guy named Estancio Rivera disappeared from a Mexico City hotel room in 1981, presumed dead. Wallet, ID, and clothes were found, but not his money or the man. ID was from Oaxaca. He worked in a Mezcal distillery and guess who owned it?"

"Arbildo?"

"Give the little lady a cigar! Currently run by Leon Arbildo, a son of the founder."

"Damn," I muttered. Did I have it? Was it that easy? Hector was the missing Estancio as well as Maria-Luz's real father. He'd vanished in Mexico City where the Arbildos lived. Then changed his name and taken a post on an Arbildo ship that sank… He'd been "dead" twice before he died for good.

The skeleton ghost stood up, tipped his hat, and walked off after wishing me "Buenos noches." I nodded at him and noticed the shadow of the church was nearly across the plaza now. The tower bells began tolling four.

"I have to run. Thanks for the help."

"No problem, but I would like to hear the story."

"I'll take you to dinner when I get back and tell you the whole thing. Right now I have an appointment in a graveyard."

I shut off the phone and ran back toward the Villaflores guesthouse. Iko barked and ran along beside me. We skittered into the doorway together and straight into a glowering Mickey.

"Thought you'd ditched me."

"No," I panted. "Just lost track of time. You ready to go?"

He frowned at me, clearly teetering on a decision.

"Come on, Mickey. You didn't come up here just for the family celebration." I leaned in close to him and breathed my words into his ear. "You want the magic."

He bit his lip.

I wanted all the help I could get, and even if Mickey didn't know what he could do, he could still be useful if things went bad. And a plain "please" was not going to work with him.

He gave a sudden, hard nod. "I'm coming."

We grabbed our coats and boxes and bundled into the car as fast as possible. Iko sat and waited patiently, then vanished to meet us at the graveyard.

The sun was already gone by the time we reached the panteon at San Felipe de Aqua. A procession by candlelight was wending to the cemetery, carried on a wave of music. We parked and joined the crowd that surged into the cemetery, Iko reappearing as before, just inside the gates.

The ofrenda and decorations were untouched and it took only a few minutes to put out the food and drink, trinkets, cigarettes, mezcal, and wash water, to light the candles and the copal. We both sat down to wait while the ghost dog circled the graves, sniffing.

The odors of food, flowers, incense, and alcohol floated into the air on mariachi music and the chatter of living humans while the Grey hummed like a generator nearing overload. The thin silver mist world seemed to quake as the ghosts flooded out, eager, hungry, happy. They rushed into the gap between the worlds with a roar. I gasped at the explosive upheaval of the Grey and Mickey stared, crouching on his stool like an angular gargoyle.

"How many do you see?" I asked.

"Thousands...more than ever. And there's...stuff. Like worms. Everywhere."

Everyone who can see it, sees it differently, I guess.

"Where's our man?" Mickey looked around, shivering. "Maybe... the dog?"

"Yeah, maybe it's time. Iko," I called, reaching down the pat the ground on top of the grave, sending up a sudden scented gust of marigold and earth. Iko ran onto the grave and sat down. Nothing changed.

Remembering the children and their chocolate, I put out my hand. "Hand me that mezcal, Mickey."

Quivering, Mickey picked up the bottle and slapped it into my outstretched hand. "You want a drink?"

"No. But I think Señor Purecete might—or Estancio Rivera, if he prefers." I twisted the bottle open and spilled an ounce or two onto the grave next to Iko. The ground seemed to swallow it, groaning and heaving a cloud of yellow and gold sparks into the air.

Someone crawled up from the grave.

He was probably a slim man in life, judging by the narrow-cut clothes his skeletal form wore in death. He had a jaunty hat on his skull and a scarf tied around the absent circumference of his neck. A shadow of flesh clung over the skeleton, giving it a blurry, out of focus look. Iko whined and wriggled at the ghost's feet, rolling in the dirt and showing his belly.

"Oh...Iko," the shade breathed, the words coming clear into my head. "Where is your mistress?" He scratched the dog as it quivered in delight.

"Not here yet," I offered. "But I think she'll show up soon."

Mickey glanced around and I followed his lead, but no one was paying us any particular attention. They were all busy and the sounds of the fiesta ramping up to last the whole night through drowned the oddness of any conversation we might have.

I held out the bottle and the ghost took it. "Gracias, Señora. It is a long time since I had a drink with a lovely lady." A spectral twin of the Mezcal bottle rose to his mouth and he poured a long shot down his transparent throat.

"Ernesto said you were a lady's man," I said.

The ghost of Hector Purecete belched and lowered the bottle. "Ernesto? From the *Dulcia*? Poor fellow. Good hearted, not so good headed. I'm sorry about the crew. It was only me Arbildo wanted drowned."

"So it wasn't an accident that the boat sank when you were on it. Jimenez found a way to sink it for Arbildo. The insurance company wasn't sure, but they suspected it. You know they paid off, eventually, right?"

"Oh si. It was an old boat. Kill two birds with one stone—heh. Or two problems with one hole in the hull. He didn't want her to know, or he'd have just had me cut to pieces in an alley in the Distrito."

"Leon Arbildo, you mean."

"Si," Hector replied, taking another gulp of ghostly mezcal. "Leon had a head for business."

"What was her name?"

"Who?"

"Leon Arbildo's wife. You met her at the Mezcal distillery, didn't you?"

"Ohhhh…Consuela. No, we met at a party. She was very bored. So was I. But of different things." Hector drew closer to the table and looked it over, pausing to scratch Iko behind the ears a pat his sides roughly. "I imagined I was so very suave she fell at my feet, but I suppose it was truly that I was new and not like Leon." He laughed and his yellow teeth snapped together with a sound like castanets. "Youth is arrogant and full of folly."

He put out a skeleton claw for the towel and water. Mickey and I watched him in silence as the ghost washed his non-existent face and combed his memory of hair. Then the specter straightened his scarf and re-settled the hat on his head before surveying the spread of food.

Mickey's eyes couldn't stretch any wider without the orbs falling out, I thought. "They never speak," he whispered. "I never hear them speak..."

"Get used to it," I muttered back. "Once they know you can hear them, they don't shut up."

The boy jerked his head toward me, drawing a breath that shook in his throat. He was more excited than the dog.

Hector—I couldn't think of him as Estancio after all this time—had torn off a hunk of phantom bread and sat on the edge of his grave, munching it. His teeth clicked and ground together. "I thought I would never taste pan de muerto again. It's very good."

"Mi—mi tia lo hizo," Mickey stammered, replying in Spanish, since he heard Hector in that language, just as I heard him in English.

Hector looked at him for the first time and the boy flinched back at the uncanny gaze from the ghost's empty eye sockets.

"Your aunt? You must thank her for me. My Carmenita—my little girl Leon called Maria-Luz—could not bring me food and drink for these many years. She was afraid the lawyers would discover her knowledge of me and of what they would do if she came here. I left my home to be with Consuela—her mother—and I hid myself as a long-dead man, Hector Purecete, who would not mind. At first I did it to be near Consuela and later, when they thought they'd killed me, to watch over my daughter."

Bones and wings rustled in the darkness and a sigh of unearthly wind brought another ghost to the party.

"Papa."

We all turned to look at the smaller spirit that had walked up to Hector Purecete's grave. She wouldn't have been very tall in life, but she had probably had her father's build. A gleaming, oil-black nimbus surrounded her, shivering off the white surface of her dress. The memory of her face was still strong, creating a translucent veil of phantom flesh and expression over the visible bones of her skull. So this was Maria-Luz Carmen Arbildo.

The dog jumped into the air and barked in joy, running to tangle under her feet.

The ghost woman laughed and patted the dog. Then she looked sharply at me. "You brought him. But what happened? He should not be loose already."

"The statue was broken at Customs," I answered. "I think Guillermo Banda paid someone to do it."

"That bastard. I hate him. More than I ever hated Jimenez for what he did."

I opened my mouth to ask her how she'd known what Jimenez had done—though I thought I knew—but was cut off by a shriek of eldritch wind.

"Don't dare!"

"Dare what? To tell the truth?" Maria-Luz screamed, turning to the latest arrival.

This skeleton-ghost was dressed in a suit—possibly the one he'd died in—much like Banda's suit. I guessed this must be Jimenez since he'd come when named and he was royally pissed about it.

"Bruja. Your father knew what you were up to. We followed you for your own good!"

"Liar!" she shouted, smacking him across his grinning, naked jaw with her bone-claw hand. "Leon Arbildo was not my father. That's why you followed me. That's why you spied on me and my real father. You said you were looking for him, but you weren't. You tried to hide him from me—you tried to take him from me when I was still a child. That's why you wrecked the boat, why you killed all those people. To get rid of my father!" So she had known about Jimenez, about Arbildo's sinking of the boat, and about the graves Jimenez had not reported to her. No wonder she'd been mad when he died.

"You don't know the truth, Luzita. The *Dulcia* sank because it was old."

Still more ghosts flooded toward our little huddle of misery, perhaps a dozen, all drenched in sea water. I spotted Ernesto Santara, but he didn't look at me. He kept his empty gaze on the ghost of Jimenez. He was no longer a pleasant haunt, but an angry one. The drowned crew moved toward the dead lawyer and Iko stalked along with them, hackles raised, teeth bared.

"My dog!" Maria-Luz screamed at me. "Give me my dog!"

I held up the bundle of hair and pot shards. "This?" I asked.

Maria-Luz lunged at me. Mickey leapt to his feet but I'd already pulled a bit of the Grey between us and the furious woman's shade recoiled with a screech.

"Mickey, keep her back," I said, in the calmest voice I could muster. "Me? How?"

"Just like you kept Señora Acoa from dying. Just put out your hands and send that feeling toward Maria-Luz."

Jimenez was backing away, starting to fade, but I grabbed him, sinking my fingers into the stinging electrical fire of his ghostly form.

"No, no. You have to face the music, Counselor," I said.

Mickey was talking as fast as he could, crooning, and holding his hands between himself and Maria-Luz. The gold strings spun out from his fingertips, stroking over her, making her more solid, more alive-seeming. She began to cry.

Jimenez struggled in my grip. "Let me go, puta loco!"

I waved the bundle of Iko's figurine at him. "You want me to give this to her? You dodged this bullet before, but I can make sure it hits you this time." I was guessing, but I knew Maria-Luz had not meant any comfort for Jimenez when she'd tried to have Iko sent to him before. Iko jumped and snapped at him, snarling.

Jimenez froze and the crew gathered tight around him. I let him go so they could hold him prisoner, themselves. They muttered to him and the sound raised the hair on my arms.

Mickey shot me a panicked look over his shoulder and I stepped closer to him. Maria-Luz was still standing in front of him, looking almost solid, while Hector hovered just behind her, clucking and making the soothing noises people murmur to upset children.

"It's all right, Mickey. You can stop."

"But—I—what—?"

"Ask Tio Muñoz."

Mickey jerked his gaze back and forth, searching for the boogey man. We were creating a ruckus. The other partiers in the cemetery were beginning to look our way with curiosity and even the vampires were drawing closer.

I sat down on my stool and tried to act like there was nothing at all strange at our feast of souls. I bobbed my head and let my feet tap in time with the brass and strings of the mariachis nearby. I motioned to Maria-Luz, who wafted closer. Jimenez was still petrified in the circle of dead sailors.

"All right," I started. "You tried to give the dog to Jimenez before, then you decided to give it to Hector, and then you gave it to me to give to Hector. Why?"

She hung her head. "At first, I was angry. Iko never liked those lawyers—"

"A good judge of character," Hector injected.

"Iko was all I had after Papa—went away. And when Iko died, that was all I knew how to do, all I could think of to keep him for a little longer—to take me to Mictlan someday."

"Some people think this is a very bad kind of magic."

"It's not. It's just...the dark kind. The death magic. What is death but part of life? And my dog was dead. I had done bad things with the magic when I was angry at that...man who called himself my father," she spat, "but I never meant harm with keeping Iko. But I found out Jimenez had lied to me. He had never tried to find out what happened to my father. He spied on me and he took the information to Leon and they tried to kill my father a third time so he had to run here and hide. I was so angry when I found out what he had done, I wanted to punish him! I thought Iko would keep him from Mictlan. Keep him in limbo and torment, forgotten but never released to the third death, wandering the way he had done to the sailors on the *Dulcia*."

"Tell the rest, pequeña," Hector urged.

She sobbed for a moment. Mickey sat next to me, wide eyed and still, watching the ghostly woman weep until she raised her head and looked at him. "You understand the magic, you know how hard it is... to be good. It was so hard, but I thought I should do a better thing. I changed my will so Iko would go to my father, to help him find the road, and I gave all the money for the families of the sailors. Leon and the insurance company gave them nothing. I thought I could repair the wrong, even if the magic was a little...dark."

"But the will I saw doesn't give the money to the families of the *Dulcia's* crew."

"No." She hung her head, ashamed. "Banda changed it. I don't know why I thought he was different than Jimenez. They were both charming liars..."

"Banda forged your will."

She nodded. "He is my father's man, even after death. Just like that pig," she added spitting in Jimenez's direction. Her spittle hissed and raised a red spark on the ground where it hit.

Jimenez recoiled, but kept silent.

Hector tapped her again and motioned her on.

Maria-Luz sighed the smell of earth and copal. "The spirits told me of you. I was sick with the cancer that killed me, but they came when I called and they said you could fix the horrible mess of this. I believed them. I told Banda to give the dog to you. I thought you could solve my puzzle of the graves, find out what had happened and make it right. And my Papa and Iko could be together again."

"So...this bit of junk controls Iko's soul..."

Maria-Luz and Hector nodded together.

I studied the bit of hair and thread. I glanced at Mickey.

"What do you think? Eternal torment for Jimenez? Or can we do something else with this?"

The boy was trembling. "Why are you asking me?" he demanded.

"Because you have the magic. And Maria-Luz doesn't anymore. She's dead, Mickey. She can't change the things she did."

"I don't have any magic! Just the ghosts! That's why I read up on Santisima Muerta—so I could use the ghosts for magic," he finished in a harsh whisper.

"You already have the magic. You do. Look at your hands."

"They're just hands!"

"Look at them the way you look at the ghosts—sideways, through the worms and lights and crazy mist. Look softly."

He stared down at his gangling, oversized paws, flexing them slowly in and out of fists and turning his head side to side. Tears began to well and fall over his lower lids as he stared without blinking. "It's—there's something on my fingers..."

"Yeah. That's it. That glowy stuff. Real magic, brat-boy. Live magic."

He stared at me. "Do you—?"

I shook my head. "No. I don't have anything like that. I just see ghosts." That wasn't strictly true, but that wasn't the time for messy little details. "But I can tell you that's life magic, not death magic. If you die, it goes away. That's what's happened to Maria-Luz."

He glanced all around the panteon, taking note of the ghosts, the living, the dead...and Tio Muñoz who sat on the ground among the tombs of the Arbildos and smiled at us, glimmering with a golden sheen.

"What do you think?" I asked again. "Should we sic Iko on Jimenez for eternity? Poor old Iko, faithful unto death and beyond. I'm not sure he deserves an eternity spent snapping at the heels of this scum."

"No," the lawyer agreed, and was silenced again by the drowned crew that surrounded him.

Maria-Luz and Hector hung on the moment, watching Mickey.

"What...what about the other one? The guy who faked the will?"

"Banda," I supplied. "Yeah, he's a piece of work."

"Can you—?"

"You, Mickey. I can deliver the bomb, but only you can build it. Iko hates him. All you have to do is make the magic go the right way so it's alive. If the magic is tuned for Banda, Iko will seem to be alive to him, but he'll still be a ghost-dog to everyone else."

I cut a glance at Maria-Luz. "Then all we have to do is tether Iko to Banda..."

She nodded. "I think...it can be done. If you rewind the thread just right."

"But what will happen to the dog? Will it...be..."

"Doomed to eat lawyer in hell?" I added.

Mickey nodded, but he was looking at Maria-Luz, now.

"Wind the thread the other way, wind it to the life of the man," Maria-Luz whispered, beginning to fade. "Iko will come to me when his job is done. Or when you break your binding."

Was it so late...or so early that the night was ending already? No, I could see it was still dark. But she was tiring, her energy fading after such an evening—her first and probably last return from the Land of the Dead. Only the sailors and Jimenez were as present as ever. Hector and his daughter had started to slide away.

"You'd better start before Maria-Luz is all gone, or you might lose the chance," I prompted Mickey.

"But..."

"Try it. What's the worst that can happen? You let the dog go. Right?"

"Yeah. Right."

I handed Mickey the bag of Iko's shards. He took the bundle of hair out and began picking the red thread loose. He concentrated, pulling the thread loose, unwinding it with care.

Iko began to fade with a whimper.

"No, Iko," Hector called to the dog in a singsong voice, thin as steam. "No, perrito, stay. Good dog..."

"Think of the man," Maria-Luz whispered. "Think of him, Jimenez's partner, Banda, the lawyer, the thief, the fraud..." she pointed toward the thread, a stream of her knowledge flowing out of her skeletal fingertips, touching the boy and the bundle of hair.

Mickey rewound the red strand the other way, muttering under this breath. The gold threads from his fingers caught on the hairs in the bundle, caught in the twist of the thread and bound up, muttering with Mickey, singing magic, alive and golden and hot as the sun.

Hector and Maria-Luz stepped backward, back, back, fading as they went, until they were only a whisper and a shred of smoke on the air. Iko stopped whining.

A hush fell, as if all the spirits of San Felipe de Aqua held their breath.

Mickey tied off the string. "There. OK? You think?" he asked, holding it out. But there was no one left to see it but me and Tio Muñoz.

The old man had come up on us without any warning or apparent movement.

"Muy bien!" he cackled.

Mickey started with surprise, jumping to his feet. The old man backed away, chuckling.

"Where did they all go?" Mickey asked, bewildered.

"Back where they came from, I'd guess. The sailors took Jimenez—I think he may be in for some trouble in the afterlife," I said.

"Good!" Mickey spat.

"And Maria-Luz and her father went...wherever."

"To Mictlan," Mickey corrected. "I think."

"Not so sure now?"

"I—I'm not sure about much..."

Well, that was a change. But I didn't comment. Instead I said, "I think we can go now, if you want to."

"I guess. We can leave the ofrenda. No one will steal from ghosts."

We started back through the crowds, the music and laughter jarring against the strangeness of the night. Mickey handed me the bag of clay pieces and the knotted bit of hair, magic, and string as we approached the gate.

"Where's Iko?"

I pointed at the gate, where the dog had appeared again, looking more like a real dog than ever. Mickey grinned and went to pat the little mongrel, carefully, as if he wasn't sure his hand could really touch it.

"Gracias, Señorita Blaine."

I turned, not at all surprised to find Tio Muñoz behind me.

"For what?" I asked.

"For helping him find a better path. He was headed for bad things."

"I just do what the choreographer tells me. What are you going to do now?"

He laughed. "I think that is up to Miguel. What about you? You are finished here."

I nodded. "Yeah. Here. But there's one thing left in Mexico City."

Muñoz shook his head. "Justice may be hard to serve with only the word of ghosts."

"That depends on which sort of justice you're talking about."

He seemed pleased by that and nodded his head. Then he turned and walked away into the night.

Mickey and Iko ran up to me, the dog grinning a satisfied doggy-smile, not nearly as tentative as Mickey's.

We walked back to the Chevy and got in. This time, Iko jumped in and curled on the floorboards at my feet.

As we drove back down the hill, Mickey cleared his throat and glanced at me.

"What?"

"Uh...so. What now?"

"Now, I'm done. I get to go home. By way of Mexico City. And Mr. Banda's office. Maria-Luz and Hector still have a little payback coming."

"And the guys from the *Dulcia.*"

I nodded. "I think I have a way to set things up as Maria-Luz wanted them. And I won't mind giving Banda a good scare."

"How's it going to work?"

"I'll give the bundle to Banda, so he becomes the vessel—I can figure out how. Then he'll be stuck with Iko until he dies, or you let Iko go."

"Can I do that?"

"Yeah. You'll figure it out." I had.

He made a thoughtful frown and was silent for a while. Then he said, "I think I must have missed something. Why did they kill the sailors?"

"That was an accident, but it didn't matter to Arbildo and Jimenez that they died. The boat was old and the company was in a temporary financial crisis. So Arbildo decided to sink it—have a little accident at sea—and collect the insurance. The sailors were just in the way. Except for Hector. Who'd been having an affair with Arbildo's wife."

"Yeah, I got that. Maria-Luz was Hector's daughter, really."

"That's right. He followed her mother to Mexico City. I think Arbildo must have caught on and so Hector did his first disappearing act. He abandoned his real identity as Estancio Rivera and took on the name Hector Purecete, Señora Acoa's long-lost relative. Estancio was from Oaxaca—he worked in the Mezcal distillery down the mountain —and he'd seen the name on the headstone in the panteon San Miguel just like we did. He got a job with the Arbildo shipping company as Hector so he could still be near Consuela and their daughter. While he was at sea, Consuela died and she probably let his new identity slip as she was dying. So Arbildo decided to get rid of his wife's lover once and for all."

"But...Hector called his daughter 'Carmenita'..."

"That was Maria-Luz's middle name: Carmen. They probably called her that so it was less likely they'd trip up in front of Leon Arbildo—but he knew."

Mickey continued to frown. "I'm still not sure I get it..."

"Arbildo sank his own ship with the help of his trusty henchman Jimenez and he didn't let on to anyone that Maria-Luz was not his daughter."

"Why didn't he just...have another kid?"

"Last night, I saw hundreds of dead kids in the cemetery. They were all Arbildo children. I'm not sure what the problem is, genetics, bad luck, a curse...but whatever it is, the Arbildos don't have healthy kids. They die young. Only one or two make it to carry on the family name. Consuela had four children, but only Maria-Luz made it past the age of four. Leon Arbildo didn't have any surviving brothers or sisters, or any other kids. He had to have Maria-Luz and she had to be his daughter, unequivocally."

"He was a very proud man—a jealous man too," I continued. "And Catholic. The illegitimacy thing was not acceptable. He had Maria-Luz watched, the same way he'd had Consuela watched. She must have known and been resentful. She started doing black magic to hurt him—she got thrown out of school for it a couple of times. When she finally met Hector and found out he was her real father, that's when the hate started. But Arbildo got even: he died and he left the estate in the hands of the lawyers who'd helped him in the past."

"And they kept on watching her and manipulating her, right?"

"Yeah. And they kept right on doing all the same things they'd done for her father and not telling her they did it. They drove Hector into hiding and when he died, Maria-Luz had nothing left but the dog and her hate. She started trying to find out about her real father, so she went to Oaxaca a lot, looking for his family or his grave or whatever she could get. She laid all that false trail for us with the Registrar of Deaths, to confuse her lawyers in case they were keeping track of her. We know Jimenez had tracked the graves, but so long as she didn't show up there, he'd never know she'd discovered the truth and he'd never be able to stop her plans for revenge."

"But she changed her mind!"

"Yeah, she did. Because she found out about the *Dulcia*. She decided justice was better than vengeance and, again, she left a puzzle for someone—me—to solve that would reveal the truth."

"She was devious, that Maria-Luz."

I smiled. "Yeah."

We pulled into the tiny covered carriage way of the guesthouse and I stumbled out of the car, suddenly exhausted.

Mickey caught my arm. "Hey…uh…you leaving soon? 'Cause I still got a lot of questions."

"Sorry, Mickey. I have to go tomorrow."

"Oh."

The church bells from the zocalo rang the quarter hour. I checked my watch; it was still early for Oaxaca on el Dia de Muertos—only ten fifteen. But it felt like two a.m.

We walked up the stairs to my room, the house still quiet while everyone was at the cemetery. I stopped and studied Mickey as he waited for me to unlock my door. He was tired, but standing straighter. His sullen look had changed into a thoughtful frown as he tried to understand what had happened and what might happen next.

"Hey," he said again. "Is Iko…going to…chew on lawyer in hell?"

"I don't think so. When Banda dies, the dog gets to go free."

Mickey grinned. It was really a nice grin. I smiled back.

Then I stumbled into my room and fell onto the bed and into sleep.

In the morning, I returned to Mexico City with only a short pause to lay some plans and then say good bye to Mickey and his aunt. Mickey was grinning again, though this time, there may have been more malice in it than the night before.

It was pretty early, but I managed to call Banda's office and get an appointment through his secretary. If he skipped out on me, I would hunt him down.

But he didn't. He was there when I arrived, even if he seemed a little puzzled about my appearance in his office. With a dog.

He looked at the strange dog and frowned. "Did you pick up a stray in Oaxaca?"

"No. Don't you recognize this dog, Mr. Banda? A former client of yours was sure you would."

Iko began to growl like he had at the airport and stalked toward the desk. Banda stood up, looking nervous. "I think you should call off your dog."

"He's not mine," I said, closing the door behind me. "If you take a good look at him, I think you might recognize him. He's Maria-Luz's dog. And Hector Purecete's. Who used to be Estancio Rivera. You know: the guy your partner tried to kill by sinking the *Dulcia*."

"I think you should be more careful what you say, Ms. Blaine. That's slander." He didn't look at me, just at the dog. The dog his secretary hadn't noticed. Nor anyone else we passed on the street or at the airport.

"Truth is a complete defense, I'm told. And the insurance company was never that convinced it was an accident," I replied. "But you know that. Because you helped cover it up. And still are. Which is how a guy in a two-man office can afford to fly to New York to watch the Yankees all season, every season. Because you steal, and you black-mail, and you pay people off. Like you paid off the guy at Customs to break the dog so I'd go home. Didn't you?"

He was backing up as Iko kept coming, inexorable as death.

"Don't know what you're talking about…"

"Oh yeah, you do. And so do the federal investigators who drop in to chat with you once in a while, and the petty officials, and everyone else you pay off so they won't pull your license and throw you in jail to rot. There's a long list of your transgressions if you know where to look. Like I do."

"What the hell do you want, Ms. Blaine? I'm sure we can settle up and go our ways. You and your dog," he added, as if he'd like to spit, but didn't dare. He was sweating and turning pale. "Will you be happy if I admit I paid to have the dog broken? Is that it?"

"No. I do like hearing you say so, but it's not enough. What will make me happy is if you were to suddenly remember Miss Arbildo's amended will. The one where she leaves everything to the families of the sailors who died on the *Dulcia.*"

"There's no such will!"

"There was."

"No there wasn't! Just the ones I showed you. Who's word are you taking? Mine or some…informant living in the hills?"

I walked closer to him. Iko had backed him to the wall. "I am taking Maria-Luz's word for it. And in a few minutes, I'll take yours, because I think you'll want to make a clean breast of the whole thing."

"You're crazy! Just as crazy as she was."

I gave him a cold look. "Iko, rip his throat out."

The little dog let out a banshee howl and leapt for Banda's chest.

Banda screamed, and tried to cover his face and neck with his hands, falling over his desk chair as he flailed at the ghost-dog.

The secretary, pounded on the door, yelling.

I stuck my head out. "He fell. He's OK," I added, pointing to the thrashing man on the floor. "Or not." I shrugged.

The secretary stared at her boss, shrieking and writhing on the floor and backed away muttering about the police and the doctors. I wasn't too worried. They wouldn't find a scratch on him.

Iko was biting savagely at Banda, who seemed to be feeling every snap of the little dog's incorporeal jaws. I have to hand it to Mickey and Maria-Luz: they did fine work. Iko was only "alive" to the man whose life he was tied to: Banda.

"Iko," I called. "Get off that piece of trash." I clapped my hands for the ghost-dog's attention. "Iko!"

Reluctantly, the dog jumped to the ground and stood on stiff legs in front of the lawyer, growling. Banda dragged himself upright against the wall, panting and shaking. He stared at the apparition with horror.

"Wha—what... is that?"

"It's retribution, Mr. Banda. That is Iko. He was on board the *Dulcia* when it sank. But Hector Purecete saved him and left him to Maria-Luz when he died. Or that's what the dead say. I don't think there's ever been a dog in this world—or the next—who hates you the way this one does. And he's all yours."

I elbowed him sharply in the gut and he gasped. I pushed the bundle of hair into his mouth and shoved his jaw shut. Convulsively, he swallowed.

Then he gagged for a moment, staring at me, until he caught his breath again.

"Jesus. What was that?"

"It's Iko. It's the little bit of magic that was in the dog you were so scared of. And now it's yours. For the rest of your life. And maybe a little longer."

He ran for his washroom and tried to throw up, but there was nothing to toss. He shook and prayed and babbled for a moment as Iko circled him, hackles raised and teeth bared.

"Payback's a bitch, isn't it?"

He glared at me as a renewed pounding started on the door. I backed up and leaned against it. "You want to talk to these guys or do you want to get out of this mess?" I asked.

"I want to get the hell rid of you. And your damned dog!"

"Your damned dog, now, Banda. But I can tell you how to get rid of him. If you do what I want."

"I'll have you arrested," he growled, rubbing his throat as he staggered out of the washroom.

"Oh, come on. You know my lawyer. You think that's going to fly? And if you think you can arrange an accident for me like Jimenez did for Purecete, consider that you currently have a ghost dog waiting for a word from me to start biting the living hell out of you. It won't kill you. But I'd bet you'll wish it would. Whoever is on the other side of this door is going to think you've gone insane when they see you rolling on the floor with an invisible dog. Because only you and I can see Iko."

If hate were a living thing it would have leapt for my throat from his eyes. "Salga!" he shouted at the door. "Salga! Estoy bien!"

The knocking died away.

"What. Do you want?"

"Ms. Arbildo's real will. I want it registered and entered for probate, or whatever you need to do to execute it. Today."

"I don't have it," he spat. "It's gone. I burned it!"

"Then forge it. Like you forged the ones you showed me before. The estate to be divided among the families of the crew of the *Dulcia*."

"There is no estate to divide! Don't you get it, estupida gringa? It's all gone. The estate is bankrupt. The money is gone!"

"You told me Maria-Luz was loaded. That thirty thousand U.S. was a 'drop in the bucket.' And her money didn't disappear until you were the sole executor. So you can un-bankrupt it the same way you broke it in the first place, Banda. And if you don't, you won't just have an angry ghost-dog on your ass. Because even you and your dead partner and your cheap secretary can't possibly have blown that much money and certainly not without leaving a trail wide enough to march the Mexican Army down. So, you still have it. Which means, it can be returned to its rightful owners."

He glowered.

"Iko," I said.

He threw himself into his chair, saying, "No, no! Please." He snatched his keyboard and began to type.

I came and stood over his shoulder, watching, while Iko growled non-stop. I looked the finished document over.

"That's pretty good, Banda. I see you'll still be able to feather your own nest, if less regally than before," I added, glancing around his very nice office.

He muttered under his breath.

"Knock it off. You lost. Man-up and live with it."

I hung around while he finished up, printed the forms, forged the signatures and got warily to his feet, eyeing the threatening little hound that dogged him unceasingly. Stifling his fury, he led me a long damned walk around downtown Mexico City to register the will and rescind the previous one.

Just outside of the courts building he stopped and turned back to me.

"Satisfied?"

"Mostly. But I know you can walk right back in there and pull that paperwork by saying you were coerced. But this is the thing you need to remember, Banda: the dog is forever. And once I'm gone, you're not off the hook, because there is someone in Oaxaca who knows all about the will, the *Dulcia*, the dog, and all the rest."

"Another of your ghosts?"

I laughed. "Oh no. A very real, solid, living person. I know you can find out who it is, but don't be hasty. Remember I said there was a way to get rid of the dog?"

"Yes," he snapped.

"That person knows how to set you free. But they won't if you screw over the survivors of the *Dulcia's* crew. And they can't if you decide to kill them. That person—and powerful friends—will be keeping an eye on you. If that person dies, or if that person chooses not to help you, you and Iko get to spend this life together, and the next one and the next one, until there is no one left on the planet who remembers you, or the dog. Until the third death."

He howled and threw himself at me. I just stepped back as Iko lunged.

I walked to the edge of the plaza and flagged a cab, ignoring the crowd that had gathered around the convulsing, screaming man on the ground. "Airport," I said, turning on my cell phone.

I waited for an answer to my call and finally someone picked up. "Villaflores..."

"Hey, brat-boy. It's the GP. It's done."

He laughed. "I'll be on the next flight. Don't want Iko to have to chew on that lawyer for too long."

"Yeah, poor, faithful Iko."

It's rare for Justice and Vengeance to stand in the same place, but I thought this time, maybe they would. At least for a while. Until the will was executed and Banda's embezzlements were restored to the proper owners. I hadn't told Banda the truth, but that wasn't bothering me too much. Whether he lived with Iko for a day or a lifetime, whether anyone remembered Banda or gave a damn in a year's time or thirty, there was at least one thing that made me smile: it would be a long time before the third death of the little clay dog.

# 10

## PEACOCK IN HELL

They'd fled into a cul-de-sac and the barrier built of eternally-tormented bodies of the damned moaned and writhed on three sides, rising toward the billowing fire of the sky for at least thirty meters. Peacock turned back with her knives at the ready, but the only thing still behind her was Lennie Redmayne. He was as dark-skinned and blood-covered as any hellhound, but he was the spoils, not the spoiler. She flicked smoking ichor off her bane-forged blades and they gave off an eerie green glow before she returned them to their sheaths. Then she pushed against the cliff to test its stability.

The wall shrieked from its all its mouths as she touched it. Redmayne jumped and spun in panic, his thin dreadlocks swinging and spattering gore against the rampart and Peacock. "The bloody hell is *that*?" he croaked. His voice hadn't recovered much yet—years of screaming in agony wasn't repaired in an hour.

"Lost souls," Peacock replied. "Just the garden variety, nothing fancy like you. Pile up like garbage here." She ignored the blood now streaking her messily-cropped blond hair and disappearing into the surface of her red leather garments as she studied the barrier a moment. "We'll have to climb."

Redmayne goggled at her. "Climb...that? It's undead bodies as far as the eye can see!"

Peacock shrugged. "It'll be a little slippery, but there're plenty of handholds. Not too bad, unless you put your hands or feet in their mouths—that could get messy."

"Fucking hell," Redmayne muttered.

"Where else did you think you were?"

"Smart arse." He was healing quickly—his voice more south London gutter and less advanced case of throat cancer now.

Peacock grinned. "Sometimes. Up you go," she added and crouched, offering Redmayne a leg up. He was a few years older and nearly a head taller, but he was thin and couldn't weigh much in his current condition, though physics didn't always function normally here.

He glanced between her and the writhing wall with his singed eyebrows raised in horrified bemusement. "Me?"

"Unless you'd rather be tail-end Charlie. We stay down here, those hellspawn *will* find us. I don't see any other way out that doesn't put us back where we came from. Frankly, I prefer the climb."

"Bugger," Redmayne grumbled and put his bare foot into her open hands.

His naked and savaged groin was uncomfortably close. Peacock closed her eyes and turned her head aside. "Don't get any idea that I'm enjoying this," she said as she hefted him upward with a mild grunt. "The view's not spectacular."

"Sod off." He sank his hands and off-side foot into the wall's bleeding flesh. "It in't you who's had his skin peeled off in strips every day for eternity."

"Don't be melodramatic—it's only been eight years."

"I'd tell you to go to Hell, but as we're already here..."

She chuckled as she pulled the crimson hood over her light-colored hair and then scrambled up below him. "Think brutal thoughts, Redmayne—it keeps *me* going."

"I am. I'm just thinking 'em out loud."

Peacock rolled her eyes.

The damned shifted and howled as Peacock and Redmayne hauled themselves upward until the noise became background. They climbed for unmarked hours wrapped in the stink of blood and bones and brimstone. Their motions became mechanical—tug free of one hand-or foothold, sink into the next, and on and up, on and up...

Teeth bit into Peacock's foot and she jerked loose to drive her boot heel into the dead thing's head. As she glanced down, Redmayne's foot flailed past her face. She jammed her toe into the massive scarp of bodies, anchored herself deep in unseen flesh and bones with one hand, and looked up. "Careful," she said, grabbing his loose heel with her free hand. "You don't want to fall now." She drew in tight against the grotesque cliff face to keep her hold and didn't flinch as teeth gnawed at her leathers.

"What? You think it would hurt? I'm fucking dead, mate."

She held steady until he got his foot planted in the grim cliff again, then she pulled loose from the hungry dead and continued upward. "You know that there's worse can happen. Only hellspawn and lords can die here—for fairly weird definitions of 'die' that is."

"And you know this how, Miss Peacock?"

"I've been here before."

"You're dead?"

"At least mostly dead—pretty much the only way to get here."

*She remembered falling. She even remembered hitting the pavement, though some other details were fuzzy now.*

Run...just run like hell. *She'd bolted across the rooftop, vaulting the vents and dodging behind any available cover.* They're back there and gaining.

*She'd glanced over her shoulder as she'd run and spotted the men behind her.* Holy shit...that can't be... *The recollection was foggy, but the roof's edge had been coming up and she'd burst desperately for it. She'd dug her toes into the graveled surface and pushed off...*

*But she'd stumbled, or the parapet was slippery and she'd launched wrong. She'd flailed and smashed against the next building with her full force. Pain bloomed in her chest and back. Then she'd slid down.*

*The giant terra cotta faces around the upper story had projected her out into empty air and she'd tumbled down without control. Only three stories, but enough to smash her like a ripe plum.*

"Answers how you got here, but not why."

Peacock shook off her memory. "What?" she asked.

Redmayne kept climbing, but called down, "I'm asking why *you*, in particular, are pulling *my* raggedy arse out of Hell."

"Because Peter Fiore wanted you filched, which would take the best thief in the business. And that's me."

"You? Work for that bastard?"

"Whether I like it or not."

"He heads up the Directorate of Occult Incursion Control now, yeah?"

"Thaumaturge-in-Chief," Peacock replied. "But that begs the question, what does *he* want with *you*?"

Redmayne scoffed. "Couldn't just call him Lord High Inquisitor could they? Right. So...I'm an artificer—was at any rate. Worked with him at DOIC back in the day."

"Jesus..."

"Watch it."

"Things must be worse than I thought if he's fishing guys like you up from the pit."

"*Guy* like me—singular. No more left, living or dead. That's my 'get out of Hell free' card."

"Free I can't manage—Fiore owns me," she added, bitterly. "I'm taking you straight to him as soon as we're on the other side."

"Well, that's proper fucked, in't it?"

"Proper as it comes."

They climbed in silence for a while.

"Hey, you got any other name?"

"Peacock."

"A first name, wisearse."

"Why do you want to know?" she asked.

"As you're half-dead and I'm all dead, and we've both worked with Peter Fiore, I was thinking we might have a few other things in common. I'll trade you a bit of magical blackmail for it."

"I already know your first name, so that's not gonna wash."

"Nah, this is better—secret about me no one but me mum knows. C'mon…it's worth it. I promise."

Peacock considered the offer for a couple of meters. "You ever call me by it, I'll shove you back down this cliff and let you make your own way up."

"Deal."

"It's Emily Anne."

"Peacock suits you better. I'm Lennie."

"Yeah, I know."

---

"Lennie Redmayne must be retrieved. I can't send an army into the Nether to get him, so it'll have to be done by stealth. Which is exactly the sort of job I hired you for."

"One of which got me killed." Peacock looked at him askance. "Thanks for the reminder."

Peter Fiore was a big guy, bald and white-bearded, and he was good at intimidation, but Peacock wasn't having any. Once you've been dead, your shit-taking limit drops way down—even with master magi.

Fiore narrowed his cold gray eyes at her. "Don't blame me for your mistakes. I had to scrape you off a sidewalk, Peacock, so I don't see where you have much cause to complain. I gave you that power—"

"I already had the veil talent. That's why I'm the best thief in the country."

"Best in the *worlds*, now," Fiore added. "And that you *do* owe to me. Along with the fact that you're up and breathing."

Peacock snorted. "Breathing…in a manner of speaking."

Fiore sneered. "Don't get bitter, Emily. Would you rather I'd abandoned your broken body in that alley? I don't leave my assets behind —even if I have to raise them from the dead."

*"Asset"…you smug bastard.* Time to change the subject, before she

gave into her continual urge to throat-punch him. "This Redmayne—he's one of yours?"

"One of *us*," Fiore corrected and glanced away. He wasn't capable of embarrassment, so it *might* have been remorse. "And yes, he was."

"I notice you didn't raise *him* from the dead, oh, mighty necromancer."

He cast a glare back at her. "I didn't have that option."

"What's so important about him that I have to go to Hell to get him back?"

"That's not something I can tell you. You know how this works. Just remember—there's a reason he is where he is, and you can't trust what the damned tell you."

Peacock rolled her eyes—*like we aren't all damned*. He was laying it on thick, but she couldn't refuse—he was the only person who had the literal power of life and death over her and, bitching aside, she'd rather have the former than the latter, even if it required putting up with Fiore.

"All right, I'll go get him. Where am I gonna find your tortured soul? Hell's a big place."

"Are you familiar with Dante?"

"Not really."

"Good, because he only got close."

---

"Is this secret what got you sent down here?" Peacock asked.

"No, I—Oi! I think we made it!" Redmayne kicked and disappeared over the cliff top as if he were swimming away into the cinder and flame of Hell's sky. Then he choked back a scream.

*Something nasty up there...* Peacock hauled herself over the last of the damned and onto the upper surface. Her left palm sizzled on something hot, but there was no place else to put her hands. She sucked her breath through her teeth and endured the searing until she'd cleared the drop-off. Then she got to her feet and searched for Redmayne.

Beyond the crumbling edge the land was as black and gritty as an ancient stove top. Intense heat and the reek of burning iron rose from it. Peacock spotted Redmayne a few meters away. He whimpered in pain as he stumbled toward a line of low, gray mounds and scattered rubble nearby, leaving burned footprints on the dark surface. Peacock's leathers and boots smoked as she jogged forward and grabbed him. She wasn't strong enough to carry him, but she could haul one of his arms over her shoulders and get him to cooler ground quicker.

She dumped him on rotting stone in the shadowed slope of a chalky mound. Then she crouched near him and studied the area.

Redmayne crawled away from the iron plain's heat and huddled on his backside, watching her. "Your cheek's burnt," he said.

Peacock held up her palms without turning her attention. "Yeah. These, too," she said. "But not as bad as you. I think we've got a little breathing room now, so long as nothing flies by and spots us before we're healed up enough to move."

Satisfied with what she saw, Peacock sat back against the stones and turned to Redmayne. "How are you doing on that score?"

He glanced down at himself. "Major bits are coming along, but the outer layer's still right tatty. Burns didn't help."

Peacock just nodded.

"You think we're safe? I mean...don't that outfit stand out a bit?"

"Have you noticed the color scheme around here? We blend right in. And red's a short wavelength. The hellspawn don't see in color, so it looks gray to them—same as most of this place. You're dark to begin with and with those wounds you look like any other forsaken soul out here. Now, if a lord passes by, that could be a problem, but only for as long as it takes me to kill it." She paused, thinking. "Actually, that might be a good thing—since lords aren't 'he' or 'she' they just wear armor and draped cloth. You could use the cloth like a toga or some-thing and save that 'outer layer' more damage."

Redmayne laid back against the dusty scree and closed his eyes. "Well, there's a silver lining to everything, in't there?"

Peacock chuckled.

"Glad someone's finding humor in this," Redmayne grumbled.

"So far, you're the most amusing thing I've ever stolen. And you owe me a secret."

"Yeah, I do. First I gotta ask, you work for Fiore voluntarily?"

"No. It was supposed to be one contract. It turned into—something else."

Redmayne looked her over and tugged thoughtfully on one of his locs. "So, the thing is…I got this funny talent—"

"Artificer."

"Not *just* that one," he said and held up two fingers.

"You're a bi-talent? Well, that's not so rare that I'd call it 'funny'…" She trailed off as he shook his head.

"I'm a mimic," he said. "It's not something I want most people to know about. Jealous bunch, Talents. Don't like other people borrowing their stuff."

"How does it work? Clearly you don't simply touch somebody and get their powers."

"Yeah, it's not that simple. There's got to be blood contact, see, and I only get a copy of the other person's magic for a little while. But it's still like having it full-power, so I get the downsides just as hard. Magical Engineering doesn't play well with some talents—'specially not death and destruction. It's like coupling matter to anti-matter."

"That would suck. But you haven't picked up my talent and we've certainly passed blood contact by now."

"It don't work here. No one changes in Hell—trust me, I tried. You can cast an illusion—"

"But they don't work on spawn or lords."

"So you have talents."

"Only the one—I can veil—but mostly I rely on my regular skills. Best in the business."

Redmayne sat up and studied her. "A true veil—not just a light-bend?"

Peacock shrugged. "Sure. I can look like someone else or I can look like nothing at all, but it'd be a waste of energy here."

"You act like it's nothing," he said looking astonished. "Veil's rare and can't be duplicated in any sort of artifact."

*Just like an engineer—always thinking about the toys.* She rolled her eyes, then glanced around and shifted her weight onto her feet again. "We'd better get moving. It's a long way to the exit."

"Something wrong?"

"Nothing specific, but you talk too much and we've had too much grace."

"Expecting the next shoe to drop, yeah?"

Peacock nodded. "Uh-huh." She picked up a handful of incinerated stone and crumbled it. The dust stuck to her burned skin.

Redmayne winced at the sight as he crawled to his feet. "Whyn't you wear gloves or something?"

"Can't feel through gloves. Besides, all damage heals here—that's how eternal torment works—you grow back together so they can take you apart over and over."

"Yeah, I noticed."

Peacock started forward without comment.

After a few steps, Redmayne said, "With your talent, you could lose me any time you like."

She sighed. "Why would I come down here and drag you out of a pile of flesh-tearing hellhounds just to dump you?"

Redmayne offered a bitter smile. "It's all about the torture, in't it? And what's worse than hope?"

That was almost amusing and she let go of half a smile. "Spawn can't anchor a talent, so...what?" She drew the mental veil over herself, formless and reflective, and flickered out of view. He gaped and she chuckled from within her illusion. "You think I'm a hell lord in disguise?"

A shadow moved over them with a thunderclap. Peacock let her talent fall away and they both dove for cover as a lord descended. It was three or four meters tall, human in form, but winged and monstrous. The crown of Peacock's head would have barely come to its sternum if they stood toe-to-toe. The lord's incomplete black armor didn't reflect the fiery sky and its crimson drapery flowed in the air like blood in water.

"Fucking hell," Redmayne cursed.

"Secondus," Peacock said and drew her baneforged knives. "Could be worse. Run diagonally from its line of attack and stay out of the way."

She stood tall and faced the lord with both the eerie green blades held low. She wasn't an assassin, but she'd picked up a few tricks...

"Fugitive souls," the hell lord rumbled. It wheeled and folded its wings, rushing forward with the momentum of its fall.

Redmayne fled toward a nearby pile of rock.

Peacock ran toward the lord and ducked. She swept the blades out as it passed over her. The knives jerked in her hands and she dug in against the backward drag as blades cut moving flesh.

The hell lord roared and flipped a wingtip, pivoting to keep Peacock in sight as it landed. Ichor sprayed from its wounded, backward knees and it staggered left, foot twisting a little. *Got you!* Peacock danced aside. The lord swiped at her and she slashed. The creature jerked back an instant too late. A talon as long as her hand clattered to the iron ground and slid toward Redmayne. *Not so fucking invincible against these, are you?* The lord raised its sliced hand in surprise.

Peacock leaped at its weak side. She planted one foot hard on its injured knee and vaulted upward. She reversed the near blade and shoved it toward the lord's armpit with a downward swing. The creature twisted and swept its elbow down, knocking Peacock aside.

She rolled across the searing surface as the hell lord screamed, then flipped to her feet and faced it. Her blade stuck out below the mark, sunk only half its length in the lord's side. Smoking ichor poured from the wound, but the monster was still on its feet.

Peacock's cheek was blistered from the heat and her remaining blade steamed with gore. She spotted Redmayne scuttling onto the burned earth to snatch up the severed claw. "Leave it, you idiot!" she yelled. *Gonna be the hard way, I guess.* "Back me!"

The lord turned toward Redmayne and Peacock threw herself

forward. The creature whirled around, snapping out a wing with taloned tips that raked across her chest and throat.

The blow spun Peacock into the air, blood fanning from the slash across her neck. She hit the ground and sprawled onto her back in a twisted heap, carmine blood running across the black plain in wide swaths. The wounded hell lord bounded toward her. Redmayne started after it with the dismembered claw clutched in his hands.

*Her memory was much more clear now: She had glanced over her shoulder as the roof edge loomed and maybe it was the action or maybe it was the sight of familiar faces that had made her miscalculate the leap...*

*But Peacock figured it was the bullet that had been shot into her back.*

The lord bent unsteadily over Peacock, laughing in spite of its running wounds. It drew back its uninjured hand to strike.

Redmayne leapt onto its back and stabbed it with its own severed claw. The talon didn't sink in deep, but it did pierce the lord's armor and a narrow stream of ichor squirted into the air. The lord shrieked and shook out its wings to dislodge Redmayne, sending a gust of hot air booming forth.

Peacock spasmed, her head lolling and wobbling as the wound in her throat began to close. She rolled to her knees and flipped her blade upward, then lunged, shoving it hilt-deep into the hell lord's gut below the edge of its breastplate. She pushed with both hands until the pommel rang against the metal, then ripped sideways and down with the weight of her own falling body. The blade tore through the hell lord's hide to the scarlet sash that wrapped the mailed kilt around its hips. The infernal creature collapsed as its guts spilled out onto the smoking field.

Peacock lay trapped under the dead hell lord, gasping and blinking. And the damned thing stank.

Redmayne danced from one burning foot to the other as he shoved the creature aside. "I'm sorry, I'm sorry," he said as she wriggled free.

Her exposed skin was crisply blackened by the time she reached the nearest rocky ridge and her leathers were badly singed. She flopped into the crumbling stone and coughed on pain and dust as her wounds closed and her skin resolved from ash to flesh. Redmayne hunched nearby with the hell lord's claw in his hand. When she caught her breath, she beckoned him to her.

Redmayne crept close and bent down and Peacock punched him in the face. "You set me up."

He landed on his back. "No!"

She knelt over him. "Bullshit! You're an artificer—you knew my drawing the veil would send out a ripple. A hell lord won't attack another of its own kind without provocation. You really thought I was one of them! You figured that one would fly on by—"

"That's a bloody-minded assumption you're making, Sunshine."

"It was a lousy trick to pull on me...*Sunshine*," Peacock spat back. "I ought to leave you here to scream your guts out for the rest of eternity!"

Redmayne scowled. "Fiore wouldn't like that..."

"Don't you lecture *me* on what that scheming bastard would or wouldn't— Oh...damn it all," she added, winding down in disgust. "I need to get you out of here or I'll never get a shot at him." She rested on her heels.

Redmayne struggled to sit up. "Who? Fiore? He's betrayed you, hasn't he? Bloody good at that, he is."

She peered at him. "He screwed you over, too."

Redmayne avoided her gaze. "Let's just say we didn't part friends."

She studied him a minute or so longer and then sat down, crushing handfuls of fragile, baked stone and rubbing the dust into her oozing skin.

"Why d'you do that?" Redmayne asked as he watched her intently. He was less eviscerated, but still a bit flayed and gnawed.

"I don't like to drip. And, crazy as it sounds, it seems to speed up healing. You could use a little, yourself."

"Should take some out of here with us, then," he said, but he didn't follow her example.

"It's tricky getting native things out of Hell. You're gonna have to leave that." She pointed at the claw.

"Hah! You barmy? This, my stealthy friend, is pure artifact gold and worth what it took to get it." He waved the talon. "I'd rather stay here and dodge hellspawn than leave it behind."

"Seriously?"

"I'd take my chances," he replied, his expression grim.

"Why?"

He gave her an odd smile. "You ever seen one of these things in the breathing world?"

"No."

"Useful, these are—at least if you're someone like me. Goes through anything, almost indestructible out in the world, and since it's hellbound, it has a positive yen to return from whence it came; or send other things back in its place."

"Literally?" she asked. Redmayne nodded. Peacock glanced at the gutted hell lord and shuddered. "Good thing it's dead."

"Who says they stay dead?"

"I jammed a foot of baneforged steel into its guts. I've never seen anything get up from that."

"How many lords have you killed?"

"That makes two—but I admit I didn't stick around the last time." Redmayne's smile was sly.

Peacock scowled at him and growled. "There goes my exit plan."

"You really had one?"

"Of course. I never go in without having at least two ways out. But neither of my escape routes accounted for bringing anything along besides you and me. Even my blades were gonna stay behind."

"There's other doors between the worlds…if we can find one down here."

"It'll have to be a wide one, which means the hellborn probably already know about it. I'll have to check the map," Peacock said and dug into a pocket hidden under one of her scabbards. She drew out a wisp of gauze that gleamed with tiny points of colored light.

Redmayne gaped at her. "You have the Liminal Map?"

"I have *part* of the map—I stole it."

"You're a fly one."

"I'm a thief."

"Where'd you enter?"

"New Straitsville, Ohio. There's a coal mine that's been burning there for more than a hundred years. Closest superposition to where I found you. Easy in, but it's a flesh lock on the way out. Now shut up and let me look—this thing's hard to see."

Redmayne put out his hand. "Let me."

Peacock wasn't sure she could trust him, but he couldn't get far without her—and the hell lord's clothes—so she handed the bit of ethereal fabric over.

"This looks familiar." He glanced down at his still-ragged body. "That'll do." He laid the map against a strip of raw flesh on his chest. The map dissolved and Redmayne sucked his breath through clenched teeth.

"What the—" Peacock started.

"Hang on," he gasped. "It's coming…"

The map gleamed into sight—a tattoo of living silver sparked with tiny gems. It was as clear as printing and when Redmayne moved, it adjusted its North by his position.

"Well, fuck me," Peacock murmured.

"Likes a bit of flesh and blood, this thing."

She grinned. "How'd you know?"

Redmayne cocked a sarcastic eyebrow. "Artificer. How'd you think?"

"You made this map?"

He scoffed. "Nah. Nobody *made* it. Compiled over centuries. Happens, though, that I did work on this bit right here," he said, and poked one glittering portal marker. "Never used it, but should be a good door—unless a lot more has changed than I imagined."

---

The broad portal was closer than Peacock had feared and less protected. The Netherworld was riddled with caves here and she crouched with Redmayne in the mouth of one while studying the landscape.

269

"You sure this is right...?" she asked.

"Course it's right. The map can't lie and we're..." he pushed aside the tunic they'd made from the dead lord's blood-red draperies and pointed at the bright star that seemed to shine on his chest, "right here. Practically on top of it."

Redmayne had bound up his feet with more cloth and made a sort of a pack from armor parts; he'd filled it with the lord's claw and other things he deemed useful. While he'd never pass as a lord on visual inspection, he certainly smelled like hell.

Peacock shook her head. "There's no sign of a guard aside from a couple of wandering spawn, or that the portal's in use at all. I can't even see it."

"It's there. Trust me." He squinted in pain. "This little bugger burns."

"It's just...something's funny. You're certain?"

Redmayne heaved an exasperated sigh. "Look, mate, I want out of Hell as much as you do. I count m'self bloody lucky it's you got sent to retrieve me and I'm not gonna ditch you. I used to be on the side of the angels, and Fiore always thought whatever he did was justified if it kept the darkness back, but it's not. Some things are evil, simple as that. It's no accident I'm down here—I damned m'self. I did things and knew I'd end right here—"

Peacock raised a hand. "Hush! There, by that steam fissure in the hillside, there's a gleam," she whispered. "See where that spawn's digging?"

"Yeah. That's the liminal point. It's a transverse."

"A what?"

"Passes through Limbo and changes orientation. Nasty trip, but it'll get us out in one piece and the lower orders of hellborn can't follow. Must be a bit of odd there."

"Probably why that spawn's so interested. Have to get rid of it before it attracts attention." She checked position of all the spawn in view. "All right. You need to be close, so follow me until I turn, then wait."

"Wait—" he started.

She ignored him and slipped out into the shadow.

She tucked tight and ran along the wall's base. She avoided the hellspawn's sight until she reached its blind spot. Then she turned sharply, keeping directly behind the creature, and dashed across the open space toward it and the crevice. She spotted a few more spawn wandering farther out in the plain where it flattened to hot iron. They might not see her, but they could hear and smell better than any dog. They'd come running if the hellspawn by the portal howled.

Peacock timed her leap and came down on the hellspawn's back with one blade out, sweeping forward and under its elongated jaw. She sliced through its throat before it could make a sound and fell on top of it.

She breathed a long sigh of relief and glanced back. Redmayne was right where she'd told him to be. She waved him forward and turned her attention to the other spawn. They hadn't turned toward the rock face. At least not yet.

Redmayne tiptoed a path to her side and crouched. She reached for the portal's gleam and he snatched her hand away. "No. We're not done here."

Peacock growled at him.

He released her hand. "Tried to tell you earlier. Soon's we're through that door, things change. You have to cut this map out of me chest first. It'll want to stay there ever after otherwise, and I'd not like that."

She was appalled. "You're kidding."

"Wish I were. Now, quick—before that lot takes note of us."

"Have you got anything sharp and stabbity in that pack?" she asked.

"Whyn't you use your knife?"

"Baneforged. Wounds don't heal."

"Right. Bugger."

Redmayne unslung the pack and rummaged through it until he found a sharp bit of armor scale. He handed it over to Peacock and cast a nervous glance toward the hellspawn. "Just nick the edge and tear it out—that'll have to do."

Peacock winced. "That's gonna hurt."

"No doubt."

She'd been able to hear him from a long distance before she'd found him. "We'd better be ready to jump," she said.

"Put your back to the cleft—that'll be easiest."

She turned and the portal leaked a cold wind along her shoulders. Redmayne gripped his pack with both hands, squeezed his eyes shut, and grimaced in anticipation. He was silent as she sliced the edge of the Liminal Map free and caught it in her fingers. She yanked.

Redmayne shrieked, arching in agony.

The hellspawn turned as a body and raced toward them, raising a clatter on the hard ground like a hailstorm. Something roared and Peacock shot a glance toward it—clouds seemed to boil both overhead and across the searing plain. Monstrous faces resolved from the fiery sky and rushed into shape as they fell upon the two fugitives. Lords and hellspawn by the hundreds.

She threw herself back against the portal.

It resisted.

"Shit. Redmayne—"

He lurched forward, the pack falling into her lap as he bowed over her and thrust his hands into the rift. Blood spattered and ran onto her face. Amid the howls of incoming hellborn, she could barely hear him spit out a word that shook the rock face behind her.

They fell though the portal and the screams of Hell's fury cut short in suffocating silence. Redmayne twisted and caught one hand in the closing portal.

---

Limbo was a luminous gray nothingness. Two streaks of light—one ruby, one gold—showed in Peacock's vision as she glanced side to side.

"D'you hear that?" Redmayne asked.

"I don't hear anything."

Redmayne flickered as he hunched beside the thin red line.

"Bloody hell. Fiore, you bastard," he whispered. His voice was hoarse and trembling.

"Holy crap, Redmayne," Peacock muttered. "What are you doing?"

"Bleeding and holding on."

She reached for the infernal rocks in Redmayne's pack. "You're not gonna heal like you do in Hell."

"Don't!" He slapped her hand aside. "We've only got minutes before we're back in the lion's den. Could you put a finger here? Any one will do perfectly fine."

Peacock flipped him the bird and he shoved her hand into the fiery light. It burned against her flesh and seemed to gnaw on her digit.

"For the love of everything, don't move," Redmayne said. "Open your suit and give me one of your blades."

"Over your dead body."

Redmayne snorted. "Later, mate. Look, I know these are the worst of circumstances, but you have got to trust me. Fiore's a right bastard and he doesn't mean either of us any good—you don't imagine he's dragging me back to play tiddlywinks, do you?"

"No."

"Then listen. Back in the day, I didn't just work with Fiore, I was his boss. The ambitious little prick didn't like that and had plans to put me under his boot same as you are. We needed a necromancer and I couldn't get rid of him, so I damned m'self to Hell and took a hard way down so he couldn't drag me back by blood and fire. With my funny talent, you can imagine how that would have gone. Fiore wants to make this homecoming hurt and I've a mind to deny him that pleasure, but Limbo's the only place my plan can work. Straight truth—I need you or we're neither one of us coming up for air. So, what's it gonna be? Time's almost up."

She grinned and Redmayne shivered at the sight. "Oh, I'm in."

---

The carmine light whirled away and she tumbled through the nothing. They were torn apart, tossed, and spat out.

Peacock lurched into a smoking cavern and sprawled on the floor. Both her knives, the map, and the pack's contents were scattered around her, but Redmayne was gone. She yanked up her suit zipper and gathered the junk Redmayne had collected. She didn't even consider running—there was nowhere to go that Fiore couldn't follow except Hell itself and she wasn't ready to return to that venue just yet. She had other things to do.

She hiked out and found a retrieval team waiting for her in the fuming bowl of a West Virginia hillside—another unending coal mine fire. And there was Redmayne, held by two goons, bound in silver, and still wounded. Pallor turned his dark skin gray where it wasn't abraded or lacerated scarlet, and he was so gaunt he looked ready to shatter, but he snarled and fought every attempt to stanch his wounds until his captors gave up and left him to bleed.

"Hurt much?" she muttered, keeping clear of him.

"Like hell."

First a helicopter, then a plane, another heli, and they were delivered to Fiore's office. Their escort had already patted her down and confiscated her knives as well as the pack—*at least he didn't make me undress, the creep.* He marched them to the desk where Fiore stood, handed over the pack, and left. The sound-proofed door shushed closed behind him.

The necromancer smiled. "Nice job, Em—bit slow, but no harm done." He turned his attention to Redmayne. "Welcome back, Lennie."

"Fiore, you black-hearted, murdering sod." He didn't even sound angry.

"Oh come on, Redmayne. You were never really Director material, talent or not. And it was so good of you to—"

Peacock stepped between them. "You shot me, you son of a bitch." She whipped one hand out for his throat.

Fiore grabbed her wrist and wrenched her hand aside. "I always knew you'd get wise." He glanced at Redmayne. "Did *you* tell her?"

Redmayne scoffed weakly. The wound on his chest was still oozing blood. "After my time, mate. Think she couldn't figure it out herself, you silly, fat bastard?"

Peacock jerked her arm against Fiore's hold and he yanked her farther sideways with a snarl. She propelled herself into the motion, jumping and sliding onto the desktop to ram her near foot into the necromancer's gut. He dropped his grip and she rolled off with a gratuitous kick toward his face as she passed. Fiore reeled back and shook his head clear.

The pack fell and spilled rocks and bits of black armor across the rug. Peacock dove and grabbed the sharp bit of scale she'd used on Redmayne.

Fiore took a step and kicked her in the side, rolling her hard against the wall.

Peacock flipped and used her legs to thrust herself upright against the vertical surface. Fiore closed the distance and she slashed at him, back to the wall.

He snatched for her hand and caught her forearm, crushing his weight against her. He rammed her into the plaster. "Temper, temper, Emily," Fiore murmured. "I figured I'd have to scrub you soon, but with Lennie back...I won't miss you that much."

He started muttering under his breath. She felt her existence unravelling around the edges, but he'd have to cut her throat to finish it, and right now his hands were busy. She rammed a knee upward. It was feeble but enough to cut off his breath for a moment. *C'mon, Redmayne...*

"You set this up from the beginning, you rat bastard," she snapped. "Hired me, killed me, drew me back up so you could run me. You sent me to Hell for your own amusement—"

From his knees, Redmayne heaved his bound weight upward against the desk and it rocked into the necromancer's back.

Fiore twisted a furious glare over his shoulder as Redmayne staggered. Peacock seized the opening and slashed at Fiore with the sharp bit of armor. It grazed off his ear. Fiore whipped around, snapping Peacock's wrist with the motion. The blade dragged down her cheek as he flung her toward Redmayne.

Peacock tucked into a ball and her cut cheek slapped hard into the bleeding wound on Redmayne's chest.

Redmayne vanished and Peacock collapsed to the floor in his place.

Fiore strode over and dragged Peacock to her feet. He held her by the throat and shook her as she hung stiffly from his hands.

"Lennie!" Fiore shouted. He glared around the room. "Come out! You know how I'll kill her and you don't want to watch that."

There was a rough hiss near Fiore's back and Peacock choked in his grasp. She muttered, "You can fucking try, mate, but it'll be a bloody good trick when she's behind you."

Peacock's appearance melted away and revealed Redmayne snarling in Fiore's grip.

Less than a foot from Fiore's spine, Peacock herself, her leathers unzipped to the waist, yanked a needle carved from the hell lord's claw out of a slit in the skin below her breast. She jabbed it an inch into her boss's neck.

Fiore twitched and dropped Redmayne. A black cloud erupted from the floor beneath Fiore and engulfed him. The dark smoke swirled and writhed to his screams, binding him within its coil, then flowed away again like ink down a drain and dragged the necromancer with it. Only an echo and the stink of hot iron lingered to mark their passage.

The air was thick and still with anticipation. Then the desk groaned and toppled. Peacock jumped back from it with a startled hiss.

She laughed in relief and flopped down next to Redmayne in the sound-proofed silence. Fiore's guys knew better than to interrupt while he was working, so she could afford a moment to catch her breath. She picked up a hell-baked stone and crushed it in her grip to rub the dust into her broken wrist and scatter the rest onto Redmayne's chest. Blood ran down her cheek from the cut she'd put there, but she ignored it. "Well. I wasn't sure about that hell lord's claw, but it seemed to work. Where do you suppose it sent Fiore?"

"You can't guess from the reek? I'd lay odds he's having a natter with the original owner about now."

"Aww...and I didn't even get to say goodbye."

Her wrist straightened with a sound like popcorn exploding. "Ow," she yelped. She shook out her hand and wiggled her fingers, then zipped her suit closed, and helped Redmayne into a sitting position. "I have never been so glad for stupid men—the guy who frisked me was too busy copping a feel to notice that damned needle."

"To be fair it was rather small and you've got some nasty scars to hide it under," Redmayne replied and squirmed. "Could you get these shackles off me? Right irritating they are."

Peacock drew a couple of picks from the seams of her leathers and started on the lock.

Redmayne watched her work. "I'd not count him out entirely yet. Necromancers don't just walk back out of Hell, but he's still alive down there until something kills him, and he'll be looking for a way out."

"Like you did?" she said, opening up the restraints.

"Ta," he said, rubbing at his arms and wrists. "Nah. I started by looking for a way *in*, but I'd never been to Hell and I had to guess a lot and go on theory. Then I had to find the right liminal point and make sure I had someone I could trust to get rid of my remains, had to figure out exactly how black and which shade of damnation my soul had to wear to land in exactly the right place, had to leave bits of intrigue behind that only I could solve for him... I knew he'd have to send someone for me eventually. Bit of luck it was you."

"Luck?"

Redmayne nodded self-consciously. "Yeah. I didn't have much of a plan for when I got out. It was chatting you up made it come together, but Fiore laid the ground himself. If he hadn't bent you over, you'd have had no cause to throw in with me."

Peacock gave him a cynical look. "You had no plan at all? You didn't know I was coming, didn't trick me into attracting that lord's attention so you could get its claw?"

"Maybe the claw I did. The rest was mostly the happenstance of you being you and saving my arse. I'm not *so* bleeding clever or I'd have come up with some way to avoid the whole thing. At the time, we couldn't run the Directory without a necromancer and T-in-Chief didn't have the kind of power that Fiore's built up since then. And I'm not good at killing people—all that—"

"All that blood," Peacock finished. "You're a twisty bit of work, Redmayne. I'm still wondering what happens to *me* now that Fiore's gone. I'm surprised I haven't dropped dead already. And how much better off are *you*? I mean, technically you're what—some kind of hellspawn, now?"

Redmayne shrugged and grimaced. "Well, hell*born*, yeah—bit of an affinity after walking out. This body *looks* the same as what Fiore murdered—or it will when I'm not portal-sick—but I'm not sure yet on the functional details of living in this world in flesh created in Hell."

"I guess we'll find out."

"I guess." Redmayne gave her a crooked smile. "Think I can get me old job back?"

Peacock started scavenging in the wreckage for weapons. "I'm willing to help you try."

# ACKNOWLEDGMENTS

These stories came from many places, published and unpublished, and I couldn't have got them here without the help of original editors Jon and Ruth Jordan, Monica Valentinelli and Jaym Gates, Jim Thompson, Shawn Speakman, Stephen Antczak and James Bassett, Kerry L. Huges and Jim Butcher, and Anne Sowards; ditto the amazing work of Falstaff Books' Publisher and Editor in Chief John Hartness, and Melissa McArthur; the unending patience and support of my spouse Mr. Kat; and the miracle work of tech boffins at iDope Poulsbo who resurrected my [expletive deleted] laptop. Thanks to Vladimir Verano for setting the chapbook version of Chemotherapy from which the version here is adapted, and to Ken George, for whom I wrote the original draft of Shattered a very long time ago. Much love and thanks to Charlaine Harris, who has been a great friend since the beginning.

# ABOUT THE AUTHOR

Kat Richardson is currently wandering loose through the mountains of Western Washington in a trailer with two dogs and a husband. It's even her own husband. Along the way she has been an actor, singer, costumer, Renaissance Faire performer, dancer, writing instructor, seller of beanie babies, and a freelance editor. She is the author of nine bestselling novels in the Greywalker series, one award-winning SF novel, and a few unspeakable things that live in an electronic trunk. Trust me, it's better that way....

# FRIENDS OF FALSTAFF

Thank You to All our Falstaff Books Patrons, who get extra digital content each month! To be featured here and see what other great rewards we offer, go to www.patreon.com/falstaffbooks.

## PATRONS

Dino Hicks
John Hooks
John Kilgallon
Larissa Lichty
Travis & Casey Schilling
Staci-Leigh Santore
Sheryl R. Hayes
Scott Norris
Samuel Montgomery-Blinn
Junkle